Sorraya in a Coma

Esmail Fassih

Written during the Iranian Revolution and the Iran-Iraq War that followed, these events are experienced through the story of a young woman, Sorraya. Desperately injured in a road accident, she is a constant presence in a story that moves between the vanities and excesses of the wealthy Iranian exiles living in Paris — gossiping, squabbling, flirting — to unbidden nightmares of war-ravaged Iran. Haunted by these memories, Sorraya's uncle, the narrator, views his compatriots and his own predicaments with wry detachment and humour.

Satire, pity and terror are skilfully interwoven in this translation of a novel by one of Iran's leading writers.

Esmail Fassih was born in Tehran in 1935. After training in the United States, he worked for the National Iranian Oil Company for seventeen years, but was forced to retire in 1981. In recent years he has established a significant reputation as a novelist with four novels in Persian — *Raw Wine* (1968), *Blind Heart* (1972) *The Javid Story* (1980), and *Sorraya in a Coma* which was published in Iran in 1984 and is now in its third edition. Esmail Fassih and his family live in Tehran.

Sorraya in a Coma

Esmail Fassih

Translated from the Persian

Zed Books Ltd.

Sorraya in a Coma was first published in Persian in Teheran in 1984; and first published in English by Zed Books Ltd., 57 Caledonian Road, London N1 9BU, in 1985.

Cover design by Henry Iles.
Printed by Cox & Wyman, Reading.

British Library Cataloguing in Publication Data

Fassih, Esmail
   Sorraya in a coma.
   I. Title
   891'.5533 F   PJ7824.A8/

   ISBN 0-86232-525-0
   ISBN 0-86232-526-9 Pbk

US Distributor
Biblio Distribution Center, 81 Adams Drive,
Totowa, New Jersey 07512, USA.

Glossary

Abba: A long, wide-sleeved robe.

Ali-Allahis: A religious sect, who believe that Ali, the first Shi'ite Imam is actually God himself.

Asha: see Maqrib.

Bi-hejabi: The Persian word 'hejab' means to be covered and veiled, referring to women. In the previous regime this was not necessary. *Bi-hejabi* means lack of *hejab*.

Fatehah: A short prayer, said for the peace of the deceased's soul.

Gaz: A sort of white nougat.

Ghazal: A style in Persian poetry, dating from the 12th and 13th Centuries AD.

Hezbollahi: Member of the Party of Allah, refers to fundamentalist followers of Ayatollah Khomeini in Iran at this time.

The Holy Five: The Prophet Mohammad, his daughter Fatimeh, his cousin and son-in-law Ali, and the two sons of this marriage, Hassan and Hossein, are considered the Holy Five in the Shi'ite sect.

Horhori: Persian slang for atheist.

Imam Hossein: Third Shi'ite Imam, martyred in Karbala, around 700 AD.

Khamseh-Khamseh: In these shells, each fragment splits into five smaller fragments and each of these splits into five more, and so on. *Khamseh* is Arabic for five.

Khatm: Funeral and mourning service held on the third day after death.

Khorram-Shahr: Green, pleasant city, was renamed by the Islamic Republic government in the war, as Khunin-Shahr, meaning the Bloodied City.

Majnun and Leila: Counterparts of Romeo and Juliet in Arabic and Persian stories. Majnun means insane; he was said to have been driven mad by love for his cousin Leila.

Maqrib: Prayers that must be said at sunset; and *Asha* prayers may be said any time between after sunset and midnight. They are usually said in succession.

Mowlavi's story: Refers to a line of one of the stories in *Masnavi Ma'navi* by Mowlavi. The line: 'Said, oh Sheikh, you got the good prayer but the wrong hole!' The sheikh was told to write his prayer, take it to the bath house at dawn and stick it in the prayer hole. The 'wrong hole' refers to the fact that, it being dark, and a man happened to be prostrating himself to pray the sheikh mistook the man's anus for the prayer hole.

Nazr: A dedication to make a donation to a certain mosque, or to the poor or to give any other kind of help, if God would solve a particular problem or grant a wish.

Radio Vatan: Iranian language radio station run by exiled Iranians since the Revolution.

Ruzeh: Mullah preaching in Iranian tradition.

Salavat: Traditional praise to Mohammad the Prophet, usually said in chorus.

Sarat Bridge: In Islamic mythology, a bridge by which only the righteous can cross into Paradise, while the sinner shall fall into Hell.

Yazid: The Arab Caliph who is known by Shi'ites as the murderer of the Imam Hossein.

Zargari: Persian equivalent of dog-Latin.

Preface

Sorraya in a Coma concerns the plight of Iranian intellectuals in the modern world, and the confusion and bewilderment inflicted upon them as a result of the Iranian revolution. Since 1979, Iranian society has been wrenched from rampant westernisation to Islamic fundamentalism, and many intellectuals who once supported the revolution are now in exile, confused and displaced by the turn of events. *Sorraya in a Coma* is one of the first major novels to emerge from this period, and it deals with the contrasts between the realities in Iran under the impact of the Islamic revolution, the horrors of the Iran–Iraq war, and the lifestyles and uncertainties of a group of self-estranged, self-exiled Iranian intellectuals in Paris.

The Café Riviera in Tehran was a meeting place for Iranian intelligentsia. Now in exile, many Iranians gather at the Café de la Sanction in Paris. Here they cling to extreme modernism, in the hope of carrying out their artistic and intellectual obligations. In Tehran, they had been at the centre of events. In Paris, however, they are out on a limb, existing on an island of their own isolation, cut off from the roots of their past creativity. While their fellow countrymen fight for their lives in Abadan and other battlefields in Iran, while the Iranian Hostage Crisis is an international issue, they busy themselves with their own confused relationships and their own petty concerns. Their society has no faith in them, and they have no faith in Islamic Iran. Divorced from their potential source of intellectual nourishment, they frivol while Iran spurns them.

The major symbol of this novel lies in the title: *Sorraya in a Coma*. Sorraya is not a character, but an image. She is the narrator's niece, knocked down in a road accident and lying in a coma in a Paris hospital. She is a brooding presence throughout the novel, and the key which binds together the different elements in the novel. She is dissociated from the world in which she exists, she is unresponsive to outside stimulae, many characters in the novel are concerned for her welfare, yet none has any influence on her. She is an image of Iran itself.

Against the background of Sorraya's gently deepening coma, writers and playwrights squabble, would-be politicians pontificate, a professor rambles on about ancient Iranian history and culture, and serious students appear to grapple unsuccessfully with the contrasts between Islamic traditionalism and modern science. Each type is a caricature, satirically yet sympathetically presented. Each, like Sorraya, is isolated from the other and each is in isolation from the real world.

The real world is Abadan. Almost encircled by Iraqi troops, this once famous oil producing centre at the head of the Persian Gulf is now facing destruction. Battered by shells, swarming with rats, kept out of Iraqi hands by the efforts of often very young and inexperienced Iranian troops, Abadan is seen through flashbacks as the narrator relives his disturbing experiences while attempting to take care of Sorraya in Paris. Horrifying pictures of the war in Abadan hang like a pall of smoke over the inconsequentialities of Parisian exile life.

In contrast to the Abadan war zone, Paris is a bizarre, exotic and irrelevant setting, competing with the portrayals of the self-exiled Iranians. The reader is thrust beyond the world of reality into a plane of allegorical significance. The Café de la Sanction, where the Iranian group meet in Paris, is Tehrani intellectual life in abstraction. Paris, for so long the home and symbol of the intelligentsia, is a visual concept of the Iranian elite's self-estrangement. It has enabled the author to place this self-styled 'Lost Generation' of Iranian artists and to depict their somewhat excessive norms of behaviour in an acceptable intellectual environment without violating the Islamic community's religious sensitivity. Here writers and artists can drink, eat and drug themselves silly while they fail to create literary masterpieces; the religious Qasem Yazdani can safely concern himself with the wonders of modern science while he brings flowers he cannot afford to Sorraya; and the narrator can move from one circle to another, as a detached observer, while he attempts to take care of Sorraya's ever diminishing needs.

viii

The narrator, Jalal Aryan, represents the author's view. He is a moderate humanist, a Western-educated intellectual with deep respect for Islamic culture and his Iranian identity. In the world of allegory, he is the observer who makes possible the creation of characters and events. However, he is careful not to identify himself with any of the other characters, yet he is not indifferent in his observations. He is the only real, flesh and blood character; the only rational being in the islands of confusion and isolation.

The author, Esmail Fassih, was born in Iran in 1935, and went to the USA in 1956, where he obtained degrees in science and English literature. Working for the Abadan Institute of Technology, he actually lived in the Abadan war zone until he was forced to retire in 1981.

In addition to *Sorraya in a Coma*, Fassih has written three other novels; *The Raw Wine* (1968), *The Blind Heart* (1972), and *The Story of Javid* (1980). He has also written a number of short stories. In all his writings, Fassih shows a deep respect for Iranian culture and identity.

Late autumn, 1980, a cold Tuesday afternoon, around two
o'clock, Tehran . . .

At the open access to the West Bus Terminal, on the north-
western outskirts of Azadi Square, pedlars, vendors, and
passengers mill about in the dust and diesel fumes, the honking,
the jumbled noise and shouts, 'Liver . . . Mmm! Two *tomans* a
skewer!' 'Sandwiches, *Aqa*! Fresh egg sandwiches!' 'Move on,
Aqa . . .' 'Beans! Baked beans!' 'Shahsavar oranges!' 'Sweet
buns!' 'Out of the way, you!' 'Winston cigarettes, *Aqa*!' 'Biscuits!'
'Hamburgers! Sausages!' 'Handbags, *Aqa*!' 'Move your bags
father!' 'Woollen socks, hats, gloves!' 'Fresh tea!' '*Aqa*, move on!
Move aside, mother!'

Some have spread out their wares on an upturned drum, a
cardboard box, or piece of cloth on the ground. One sells
barbari bread and cheese; another *lavash* bread and boiled eggs.
An old man sitting in a corner sells plastic packets of dried
seeds, almonds, pistachios, chick-peas and raisins, dried figs
and mulberries.

The new makeshift Terminal's interior is a shapeless,
undefined space, with no buildings, no facilities, not even a
wall. Inside, it is still just a taken-over lot. But coaches heading
for the north and the north-west of Iran, and even for Turkey
and Europe, all start from this point.

To the north, under the blue sky and fat white clouds, rise the
clean snow-covered Alborz mountains. Closer, a cluster of tall,
multi-storey buildings, dusty grey and white, huddle together
like dingy monsters. Modelled on New York's skyscrapers,
these supposedly residential units are now stranded, unfinished,
worthless, useless, and empty under the autumn wind, behind

the Terminal. In the foreground, scattered around the lot are tarpaulin tents, each representing a bus company or travel agency, and in every corner, 'cooperatives' have sprouted. Behind the tents, coaches unload and reload passengers.

The crowd milling around are mostly from the provinces, or are war refugees, or just people like myself, driven from their homes for one reason of another. There are homeless Turks, Lurs, Kurds and Khuzestani Arabs, pouring into Tehran or leaving it. Where I enter the Terminal, to one side, several dusty-bearded soldiers in crumpled uniforms are drinking tea. Three Kurds in baggy trousers, wearing paramilitary jackets and their traditional polkadot turbans, are resting in a corner smoking Winston cigarettes. An Arab from Khuzestan sits in a corner, apparently with his mother, wife, and six or seven children, doing nothing, their faces empty.

I find the tent representing the TBT agency, now 'Cooperative No. 15'. There is even a bivouac counter in a corner, with a cardboard sign: 'Passengers to Istanbul'. The counter is almost deserted. I find somebody and hand in my ticket. Without even checking it, the man ticks off my name on his list. I have no luggage as such to hand in, so he allows me to keep my small case and handbag. The door of 'the coach' – a well-worn Deluxe Benz 0302 – is open, and the driver and his assistant are loading luggage on to the roof, but it is not ready for boarding. A tall man, with soft, curly beard, fine moustaches and a round white fur hat, which gives him a holy 'Zoroastrian' look, has a heap of luggage, and is haggling with the driver. One of the larger suitcases has burst open, and he is trying to tie it up with rope. I help him, and then lift it, and the other pieces, on to the roof; he thanks me. Then I wander around, light a cigarette, and wait.

Just then the red-alert siren sounds from the airport across the road. Almost immediately the nation-wide two o'clock news, on the radio in the little TBT tent, is interrupted by the now familiar, monotone warning: 'Attention, attention! The sound you are now hearing is the Red-Alert or the Danger Warning, it means an air raid is about to take place. Leave your place of business and go to shelter!' The Red-Alert is then broadcast. No one pays much attention. Save a few jeers and grumbles, more or less everyone goes on with what they are doing. After two months of war, the people in Tehran are hardly very excited by these mostly false alarms.

The tall gentleman with the beard and moustaches, strolls up and stands by me. He has stashed away his luggage, but is still loaded with bags and parcels, blankets and assorted cushions. He, too, has lit a cigarette.

He shakes his head ... 'Red-Alert!'

'Yes.'

'I don't think they'll hit, *Jenab*, eh? What is your excellency's opinion?'

I do not answer.

'They've probably seen something on their radars, no?'

'Probably.'

'Or perhaps an unidentified object has been reported?'

'All finished with your luggage?' I ask.

'Yes. Are you by any chance travelling to Europe by TBT?'

'Coach to Istanbul.' I turn and toss my half-smoked cigarette aside, retreating into my own thoughts.

'What is your point of destination?' he asks.

'Paris.'

'Are you a French resident?'

'No.'

'How did you, er ... get an exit permit in this chaos?'

He simply won't give up, so I briefly tell him about my niece's accident in Paris and the ensuing troubles. He volunteers no information. 'So,' he says, 'Your excellency's heading for Paris?'

'Supposedly.'

'You're not married, are you?'

'How did you figure *that* out?'

'Ah! I'm an expert on faces and characters. I've spent a lifetime in the Public Relations Department of the National Air Lines.'

'I see.'

'Have you had lunch?' he inquires in a friendly tone.

'I had a little something at my sister's place.'

He looks around the Terminal. 'Looks like there are no restaurants or anything around here.'

'I saw some liver kabab and egg sandwich stands by the entrance.'

'Oh, God, no!'

The siren has been cut off.

My companion says, 'Let's go . . . By God Almighty, let's get out of this Nowhere's land.'

The Arab woman sitting quietly in a corner just shakes her head in silence, steadily beating herself on the head.

We walk slowly back to the bus, and as there is nowhere to sit, we stand and wait. Curly-beard continues complaining about the state of things in Iran.

'How did *you* get an exit permit?' I ask him.

'My passport has a Pakistani permanent residency stamp. My mother's there. I sent my passport over, she fixed it.'

'I see.'

'I've got a valid US visa, too. My ex-wife, my son and my daughter are there, in Virginia and Los Angeles; according to their laws, they grant asylum to emigrants with political or religious insecurity. They fixed it for me.'

I do not understand what exactly he means by 'religious insecurity'.

We finally get on the coach around mid-afternoon, and the driver starts up the engine. The migrating Zoroastrian-looking gentleman and I are seated next to each other: he, by the window, and I in the aisle seat. Before sitting down, he arranges a couple of blankets and cushions under and around him. 'If we can't travel by 747 Jumbo, let's at least travel in comfort!' Opposite me in the aisle sits a young woman with a baby, and a not-so-young, tubby little fellow who is apparently a student in Germany.

Before we take off, the driver welcomes each and every one of us with his typical Azarbaijani kindness and good-humour. In front of him, and ranged around and above his windscreen, is an assortment of tiny pictures, curtains, tassels, artificial flowers, mottos, a radio, a box of tissues and other odds and ends. Between a portrait of the Imam Ali, and a snapshot of the driver's little son, is a poem printed in fine Persian script: 'A night at home, and a hundred on the road/Oh, fatherless Benz where doth thou lead me on?' He calls out, 'I introduce myself: Ladies and Gentlemen. I am Abbas *Aqa* – Abbas *Aqa* Marandi

4

– at your service. Anything you need, you need at all, let me know. And this here is my helper, Hussein *Aqa* – ditto for him. By his holiness, *Imam* Ali himself, the first Shi'ite *Imam*, the king of men, I hope the trip goes nice and smooth for all the ladies and gents. So, to Mohammad and his descendants, *Salavat!*'

All the passengers loudly chant the *Salavat*. Curly-beard, too, raises his voice; but he turns aside and laughs. Abbas *Aqa* Marandi calls for a second, a third and even louder *Salavat* for the leaders of Islam and for our dauntless fighting soldiers ...

After armed Revolutionary Guards have checked the bus, and the driver's papers at the Terminal's only exit-point, the 0302 Benz finally starts the journey.

Ten kilometres up the main highway, Abbas *Aqa* stops to fill up with fuel. A long queue of vehicles, stretching over two or three kilometres, are lined up at the filling station. Passenger-carrying coaches are exempted from queueing for fuel, so Abbas *Aqa* reverses slowly to the head of the queue. About ten minutes later the refuelling is complete.

Meanwhile, my travelling companion, who says his name is Vahab Soheili, tells me about his many years service with National Iranian Air Lines, how he had recently been kicked out of his job, how on several occasions they had 'barged' into his house and confiscated many of his books and albums, and how he had been kept in Evin Prison for a month and a half, before it turned out that he had committed no crimes, and so was released without a trial. His wife, his ex-wife, and his offspring were either in England or in the United States, his mother was in Karachi, and his late brother's four sons and only daughter were in Germany.

Looking around it seems that nearly all the passengers are in the same position. Except for myself and one or two of the students, the rest have gathered up their belongings and are leaving for good. Soheili, for one, is bidding adieu to his motherland, and says he has packed even the pumice-stone in his old bathroom; Mrs Kiumarspur, a micro-biology PhD from America, is going to join her husband in Paris. In none-too-rigid Islamic head-cover, she is breast-feeding her baby, which is probably a game in itself, for apart from this, her only

5

concern is flirting with the tubby student bound for Germany.

Dusk has fallen when we come out of the filling station. About half a kilometre further up the highway, a little pick-up truck has been hit and overturned. Seventy or eighty kilos of onions are scattered over the road. The driver, an old peasant, squats by his vehicle and the onions, his head in his hands, as if dazedly wondering what to do. Traffic whizzes past, left and right, nobody caring about him. The scattered onions, the overturned truck, and the old man are an hilarious laughing matter for most of the passengers.

2

Two hours after nightfall, Abbas *Aqa* Marandi pulls up in front of a large coffee-house outside Takestan city limits – 'for supper and saying of prayers'. Several other coaches are parked there. Most of our passengers rush to buy dinner *jetons* from the coffee-house proprietor, who is already helplessly crowded with customers. Soheili is in front of me.

'*Jenab* Aryan,' he says. 'They only have rice-and *khoresh-geimeh*, and *kabab barg*. What should we do?'

'Whichever. Both are fine,' I reply.

'The *khoresh-geimeh* is certain to be fat. And God only knows where the *kababs* meat came from!'

'Take it easy, *Aqaye* Soheili.'

'I don't see any dogs round here, by the way . . .'

I chuckle. 'Even if it's cricket's chitterlings from the Moghan Desert,' I said, 'I'm eating it.'

Soheili laughs. 'In that case, if I may so trouble you . . . you wouldn't happen to have a hundred *toman* or so change? If you could lend it to me, a thousand thanks. I only have dollars and pounds left. We'll settle what we spend later.'

'Of course.'

'Dinner's on me!'

'I'm most grateful.'

'Tea or soft drink?'

'Tea's fine.'

'Well, then – two *kabab barg*, two teas, two yoghurts. How's that?'

'Perfect.'

I hand over a hundred note and Soheili gets *jetons* for food and yoghurt. While, bag in hand, he goes to 'clean up', I get the food at the crowded kitchen door. Loaded with *kababs*, country bread, yoghurt and onions, I find an empty place in a corner.

Soheili comes over. We sit down to eat. The kabab is not at all bad. The rice, too, had it steamed long enough, would have been fine. Two peasants come and sit next to us, with a rice-and-*khoresh geimeh* – they don't just eat it, they make passionate love to it, their faces at kissing distance from the plate. They scoop up the food with a chunk of bread, and stuff it in their mouths; some stays in, some escapes to the loving bosom of the plate. They lick their fingers. They have nothing to do with spoons and forks. Between plate and mouth, exists a spirit of unity and intimacy. Soheili eats his white rice with a fork.

'I'm going from Istanbul to Karachi by Pan-Am,' he says.

'I see.'

'How are you getting from Istanbul to Paris, *Jenab* Aryan?'

'I have an Iran Air ticket, but ... I'll just have to wait and see.'

'Iran Air doesn't have a flight now, does it? Iran's airports are shut.'

'That's right. They said they have a contract with Turkish Air, which apparently flies Iran Air passengers.'

'Is your ticket full-price?' he asks.

'No. Forty-percent discount.'

'Are you a government employee?'

'Oil Company. In the south.'

'Could I see your ticket?'

I show it to him. 'No-cash-return, and non-transferable,' he says. 'But I've got friends in Istanbul, we'll fix it for you. If they have a new contract to fly Iran Air passengers, we'll fix it. How long are you staying in Istanbul? It's a very beautiful city.'

'I'm not planning to stay. I'll get moving the day we arrive – if I can.'

'You are worried about your niece, right?'

'I must get to her hospital as soon as I can.'

'What about your own leg? You have a limp. Were you hurt in the war?'

'It's nothing. I tripped over a bottle of Coca Cola.'

He laughs. 'If I may say, God bless you, good man. I hope that with our lord Ahura-Mazda's help, all will turn out well for you and your niece, and everything will come to a good and happy ending – right there in Paris!'

'I don't know . . .'

We each light a cigarette. A boy brings us tea.

'What happened?' he asks.

'What?'

'To your niece.'

'We don't exactly know. In the letter we had, and the few telephone calls to my sister from Sorraya's friends in Paris, we've been told that she was cycling back from a friend's house. Apparently the roads were slippery. She fell turning a corner.'

'And has brain damage?'

'Apparently.'

'How long ago?'

'She's been in a coma for two or three weeks now. I think.'

'God. As simple as that?'

'Yes . . . as simple as that.'

'How old is she?'

'Twenty-three, twenty-two.'

He shakes his head. 'How strange . . .'

I sigh. 'Yes. A fifty-year-old banana like me survives in war-torn Abadan, and in the battle areas, comes through the palm-tree plantations, gets on a dilapidated motor-dinghy by night, travelling over a hundred kilometres under heavy bombing and shelling to Bandar Mahshah. A twenty-two-year-old young woman falls from a bicycle in the suburbs of Paris . . .'

'There's no sense in anything in this world, is there *Jenab* Aryan?'

'No . . . apparently there isn't, *Jenab* Soheili!'

'And now, you're going there to take her back to Tehran?'

'Well, not while she's still in a coma, of course, but my sister does want me to bring her back to Tehran eventually.'

'Well, Lord willing.'

'You said it.'

'Don't lose hope. Ahura-Mazda himself is the resolver of ills.'

'Thanks.'

Around ten in the evening we board again, and move on. This time the passengers are mostly silent, and soon almost everyone goes to sleep. The good Soheili arranges all kinds of cushions and blankets around and under himself. I like this: he pampers himself and is excellently organized, too.

'Bless you . . . *Jenab* Aryan, if you would be so kind to hand me that cushion up there, a thousand apologies. I really have put you to immeasurable trouble tonight . . .' He places the little silk cushion against the window, so that if his head rolls in his sleep, it should come to rest against something soft.

Outside, everything is dark; the coach moves on, groaning. Soheili is soon in the Seven Golden Slumbers. I cannot sleep. Although I have taken my medicine, I feel dizzy, my head aches as if things keep spinning round inside my skull. I look out. In the darkness the night seems silent, and the earth calm. But not within me. The silent night and the calm earth are out there. Or under Soheili's little silk cushions. Or perhaps it has slipped and fallen out of the window. It is the kind of night when the passenger is the bus, and the bus is the night, and it is the night that moves. It is the Jalal Aryan night. A man, almost fifty, teetering this year between life and death. When he walks, he looks like the late Charlie Chaplin – in slow motion. His face is the cross section of a full-frontal view of something between the Long-Armed Shah Ardeshir and the inventor of carrot jelly. When he breathes, his chest sounds like an asthmatic pig. Apart from all this, he is healthy, handsome, and gorgeous.

At three in the morning, we arrivew in Tabriz. Empty streets, everywhere; cold, windy, and drizzling. Abbas *Aqa* pulls up in front of the local TBT Terminal. A couple of new passengers board here. The Tehran passengers are mostly still asleep. Only Doctor Kiumarspur takes her child out to pee by the gutter. Tonight, her Biology PhD is worth nothing. Under the glow of the street light, her gold bangles and the arc of her son's urine make the same spectral array of colours.

10

3

At daybreak, we pass through the clean steppes of western Azerbaijan, and head towards the Bazargan border. It is freezing outside, and daylight grows slowly. The steppes and the hills are bare, but it is beautiful when the first wide rays of sunlight shine out. In the plains, single, ghostlike trees stand out here and there. The hills are empty. From time to time, a bird flies up, spreads its wings in the strong wind blowing from Russia, rocking like a small dinghy in a storm. It reminds me of Sorraya.

We arrive in Maku in the early morning hours. Abbas *Aqa* stops again, and we refuel. Maku seems to have turned stiff with cold, looking shrunken and wan. Even its main street, with its low stone-front buildings, shops and houses carved into the mountain, seems more empty and diminished than ever. In this ungodly dawn hour, the people are queuing, with empty tins for kerosene, standing rigid in lines, or sitting sleepily, or dozing. There are other queues, at the baker's, at the grocer's, people waiting for bread, foodstuffs, or some other rationed items.

I swallow down my morning ration of medicine with a glass of water brought for me by Abbas *Aqa's* apprentice. After a while, Vahab Soheili – who is a fine sleeper – begins gradually to stir at my side. I am not in the mood to talk, but there is no stopping Soheili's lingual engine.

'Top of the morning to you, *Jenab* Aryan.'

'*Salaam.*'

'*Sabbah-Kum-Allah . . .*'

'Knock it off, *Aqaye* Soheili!'

He laughs. 'Any idea where we are?'

'Just past Maku.'

'Then we can't be very far from Bazargan.'

'We're supposed to be arriving there around seven-thirty, eight.'

He looks at me. 'Morning dose, going down the hatch there?'

'Morning dose, down the hatch,' I answer.

'What are those long, orange pills? Aren't they Gaverine?'

'That's right, Gaverine Rx. Three a day.'

'Dilutes the blood and regulates the body's salt. Yes, it's the best kind. My brother took the very same pills after his first heart attack. They kept him alive for years. You know something else, don't you, they must have told you. If you take these pills, then NO alcohol. Gaverine and alcohol don't mix. They're fatal enemies.'

'Yes, they've told me,' I say. And I remember, too, my promise to Farangis.

Then Soheili says, '*Jenab* Aryan, bless your little hand, would you be so gracious as to hand me down that little black bag up there . . .'

At about eight o'clock, we come into the Bazargan Border installations. A dozen or so other passenger coaches and over a hundred trucks and cars have already parked in front of us.

The Bazargan Transit building is a big, old, single-storey edifice, with only one narrow half-door now open, but controlled by Islamic Revolutionary Guards. Hundreds of travellers are crowded in front of it. There is no sign of the regular police force. Only a few boyish *Hezbollahi* youths, quiet and polite, with G-3s and U-Z machine-guns dangling from their shoulders, are assisting the passengers and attending to what has to be done. It is clear that one must wait for hours, perhaps even days, before getting through the rigmaroles here.

The good Soheili is awake now – very much so. Like the other passengers, he has come out of the coach, but is silent and worried. He is busy gathering his mountainous pile of cases and packages together. Abbas *Aqa* Marandi and his apprentice have just finished unloading all the baggage. Abbas *Aqa* collects all our passports, and taking them, along with his own papers, somehow pushes his way through the mob and into the half-door. Orders are for each person to carry all their baggage and belongings into the Transit Hall. A bearded, middle-aged man shouts out through the narrow doorway: if anyone has any extra currency, or gold, or any other valuable objects with them, they must be handed to the customs authorities and get a receipt. Otherwise, if anything is discovered, it will be confiscated, and the passengers turned back. The Iranian world travellers, who used to cruise abroad so elegantly in the years of the Shah's regime, with so much pleasure and in luxury, are now waiting, silently, like deaf-mutes. Not a peep out of anyone. All they want is to get out, somehow, anyhow. It is an emergency situation. The men are no longer 'gentlemen', they are 'brothers'. The women are no longer 'ladies', they are 'sisters'. The people are in batches and groups. 'Iran-Peima passengers, come forward'. 'Mihan-Tour passengers, get back there!' Doctor Kiumarspur, with her baby in her arms, stands next to me. The German-bound student has abandoned her, and gone off to care for his own. She looks worried and at a loss, probably because of her jewellery. Her baggage is scattered everywhere, in bits and pieces. She sighs. 'Have you read that book by André Gide?' she asks me. '*The Narrow Door?*' She's glancing at the guarded half-door.

'No, I have not.'

'He says, "Try and enter through the narrow door . . ."'

I smile at her. 'You don't have that much luggage. Brother Soheili is the one who's going to have to try awfully hard . . .' I glance at Soheili behind me.

Soheili does not laugh. He simply shakes his head. However, he is looking cool and experienced.

'Gide doesn't mean baggage,' Doctor Kiumarspur says. 'He means resurrection.'

'I see.'

'One of my sisters was a university professor, she's now on the government black list: Exit Forbidden. Another sister's in prison, we've had no news of her for months.'

After two hours, it is our turn. We somehow squeeze past the mob swarming in front of the tiny door for no reason, save perhaps anxious haste to get into the Transit Hall. We spend a good deal of time passing on Soheili's numerous pieces of luggage hand-to-hand. We all get in, at last.

It is a large lobby, ending in a corridor leading to yet another hall. A gloomy hush reigns here, suddenly. There are several queues. One for retrieving the passports. One for body-search. Another for luggage search. Another for handing in valuable objects, and another for going out and into the Transit Hall on the Turkish side. I stand in the small passport queue.

A boy with a scant fuzz of a moustache on his upper lip, and sensitive green eyes, is seated behind a very large table, with a U-Z machine-gun on his lap.

'The reason for your trip abroad?' he asks.

I explain.

'Are you travelling alone?'

'Yes.' In my hand, I have a signed copy of an official memo, on government printed stationary with the letter-head of the Ministry of Petroleum, National Iranian Oil Company, the Islamic Republic of Iran. The Tehran Committee Caring for the Problems of the Employees of the War-struck Territories, Abadan and Khunin-Shahr, instructing the deputy authorities of the passport office to render what emergency help the aforementioned (i.e. me) may need. The Deputy Oil Minister has acknowledged the note. I show it to the 'brother'.

'What was your position in the Oil Company?'

I tell him.

'Whom did you say issued your exit permit?'

I mention the name of the Deputy Minister who signed my permit from the Oil Ministry.

'Why didn't Minister himself sign it?'

I inform him that the Oil Minister is being held a prisoner of war by the Iraqis.

He hands me back my stamped passport. 'Go on, brother.'

'That's all?' I ask.

'God be with you.'

The queues for body-search lead to two booths, one for the 'brothers' and another for the 'sisters'. After that the passengers move on to the luggage-checking queues, stand by their things, and shove them gradually forward. In the body-search booth marked 'for Brothers' is a boy of small build not yet eighteen or seventeen years old. Standing before me, he is almost like my child. Without looking at anything, he begins to feel the lining and shoulder seams of my jacket, crushing them in his hands, asking the same questions about the reason for my trip, my occupation, who I am travelling with, etc. He reminds me of

Seyyed Matrud's retarded boy back in Abadan. Only this boy is plucky and alert. While he gives my shoe a thorough inspection, tapping the heel, he asks, 'How are you? Well?'

'Oh, not bad.' He himself seems tired and dry. 'How are you doing, yourself?'

He does not answer me, he just lowers his head.

'You do a thorough job,' I say. 'But I noticed one point.'

He does not pay much attention, just glances at me, dubiously. 'What point?'

'It's not that I mean to criticize the brothers' work, or anything. But I've noticed that people who come out of the body-search booths, go straight to their baggage. They could take something out of their cases and put it in their pockets. Don't you think it would be better to do the body search after?'

'We're badly crowded,' he says, scratching his head. 'We're making some changes here . . . going to have a new corridor built . . .'

He does not search the other shoe. 'Off you go.'

'That's all?'

'God's hand be with you.'

I thank him and come out. Soheili is next in line. His face is the colour of dried mustard. I could guess why. Even his moustaches seem to have suddenly grown greyer and are standing on end.

'Do they search thoroughly?' he asks.

'Thorough as you could wish,' I assure him.

He gives up his place, leaving the queue, and heads back towards his luggage. He changes his coat and shoes. (In Istanbul, he tells me he had £38,000 worth of Travellers Cheques and thousand dollar bills, sewn into the lining of his coat and shoes.) I join the luggage search queue, and because my lone case is skimpy, and the money I am carrying is within the legal limit, I get through quicker than most. I enter the Transit Hall. Doctor Kiumarspur is arguing with the *Hezbollahi* brothers at the customs desk, for they have taken all her gold and jewellery and given her a receipt. She is fuming, all in vain.

In the main Transit lobby a large, U-shaped counter turns across the hall. The door on this side of the counter opens to

Iran, the one on the other side, to quote Abbas *Aqa* Marandi, to 'Turchish' soil.

I do not see Soheili anywhere until noon, when finally he enters the Turkish Transit Hall through a side door. Not only is he now back to his normal colour – he is positively glowing. Obviously, he has sneaked through whatever it was he had with him.

This, however, is only the beginning of our trouble with the Turkish officials, who seem to enjoy their own signs of order or discipline. For a start, they have kept everyone waiting, saying the inspector in charge has gone to make a phone call. Also, there is no electricity, because of a power cut. (Iran supplies the electrical power for both halves of the border and customs facilities). Of course the Turks blame this on Iran, saying Iran's juice is gone, and find this very ludicrous. They talk and joke about it in Turkish, laughing merrily. Next, when the official inspector arrives on the scene, the first thing he says, and is translated for us, is that everyone should have had *cholera vaccinations* on the other side of the border.

The Iranian passengers, who have just been through the twelve tasks of Hercules with the Islamic Republic officials raise their voices in shouts of protest, demanding to know why no one had told them about this cholera business beforehand. The Turkish inspector is unmoved. Passports *must* have cholera vaccination stamps. The only exceptions are those with International Vaccination Booklets. This is a recent order. Harsh discussions follow, but the Turkish inspector remains adamant. He has the passports in his hand, and he waves them in the air, saying they must go back and be stamped with cholera innoculation stamps, or else. My passport is there, too . . .

'I'm not going back!' Doctor Kiumarspur declares.

'Wild horses wouldn't drag *me* back,' Soheili says. 'They should have told us this, before . . .' Then, he booms in English at the Turkish official, 'You should have notified us on the other side! You should have declared . . .' I had not heard this voice of his on the other side of the border.

'How doltish this lot are,' Doctor Kiumarspur says. 'They're even worse than us!'

'It's not right. It's not fair!' Soheili cries. Everyone joins him, throwing in some insult. But it is no use arguing with the Turkish official.

I step forward, take the passports, and, having commissioned Soheili to keep an eye on my little case, I head back towards the Iranian side of the border. Asking as I go, I manage to locate a little booth at the far end of the corridor, where I find the Iranian Quarantine Officer, sitting in the dark, smoking. I explain the problem to him. He seems to understand, even before I open my mouth. This is, apparently, nothing new. He takes the passports – there are fifteen or sixteen of them – opens them all to the next-to-the-last page, and lays them in a pile. Then he begins stamping them in rapid succession. He is a plump, sick-looking man of forty or so, and in the dark little room, he seems even more unreal than his actions.

'These passports,' he mumbles, 'will never contract cholera!'

'They probably won't,' I agree.

'Here you go.' He hands me the batch.

'Thanks, Doctor!'

'Ha! *Bon Voyage*.'

When I emerge once more into the light of the Transit Hall and distribute the passports among their owners it turns out that they have all been stamped upside-down! This does not matter, however, and everyone laughs, because now a new dilemma has come about. It is twelve-thirty, and the Turks have closed up their side of the lobby, and will not reopen till two-thirty. The officials have all gone out to lunch. The doors at the end of the Hall are closed – padlocked, chained and all.

Thus we just wait another two hours doing nothing, behind the locked doors of the Turkish Transit lobby. Most of our passengers are gathered behind the chained doors. A few are spread out on the ground, busy eating. Some offer fruit and nuts to one another. One group sit on the counter, filling out forms. Doctor Kiumarspur's baby is asleep in the arms of the student, who is sitting cross-legged on the floor. The woman herself, her eyes red from crying, is also sitting on the floor exchanging Turkish lire, German marks and French francs with another student. I sit next to Soheili, beside his mountainous pile of luggage, and light up the last of my old Oshnu cigarettes. I do not ask how he managed to get all that luggage through, or, if he had any money with him, or how he got that through. Being well-travelled, and having spent a lifetime working in the National Airlines, in close contact with customs officers, and having been the director of numerous excursion tours, has obviously had its effects.

'Do sit down, *Jenab* Aryan,' he says. 'Be patient.'

'Yes.'

'At this moment, we are actually, nowhere. Neither in Turkey, nor in Iran.' He says this with delight.

'Congratulations,' I say.

'People without a country . . .'

'Dear *Aqaye* Soheili, we are in the Bazargan Border Transit Hall,' I declare. 'Between Iran and Turkey.'

'No. Neither here . . . nor there. People without country, in this mad world. We're all dangling . . . in nowhere. I swear.'

'For the love of God, *Jenab* Soheili – don't get philosophical!'

'No, I implore you – it's true! This is our situation, exactly. The whole country, the whole world, is in a sorry, confused state . . .'

'In two hours the Turkish officials will come back and open the doors. Then your excellency can walk to freedom and be on your way to Karachi and then Washington, DC. In a week's time, all this will be just a memory for you. You will joke about it at cocktail parties.'

'They're opening up in *two* hours?'

'Apparently.'

'What do they eat that takes two hours?'

'*Dolmathis!*'

Soheili laughs, taking out a cigarette from his packet of Winstons. He lights it with a gold lighter, which I have no idea where he was hiding up to now. Then he offers me a cigarette, too. I tell him I just finished one.

'When we arrive in Istanbul, I must send a cable to my son in London,' he says. 'Tell him to send me a little money order, that sort of thing – I have none, at the moment. I'm indebted to you, too, *Jenab* Aryan. I also need something for the expenses of my journey to Pakistan.'

'I was under the impression that you had dollars and pounds left.'

'Oh, in the bank, yes!'

'I see.'

'I shall tell my son in London to send a money order immediately.'

I do not know whether he is saying all this really for me to hear, or for the others.

'I thought you said your son was in LA.'

'That's my own son. This one's my wife's son from her first marriage.'

'I see.'

'Believe me, *Jenab* Aryan – he's more sincere and more faithful and more loyal than my own son. He's a petroleum engineer. Worked in London for OPEC. Now he's working for Saudi Arabia.'

'Who's the one in Virginia, then? I thought you said *he* was your wife's son from her first marriage.'

'Oh, no, that's Robert, my son-in-law. He's American. He married my daughter in Tehran. She's an IBM computer technician.'

'Oh, then her name's Virginia?'

'No, her name's Firuzeh. Robert's working with his brother-in-law now, that's my own son from my first wife.'

'I'll have that cigarette now, if you don't mind.'

He laughs, extending the packet towards me. 'Have I given you a headache with all my talking?'

'No, but my stomach's rumbling like anything . . .'

'I do happen to have some *Gaz* and pistachios at the bottom of one of these cases, somewhere. Allow me . . . I'll be most happy to, eh, open them up, and . . .'

'No, no, please! We'll be out soon, we should be able to get a bite to eat somewhere.'

It is almost four o'clock when the last of our passengers leave the Transit Hall on the Turkish side. I expect now everyone to be as tired and hungry as myself; but suddenly the entire bus-load is restored, lively and jovial. The luggage has been reloaded, all tied up, the coach is ready. In the rear-view mirror, I see Abbas *Aqa* Marandi's beaming face as he starts the engine, and releases the hand-brake. He wastes no time with *Salavat*. He speaks only to tell us there's a big restaurant two or three kilometres up the road, which has food 'and *everything*!' and almost all the passengers burst out clapping. They know he means 'booze'.

At dusk, having eaten, rested and refreshed, we resume the journey, moving on through Turkey. It is cold again, and the sun sets rapidly, dying away into the horizon. I do not feel that we are in another country. The noises and clatter in the coach are exactly the same as before, and the passengers are the same passengers. The steppes and the hills are still naked, and the landscape seems to be the continuation of the hills and valleys on the other side of the border. The same birds seem to shudder in the heavy wind.

Soheili is now very much livelier and jauntier. He has taken out a piece of paper and is counting up the expenses he and I have shared, and for which I have paid; supper, lunch, and other expenses, and he adds them all up. He writes in English, neat figures, in fine handwriting. He then divides the total by two, and takes out an amount in Turkish lire from his wallet, handing it to me. I do not want to take any money from him, but he insists, saying all must be made fair and square ... When I put the lires in my wallet, he asks, 'Whose photo is that? Your sister's?' He is a born snoop!

'No. It's Sorraya.'

'Oh. She's very lovely. I hope to God she'll get well, soon.'

'I hope so.'

'Who's paying for her hospital expenses? Does she have insurance?'

'Well, I don't know. I'll have to look into that when I get there. Apparently, the students are insured for as long as they're at the university. But Sorraya finished her studies three months ago. She was waiting to fly back, before the war broke out and the airports were closed. And then this came up.'

'What will you do if she's not insured?'

'Pay right out of the old pocket ...'

'Do you have money, there?'

'No. Nor does my sister. We'll have to work something out ...'

'It's not easy now – sending money.'

'I guess not.'

20

He remains silent for a short while. Then: 'I expect your sister wanted very much to come along on this trip herself. No?'

'She couldn't.'

'They didn't give permission? Why? Didn't you have a hospital certificate?' By God, he is nosy!

'Yes, but they only allowed one person to go.'

'Why didn't your sister go herself? I don't mean to be inquisitive!'

'My sister has sciatica, she's practically bedridden.'

'Did you say her husband's passed away?'

'Yes, he was a doctor in the Oil Company. He had a stroke and died ...'

'Goodness me. The world is a road to pass, *Jenab* Aryan.'

'So it is.'

The student bound for Germany passes round some *Baqlava* (soft sweets), giving me a reprieve from Soheili's tireless questioning.

We spend the night in Erzerum, sleeping in the tiny Heylun Hotel, with no shortage of night-noise and bugs. Soheili and I take a twin-bedded room, in which the radiator pipes sound like the entire Ottoman Cavalry charging through. The establishment is a four- or five-storey building, with narrow wooden staircases and wide, shapeless rooms. Whenever someone passes through the corridor or up and down the stairway, the building reverberates like the Great Armenian Massacre. But I take my pills, and I think I sleep some five hours.

The next morning, after a small breakfast, we start out. The students going to Germany, Doctor Kiumarspur, who was heading for Paris, and several other passengers, have left us to catch their planes.

All that day, we travel through the Turkish mainland, spending the second night in Ankara, in a hotel not much better than the Erzerum Heylun. The third day we still travel on. Everywhere, the land is very much like Iran – bad roads, and bare trees. The small towns and villages are beautiful, but trampled in mud and poverty.

The steppes are empty, the vast orchards weather-beaten. Army trucks, with soldiers in full battle-gear, fill the roads. They stop the coach every few kilometres and make a complete inspection. Everything from their helmets down to their boots

21

and their strange weaponry, is American-made. Sometimes, near larger cities, the coach's progress is slowed down, because the trucks and tanks obstruct the traffic, the long barrels of their guns jutting out, covered with tarpaulin under the rain.

It is a long and very tiring bus journey, from Tehran to Istanbul, but every few hours, whenever it takes Abbas *Aqa* Marandi's fancy, he makes a stop and gives us a rest. He is a free and jolly spirit, and I get to like him. I wish I knew what he had behind him in Tehran, what sort of a life he leads, and I wish I could make him my guest, sometime, buy him a bottle of something, somewhere. 'One night at home and a hundred on the road,/Fatherless Benz, to where doth thou lead me on?'

But within three days he somehow gets us all the way from Tehran, tired and travel-stained, to the furthermost tip of Asian Turkey, and across the Bosphorus, to the European side of Istanbul.

It is just after nightfall when we get off the coach at the 'TBT' Istanbul Terminal, in a busy section of the city, surrounded by hotels of all sizes. One by one, the passengers fade away into the misty Istanbul night. Soheili and I, still in the spirit of the journey, come to a small hotel near the Terminal, where the owners are pleasant, friendly and humorous like most Turkṣ. When they learn that we are Iranian, coming all the way from the Islamic Republic at war, they treat us with kindness and sympathy, giving us a 'good' room with two 'nice' beds.

The room is, in fact, little larger than a telephone kiosk. After a brisk shower, however, the only thing I care about is a good, long sleep.

4

In the dark of night, we are on the first floor of the National Iranian Oil Company Hospital No. 2, in Abadan. We are in the old clinics section, behind the large room that once belonged to the Ward Master. Tonight, they have moved us temporarily to these rooms facing the city water-tank. This part of the hospital, they say, is better sheltered from shelling and shrapnel.

I have been feeling better lately, and even been able to move around and help the staff, moving the injured or the corpses, or assisting with stretchers and wheelchairs, but since this afternoon old pains have weighed heavily in my skull, and I have come to lie down. After the dusk, the Iraqi armed helicopters hit the water-tank, and most of the glass doors and windows on this side smashed and shattered, and the sound of the explosion reverberates within my head all night. This is the night that Mr Katuzian's daughter, hit by scattering mortar shell while sitting in the car in front of their house, had the emergency operation. They have amputated her leg and put her in the room next to me.

The storm roars all night; strong, turbulent winds scream outside the window. We hear the sound of frightened dogs howling out there, somewhere. The wind blows the rain in through the broken windows, and the cardboard and news-paper we put up against them are useless. The exchange of artillery fire is heavy, maddening at times, especially on the right side of the building which is not far from the waterfront and the Iraqi border. I lie in the dark, numb and senseless with the many pills I have swallowed, but still unable to sleep, listening to the sounds of the storm, and the wail of falling shells and other explosions. Sometimes, the sounds are confused, mixed together, so that we cannot tell whether it is gun-fire or thunder.Time and again a violent burst of lightning illuminates the room, and I can see the rain, and the smoke suspended in the air, over the tops of the ailanthus trees. The Katuzian girl, who has been brought out of the operating theatre to be informed that apart from the amputation of her left leg, her father has been killed and her mother hit in the stomach by shrapnel, sobs unceasingly.

After midnight, the storm grows worse, rain floods into the room in torrents. The room next door must be even worse, because they bring out the few patients – including the Katuzian girl – and leave them in the corridor. The shelling and heavy artillery fire has stopped, but we can still hear machine-gun firing; they are still fighting, in the dark. The effect of my early evening pain-killers has worn off, and I lie aching, trying to think that my pain is nothing, compared to that of the Katuzian girl. Her hysterical, tormented sobbing and her delirious cries are heard all through the night, in the dark, storm-stricken corridors.

Friday morning 28 November 1980, in the city of Istanbul. We are in the one-star Ebrular Hotel – or maybe even no-star. We are in the lovely, quiet Mustapha Kemal Bulvari. No shelling, no explosions, no bloodshed or dying Abadan; nor of the honking and the hooting of Abbas *Aqa*'s TBT Benz's engine, or of its passengers. There is only the good *Jenab* Vahab Soheili and he has risen from his bed next to mine, is washed and spruced-up. He has shaved away his beard, leaving his moustaches immaculate. He is now sporting a smart suit, chic and elegant. At the moment, he's busy combing his moustaches. In time with the movements of his hand and comb, he is whistling an accompaniment, softly between his lips.

Seeing me waking up, he gives a 'Top of the morning to you, *Jenab* Aryan!' then: 'Ah! What a beautiful morning! *Jenab* Aryan, my dear friend, what do you say, shall we go down and have ourselves a real, proper breakfast in the beautiful city of Constantinople?'

'Good morning.' I manage to put in. 'Yes, certainly.'

'A proper breakfast, mark you, not the sort of transit garbage we had to put up with in those tea-houses Abbas *Aqa* Marandi made us stop at . . .'

'I agree.' Then I ask, 'I've got to get to National Iranian Air Lines' offices as soon as possible. Are they open today? It's Friday.'

'They're open today. Here in Turkey, Sunday is the week-end holiday.'

'Then I'll go there at once.' I sit up and yawn.

'How's your head, *Jenab* Aryan?'

'Fine.'

'You kept starting out of your sleep last night. Bad dreams?'

'It's nothing.'

'It was as if your breath suddenly caught in your chest, like a long groan, it woke you up. I mean it actually brought you up off the pillow.'

'I'm sorry I disturbed you.'

'Not at all. Don't apologise. What is it, a souvenir of the war in Abadan?'

'Is what a souvenir of the war?'

'These nightmares and sudden wakings . . .'

'Some of them . . . How are you, yourself?'

'Splendid! Thank you.'

I did not want to talk about the nightmares. Since the first nights in the hospital, they had become so bad that I hardly dared lay my head down without my damned brain starting off.

'I'm at your service,' Soheili says. 'I know some people in the Iran Air office here.' I recall him telling me of the lifetime's work in 'Iran Air', etc., etc.

'I'll have to check if Iran Air does have a contract with the Turkish Government to honour our tickets in Europe.'

'We can check that with the Iran Air agency's employees here. I know most people there. After all, yours truly was an old hand in that outfit. I, myself, must book a reservation for my flight to Karachi. My visa's ready in the American Consulate there. My friends in Washington fixed it for me. But I'm in no hurry myself. But as you have some urgency, in reaching your unfortunate niece in Paris, I shall be glad to settle your business first.'

'That's very kind of you.'

'So! In your company, a real breakfast to start things off!'

'Are you going to ask to have it sent up, while I wash?'

'No, indeed! If you wouldn't mind getting dressed, we shall go to the Continental Restaurant. We're back in civilization now!'

About an hour later, after fruit juice, three fried eggs, sausages, tomatoes, toast, butter, jam, cheese, and large quantities of Turkish coffee, Soheili (who in his own words, has 'an excellent stomach') is feeling even better. He has brought with him a Canon Super-8 movie camera about two feet long, and is asking the hotel waiter where he can buy films.

'*Aqaye* Soheili,' I tell him, 'I'd better hurry on for the Iran Air office.'

'Yes, certainly. In a moment. I'm at your service.'

'Do you know the address?'

'I don't have it just at this moment. But we can ask at the hotel information desk, or find it in the phone directory. Then we can set out. I should like to buy a couple of reels of Super-8 film myself. The scenery of this city has always fascinated me. I've never had ample time to take any films of it. Now I have nothing but time . . .'

'So let's get started.'

The Iran Air Istanbul office is located somewhere in Republic Avenue (Cumhuriyet Caddesi). We go by taxi.

Soheili is right, the city is picturesque, and it is a clear, fine, beautiful morning. The taxi takes us through the People's Avenue (Milet Caddesi) into Ataturk Bulvari, then comes up across the water over Ataturk Köpruŝü and enters Cumhuriyet Caddesi. On either side of the water, rows of tall, sturdy houses, built in all different periods and styles, oriental and western, new and old – Byzantine, Roman, Ottoman, Modern Ataturk, and American skyscrapers – stand in a row. On our right, is the Gatala Bridge. Further in the background, the strait of Bosphorus lies calmly under the blue sky with little puffs of white cloud. It is really fine. I would not mind spending a few days here myself, but thoughts of Sorraya, in hospital, in Paris . . .

The Iran Air office has been open for some hours when we arrive, but there are no customers. Along with his greetings and salutations, Soheili shakes hands and kisses almost the entire male staff, eastern style. He then ushers me to an official, who is sitting idly, like everyone else, behind a computer viewer. Soheili exchanges greetings and kisses, and chats with him, too.

'Nothing to do *Jenab* Azari?'

'Not a thing, *Jenab* Soheili.'

'Do something for our *Jenab* Aryan, here.'

'Of course!' Azari has a beautiful Turkish accent, a very smart gabardine suit, a snow-white dress shirt with a crisply starched collar, a Christian Dior tie, and, in the fingers of his left hand, a delicate rosary of amber beads.

Soheili says, 'He's travelling to Paris. He's got an Iran Air ticket. In Tehran, he's been told that, apparently, Turkish Air accepts our tickets. If you would be so kind to check that and book our *Jenab* Aryan a reservation . . .'

'His ticket and passport, please,' Azari says not looking at me.

I hand them over. He gives everything a thorough inspection. The ticket has a forty-percent Oil Company discount. Azari shakes his head. Impossible.

Soheili murmurs a few words about the fix I am in and reason for my going to Paris.

Then Azari looks up at me, and asks, 'When must *Jenab* Aryan leave?'

'*Jenab* Aryan would like to leave as soon as possible,' Soheili says.

'Today, if possible,' I add. 'All I have to do is pick up my suitcase from the hotel.'

'Turkish Air Lines have daily flights to Paris, at eleven-thirty and at three-thirty.'

'Three-thirty today is perfect,' I say.

Azari picks up the phone.

While Soheili and another employee chat in hushed voices in a corner, Azari makes a reservation for me: THY (Turkiye Hava Yulari) Flight 616, Boeing 727. Departure 15:30 from Istanbul Airport, Arrival 18:55 Orly Airport, Paris, same day. He writes down all the information on an orange-coloured sticker, attaches it to my ticket, stamps it, then offers it to me, with both hands.

'Okay . . .' he asks.

'Finished?' I wonder.

'Good-bye!' His accent is becoming more and more pronounced by the minute.

'No other formalities? Handing in passports in advance? Exit permits? . . .'

'Oh, no, sir. We don't have any of that red-tape nonsense here! Just go to the airport and hop on.'

'Thanks. I will. Is the airport far?'

'Twenty kilometres . . .Take a taxi, sir.'

'Anything else?'

'Yes, enjoy yourself like hell in Paris!'

'Thank you, *Aqaye* Azari.'

And now, it is time also to say good-bye to Vahab Soheili. Soheili pumps my hand in both of his, and gives me his sincere wishes for my niece's speedy recovery with the good Ahura-Mazda's grace. He gives me other bits of advice and suggestions, and wants us to keep in touch in the future. But he is leaving for America, and I am returning to Iran. When we want to exchange addresses, we realize that neither one of us actually has a home, or a fixed address. I am a war refugee, and will probably never go back to live in my old Company house in Abadan. Vahab Soheili is taking permanent refuge in the US. I give him the only address I have in this world – my sister's. Soheili jots it down, then kisses me. His light brown eyes sparkle in sunshine. I do not believe, now, he ever hid £380,000 in Traveller's Cheques or thousand dollar bills in the lining of his coat. Nor do I believe he has an American visa awaiting him at the US Consulate in Karachi; just as I had not believed Islamic Revolutionary Guards had broken into his house, arrested him, or kept him in Evin Prison. After kissing and all, we bid our final farewells.

I go back to the hotel, pick up my bag, settle the bill, and get to the airport by taxi a few hours ahead of time.

At Yesilkoy Airport, at a Turkish Air Lines counter, I am told that Flight 616 to Paris will depart on time; I am the first person to check in. After preliminary formalities, I walk the transit lobbies. I make a telephone call to Farangis from the Airport's communications booths, and give her the news of my flight being okayed and set. When she hears that in a few hours' time I shall be in Paris, by Sorraya's side, it makes her very happy. I promise to call her as soon as I have seen Sorraya with my own eyes.

I have a pleasant feeling of security now. Just two hours before the plane takes off. At the exchange bureau I cash in my remaining Turkish and Iranian money for French francs. Then stroll to the bookshop, buy a novel to keep me busy: *The Dogs of War*, by Fredrick Forsyth. I sit in a corner in one of the bars and order Turkish coffee.

At three o'clock, the passengers for THY Flight 616 are called. Two *Turkiye Hava Yulari* officials line up all the passengers, check boarding passes, and march us out in single file, through Departure Gate No. 26 and on to the plane. Exactly at the appointed time – to the minute – the plane takes off, without the least bit of fuss.

Beautiful, warm sunlight shines in through the little oval windows. The sky is bright, clear sapphire, creamy clouds below, and the earth further off beneath them, thirty-two thousand feet away. While we are flying over Bulgaria and Yugoslavia, an interesting meal is served: seafood hors d'oeuvres, chicken and peppered rice – and fine, hot coffee. After dinner, I take out *The Dogs of War*, and start reading. Good action narrative, about a group of international ex-army mercenaries, but, unable to concentrate, I am not making much progress in the story. Thoughts of Sorraya weigh on my mind.

Under the bright sunshine, *The Dogs of War* in my hand, I close my eyes, and we pass, I think, over Austria and Germany.

. . . In the hour of the wolf, the bodies are brought into the old Children's Ward, now in use as the Emergency Unit for the wounded. Abbas, Morteza, and the rest of them are brought in, on separate stretchers. I help carry Morteza's stretcher to the operating rooms. Blood still oozes from his slashed neck.

They are two brothers, who had been sent to Ahvaz by the Mobilization of the Meek Organization (*Baseeje Mostaz'afan*) in Aligudarz. They have had six weeks training in the 3rd Brigade Revolutionary Guards Division at Camp-e-low, Ahvaz-Abbas and Morteza Shabestani. Abbas, at nineteen, had recently developed a passion for martyrdom, left his job as an

29

apprentice mechanic, and was serving out his regular, two-year military service in the Revolutionary Guard Force. Morteza was three years younger. He had left secondary school to join the Guards, as a volunteer. He idolized his older brother, Abbas. Anything Abbas did, Morteza would do the same. Following his brother, he had joined the '20-Million Strong Soldier Army' of Khomeini.

They had come into Abadan just before the outbreak of the War, and worked in the *Kommiteh* of the Zanguli Mosque, near the Abadan Refinery shipping offices. On the night of 11 October, Abbas and Morteza, along with four other Guards, were in their little trench, in front of the gardens of the old Naft Club, right on the water-front. The six battlers stood watch in two groups of three, relieving each other every three hours. Young Morteza and two older Guards from the Esfahanis Mosque's *Kommiteh* had done watch duty from nine o'clock to midnight, standing with G-3s, RPG.7s and hand-grenades at the ready. It was one of those very tense nights when an Iraqi surprise offensive across the water was expected at any moment. But until near midnight, nothing had happened. The watch had passed quietly, in fact, it was so quiet, that young Morteza, waiting to be relieved of his watch, fell asleep. He was in the trench on his knees, the G-3 in his arms. He slept with his hand on the butt of his machine-gun. The others in the ditch were awake and alert, even though they, too, were tired in the last minutes of the watch. One of them, Najaf Karimi, was a lad from the Lane One Oil Company Labour Residential Area – the old Ahmadabad. He now had his eyes on the Annexe Recreation Center Building, where, in the kitchens, the other Guards were encamped. Najaf, too, was waiting to see when the relief group would arrive to take over.

Two or three minutes before midnight, as Morteza still sleeps, Najaf sees shadows moving in the dark. The shadows appear from behind the huge brick walls of the Annexe Building, then slowly creep forward along the hedgerows, coming from behind the parking lot. Najaf recognizes his fellow combatants – Abbas Shabestani in the lead, then Mostafa Khabbazi, and then Ja'afar Cheraghi. The long wait is over. Najaf nudges young Morteza Shabestani in the shoulder. 'Wake up. They're here.'

In a split second, Morteza starts awake, befuddled and alarmed.

'They're here?'

'Yes, don't be scared. Over there, by the hedges.'

And Morteza turns and opens fire. All three approaching Guards are killed instantly by Morteza's G-3 gunfire – first of all his own brother, Abbas.

In the morning, when the bodies are brought to the hospital, I see Morteza among the wounded. He has tried to cut his throat. He barely looks his sixteen years – with just a covering of soft down near his ears.

In the Ward, one of the 'Holy-War' mullah brothers tries to comfort Morteza, assuring him that in the eyes of Allah, and in His divine justice, young Morteza is not to be blamed for what is done. His brother Abbas' martyrdom has been the Will of Allah.

The only way for Morteza to rejoin his brother, would be for him, too, to be martyred, fighting the 'Infidel Ba'athists', and thus go to Heaven.

5

It is getting dark by the time we land at Orly Airport. Once we are in the corridor of the Terminal, I briskly follow the signs marked 'Arrivée'. My heart beats fast, and something in my brain whirls like a crippled windmill. I get to the section where Passports are controlled. I have already filled in the necessary forms we were given in the plane, and my passport has a French visa good for a three-month stay. The uniformed Customs official at the check-point examines and acknowledges the validity of my documents. He shoots a gloomy glance at my face and does not smile, but clack-clack, he stamps them all. '*Merci*, Monsieur!' He waves me in. I waste no more time. I rush to the turning luggage counter and grab my case. Night has fallen when I finally come outside. There is a light drizzle, and the cold November wind of Paris strikes me in the face.

On my way to the taxis, I bump into Nader Parsi, the Persian poet, author, playwright, translator and stage and screen actor, who is coming in through one of the Terminal gates with a short, plump woman. He stops to kiss me and say a hearty *salaam*. I knew Nader Parsi many years ago, in school in Tehran, and we were still on casual, friendly terms. After exchanging greetings, he introduces me to the woman, his wife, Sara, explaining that they have come to meet her sister, who is flying in from the States. Both are smartly dressed: she in fur coat and a pill-box hat; Parsi in a black leather coat and a feathered hat. In my old, paramilitary khaki jacket, I might well be taken for an old crony of the porter coming to take their cases.

'Well, Nader,' I start to say goodbye.

'You scarpered off too, eh?' he asks.

'Yes!'

'Where are you going? Where are you staying?'

'Right now, I'm going to the hospital ... I don't know yet where I'm going to be staying.'

'Hospital?'

'My niece has had an accident, she's in pretty bad shape. There was nobody, so they sent *me* out to see what can be done.'

'In that war and all? With all the borders closed, how did you ever get a permit?'

'Yeah, well!'

Parsi laughs. 'Well, I hope your niece gets well, Jalal. You look like you're in a hurry now. Take my phone number ... Jot it down somewhere, quick. Give me a call sometime tomorrow evening.'

I make a note of his number on the back of my ticket. 'All right.'

'Make sure you ring, now.'

'Right.'

'We're quite a crowd here ... Come and meet everyone.'

'Okay.'

'We often gather round, do some reminiscing. Maybe we'll even have a few laughs. Why not have a laugh, eh? What do you say? All right?'

'All right.'

'Look at him, Sara,' Parsi turns to his wife. 'The only thing this man can say is "Right" and "Okay". If you tell him: "Jalal Aryan, take this sackful of nails on your forehead and get yourself up Mount Nowhere, on the double, because there's a man up there who needs nails for his coffin" – he'll say "Right, okay!" ... So! Come over, let's see you sometimes.'

'Do you ever see Leila Azadeh?' I ask him. 'Is she still here?'

'Yes. Leila *Khanom*'s still here, too. I heard she's been ill, but she's fine now, and out of hospital.'

'Well,' I say, 'I'll be seeing you.'

'So, then. Make sure you call,' Nader Parsi says.

His wife adds, 'Yes, please do give us a ring.'

'Right.'

'Keep in touch.'

'Goodbye.'

He and the wife disappear into the Terminal, while I find the taxi depot.

My heart is pounding again – it's almost ridiculous. As quickly as I can, I hop in a yellow Citröen cab, and give the driver the name of the hospital. The rest is simple.

'Hospital *du Val de Grace*, please. Very quickly.'

'*Oui*, Monsieur.'

My briefcase and the small suitcase do not have to be put in the boot, and – unlike Tehran – the taxi driver does not waste time picking up four other passengers. I slam the door closed and we start.

It is a miserable, windy night, and still drizzling. The taxi driver manoeuvres so fast that I cannot make out the route he is taking. After a while, we enter heavy traffic, and it's half an hour before I recognize the Boulevard Montparnasse. A few minutes later, the taxi stops in front of the hospital. The driver shows me the entrance, at the junction of Montparnasse and Rue Saint Jacques.

The hospital building is like some ancient cathedral or castle – with dark, Gothic arches, gloomy under the rain and the play of shadows from the lights; more like a Hitchcock creation than a modern hospital. With my own hard-up refugee appearance, rusty case and luggage in hand, I'm not such an exciting, gorgeous picture either.

Asking everybody as I go in, I make my way to the '*Renseignements*'. There are three women in the room. In broken French, I try to explain which patient I want to see. I tell them who I am, where I have come from, and why I am here. The three women – one of whom is a nun – listen to me in awe, and when they hear of me leaving Iran in a bus, they stare as if I had appeared from the depths of wherever it is the Biblical plagues are kept in moth balls. At this moment, another woman, in nurse's uniform, with a scarlet cape over her shoulders, enters the room. She is obviously coming off duty and ready to leave. One of the women points me out to the nurse, presenting me as 'The Monsieur from Iran' and 'The uncle of *la Comatose*'.

The nurse – *Nourrice* Georgette Jardin, I soon learn – works in the ward where Sorraya is kept. She too, gives an exclamatory '*Mon Dieu!*' but greets me warmly. Sorraya is still, unfortunately, in a coma, she tells me. But Dr Paul Martin has been trying out some medication and treatments on her, I think she says. Three weeks have passed, since the *tragique* incident, but they were not yet clear what exactly had happened. Oh, yes, Sorraya had been cycling round a corner, and had fallen on the slippery street. Or, perhaps, there was an accident, with a car or something – though this seemed 'doubtful', but not 'improbable'. The driver of the car who found her said she was unconscious, and only her forehead and temple had been lightly grazed. That night, a Madame and Monsieur – Christienne and Phillipe Charnaut – friends of the patient, whose names and address were in her handbag, brought her here. They have since taken care of her and visited her regularly. Don't I know them? Yes, I tell her, I have heard of them – they had notified my sister. *Nourrice* Georgette Jardin of course knows of this. But, oh, it is very sad, she says, that Sorraya has not come round yet, to tell exactly what happened. It is absolutely terrible, no? Yes. How is she now? The same, unfortunately. *La même condition*. I ask if I could see Sorraya – for just a few seconds tonight – I do realize it is late, but I have come five thousand kilometres for this. Nurse Georgette Jardin understands, and accepts, with sympathy and kindness and leads the way. Leaving my bags in a corner I follow.

In the lift, on the way to the third floor, Nurse Jardin talks non-stop, about coma, I think, the causes of coma, the various conditions of the comatose patient, the side-effects on the body . . .

The moment I enter Sorraya's room, the anxiety and the dread which has been building up in my heart since I set foot on French soil becomes an almost unbearable wave of pain . . . The moment of bitter truth.

Sorraya is there . . . or, what is left of her. She is lying on a narrow bed, at the far end of the room, away from the window. Only her head and one arm are uncovered. Her face is drawn and colourless. There are dark circles under closed eyes. Her thin arm lies on the sheet. Silent, still and cut-off. A needle carrying some fluid is attached to the middle of her wrist. The urine decompression pipe hangs down over the side of the bed to a plastic bag. From her nostrils, a pipe leads to an oxygen cylinder, obviously easing her breathing. The rain outside is heavier, beating down on the windowpane. I can no longer hear Nurse Georgette Jardin's voice. I step forward and touch

Sorraya's hand. Her palm is cold, almost lifeless, like a clam. It is as if there is no blood pressure, or any blood, for that matter. But her pulse beats rapidly. I lean down and kiss her cold forehead. In that moment, I am not even thinking of Farangis. All I think of is this poor creature. Something burns in my eyes. I try to control myself.

The nurse says: '*C'est trés malheureux,* Monsieur' This is very sad, sir. I know ...

I turn to look at her.

'Thank you,' I say. 'Mademoiselle, is there anything I can do? Tonight?'

'No, no. You can come back tomorrow morning and talk with Dr Martin.' She adjusts her *manteau* over her shoulder. We leave the room. 'Yes. Come again in the morning.'

'Yes. I'll be back in the morning ... I'll also take steps about the bill.'

'Of course. I don't imagine there's any urgency. Madame and Monsieur Charnaut have filled out a guarantee form, I think. I shall give you their address and phone number ... Unless you have got it yourself?'

'Thank you, I have got it.'

On the ground floor, we come across Dr Martin, who has just come to look at some of his patients.

'Dr Martin, may I introduce Monsieur Aryan – Sorraya's uncle. He has just arrived from Iran. Monsieur Aryan, Dr Martin.' Dr Martin extends his hand. 'Ah, Monsieur, *ça va.* How are you? It's a pleasure.'

'Fine. A pleasure for me too, doctor.'

'Welcome to France.'

Dr Paul Martin is a man of short stature, in his forties, balding, and like Georgette Jardin and almost all French, loquacious. He soon starts to talk about Sorraya, and about the conditions of comatose patients in general. I don't comprehend much, not only because of my poor French, but also because tonight my brain power is at its low ebb. I made the entire painful journey, from Tehran's Azadi Square and the ramshackle Bus Terminal to Paris to *Hôpital* du Val de Grace with hope. Now this. I am no longer capable of listening, discussing, or even functioning like a normal human being. Dr Martin, however, goes on inexorably. After explaining that they now know exactly to what extent Sorraya's brain has been damaged, he reflects that these cases have no fixed pattern.

'Monsieur Aryan,' he then concludes, 'you have been to see Sorraya, no?'

'Yes.'

'Did you touch her?'

'Yes.'

'Was there any tangible reaction?'

'What do you mean, doctor?'

He asks in English, 'Did you hold Sorraya's hand or speak to her?'

'Yes, I did.'

'Did she show any reaction? Or move?'

'I don't think so. There was no response.'

'Are you quite certain?'

'I don't think she felt anything – or at least, if she did, I didn't notice.'

'Come, let's go back, please. Repeat what you did in my presence – I'd like to record this on the *SSR* machine, and take a look at the graph. You have time?'

'Of course.'

'*Eh bien. Allons*! Very well, let's go.'

The doctor and I, along with Nurse Georgette Jardin, go upstairs again. A machine of some sort is brought into Sorraya's room; they connect little gadgets and wires to Sorraya's hands, forehead and temples. I am excited that my presence in the hospital tonight has caused some positive action.

The Doctor asks me to take Sorraya's hand, to kiss her, to talk to her about the most personal and intimate things. I do as he asks, spending four or five minutes talking gently to Sorraya, about Farangis and me and all, caressing her hands and face. After a while, the Doctor removes the graphs from the machine, saying he must study them carefully later. But, obviously, he has not found whatever it was he had been hoping for.

Again, I thank them both, and reassure them that I have no intention of moving Sorraya until her condition is improved. We arrange for me to come back in the morning and see to 'things' (that is, the hospital bill). Neither Dr Martin nor Nurse Jardin seem very concerned about the bill. I get a feeling, however, Sorraya is not eligible for government insurance. And

Charnaut has signed a guarantee. Just perfect! The doctor shakes my hand warmly, wishes me an *enjoyable* stay in Paris, expressing his delight that I have come to Paris, to see Sorraya, and help. *Merci mille fois*. A thousand thanks. I thank him, too. Ten minutes later, I leave the hospital.

The rain is pouring now, but I don't feel like taking a taxi. I feel like crawling in the rain, up the Rue Saint Jacques – getting soaking wet! I know this part of Paris. I walk up to Jardin du Luxembourg, and on to Boulevard Saint Michel and turn into small, dark Avenue Monsieur le Prince, and the Hotel Palma, which I also know. It is still there and there is a vacancy. There is always a vacancy at the Palma, because it is a dump in the Latin Quarter. When I get in, I am dripping like a drenched alley cat. Madame Sumunjou is also still there, small and delicate as ever, with her fragile, ageless Swiss face. Reminiscing, she shows me to my room.

If it were any other night, at any other time, and I had not made that promise to Farangis, I should fetch a bottle of the old 'medicine' and get tight as an owl, but not now.

6

When I wake in the morning, it's still cloudy, and the little Avenue Monsieur le Prince is empty and quiet. The naked tree-tops quiver in the wind outside my window. I can see nothing else of Paris.

I shower, shave, dress, and sit by the window, opening it just a crack, to let in some fresh air. I breathe deeply, trying to think out what I must do next.

First I write a long letter to Farangis. I did phone her last night, but now I describe Sorraya's condition, and write all the things I couldn't say on the phone. I try to sound hopeful – without lying – but when I read the letter over, I find it so cheerful and inspiring it's positively absurd. In one place, I have written 'Feri, not only is Sorraya's condition not dangerous, I even think it is promising. The only thing is we must be prepared for anything – even for things to get worse, and I swear to God I have no idea what I am talking about!' I close the letter with kisses, etc., put it in the envelope, address it, seal it, and put it in my briefcase. I go downstairs, wearing a new shirt and a smart new sweater, knitted by Farangis herself. The box of pills I take before meals is in my briefcase too.

In the illustrious Palma Hotel, breakfast is included in the room rent. There are, however, no garçons about. In fact the receptionist, who doubles as chef and garçon, brings the breakfast trays. All one is asked is 'Tea or coffee?' The rest is fixed: French bread, croissants, butter, cheese and jam, served in little packets. Milk with coffee or tea. Today, the receptionist is old man Duval himself, the proprietor, manager, chairman of the board of directors, chef, garçon, bellboy and *maitre d'hotel* of the establishment. He wears his mismatched coat and trousers, bow tie, felt hat, and the eternal pipe in his mouth. 'Coffee,' I say, and he brings the tray into the little room, to a table by the window. The bread and butter, and the sour-cherry jam is fine.

After breakfast, I go out, walking down the Boulevard St Germain to the post office at the corner of the Rue Danton. I go in and ask about the state of air mail delivery to Iran. The air mail delivery to Iran has its difficulties, that is to say, it does not actually exist. Due to the Iran–Iraq war, and the airports being shut down, they are not accepting any air mail to Iran. However, there *is* a postal service: they take the letters by air to Turkey, and then send them on by land. It takes about ten or twelve days. I post Farangis' letter, and from there I take the metro to the Franklin D. Roosevelt Station, which leads out to the Avenue Montaigne, and the Bank Melli Iran.

Inside the bank is a hubbub of penniless Iranian students. I open a temporary deposit account, and with a French franc cheque carried on my passport, draw a cheque for ten thousand, for part payment of Sorraya's hospital fee, although the bill so far – when I saw it yesterday – is around a hundred and forty-two thousand francs. *Merci mille fois*!

When I come out of the bank, an Iranian youth accosts me and explains how sorry his state of economics are. Having just now a pleasant feeling of economic power, I pass him a fifty. But I get out of the neighbourhood quickly, because it is full of down-and-outs and vultures. I walk to George V Street and buy myself a brand new, three hundred franc raincoat. I take a taxi to the Rue Saint Jacques and Boulevard du Montparnasse.

It is still cloudy and dull, and I cannot get the image of Sorraya on that sad hospital bed off my mind. However, under my skin, I feel somehow secure and trustful. I light a new cigarette, while the taxi passes the crossing at the Rue New York, over a bridge, and comes to Montparnasse. I get out at the Val du Grace hospital. Today, the old building, with its dark vaulted roof, its ancient columns, its crescent-shaped, colourless corridors, and baroque style, appears even more depressing than it did last night. One gets the impression of entering a monastery or a convent, instead of a modern-day hospital – although the one hundred and forty-two thousand franc bill is quite modern and bears the heavy footprints of Giscard d'Estaing's capitalist government.

In Salle Three corridor, I catch sight of Nurse Georgette

Jardin coming out of the noisy metal elevator. Her uniform is immaculate, almost blindingly white. She sees and remembers me. She comes up to me, beaming widely, almost as though she was about to start embracing me. Her face is pink and nice, like a freshly sliced *jambon*, and her small hazel eyes shine like two fresh olives. '*Et alors, comment allez-vous aujourd'hui*, Monsieur? And how are you today, sir?'

'Well. Thank you. How's my niece – Sorraya?'

She shakes her head. 'The same.'

'No ... no change?'

'No, I'm afraid. You want to see her, no?'

I fear it might be against the regulations. 'I wanted to give a cheque,' I say. 'It's not much ...'

'It's fine...*Merci mille fois*. Oh ... I forgot! Do you know who is here at this moment? Madame Christienne Charnaut. You would like to meet her, no?'

'Charnaut? ... Oh, yes. Madame and Monsieur Charnaut ... Sorraya's friends.'

'Yes. Your niece's friends.' She says they are very kind. They have been to visit Sorraya regularly. 'They have looked after her, you know. Madame Charnaut is here today. Upstairs. It is good, no?'

'I would like to meet Madame Charnaut.'

'Certainly. In fact, she's with Sorraya right now.'

I do not know the French for cash office, and I do not want to speak further to Georgette Jardin about paying a meagre ten thousand francs to the hospital by the name of 'Valley of Grace'. I decide it would be best to use the phrase '*Monsieur le Directeur*,' or something.

'Can I see the hospital director later, about paying in this cheque, and have a word or two with him?'

'About the cheque?'

'Yes.'

'Oh, of course. You must see Monsieur Macadam. In this very building, the basement, Room 12.'

'*Merci.*'

'Well, best of luck!'

'What about Dr Martin? Can I see him today, do you think?'

'Dr Martin is upstairs as well.'

'*Merci.*'

She still stands there, looking at me.

'Mademoiselle,' I say. 'Is there . . . is there something else you ought to tell me about my niece?'

'No . . . Not really. Poor thing! You have been told all there is, I'm sure. With this sort of thing, of course, one has to wait and see . . . We all hope she will recover.'

'Well, all right. *Merci.*'

'Take care – the stairs may be slippery.'

'Yes, I will.'

I climb the well-polished, tiled stairway leading to the third floor.

Even the Out-Patients Department (OPD) of the Abadan NIOC Hospital was better than this The waiting room was as big as an airport lobby, with twenty-two specialist doctors, and two separate, well-stocked, prescription centres – one for labourers and one for staff employees. The floors, rooms, and even the toilets were cleaned and disinfected at least three times a day, and everything was polished until it shone. But that evening, after the Hospital's main entrance was hit by rockets, and we were moved into the OPD, things had changed.

The long corridor on the third floor of the *Hôpital Val de Grace* is almost deserted. An assistant nurse enters one of the rooms, with a medicine trolley. A janitor moves a little electric floor polisher across the worn tiles. On a wall, the stereotyped, golden-haired, blue-eyed nurse in the poster raises a finger to her painted lips. 'Silence!' At the end of the corridor, Dr Martin stands, speaking to a young woman of petite build. He sees me, and signals with a sweep of his hand. Instead of interrupting them, I enter the doctor's spotlessly shining little office, and sit down, waiting for him. Only the very tips of the bare trees are visible through the long window. The sun breaks through the clouds and is suddenly almost glaringly bright.

. . . It's early evening, and I'm helping two volunteer students working in the OPD rooms. Among the wounded is a labourer's wife and her baby. The child lies in the mother's arms. The mother is unconscious. Both her legs are deformed by burns, full of pieces of shrapnel. The baby is clinging to the mother's neck, wide awake, feeding; the mother's breast still in its

42

mouth. The mother's face is covered by her *chador*, but her legs –
or what used to be her legs – are apart, red and black and
charred. On one leg, the stocking has melted and almost
dissolved into the flesh. The floor of the OPD Hall is filthy,
disorderly, and tonight, everything reeks of blood. The glass in
the tall windows has been shattered, and black smoke is rolling
in. The wounded have by and large been brought in and laid
down along the wall, until the doctors can get to them. Almost
all of them moan and cry out *'la ilaha illa allah'*, or say their
shehadatein. Everywhere you hear the sound of moaning, and
the crying out. There is no electricity, but a generator supplies
power for the drugstore and rooms on one end of the hall. The
other end, where the windows are, is dark, and in a corner,
beside me, a lad from the Security Guard, whose head has been
damaged by explosion shock-waves, talks loudly and deliriously
about hauling an ice-making machine – without even having its
keys – from the Annexe building by the waterfront all the way
to the Maintenance Building in the Petrochemical Plant
Road.

Footsteps, those of Dr Martin and the lady with him,
approaching, bring me back to the room. I get up and we shake
hands.

'Aha! Monsieur ... Good day to you. *Ça va*? Are you well? ...
Not tired any more?'

'No, thank you. How are you, Doctor?'

'Fine, thank you. Listen. You two people would like to meet
each other.'

The small woman looks me over with a smile and with
curiosity. She is wearing jeans and a gold-coloured wind-
cheater. Her black hair is in a ponytail, and she has small, but
fine, sensitive eyes.

The doctor says, 'Monsieur ... I have forgotten your first
name.' I know he has forgotten both my names.

'Jalal Aryan.'

'But, yes. Forgive me, Monsieur Aryan.' Then, turning to the
small young woman, he says 'Madame Christienne Charnaut,
let me introduce Monsieur Jalal Aryan. He is Sorraya's
uncle.'

'Oh, yes, that's right,' Christienne Charnaut says with a wide smile. 'I recognized the Monsieur from his photographs. Sorraya showed several snapshots to me. She spoke often of you.'

I nod and exchange pleasantries with Christienne Charnaut.

'*Enchantée*, Monsieur Aryan,' she says.

I reply with an '*Enchanté*, Madame.' Her hand is bony, but firm, like a peasant's. The doctor stands back, beaming, letting Madame Charnaut speak to me.

'*Mon Dieu*,' she says. 'What is happening in Iran?'

'Revolution ... war ... and many other things.'

'*Mon Dieu*!'

'Mademoiselle Jardin told me how you have cared for Sorraya, and helped her while she has been here ...'

'Bah! We have done nothing! Sorraya was my friend. We were in the university together. Of course you know, we went to the Sorbonne. The least we could do for her after that tragic accident was to bring her here ... What a terrible, heart-breaking accident ... Of course you know. She was ready to go back to Iran, she wanted to go to Tehran by land ...'

'Yes, her mother is very upset and worried.' Turning to the doctor, I ask 'How is she today?'

'There's been no change, I'm afraid ...' He now goes into further explanations. Apparently none of the treatments and medicines have affected Sorraya's condition. He asks, 'Did I hear correctly last night that you planned to move her from here?'

'No. Oh, no,' I say. 'Not at the moment. Besides, Iran's airports are all closed ... Even if her mother wants her moved, that's not possible.'

'Very good, that's a wise decision. Well I have to be going.'

'Thank you, Doctor.'

He leaves, and involuntarily I enter Sorraya's room. She is still there, in coma, cut off from the realities of the world, lying in that corner. In the daylight her lovely face is like a piece of parched, yellow paper, worse than what I saw last night. The chart at the foot of her bed bears weird curves, marks and lines, incomprehensible to me. Christienne Charnaut is behind me, speaking. I have quite forgotten her.

'You had better not move her from here,' she is saying. 'She's very ill.'

'Yes, I see that.'

'Well,' she says, 'I must be going. My two children are alone in the car! I stopped by to see Sorraya and speak to the doctor, but I always talk too much! My car is by a parking meter and it's certainly run out by now! Where are you staying?'

'Hotel Palma ... Avenue Monsieur le Prince ... The number's in the phone book, of course.'

'When did you arrive? Yesterday?'

'Yes, yesterday.'

'Here is my address, Monsieur Aryan. Phillipe and I would like very much to see you some time ... Sorraya's belongings, and valuables – her gold and jewellery – are in my safe keeping. You must come and collect them.' She hands me the slip of paper, bearing her address. 'I've written our phone number, too. Do give us a call before you come. Phillipe can come and pick you up. We live in Saint Remy – about seventeen kilometres outside Paris. The Metro station is Saint Remy les Chevreuse.' She speaks so rapidly and bombards me with so much sudden information that I am quite confused. Phillipe, I have to assume, is the husband. 'Thank you,' I say, 'I shall certainly phone.'

'Listen! Tomorrow's a holiday. Be sure to call us. We have guests this evening; my two sisters and their husbands are coming with their children. I've got a headache already – but Phillipe is fond of them. Do you know in France they call the sister-in-law 'the beautiful sister'? Phillipe works in Robinson but he comes to his company's other offices in Port de Versailles, which is near here ... It's not far from your hotel, either. Avenue Monsieur le Prince is near the Odeon Station, isn't it? Phillipe can pick you up and bring you over. Around six or seven in the evening would be very good. *Non*?'

She has to look up in order to speak to me, but this does not bother her in the least, and in no way deters the flood of words pouring out. French always sounds 'too fast' for me, even when spoken by someone other than Christienne Charnaut. I don't understand a good deal of what she says, but I have understood enough. Besides, I don't want to keep her any longer while her two small children (they must be less than five at least, or they would be in school) are alone in the car.

'Thank you,' I say. 'Yes, I will. I'll certainly call.'

'The day this *tragique* accident happened, Sorraya was at our house,' she continues. 'In the afternoon, she was cycling back to

Paris, when it happened. Fortunately, our address was in Sorraya's handbag. Phillipe and I went to the Montparnasse Belle Vue Clinic straight away, and brought her here. The police, they don't care. All they can do is cough, rub their moustaches, take addresses, and file reports. Unfortunately, Sorraya had no insurance of any kind on her. She had finished her studies by the end of July. Phillipe and I signed the papers, guaranteeing payment of the hospital fee. If it weren't for Phillipe, God knows what would have become of things.'

'Sorraya's mother and I are indebted to you for ever, Madame Charnaut,' I say. 'Now that I'm here, I shall take over full responsibility for her expenses. At this moment, of course, we haven't got much money in our hands; but I will get enough soon. We are very grateful for your assuming the responsibility. Many people wouldn't have done that. You are noble people.'

'We were glad to do it.'

'I will call tomorrow and thank you properly – goodbye for now.'

'No need to thank us. Sorraya was my best friend, and what a fine, free spirit . . . With all the experiences she has had, losing her husband in the Revolution, and all that she has behind her . . . She has interesting ideas and outlook on life. She's been a fantastic friend to us . . . It's a great pity that fate has dealt her such a dreadful blow. Terrible luck! Well, I *must* hurry! My kids are alone in the car! I hope the police haven't stuck a ticket on my windscreen. Phillipe will be absolutely mad! So – you will call?'

'Yes, absolutely.'

'Tomorrow?'

'Yes, tomorrow.'

'Very well then, *Au revoir*, Monsieur Aryan.'

When Christienne Charnaut has left, I go back into Sorraya's room. Two of the four beds are empty. The patient in the third bed is asleep. The room smells of Dettol. I stand for a while, at the head of Sorraya's bed, holding her hand. Her lovely, dark face is small as in the days after her birth. 'Sorraya,' I whisper. 'Get up, girl! It's uncle Jalal. The dumb one. We'll go back to Tehran . . . Back to Farangis. You don't want Farangis to be alone and unhappy – in these rotten conditions . . . Wake up, girl. Wake up, my lovely . . .' It is useless.

Later, I go downstairs, to Monsieur Macadam in Room 13, and pay the cheque towards Sorraya's expenses. Monsieur Macadam is a dour, silent man. He is happy to see me, he says, and he manages to keep me waiting for over an hour and a half putting the accounts in order, and giving me a receipt for the present payment. He says he hopes the payment of the rest of the bill can be arranged soon ... Rules are rules.

It is three in the afternoon when I leave the hospital, and my head is aching again. When I get to the Avenue Monsieur le Prince, I feel hungry, thirsty and empty, but it's too late for lunch, and too early for supper. Near the hotel there is a MacDonalds café. I think of going in for a 'Big Mac' and some french fried potatoes, but the place is full of Spanish tourists and dark Hindustanis; there are no seats, just stand-up counters, so I go back to the hotel and swallow down my pills with a cup of hot chocolate which Sumunju brings me.

Afterwards, I lie down on the bed, and light a cigarette. I must do something, soon, about the hospital bill. Nader Parsi was the first person I saw after my arrival in Paris, and he is now the first person I think of.

Nader Parsi was a Pamenar neighbourhood boy, the son of Mash-Gholamreza the building contractor. In those years he was at the Rahnema high school, too, and both the president of the school's so-called 'Theatrical Society' and the 'Sports Council', yet he was always in fights and squabbles with everyone. After he was given a good beating by Alikhani with his knuckle-duster, he left the Sports Council. In 1956, at the expense of the then free-spending government of the Shah, he was sent to France, where he stuck around universities for seven years and got his Masters in science, and, I think, another degree in neo-classical literature – so he said. When I next saw Parsi in Tehran, he was the chief editor of a major publishing organization – although he was still into collusions and rackets – and had written some short stories and plays, making a name for himself among the younger generation, especially those drawn to his tradition-breaking prose style. He had also set up a small, modernistic bookshop opposite Tehran University, and he sometimes staged his plays in the University Amphitheatre.

He'd translated several Hemingway short stories, too. Then he went into television, and returned to France – at the expense of the Iranian Television Corporation – for a six-month course, after which he began to produce 'artistic' short movies. Then newspapers and magazines spread the news that one of Nader Parsi's films had won first prize at a New York film festival. I was working in the oil fields in the south then, and was really pleased when I heard the news. However, having known Nader Parsi for a long time, and always been suspicious of foreign 'Festivals', I got in touch with Bill Quentin, a University of New York professor who was conducting a management seminar in the South at the time – he'd had a hand in that festival. I asked him about Nader Parsi's film; he not only remembered Nader very well, he affirmed that his film had received an award – he also recalled how Parsi had got into an argument with Jack McCoy, one of the judges, on the night of the awards presentation; they had almost come to blows.

In the early 1970s, Nader began making 'Guest Appearances', in glossy Iranian feature films, bearing his name at the end of their cast list – 'Also starring ...' Later, with the financial support and the fame of another already well-known actor, Parsi made a few big, real money-making films himself. He had by now married several times, and had two sons rejoicing in the names of Hum and Tahmaj, dug up, God knows how, by their father from the depths of the *Shahnameh*. His children went to school in Lausanne.

I give Nader Parsi's telephone number to the hotel receptionist, and he connects me. Parsi's wife answers first. I give my name, and ask is *Aqaye* Nader Parsi at home?

'Yes, he just got in.'

'May I speak to him, please?'

'What did you say your name was?'

This is plain nosiness. I repeat my name, and wait until I hear Nader's voice.

'Howdy, pardner, as John Wayne would say!'

'*Salaam*, Nader.'

'How are you, Monsieur Jalal, eh?'

'Tired.'

'Tell me everything, now. What have you done? Where are you? When are you coming to see us? How is your niece?'

'My niece is the same.'

'What do you mean?'

'She's in a coma – as they say.'

'You're not in a coma, yourself! I hope?'

I laugh. 'Not only am I in a coma, my entire family and damned ancestry's in a coma.'

He laughs, too. 'What about the expenses?'

'Well, I gave them a cheque for ten thousand francs; they said *"Merci mille fois!"* '

'They always say *"Merci mille fois"* when they get the money.'

'I have to scrounge some money together, Nader.'

'From Tehran?'

'Yes – from anywhere.'

'It can be done. Come to the Café de la Sanction tonight. The crowd usually meets there. We'll talk about it.'

'What was the name again?'

'Café de la Sanction. Come at around nine or ten, that'll be great.'

'Where the devil is it?'

'North end of the Rue Saint Jacques, before you reach the river bank, opposite the Raoul's Cinema. You can't miss it.'

I jot something down. 'Ten o'clock?'

'Yes, nine-thirty or ten. We're all there. Be sure to come. It's the hang-out, you know . . .'

'All right, I'll be there.'

'Did you see Leila Azadeh?' he asks.

'No. Where should I see Leila Azadeh?'

'I just thought you might have seen her; since you were asking about her yesterday.'

It's clear that he wanted to see Leila Azadeh, himself.

'No,' I say. 'I was just asking about her.' Then I ask, 'You said she was ill . . . You said she had to spend some time in hospital. What was wrong?'

'I don't really know . . . That is, no one really knows. I just heard she had an operation. All very hush-hush. Her parents are here, too. But they live in Marseilles. Leila lives alone. Anyway, whatever her illness was, we never found out.'

'Well, I'll see you later, Nader.'

'Be at the Sanction at ten.'

'All right, I'll try.'

'Don't *try, be* there! Come and see The Screwed-up Generation.'

'What on earth is The Screwed-up Generation?'

'The *Lost Generation*, idiot. To quote Hemingway, that is.'

'Oh!'

'So. Come and see the homeless exiles. They usually gather there in the evenings. Far from the homeland, they come to exchange news about home and see each other. As Mowlavi says:

> Listen to the flute, as it narrates,
> Moaning from the pains of separation
> Ever since they cut me off the reed-bed
> People have wailed because of my lamentation.

'Flute, be damned! Tell them to come and lament to the blowing of shells in Lane One of Abadan's Ahmadabad, labourer district!

Parsi makes an obscene remark about the regime and the war-mongers. I laugh, saying, 'All right, then – ten o'clock in the Homeless Wailers' Café.'

'Yes, ten o'clock, Café de la Sanction.' He sounds insulted, but has enough manners – or is graceful enough towards me – not to hang up first. I put down the phone, lying back in the bed. I cross my hands over my forehead.

I try to bring Leila Azadeh to my mind, as I knew her thirteen years ago, or the way I saw her once again here, five years after that. It doesn't work. Only Sorraya's pale, yellowish face, remains imprinted on my mind.

I am driving up the Petrochemical Plant Road towards home, in a Land-Rover borrowed from the Volunteer Helpers *Kommiteh*. I have to get my travelling documents, and a few things together for the emergency trip to Tehran.

I turn through Ahmadabad Street into the Petrochemical Road. Like a giant lying, wounded and burnt, in the sleep of death, the huge Abadan Refinery is spread out, sending up clouds of smoke. The Petrochemical Road and the winding streets of Breim itself are deserted, and still as death. The houses have been abandoned, mostly with the furniture in them. The burglars, or the buzzards of the war, have raided them. Here and there, walls and the roofs have been hit by shells and rockets. The lawns are either burnt, or overgrown and parched, the trees broken. A tree felled by enemy fire is still there, blocking the road, no one has bothered, or dared, to move it. Even the dogs and cats have fled.

My own house is by the Arvand River, little more than seven or eight hundred metres from the shores of Iraq. The last time I was here, about a month ago, I came to drive my servant-gardner, Matrud, and his retarded son, Idris, to a 'safe' place in Ahmadabad's Lane 12. They had nowhere to go. They *have* nowhere to go. The rooms at the corner of my garden have been their only home. The little I paid Matrud these past years was their living. Outside of Abadan, they would die.

I can hear gunfire overhead and all across the region, but nothing comes my way. I park the vehicle at the end of the drive, and get out. The four outside walls of the house are still intact, though every single window has been shattered by the impact of shells falling in and around the garden. In the distance, somewhere, dogs are howling. I open the front door and go in. There is no electricity; there is no water in the taps. Most of the furniture is still there. The house is so near the Khorram-Shahr Road and the waterfront, and so exposed to enemy fire that not even the burglars and the war buzzards have dared to break in. But it has not been too dangerous for the rats! They are here. I can hear them racing around the rooms. And they have been at work, too. Apart from the food in the kitchen cupboards, they have gnawed away most of one carpet, several armchairs and even some books. It is quite a scene; but I have come fully prepared. Having heard tales of rats in many other houses, I have brought along a large packet of rat killer! I close the bathroom door and the front door. I tear open the poison packet and get to work, sprinkling the powder all over the floors, and sometimes right on top of the creatures' heads. Some of them stagger about and drop dead on the spot. This gives me some satisfaction.

I get out a small suitcase and start packing the things I came for. I have to get out fast; the Iraqis may show up at any moment! The sewage rats I could send to hell with DDT but Iran had yet to invent a DDT for Saddam Hossein's rats.

A man's shadow appears in the doorway, and I turn with a jolt. But it is Matrud – the old, short and shrunken stature, dark face, pale moustache.

'It's you, *Aqa*!' he says. '*Selaam*!' (the old Abadani dialect has an 'e' sound for 'a' in the first syllable).

'Matrud! For God's sake – what are you doing here?'

'I, er . . . We came back . . .'

'You're back living here?'

'Aye, *Aqa* . . . I've made some tea. You want a coop?'

'Didn't you promise me you'd stay in Lane 12 with your brother? You didn't stay in Aqa Jari either! Got up and came all the way back here again, for nothing. You were damned lucky the Iraqis didn't capture you as prisoners of war on the damned road. This place is dangerous!' I am really angry with him.

'They hit der, too. They hit it every day. Here seem better'n der.'

'They can shoot you here with a goddam Kalashnikov from across the river!'

'Death is in God's hands, *Aqa*!'

'Where the hell's Idris?'

'Idris boy here too, in Dr Nurbakhsh's house.'

'Idris is here, too?'

'Well, er . . . Where can I put 'un? Won't stay anywhere. Has to be with me. He's got no proper brain.'

'Are you minding Nurbakhsh's house, too?'

'Aye. Have some tea?'

'Matrud, listen! You must go back to Lane 12 at once.'

'Aye, *Aqa*. Where should we go? When death come to take you, well, he take you.'

'You haven't even got water here.'

'Tap in garden has some. Electricity's off. But a little water. Pressure's not much, though.'

'Look, Matrud,' I say. 'I have to go to Tehran. I *must* go. My sister's child has had an accident. You know they don't have anybody else. I may have to be away from Abadan for two or three months. I don't want you staying here.'

'Are you sending us away, *Aqa*?'

'Matrud – what a hell of a thing to say! This house belongs to the Oil Company. It's public property. But it's *dangerous* here. Damn it, this is a war zone!'

52

'What can we do?'

'Go somewhere else.'

'Where else have we got? It's us, the poor, who have all the troubles.'

'What became of your brother?'

'He's gone . . .'

'What?'

'He left this world. He died. His house is flattened to the ground, too.'

'God, I'm sorry, Matrud. What about his son, the one in Khosroabad?'

'He's gone, too.'

'He was killed fighting?'

'Aye, *Aqa*. Sit down. I'll bring 'un tea.'

'Oh, Matrud! Matrud! I'm saying there's bombing and there are rockets and shells falling from the sky – you tell me to sit down and have a cup of tea. I tell you to get out of here, go find somewhere sheltered – you tell me to sit down and have tea! I tell you think of your son, Idris – you tell me to have a cup of tea . . .' I lower my voice. 'You must go to Ahvaz or to Masjed-Suleiman or somewhere like that, away from Abadan, till the fighting dies down.'

'We've nowhere to go.'

'*Find* somewhere!'

'We was born in this town, we'll die in this town.'

'Is there anyone in any of these houses round here?'

'No. Dr Nurbakhsh 'un gone too.'

'Nurbakhsh was killed?'

'No – gone to Tehran. Aye, *Aqa*! What's all them rats?'

I am about to explain to him about the rats, when an explosion shakes the house, with an intensity that makes me think the hospital Land-rover must have been catapulted into the sky. I hurry outside. The Land-rover is still there and so is Idris. Idris is in his tennis shoes. With his Pan-Am handgrip, from which he once used to sell Winston cigarettes, and that meaningless, Arabic song he always sang. He's polishing the Land-rover. Against the background of burnt hedges and fallen, charred trees, his little fat figure, with the blank face and crazy eyes, completes the picture.

When I reopen my eyes in the Hotel Palma, it is dark. The street noises have died down. I look at my watch – it is nine-twenty. I get up, wash, and dress. By nine-thirty, I am sitting on the bed, with a fresh cigarette, tuning my tiny short-wave radio to the Iranian news, especially broadcasting for 'dear compatriots' abroad. The news is solely about the Iran–Iraq war. The war which has for the time been labelled as a battle 'between Islam and the Saddami Infidels'. The Iraqi forces have now completed the blockade of Abadan, and are attacking the homes and residential areas of this 'resistant, martyr-breeding town' and its 'defenceless people' from all sides, with guns, rockets, shells and bomber planes. The 'Mercenaries of Saddam Hossein, the American Infidel', have advanced towards Ahvaz and Dezful, and are now just ten kilometres outside these towns, but faced with the strong resistance of 'The Guards of Islam', the Islamic Republic of Iran Army, and the 'martyr-breeding people'. 'The Forces of Islam' have succeeded in destroying one armoured vehicle, two personnel carriers, and a tank belonging to 'The Infidel Ba'athists'. They have sent hundreds of 'those tricked by the bribes of the Regime of Saddam Hossein the Aflaghi' straight to hell.

7

It's nearly ten when I come out of the hotel and swing through Avenue M. le Prince and into Boulevard Saint Michel. It's cold, but the sky is clear and full of stars. A breeze wafts from the Seine, not far to the north. Scores of cafés, restaurants and cinemas are alive with lights and sounds and glitter. The smell of roast chestnuts, and hamburgers and french fries from the MacDonald's joint on the corner, fill the sidewalk. My date with Parsi is for ten o'clock.

A strange, painful dizziness suddenly appears in my forehead – this is unusual. I lean against the wall, at the corner of Rue des Écoles, waiting for the pain – or me – to pass away. In Abadan hospital – especially in the first days – I used to have such pains. Sometimes, they made me lose consciousness. But they had not appeared now for some time. Tonight, the fuzzy feeling is unusual, and the pain is bad.

Somehow, I manage to sit down at one of the tiny sidewalk café tables. Despite the cold and the windy night, I don't mind sitting out here alone. One or two of the tiny, round tables are occupied, but most of the customers are huddled inside the café. My head still aches.

An old but fresh-faced *garçon*, in a claret-coloured coat, with a white towel draped over one arm – looking as if creeping out of the pages of Balzac – comes up to me. There's always a white towel draped over one arm.

'Yes, Monsieur?'

'*Un Expresso, s'il vous plait.*'

'*Un Expresso.*'

Paris ... the cradle of civilization.

I pretend I'm really somebody. I take *The Dogs of War* from my pocket, and open it. The Zangaroo Republic has become a plaything in the hands of the British. A London merchant, Sir James Manson, discovers through his spies that in one of the mountains of Zangaroo – Crystal Mountain – are platinum mines worth millions of dollars. With a small army of professional mercenaries – American, Irish, German, French and English – Manson decides to overthrow the Zangarooan government, and set up his own puppet state. But after the internal rebellions are set in force and the mercenaries enter into action, Manson's pawns soon find themselves faced with KGB agents and realize that when the bait is large, the West is not alone. However, tonight, here in Paris, I'm at the beginning of chapter eight; two of the mercenaries have just had a telephone conversation with Manson, and I can't even read the first sentence to the end. The thought of Sorraya, lying in coma, seeps through what is left of my brain. The headache, the cold night breeze, the loneliness, the coma, and *The Dogs of War* . . . I hear Nurse Georgette Jardin and Dr Paul Martin talking fast, and the sight of Sorraya's comatose form moves in waves around my head. Dr Martin expounds his vocabulary of medical terminology for my benefit.

'Coma is a "sleeplike" state of unconsciousness that is caused by a malfunctioning of the brain. This may be temporary, or it may be permanent and fatal. No one can tell how long it may last. A state of coma that lasts for more than two or three days, and causes deterioration of the brain cells, is the sign of severe damage and is probably fatal . . .' Sorraya has been in a coma for twenty-three days. 'The damaged cells may be in the outer layers of the brain (cerebral cortex), or in the deeper parts (the cerebellum) which is the brain's centre.' Poor Sorraya! . . . I raise my head and exhale a thick cloud of cigarette smoke into the cold air. The dizziness has now pervaded all of my skull, the back of my neck, and even behind my ears.

A tall, red-headed woman sits down opposite me at the tiny table. She puts her handbag down on the edge of the table. Slowly, she begins taking out a pair of none-too-white gloves. I try not to look at her. She looks like a prostitute, and God knows how many thousand walk the streets of Paris. She springs a *'Bonsoir'* on me, and I reply with a nod, unleashing something on my face that might pass for a smile. She begins excavating in her bag for a cigarette which she pokes between her lips, then rummages around for the missing matches. She is in need of a light. She takes the cigarette from her mouth and starts to cough. Her coughing, worse than my own, is like a raucous groan. Give me the gasoline-burning Vahed Co. buses in the chaos of Tehran's Revolution Square any day.

'You have light?' she darts at me in broken English.

I strike a match for her.

'*Etes-vous Parisienne?*' I ask.

'*Mais oui!*' Of course she's from Paris.

Her teeth are brownish and her eyes, like those of an anaemic's or worse, are yellow and dirty. The lines on her face are not so obvious, but her extreme thinness, the teeth, and the barking coughs, make it all too clear that she has worked for at least twenty years in 'the oldest profession in the world', in this cradle of *Humanité, Egalité, Fraternité*.

'Don't you want to buy me a drink?'

'What do you drink?'

'*Une* Bloody Mary.'

'Smirnoff and tomato juice?'

'Could be.'

'Why Bloody Mary?'

'I'm made of Bloody Mary.'

The waiter arrives with my *expresso*. He places first a paper napkin and then the tiny cup and saucer before me. The tab bearing the price of the coffee (service included) is in the saucer also. Three francs and sixty-five centimes.

'And for madame?'

'*Une* Bloody Mary, *s'il vous plait.*'

The waiter repeats the order indifferently, and vanishes.

She asks, 'Don't you drink?'

'No.'

'Why?'

'Lots of reasons ... Doctor's orders, for one.'

'Where ...?'

'Pardon?' I cannot understand the French phrase she has used.

Like some grammar instructor, or like one speaking to the mentally retarded, she enunciates, 'Where? ... Where are you sick?'

'My head,' I say fingering my skull. 'I'm sick in the head.'

She laughs. 'I'm sick in the head, too!' Then she rubs her hands together and shivers with the cold. '*Rrrr . . .*' She says, '*Il fait froid!* It's cold!'

'Bloody Mary warms you up?'

'I hope so.'

I don't mind her turning up in the middle of my lonely night. She somehow senses that I have just taken an interest in her for the first time, and smiles. It's as though French women are fitted with a radar complete with Mirage scanning computer devices, for these sorts of perceptions.

'Where are you from?' she asks.

'What do you think?'

'You're not American?' She's looking at the English copy of *The Dogs of War*.

'No.'

'I think I'm going to like you.'

'God help *you*!'

'Thank you.'

'What are you called?'

'Adèle.'

Her drink arrives and Adèle behaves with it in a not too ladylike fashion. That is, she picks it up and tosses it down the throat, the way old Tehran roughnecks used to toss it down. Or maybe she thinks it's the last government ration and at any moment the foreign legionnaires might swoop down and take it away from her.

Then she say, '*Alors, comment vous-appelez-vous*? Well now, what is your name?'

'Horse,' I reply.

'What?'

I repeat.

'Horse,' she says. 'That's a nice, simple name.' But I don't think she believes me.

I glance at my watch, and tell her apologetically that I have to meet some friends at the Café de la Sanction at ten o'clock. Oh, of course, she says, and she's ready to come with me, if I like. By nature, and by way of not wanting to turn down an offer, I say yes, and immediately regret like hell.

We enter the Rue Saint Jacques at a stroll, and walk uphill.

The street passes behind the grounds of the Sorbonne. The area is a mixture of the ancient stone buildings, cafés, restaurants, cinemas and cabarets. Adèle is telling me her life story. She is from a little village near Bourget ... I don't remember where. She has been living in Paris for eighteen years. She has no other 'occupation'. Not only does the government forbid Adèle her social rights, each month she is called in on various pretexts, examined, and threatened with having her licence removed unless she makes better efforts to keep in good health, and keep her living quarters in better sanitary conditions. She speaks vulgar French and I cannot understand the meaning of most of her words. I just remember one French slang word meaning excrement, which she uses as an adjective for every noun, proper and common, in her sentences. Two or three times, too, she uses the phrase 'I make nice love', which, of course, I understand well.

At the top of the street, past a string of movie theatres, there is a pedlar with a hand-cart, selling hot food. Adèle's steps falter. Her eyes are glued to the cart.

'*J'ai faim.*'

'You're hungry?'

'I'm *dying* of hunger.'

On the side of the cart it says: HAMBURGERS ET HOT DOGS.

I think Adèle says 'A penetration of the corrupting American features of culture in the aged civilization of France.'

We stand in front of the cart.

'A hot dog, please,' Adèle says . 'With lots of mustard. 'Then, to me. 'The mustard is from the Bourget area. It's really terrific. *Un peau trop fort, ça.* It's a bit hot.'

'Good?'

'Mmm! You want some?' she offers me a bite.

'No, you eat it.'

8

A little way past the intersection of Rue Saint Jacques and Boulevard Saint Germain, I spot the long and ancient sign of Café de la Sanction. Adèle has just devoured her hot dog, and she wipes her mouth as we enter.

Café de la Sanction, unlike its impressive name, is hardly a sacred or authoritative hideaway of the refugee. It's an old, dilapidated dump, with roofing, floorboards, wall-paper and curtains reeking with age, as if nothing has been changed or even mended since the Great French Revolution. Adèle, however, is exultant with joy, and seems to be having more hunger pangs in front of the food *vitrines*. Inside, the café consists of numerous interlocking rooms and lounges, accommodating several bars and food counters, etc. American rock music blares out from one of the juke boxes.

I am having a look around when Adèle says: 'First we eat something, no?'

'Sure.'

She stands frozen in front of a glass case filled with various seafood delicacies.

From behind me, I hear Nader Parsi's voice with it's heavy accent.

'*Bonsoir*, Monsieur Aryan!'

'*Bonsoir*, Monsieur Nader Parsi!'

Then, in Persian, he says: 'Come on to our table. There's plenty of food and drink and everything, ready at your service'.

'All right,' I say.

'Bring your friend, too.'

'Sure.'

He looks at Adèle, with admiration and even a little astonishment. In the glare of the café interior, she has put on a huge pair of dark glasses. With her tall figure and reddish-gold hair, she has made an eyecatching sight all right. Parsi leads us to their table in the rear of the café, near the small dance floor.

About eight or nine Iranian couples are gathered round the table. Nader Parsi presents me to them – whom he jokingly calls the Iranian 'Lost Generation' – and he introduces them briefly to me.

I know four of the men by name, though I don't think any of them had heard of me. One is Dr Ahmad Reza Kuhsar, author and Tehran University professor, and his wife; then Bijan Karimpur, Iran's modern-set poet, and his wife. Another is Majid Rahnama'i, the executed Prime Minister Hoveida's art-loving friend, and still another is Reza Majidi, Empress Farah's special librarian, each with their wives. Then there is Jalal Keshavarz, Iran's famous Zoroastrian authority and one of the original founders of Iran Novin Party, and his European-looking wife. There is also Colonel Javad Alavi, whose wife is related to Keshavarz. *Khanum* Homa Ala'i is also there with her husband who was a managing director of the National Iranian Oil Company. There is an Ahmad Qandi – Reza Majidi's nephew, who is awaiting his US visa – with slick, oiled hair, velvet suit, loud tie and a little portable radio glued to his ear, listening to the Voice of America. There is also a Dr Kazem Makaremi, and last and certainly the least, diminutive, chubby, pink and white Dr Qassem Khatibi, both without their wives. Food and drinks, French and American, are plentiful on the table. The gathering is, as Parsi hinted, not unlike a scene from the Hemingway novel. Before Adèle and I seat ourselves, in keeping with the atmosphere, I introduce Adèle as 'Mademoiselle Adèle Françoise Mitterand.'

Heads turn furtively in our direction. Some eyes practically pop right out of sockets.

Adèle simply smiles. Most people near shake our hands with respect. They all scrutinize her carefully, and exchange pleasantries. Adèle merely says *Enchantée* to everyone and sits down. Karimpur offers her some white Bordeaux which she quickly accepts. He asks to pour me some, too. I say 'Just mineral water, tonight. Doctor's orders.'

Karimpur says in Persian, '*Aqaye* Aryan, as our dear Moshiri says "Fill up the cup to the brim . . ." Don't break an estranged man's heart . . . We're afflicted, too.' He has a drawn, sorrowful countenance, with thick, droopy moustaches like those of Maxim Gorky, and a mass of long, curly grey hair down to his shoulders.

'I'm sorry, too,' I say.

'*Jenab* suffered a stroke early this year,' Parsi explains. 'So we must have a care for him. He has a worry of another sort, too.'

Doctor Ahmad Reza Kuhsar says, 'Allah willing, nothing serious I hope, eh, friend?' His face is aged, but truly magnificent and dignified, with long, full white hair, thick, Kamal-al-Molk moustaches, and large, honest eyes.

'Thank you,' I say.

My official spokesman, Nader Parsi, adds, 'His niece, who has been studying here, has had an accident. She is hospitalized at the Hospital du Val de Grace, and she's in a coma and not very well. *Jenab* Aryan has come to help her.'

'Allah-willing, she'll get well . . .' Dr Kuhshar says.

'Allah-willing,' Parsi says.

Karimpur speaks up. 'In any case, as our Moshiri says "Come fill the cup . . . For in this land of ruins, no more the wine will show me the way out . . ." '

From the adjacent table, Majidi's wife, who has not heard our conversation, asks, 'Have they come from the Elysée Palace?' She speaks Persian with a French accent.

I do not answer her.

Dr Kuhsar's wife asks Adèle: 'Mademoiselle, are you related to Monsieur François Mitterand?' This one speaks French with an Isfahani accent.

Adèle, whose mouth is full of bread and caviar, swallows unhurriedly. Then issues a simple, '*Non*.'

'No relation at all?'

'Which François Mitterand?' Adéle asks.

'. . . The leader of the French Socialist party . . .'

'No,' Adèle says. 'I'm related to no one by the name of Mitterand.' She is spreading a biscuit with butter and a sort of paté Doctor Rahmani has offered her. The glass of Bordeaux, which Karimpur has refilled, is close by her elbow.

Majidi's wife says, 'But I'm certain that Monsieur Aryan introduced you as Mademoiselle Mitterand!'

'Monsieur Aryan . . .' Adèle asks. 'Who is he? Am I related to him as well?'

'That tall monsieur you came with,' Majidi's wife explains.

'Ah . . . that monsieur,' Adèle says.

'Well?' asks Majidi's wife.

'Monsieur is sick in the head,' Adèle says now.

Majidi and his wife, and two or three others who understand French burst out laughing.

'So it was a joke?' Majidi's wife asks.

Adèle says, 'Monsieur himself said that he was sick in the head.' She points to her own head.

By now, everyone is laughing – even a few, who clearly don't speak French and have no idea what was going on.

Majidi asks, 'Then, what is your name?'

'Adèle Formulu.'

'Adèle Formulu?'

'Adèle Christianne Lafoure Formulu.'

'So . . . It was a joke! Yes?'

Adèle shrugs.

Majidi's wife says, 'Well . . . A funny sense of humour *Aqaye* Aryan has.'

I am now sorry for what I have done, mostly for Adèle's sake – it wasn't such an original thing anyway. I even hear Hemingway's bones rattle in his grave in Ketchum, Idaho.

Adèle, however, not only doesn't look upset, she's eating and drinking away, having a jolly good laugh herself, and is obviously very pleased to be in this ridiculous game with a bunch of foreign 'intellectuals'. All this is a joke. A laughing matter. Everyone here is gathered solely for the purpose of having a few laughs and a good time. Majidi gets up still laughing and dances with *Khanum* Ala'i. Dr Kuhsar dances with his wife. I lean back in my chair, feeling empty, and ask myself what in the name of the Seven Mad Gods I'm doing in this place. Traces of dizziness are still with me. I take out two of my good old pills and knock them back with soda water, but later they just make my mind even foggier.

Parsi stealthily hands me a packet of strange cigarettes. He says, 'Now that you don't drink, here – light one of these. Put the rest in your pocket ...' I look them over.

'These are the ones that turn wolves to courting jackals ...
Right?'

'Even beyond.'

'The Cloudlands?'

'The Cloudlands 2000.'

The Cloudlands 2000 is all I need tonight.

9

I don't remember how much later Leila Azadeh entered. She is still small and delicate, very little make-up, light chestnut hair, black raincoat, white silk scarf. She still has that dream-like quality, and is still attractive. Most of the people around the table know her, and are happy to see her. Judging by Nader Parsi's staring, and his droopy mouth, it's obvious he would like to know Leila Azadeh better. Leila and I have not seen each other for eight years now, even then our acquaintance was not firmly rooted. I don't think she remembers me at all.

She exchanges a *Salaam-Aleik* with each and every one at the table, kissing the women, shaking hands with the men. When she comes to me, she cries out a long '*Sala-a-am!*' and not only remembers me, but is also evidently happy to see me here. She sits next to me. 'Mr Jalal Aryan! You, here?'

'I came, that's all.'

'Good, good!' Her eyes seek something in mine.

'It's good to see you,' I say.

'Seeing you is goodness itself.'

'Okay.'

'This is good, it is good.'

'You haven't changed at all,' I say.

She looks at me.

'Are you ill? Or just older and wiser?'

'Just dumber.'

'Really, how are you?'

'I don't know, a little more aged. A little more confused.'

'When did you leave Iran?'

'Three days ago.'

'By bus?'

'By Cooperative 15 Benz.'

'Fled from the Islamic Republic? No, no! Sorry, you don't run

65

away. Running away is for chickens like . . .'

'Leila!'

She giggles.

'Well. I hear there's war.'

'True!'

'How is it?'

'Dirty and insane . . . The maniac dogs are shelling the towns, the streets, the houses and the innocent people.' For the first time, I have found someone I feel like talking to.

'The Arabs?' she asks.

'Saddam Hossein's "infidels"!'

'Who's to blame? Who are we fighting? Saudi Arabia?'

'No, with "The infidel Saddam Hossein Aflaghi"!'

She giggles. 'Tell me about it.'

'One problem is that while the storm of the Revolution is taking its course in the land of the Rose and the Nightingale, the neighbouring country is being ruled by a maniacal beast . . . There's no saying what a maniacal beast won't do, when he is provoked.'

'You weren't hurt?' she asks, looking at me.

'No.'

'Are you lying?'

'Yes.'

She laughs. 'Ah! *C'est bon* . . . That's good.'

I look at her. She's still perfect and lovely.

'Jalal, where are you now? In Abadan? Or have you come out? Or are you on the sidelines?'

'On the sidelines.'

She sighs. 'It's better to be on the sidelines, than not be there at all.' Then she lowers her voice. '*Mesdames et messieurs* here, whom you see eating and drinking and dancing – half of them have fled from the Iranian Revolution. The rest from the war. That is . . .'

'Say no more . . . I know.'

'Me also . . .'

'Not you. You came here long before the Revolution, eight or nine years ago. You're not one of them.'

She sighs again and leans back on her chair. 'I'm always running away from *myself*. Within me, I have a thousand revolutions and a hundred thousand dirty, insane wars.'

Nader Parsi, who has been listening, remarks 'Leila, dear . . . Hafez says: "We are not come here in search of position/From the ill of chance to refuge here we come".'

Well, I don't know, *Jenab* Parsi,' Leila says. 'In your case, I'd think that it's from all your relatives and in-laws to refuge have you come . . .'

Parsi reddens. 'Don't say that, Leila *Khanum*.' He lifts his brandy and knocks it back at one gulp. But his eyes never leave Leila. Bijan Karimpur brings Leila her favourite drink. A thin glass filled with a greenish liquid.

'A Pernod,' he says, 'with a dash of lemonade.'

Leila Azadeh says: 'Thank you. You remembered . . .'

'Who could forget?' Karimpur replies. 'Pernod and lemonade is the thing our Leila drinks.'

'Among other things!'

'Whatever Leila Azadeh wishes, Leila Azadeh gets. I shall personally, with all my heart, produce it for her.'

'In your future regime, the only thing you'll produce will be the hard Bolshevik vodka.'

'There's plenty of that, too!'

'With coupons!'

Karimpur laughs. 'There will be plenty without coupons, too.'

Parsi listens, and it is obvious in his eyes that but for his wife's presence, he would get up and twist Karimpur's head off, for preening himself for Leila Azadeh's benefit. I glance in Adèle's direction. She is getting close with Qassem Khatibi and Kazem Makaremi. Since Leila came to sit beside me, Adèle has begun to flirt.

Leila gets up and goes over to *Khanum* Ala'i, speaks with her for a few minutes and returns. I think she has been to find out who Adèle is. 'So, you have a fiancée!'

'We're one soul in two bodies.'

A tall man, whom everyone addresses as His Excellency Colonel Javad Alavi, comes up to my chair and with great modesty, inquires how I am. At first I think he, too, has come to flirt with Leila Azadeh. He says, 'I'm most honoured, *Jenab* Aryan, I am Colonel Alavi.'

'My pleasure.'

'You are still with the Oil Company?'

I tell him that I am.

'Anything left of the Oil Company? I hear they are now calling it the Spoiled Company.'

'What can I say? You'd have to come and see for yourself.'

He does not smile. 'Tell me,' he says. 'What's the story of the Abadan Zulfaqari? What was the situation? I had a brother – Lieutenant Alavi – martyred there!'

'Congratulations and commiserations!'

Zulfaqari was a newly constructed suburb – near the cemetery, or as the Abadanis called it, the *Khakestan* (Dust-land). It had come under brutal attack in early November. The Battle of Zulfaqari is now famous. I tell him, 'Zulfaqari's next to the Abadan Cemetery.'

'So there have been attacks as far into the island's centre as that?'

'They crossed the Bahmanshir River by night with a mobile bridge, but the people and the guards and the army defeated them. There was a lot of killing.'

The Colonel shakes his head. His glass shakes too, and the drink within it. 'What about the rest of Khuzestan? How much of it has been occupied? Tell me.'

'I don't know, sir.'

He is a bloody Colonel in the Iranian Army, and he is sitting here gorging himself with Bordeaux, asking me for news on the war in his homeland.

'Have they taken Meidan Tir in Abadan?'

'I'm just a simple Oil Company employee on the sidelines. I'm not into war or politics. Yes, the Iraqis have not only taken Abadan's Meidan Tir, they've advanced as far as 20 km into the Mah-Shahr Road.'

The Colonel is, of course, not pleased. However, with some pomposity, he exhibits his tactical and military knowledge, and throws in some disparaging insults about the ruling government. With a few more pleasantries and courtesies to me and Leila, he returns to his seat.

'Don't mind him,' Leila says to me. 'Shall we go out and take a walk?'

'All right ... There is something I want to tell you anyway.'

'What about your fiancée?' She gestures towards Adèle.

'My fiancée's doing fine.'

'Been engaged long?'

I look at my watch. 'Thirty-five minutes.'

'Where did you pick her up?'

'Off the sidewalk on Saint Michel.'

'You horror!'

We rise. Leila Azadeh announces that we are going for a walk. Many eyes follow her.

'Coming back here?' Parsi asks me.

'I think so.'

'... About that little economic matter ... You know ...'

'Don't talk in mysteries,' Leila says.

'There was something Jalal and I were discussing ...'

'Don't go counting on anything, *Jenab* Parsi.'

'As Fitzgerald says, I'm counting on the fact that "Tender is the Night".'

Karimpur breaks in: 'Long is the Night ...'

'And the *Sufi* wakeful,' Parsi adds.

'And the Sufi snoring!' his wife says. 'Within half an hour, you'll have drunk so much you'll be snoring out loud right in this very seat.'

Bursts of laughter greet this attack. Parsi casts an angry look at his wife, but says nothing.

'Well, *au revoir*,' Leila says.

'Goodbye,' I say.

10

We walk straight up the Rue Saint Jacques.

'It's strange,' Leila Azadeh says.

'What's strange?'

'I was dreaming of you last night!'

'What were we doing?'

She nudges my elbow. 'No, seriously. I dreamt of you. I dreamt we were back in Tehran.'

'Then it must have been a nightmare!'

She laughs. 'No! But it's odd. So many years have passed – and yet I have to go and dream of you last night, and here you are – after all these years – in the same month of November, I think it was, when I met you first, maybe even the same day, I don't remember . . .'

'I told you it was a nightmare!'

'It was no nightmare in those days, Jalal,' she reaches for my hand.

'No . . .'

At the end of the Rue Saint Jacques is a wide street, on the river bank. Across the water, the Notre Dame is brilliant with many lights, for the tourists' benefit. White yachts, lit up and twinkling, bob up and down on the water, moving to and fro.

'So. Have you come to take your niece back to Tehran?' Leila asks.

'If possible.'

'Would it be better for her to stay here? . . . Till she gets well . . .'

'I don't know. My sister wants her home.'

'Listen, Jalal. Start at the very beginning and tell me the whole story, I want to know what happened.'

'Well – forty-six or seven years ago, one night my old man, Arbab Hassan, sleeping out on the roof-top of our house, in old Tehran, under the stars, felt like making –'

'Jalal! Not that far back, thank you!'

'How about the beginning of autumn this year?'

'That's far enough.'

'When the war broke out on the first day of autumn, or the last day of summer, to be exact, I was lying in Abadan's No. 2 Oil Company hospital.'

'Why?'

'Recovering from a stroke.'

'No!'

'I didn't think I had one, either.'

'Had what?'

'A brain or anything to have a stroke in the first place.'

'Be serious! Well, then what?'

'Two weeks into the war, I managed to get about a little, and have myself discharged. But you see, with the flood of the dead and wounded pouring into the hospital – like all the patients who could walk – I began to help around, and gradually became like a member of the hospital staff. Later, after the Iraqis captured and blocked all the island's exit routes, and we were besieged and surrounded . . . there we stayed, till about the last week of October. My sister managed to call one night from Tehran, telling me about Sorraya's accident here in Paris, that she was in hospital, in a coma, possibly dying, and I was to come to help her. Something she said that night still sticks in my mind: "I've got no one in this world, and before they wrap me in a white shroud and lay me in my grave, I want to see my child one more time!" '

'Tsk, Jalal! Don't talk like that.'

'You told me to tell you everything.'

'I know! Well, what then?'

'The next night, I took the only route left – that's from the south side of the island, along the Bahmanshir River, into the mouth of the Gulf. This was the only outlet from Abadan which the Iraqis had not yet captured. Under the shelling and gunfire, we came out into the Persian Gulf, in a tiny motor dinghy, and reached Bandar Mah-Shahr. I got myself via Behbehan,

Kazerun and Shiraz to Tehran, to see what could be done for my sister and my niece. That's the story, and the reason for this mission.'

'And now you want to take her back to Tehran?'

'I'm not going to move her till she's better.'

'Good. So . . .?'

'Sorraya herself was about to come back. She was all ready to return, when this accident happened.'

'What's exactly happened to Sorraya? You say she's had brain damage . . . how is she?'

'Bad . . . I don't exactly know, yet. She's had concussion, and the doctor says it's both in the cerebral layer and the internal sections – somewhere.'

'How awful.'

'Yes, and she's a damned fine girl, too.'

'How old is she? Tell me about her.'

'Twenty-three. Sorraya . . . is the only daughter of my only sister. Her father died a good many years ago.'

'She's not married?'

'Sorraya? Yes, she was married in Iran. After graduating from the Sorbonne, here, she went back to Iran. This is about three or four years before the Revolution. She got married. Her husband was a fine young man, too, Khosro Iman. He was a university graduate too, with a good job. They were very fond of each other.'

'What happened?'

'He was killed in the early street demonstrations of the Revolution.'

'Martyred?'

'Yes . . .'

'So then Sorraya came back here to continue her studies?'

'Yes. Farangis said that would be best. She thought it might help her get over Khosro's death. After the Shah's fall, in the days of Bazargan's provisional government, she came back here. She had just finished her studies, was planning to return home. One evening, she fell while cycling and got hurt. She went into a coma that very night.'

'Then she must have had a concussion. Was her skull fractured?'

'Well, yes, I suppose so.'

'Go on.'

'Apparently, the fracture is not serious. But the damage inflicted on the brain itself is. Her doctor and the nurses have explained it to me. Apparently, in layman's language, she's had internal bleeding. Even some of the brain's soft matter itself has been crushed.'

'Oh, my God!'

'Yes, it's not a thing we want even to hear.'

'No.' She presses my arm to her. We stroll in silence, she looking at me.

'What are they doing for her?'

'They've drawn out the blood from under the skull. Concussion of this sort can almost totally paralyse the brain – which, in this case, it has. They're just keeping her vital organs going. She's connected to life-support machines, for oxygen, food, water, drugs . . . They're giving her cortisone, and glucose, and vitamins, etc . . . They take an EEG daily. Also something they call neurotherapy, taking SSR tapes . . . They're working on her.'

'Will she get well – do you think?'

'Yes, she will. I hope.'

'Good.'

She smiles. 'Is she very pretty?'

'Very much so . . . Maybe as beautiful as you.'

'Which hospital is she in?'

'Hospital du Val de Grace . . . Did I pronounce it right?'

'Good enough for me. I have to go to the hospital tomorrow myself, the Sacre Coeur.'

'Whatever for?'

'See the doctor . . . I had an operation recently.'

'. . . What operation?'

'One cannot talk about everything.' She looks away.

I pry no further. I remember Nader Parsi saying something about Leila having been ill and a problem of which she had told no one. I glance at her. Her head is down, I cannot imagine beautiful Leila Azadeh, young and rich and healthy, here in Paris, could even run a fever, let alone have a surgical operation. Troubles are in Iran, for little, old, war-stricken me, and my sister, and her child.

We cross the Pont Neuf, walk down the steps, and stroll by the river. It's quiet and deserted now, save a few lonely wanderers here and there.

Then she says: 'Well. How are you, yourself, these days?'

'Don't ask!'

'Still alone?'

'Yes. And tired.'

'No wife, no children, no home ...'

'No star, no nothing.'

'Why did you *stay* there, Jalal? I mean in Abadan, and all that? ... You could have come out, come here, or anywhere you liked. You worked there for so many years ... More than enough. Why did you stay?'

'No reason. How was I to know there would be war? I was nobody. I was in the hospital, reading, when damned Saddam started pouring bombs and shells ... How are you, yourself?'

She sighs. Then she shakes her head, looking out across the water. 'I'm all mixed up. God ... I'm ... muddled and befuddled.'

'I heard you remarried. I heard you married several times, after Eftekhari. Making a collection?'

'Yes, a collection of dried husbands ... Those days when I was with you, I really wanted to be your wife.'

'No! ...'

'And since you didn't marry me, I love you forever and absolutely.'

'*I* didn't?'

'Well anyway, it didn't work out. I mean ...'

'Then ... Hush ...'

'Why?'

'Nothing is ever absolute.'

'The ones I married were all absolute. Absolute disappointments! To quote Fertidun Tavalloli ...'

'Now you're getting melancholy.'

'OK, so I won't get melancholy.'

'Is there no one at the moment?'

'No. There really isn't.' She falls silent.

'Is there something wrong?'

'Nah.'

'Something's troubling you.'

'I'll tell you later. There's a Doctor Abbas Hekmat, you've

surely heard his name. The *famous* author.'

'Of course – *The Candle in the Mosque, The Dust of the Tavern Door*. Where is he now?'

'Working in London. Wants to come and take me there for a year as his, ahem, assistant, to help him put together a glorious four-volume book on the history of literature in Iran. He works for an English publisher. Maybe I'll go. Maybe I won't. I'll have to see.'

'Sounds good.'

After a while, Leila wants us to go up some steps to where they take short cruises on little tourist boats on the Seine.

'You know, I've been here for years and I've never ridden in one of these silly things.'

'You want to ride one?'

'Don't you want to?'

'All right.'

'Don't you want to?' She looks at me.

'Okay, let's go . . . You twisted my arm enough.'

'Thank you, Jalal.'

It's still not too late for a river cruise. In a corner, several tourists are waiting for the boat to come; two or three talk together in Spanish. A soldier and his lover are whispering. A couple of Hindustanis stand crumpled up to one side. It is chilly and breezy, but nice. The river ripples along with tiny waves, flowing. Lights are glowing. The night is silent, and the world is calm.

In the ticket office, there is a tiny woman in a navy blue sweater, with a little beret of the same colour on her short, golden hair. Her face is red with cold. She is reading the *France Soir*. Like most Parisiennes, her face is painted and yet childish.

Before I have time to reach for my wallet, Leila calls out, 'No, leave it. Let's go on walking.'

'Don't you want a ride?'

'I changed my mind.'

'All right.'

'I'm afraid you'd get bored.'

'No . . .'

'Look at me! The same old fickle Leila Azadeh. Restless and moody.'

'Which way shall we go?'

'We'll walk down the Seine, here. Along the Jardin des Tuileries. Then along by the Louvre. Then we'll cross the river by Notre Dame and the Île Saint Louis, and be back in Boulevard Saint Germain. Don't you want a half-franc night tour of Paris?'

'No!'

'Well, I'm all yours tonight. Aren't you going to ask me if I've written anything lately?'

'Oh, Leila. What have you been writing lately?'

'Zero. I'm far away from life in Iran. Nothing there affects me any more.'

'Don't say that. You could create a masterpiece any time.'

'With the changes there, the Revolution, the war, and the aftermath, who wants my kind of work any more?'

'Thousands of people . . . Your writings will always have an appeal.'

'That society is no longer the place for people like me. At the moment, the only place for us to be is in a cocoon. Or in a coma.'

'Leila! . . .'

'I wish we had something with us.'

I offer her one of the cigarettes Nader Parsi had given me. She takes one. I strike a match, cupping my hands, and light both our cigarettes.

'These are really strong stuff,' she says. 'And very expensive.' She coughs.

'How do *you* know?'

'When it comes to this sort of thing, there's very little I don't know. Where did you get them?'

'A gift from Monsieur Nader Parsi. Do you you know him well?'

'Splendidly!'

'He said he was at your service. The way he kept looking at you, I expected him to start drooling any minute.'

'He can drop dead. After he divorced his former wife last year – his French wife – and before he married his present wife – the money wife – he was smooching around me for a while. But I hate his type. Settled. Wise. Mature. Man of the world. Manager. Answers for everything. Ugh!'

'I heard he has a nice house here?'

'He's got a smart flat in Neuilly suburbs, north of Paris. But it seems his ex-wife wants to go to court and take it away from him. Parsi's in a hurry to sell. He's looking for a bargain. As for his money, I've heard it's mostly in Barclays Bank in London.'

'He said he and his cronies are the Screwed-up Generation of Iran, like Hemingway's Lost Generation here in the 1920s.'

'He blabs nonsense. Hemingway's dead. So is his Lost Generation. Besides, that was a different world, a different culture. They were a different breed from us, decades before we were born. We're muddled and befuddled.' But then she sighs, and says, 'Well, perhaps we *are* lost, too. We're in Paris, too. We wander round, aimlessly, ride in taxis, sit in cafés, drink Pernod, chatter and argue forever, too. We're shattered and broken, too. Perhaps we *are* the Screwed-up Generation of our crazy era . . .'

I look at her. The soft breeze, blowing from the river, ruffles her hair. In the shadowy glimmers of the Paris night her own face is like that of a Hemingway character. Or maybe she tries to look like one.

'Well,' she says. 'Now that you've come here, I'll be your Maria and you be my Robert Jordan!'

'Leila!'

'Now *I'm* blabbing nonsense. No?'

'You were right when you said everything is mixed-up, muddled and befuddled.'

'Why – because they were in Spain?'

'Maria was a guerrilla. And she had her hair shaved by fascist rapists.'

'Well, I'll have my hair cut short, for you, *à la garçon*. Or *à la Maria*!'

I take a deep breath. 'Don't you change a hair, girl. Just stay as you are.'

'All right.'

'Shall we talk about Nader Parsi?'

'No – stuff him . . . I feel something's twisting around in my head.'

'It's Parsi's damned cigarettes.'

Something is twisting around in my own head, too. Leila

stops under a tree, and leans against it. She is tired of her cigarette. 'Here, you finish mine.'

On the waterfront, the cold wind feels more cutting. The tree we are standing under is bare; it doesn't offer much shelter. She holds on to me.

'We're both of us old, and here I am acting like a lovesick schoolgirl.'

'More like a rag door-mat.'

'A Kerman carpet.'

'I can't be a Kerman carpet, I'm from Shiraz.'

'Then you're a genuine vintage *Khollar*!'

I feel good, smoking both cigarettes at once, like a twin-carburettor. I fill up both lungs, and make no undue haste in exhaling the smoke through the exhaust pipes of my nostrils.

'Look at your hair,' she says. 'A handful of ashes.'

'I may be old, but . . .'

'Jalal – do you think we . . .'

'Yes!'

Her face is close to mine. It still holds the same magic it had in those days. I look at her, and touch her face. Suddenly she starts, as if stung.

'What is it?' I ask.

'Nothing. You don't know . . .'

'What's the matter? What's happened, Leila?'

'I'll tell you later . . . In fact, it's better that you don't know at all . . .'

'I thought there was something . . .'

'Yes, there is.' She gives a long sigh. 'You said we don't have to pay for our sins . . . but we do.'

'Put this sort of nonsense away, Leila.'

'Then why do we take so much agony and suffering?'

'Come on, let's sit over here on this bench.'

We sit down. In the café, she didn't seem to have the slightest care, much less agony and suffering. I feel suddenly, unreasonably put out.

'Leila, listen. Anybody looking at the way you all live here, like back there, in the Café de la Sanction, would never believe you could possibly have a care in the world. I mean, compared with people out there in Abadan, or in Khorram-Shahr, Hoveizeh, Dehloran, Shush, Dezful, Ilam, Sumar, Naft-e-

Shahr, Gilangharb, or in Qasr-e-Shirin, or in –'

'Sh-sh,' she says softly. 'I know.'

'I'm sure *you* understand.'

'But Jalal, everyone has to face the algebra of his own fate . . . You said that yourself one day. I remember it.'

'Well, yes, we do, but just compare.'

We are silent for a while. She looks at me, not only at my face, but almost searching my thoughts and depths.

'You never had this trace of anger and bitterness, Jalal. How are you, really?'

'I'm alive.'

'Are you completely recovered from that stroke?'

'Just about.'

'Any side effects?'

'Only sometimes – my memory doesn't seem to work so readily as it used to.'

'That's not unusual. My uncle had a stroke, too, here . . . His memory's mixed up a little, too.'

'Sometimes, when I want to remember something, quickly, it won't come. But what's worse is that sometimes scenes I don't want to remember suddenly rush to my head and stay there.'

'From long ago, or recently, like from the war?'

'Mostly recent ones. The old ones, I'm used to by now.'

'Do they come in your dreams, too?'

'There's plenty, there. What's odd is the way they come when I'm awake – and stay. Like yesterday, or . . . whenever it was, I was sitting in the hospital, alone, suddenly a scene from the hospital in Abadan came back to me, and I was actually there for a minute or two . . .'

'Tell me about it.'

'No!'

'Tell me of the war.'

'You don't want to hear about the war.'

'You know, I have absolutely no feelings about the Revolution in Iran or the war with Iraq. None of us here really have.'

'You, personally, are not at fault, Leila. You left Iran long before the Revolution and the war. You were then free, and you chose your own place to live, the way you choose your own men . . .'

'Oh?'

'Oh.'

'I want to hear about the war.'

79

I feel hazy.

'There's one scene I can tell you about now,' I say. 'About a month after the start of the war, I was still in Abadan. The Iraqis hadn't yet completely blockaded the island. The ordinary people were panicky – just dropping everything and leaving in groups. The Mah-Shahr road was still in our hands. Downtown Abadan and the residential areas around the Refinery were bombarded around the clock. Everywhere was full of smoke and fire. Huge columns of smoke rose from the Refinery day and night. Bavardeh crude oil tanks were burned and smoked continually. The shelling, long-range artillery and explosions never ceased. Even the hospital had been hit several times. One evening while I was there, I had gone to help some of the Abadan students who were working as volunteer helpers. A company labourer was brought for help. The yard of his house had been hit by a *Katiusha*. His wife, mother, and four or five of his chidren had been killed. He had been in the kitchen and was hurt only in the leg, and that not too badly. They had brought the bodies of his wife and children, and the mother, by jeep. He came in a corner of the jeep with them. He held a large cardboard box marked "Salted Puffs". He was crying and he handed this box to one of the students. The student, who knew what had happened, asked, "What's in here, father?" The labourer kept beating himself on the head. "I don't know which one's it is," he wailed. The student opened the box. We looked inside. "I don't know which one's it is!" the man kept moaning. Inside the box was a child's arm. It was chopped at the shoulder – evidently by flying shrapnel. The man kept hitting himself on the head, crying, "I don't know which one's it is! . . ." These are the sorts of things happening out there.'

11

Leila's head is down. I think she is crying. But when she looks up, her face is dry, just horrified and stunned.

'We should be there, writing these things,' she says.

'Maybe.'

'Not sitting in cafés, moaning and groaning, reciting poems and sighing, intoxicated with wine, listening to the BBC and Voice of America.'

'Maybe.'

'Do you want to hear something less horrible?'

I look into her eyes. She is really trembling now. I do not touch her.

'Do you want to know why I shivered like that when you touched me?'

'Yes.'

'I thought it might be best if you didn't know – but do you want to hear about it?'

I remain silent.

'There's this Nosrat Zamani here, you've probably heard of him. He wrote poetry and played in Persian movies. He was here this year – probably still is – though I heard he ran away from the French police, to England. This spring he grovelled around me a good deal. I disliked him, disliked his type – but in my silly, stupid way, I never learned to say no to men. I joked and laughed with him, as I did with the others. I mean I was *sociable*, so he thought he could do anything he liked. He raised his voice at me a couple of times, here and there and started playing the tough guy. About a month and a half ago, we were all guests at this Dr Matin's house – the former director of one of these foreign companies, now escaped from Iran. He has a house and some gardens somewhere near the Porte d'Italie. Everyone was plastered, stoned, drunk. This Nosrat bastard is one of those Iranian creeps who think women are dish-cloths, that should be kept in a corner to be used occasionally, then thrown back. Anyway, he kept getting funny with me that night ... When everyone began leaving, he said he'd drive me home – look, just speaking of it makes my heart thump like mad – I don't know how the police didn't get him, driving in that condition. I was pretty far gone myself, and fell asleep. At the door, he said he needed to come upstairs and make a phone call. He brought a bottle of whisky out from his car, and came up, sat down, and started drinking again. The witless baboon came into my room, with his blasted bottle of whisky and two glasses, and started insisting that we had to get married. – I haven't told this to a soul yet. You're the only person hearing it for the first time. – I told him I wasn't feeling well; that we'd talk about it tomorrow, sometime. He kept on drinking, getting more garrulous and nasty by the minute. I don't know what sort of answers I was giving him by then – I just wanted him to shut up and get out. My sister Pari wasn't in Paris then, she'd gone to Zurich. Mother and father were in Marseilles ... Anyway, all of a sudden I see he's got the empty bottle in his hand and he's threatening me. I can't think why I didn't scream then, and wake the neighbours. I just cursed at him. Then he got in a rage. He slammed the end of the bottle against the wall and smashed it, like they do in films. He held the broken half by the neck ...'

Leila falls silent. In the quiet of the dream-like night, beside the Seine, another white boat sweeps past dove-like on the water. The boat's entire length is decked with lights. From inside, soft sounds of music and singing drift over. The tricolour, red, white and blue flag of France, at the top of the mast, ripples slightly.

'I was in the hospital for a month and a half. Eighteen stitches just on the outside, under my liver. God knows what they've had to patch up inside ...'

'Shshsh.'

'So you know. You know what's been done to me.' After a silence, she adds 'I'm not Maria, but we've got our algebraic formula, too.'

82

I still do not touch her. 'Where did you say the bastard is now? England?'

'Yes ... I feel ... I don't know. I feel now as if ... I'm not a whole woman, or myself any longer. I feel the woman which was me, has been torn, destroyed – and killed.'

'Don't be a child, Leila. Of course you are yourself. Accidents happen, little accidents, big accidents. That bastard ...'

'I'm not thinking of him. I'm thinking of me. I've been thinking a lot about myself. It was my own fault.'

'You've picked the hard way out, Leila. The easy way is to always lay the blame on other people.'

'I thought about myself during the days and nights in the hospital ... I thought about the kind of life I've led since I was fourteen or fifteen, the life that finally came to this ... Only I never thought it would be so soon. What freedoms and liberties I used to have, God! Too much money, too much liberty ... Everybody's darling ... Father was a big spender, and always one for a good time. Mother was from an aristocratic Shirazi family. I was a brat. At seventeen, I was sent to France, to stay with my father's sister. At nineteen I married the supposedly greatest Iranian film director of the time. I was the cream of Tehran society. I translated books, wrote stories. Publishers, film and TV people spoiled me even more. I felt lonely and unhappy inside, but as long as the flattery, the drinks and the parties were there, it wasn't so bad. No ambition, no faith, no morals, no values ... just be happy, drink, sing, enjoy, because we will die soon.'

'But now you've changed,' I say.

'No. Just defeated.'

'Of course you've changed. You speak with new maturity, new reflections.'

'No. I'm the same. You saw for yourself, this evening. One doesn't change after thirty. I'm thirty-seven now.'

'One can always change. Unless one doesn't want to.'

'I don't want to.'

'Well, that's great.'

'I couldn't, even if I wanted to.'

'With that pack of friends, you probably couldn't. God knows, they are a dissipated crowd of has-beens. Like Nader Parsi said, they're the "Screwed-up Generation". Do any of them know ?...'

'No. None of them. I don't think so. I got myself to a private hospital that night. My aunt and her husband know only the generalities. Even my own parents don't know the facts. At least living in a foreign land you can die and go to pieces and no one will ever know. As for Nosrat Zamani – I've told the police I'm not pressing any charges, as far as I'm concerned. I want this thing forgotten. He ran and hid that very night. Karimpur and Parsi and Dr Kuhsar and Bahman Qaraguzlu only found out about it after three weeks. Of course they all jumped to the worst conclusions – they thought I'd had an abortion.'

'How are you now? What do you feel?'

'I'm not sure . . . I feel as though everything's over.'

'Come off it. Aren't you cold?'

'No. Only my throat feels dry.'

'All right, let's get going and have a drink somewhere.'

'Let's go back to the Sanction, and see what the Screwed-up Generation is doing.'

'Okay.'

She was right when she said she was unchangeable.

We come up the steps away from the waterfront.

'Let's get a taxi,' Leila says. 'I feel a bit weak.'

We wait for a taxi. The streets are empty.

'See that tall, black building over there?' she says. 'That's the *Palais de Justice*. At the end of it is where they imprisoned Marie Antoinette before her execution.'

'Good for them!'

'Jalal – don't be asinine!'

'Come on, here's an empty cab.'

The taxi stops and we get in. Leila gives directions. The driver is a woman, and has her dog with her in the front seat. She drives around the Place du Chatelet, behind the Notre Dame and then across the bridge on to the northern corner of the little Ile Saint Louis. Leila talks non-stop. The cathedral and the island are brilliantly lit. The tall, ivy-clad stone walls glisten in the light. The cathedral with its gardens is so immaculate and shining it hardly seems a place of worship and prayer. Close to midnight we reach the Café de la Sanction, and after much insisting, Leila pays the cab fare. I don't really want to say good-bye to her now, but I know I must.

'I'd better get back to the hotel,' I say, 'and get some sleep.'

'Come in just for a minute – have a coffee.'

'No. Your number's in the phone book, isn't it? I'll get in touch.'

'Aren't you going to take your fiancée – Mademoiselle Françoise Mitterand?'

'No!' That's why I don't want to come in!'

She laughs. 'You said you wanted to talk about something?'

'Talk? Oh, yes . . . My sister wants to send some money, for Sorraya's hospital expenses – about a hundred thousand francs . . . Of course, she doesn't have any means of getting the money out herself. Is there anyone among your friends who could handle something like this. Someone you can trust?'

'I can give you some myself.'

'No. Say one more word about that and I won't even get in touch with you again.'

'Why . . .?'

'You don't talk money with someone you love.'

'Oh, don't be silly!'

'Forget it then.'

'Well, there are a couple of people . . .'

'Of the Screwed-up Generation?'

'Yes, Dr Kuhsar does this sort of thing. So does Parsi . . . and Bahman Qaraguzlu . . . Colonel Afshar as well . . . Come and have a chat with one of them.'

'All right. Let's see.'

Thus we enter the Café de la Sanction again.

Most of the people are gone from around the huge 'Iranian' table, only Majidi and his wife, and a few others are left. A couple of other gentlemen have arrived; one is extremely large and fat – it turns out he is General Doctor Qa'em Maqami Fard. He, too, is well acquainted with Leila Azadeh. Another is a middle-aged, unprepossessing midget, and I get the impression that he must be the General's chauffeur or errand boy. I ask for hot chocolate and Leila orders a Pernod. The huge General Doctor gallantly orders a whole bottle of Pernod to be brought to the table – though, in his opinion, ladies ought to drink champagne, which he is drinking now himself.

'From here, we go straight to my house, Madame Leila Azadeh,' he says. 'Bring your friend, too. If he so wishes.'

'My friend wouldn't even come in here. I had to drag him.

He wants to sleep.'

'Sleep! Don't talk nonsense, my girl. Sleeping's after dying. We'll sleep after we're dead. "Drink wine, for you shall sleep beneath the dust"!' His poetical and romantic jargon are spoken in a military tone; and his battlefield, the Café de la Sanction.

'But *Aqaye* Aryan has a sense of humour,' Majidi's wife joins in. 'Bravo for him.'

'Yes,' Majidi replies. 'Mademoiselle Adèle Francoise Mitterand ... She waited a long time for him.'

Everyone laughs. Evidently Majidi or somebody, has told the General and his friend about the joke of the early evening.

'Dreadful language, too,' Majidi's wife says. 'She swore like the Paris layabouts.'

'And of course, the good Dr Qassem Khatibi came into something good.'

Ahmad Qandi is still there; he is now playing what must be a tape of the 'Voice of America' Persian language programme. The disc jockey's nauseous voice says, 'Our warm and hot Salaam from Washington, the sunny Capital of the United States of America to the fine boys and faithful girls of Iran ... In Tehran, Ahvaz, Shiraz, Abadan, Golpaigan, Mashhad, Kermanshah, and the other beautiful cities of Iran ...'

'Where's everybody gone?' Leila asks Majidi's wife.

Dr Majidi, whose Persian is more intelligible now he is completely stoned, says, 'The good Nader Parsi, who was falling asleep, was taken off home to Pont de Neuilly by his wife, where they are probably now in bed, fighting over money. Dr Kazem Makaremi expounded so many of Einstein's theories for Madamoiselle Adèle's benefit that she finally left with fat Dr Khatibi. You will of course appreciate that Khatibi has taken his wife to England and deposited her in a free lunatic asylum. Kazem Makaremi's wife is touring Sweden with the Doctor's nephew. Makaremi himself has this night accompanied Dr and *Khanum* Kuhsar to the home of Brigadier General Farrokhi – who used to be His Majesty's Head Cook. They didn't quite get enough to eat here, you see ... What I'm wondering is whether fat Khatibi will manage anything?'

'I doubt it!'

'Mademoiselle wanted *Aqaye* Aryan!'

'Yes, Mademoiselle Françoise Mitterand wanted *Jenab* Aryan!'

'Not fat Khatibi!'

Hoots of laughter rise from around the table.

'Nasrin,' Leila says to Majidi's wife, 'start at the beginning and tell me everything!'

'I'm afraid you'll split your sides laughing.'

Majidi declares: 'Our *Jenab* Parsi is of the opinion that we are all "a Lost Generation", like that writer, what's-his-name, said. . .'

I look at Leila.

'We are *all* Balzacs,' Majidi says.

'Balzac, *Jenab* Majidi?' says Leila.

'How the hell should I know.'

'We are all Ball-zacks!' says the General Doctor.

I get up to my feet. 'With your permission . . .'

'Jalal!' Leila says. 'Don't go so soon.'

'I really must.'

'What about that thing about the hospital?'

'I'll call tomorrow – about ten?'

'Ten's fine.'

'Good-bye, then.'

We all say good-byes and I go outside. Thank God the pavement still stays firmly beneath my feet. I walk back to the Hotel Palma, which is also still in its place. Only I am tired and dead.

12

The boy who sits behind the tiny reception desk at night is busy reading. I get my key from him and take the lift upstairs. My room is warm, and without turning on the light, I undress and slip into bed. The sheets are snow cool and stiffly starched. I turn on my transistor, tuning in to an English-speaking station, for the news. My head is still woolly. I reach for a cigarette from the bedside table, light up, and think about Leila.

Lying there in the dark, with the ashtray balanced on my chest, I wrap up little bits of my mind in layers of smoke, letting it drift in the darkness. When I was very young, and gone away from Darkhungah and Shahpur Street in Tehran, to a college in America, I didn't like to sleep without a light. I was afraid. In the dark, bits of Darkhungah would creep in and eat away at my brain. This year, however, I detest the light. Now, light is bad – like many other things which were once good, and are now bad. Now, in the dark I see many things from the past which were never as bad as today – even phobias from my Darkhungah childhood ...

By the time I stub out my cigarette, my head feels full of smoke. But when I close my eyes, lying between sleep and wakefulness, Leila Azadeh's face and memories of her crowd into the very centre of my brain, and this is not bad ... Then other memories are confused with them. Memories of the days when I had returned to Iran from America after my wife's death, and I was alone, looking for work ... memories of my young brother Yusef, his illness, his death. Then I am back in the autumn when Leila Azadeh and I were together. She had just divorced one of her husbands, and wanted someone – a stranger, remote from her family circle and friends – to whom

she could pour out her troubles. She was translating a novel . . .
she was young then, very sensitive and very beautiful, too. She
had taken an interest in me, though it was obvious that nothing
lasting would ever come of it – she was what she was, and I was a
dumb nothing. Besides, no one connected with Leila Azadeh
ever went for the simple things in life. Her world was one of art,
of feeling, creative impulses, of the very essence of love, passion,
and the thousand thrills of living. I was just an extra. A lonely
hunk of man, someone to be with, to fool around with in bed,
have a few laughs and then later empty out the ashtrays.

The phone gives a short buzz. Or perhaps I dream it. I cannot
tell how long I have slept, or whether I slept at all. Leave it, I say
to myself, do not answer. Then I fear it could be something
important, from the hospital, maybe, or from Tehran. The
phone is no longer buzzing. All the same, I pick up the receiver.
'*Allo?*'

'*Allo*, Monsieur Aryan? I'm sorry.' It is the boy at the reception
desk. 'Sorry to bother you.'

'I was awake,' I say. 'Yes?'

'A Madame and Monsieur are here – they wanted to know if
you were awake; if you are awake, they would like to see
you.'

'Very well.'

'So you don't mind seeing them?'

'No. Did the Madame and Monsieur give their names?' With
all the dizziness and sleeplessness, my head feels like a cageful
of panicking rats.

After a moment a woman's voice says '. . .*C'est moi*, Jalal.'

'Leila? Is that you?'

'*Mais ouiii.*'

'Are you all right?' Judging by her voice and speech, she is
obviously as high as a kite.

'We're absolutely terrific,' she says. 'Me and this General
Doctor Qam-Qami . . . Oh, God! Me and this Doctor – oh what
a name to have to pronounce, at this hour – General Doctor
Qa'em Maqami Fard, and our friend *Aqaye* Hakimian, were
passing by . . . Thought we'd drop in on you . . . You weren't
asleep, or anything, I hope? Were you asleep?'

'Asleep? At this time in the morning?'

'How's your head?'

'My head? I think it's still stuck on my shoulders.'

She giggles. 'Can we come up?'

I have never been able to say no to her. 'Sure.'

'Or maybe you could come down. We can go for a little spin in the General Doctor's car.'

'All right.'

'Come on, then.'

'Give me two minutes to put something on.'

'This *Jenab* Hakimian is what you want.'

'Want for what?'

'Ah – you know!'

'That's what you think!'

She giggles again. 'Well! Hurry then. I'll explain later.'

The way my head spins, it is a miracle I can even manage to get my pants on. I throw on my woollen sweater. While I am bending over, working on my shoelaces, an even sharper pain attacks the top of my forehead. This is it, I think. I straighten up, lean my skull against the wall, and feel the dizziness slowly passing. I hear the lift coming up in its shaft, which is just at the back of my room. Someone raps on the door. For God's sake, no, I whisper.

'Jalal?' It is Leila's voice.

'Yes?'

'It's just me. Open up.'

'The door's open.'

Leila comes in. She is still wearing the black raincoat and white scarf she wore earlier in the evening. She is also wearing a *beret* at one side of her hair.

'Why are you sitting there with your head against the wall?' she wants to know.

'It's nothing.'

'You got a headache?'

'I bent down to do my shoelace up, blood rushed into my body's smoke circulation.'

Leila bursts into peals of laughter. She herself seems to have nothing in her blood other than Pernod-and-lemonade.

'You weren't asleep, were you?'

'What do you think I was doing, girl?' Then I ask, 'How the devil *are* you? You look terrific!'

'I'm fine. I'm just thirsty.' I stand up, and she comes forward.

'Do you want a glass of water?' I ask. This is stupid, I know.

She looks into my eyes. Her own are tired, sad and desolate. 'I said I'm thirsty. I didn't say I wanted to wash my hands. *God*!'

'You came here at this hour of the morning to crack this joke?'

'No ...' She smiles, 'There's a gentleman by the name of Monsieur Abbas Hakimian downstairs. You'll want to speak to him. He's brought his cheque book along.'

'Oh, that. Thank you ... But I really didn't want you to put yourself to trouble, at this hour.'

'Don't keep repeating what hour it is ... Come on.' She pulls my sleeve, trying to take me in her arms. This is Leila Azadeh all right. When I touched her over by the riverside, she had trembled like a leaf. But now, with two men waiting downstairs, she is like melting fire itself.

'What does the General Doctor Qam-Qami want?' I ask.

'We came in his car.' She sits down on the bed and begins to brush her hair. Then she looks around my tiny, almost empty room. Perhaps for want of any other comment – she says, 'It's clean. I like it.'

'It's a dump.'

'It's just a bit small.'

'I've lived in big places, too. Like hospitals. Like lunatic asylums.'

'Lunatic asylums?'

'I spent three weeks in the Shafabakhsh Lunatic Asylum, in Shemiran, the year before last.'

'Bully for you!'

'Have you known the General Doctor long?'

'This is third time he's cornered me.'

'Which is he – a political escapee, or just a nobody loaded with dough?'

'Both.'

'And now his heart is lovesick for you, eh?'

'I don't know if it's his *heart* ...' She chuckles.

'So he's a Doctor?'

'Sort of. He *was* an army veterinary. He did his studies right here, took several specialist diplomas – all at the Iranian

Shahanshahi Army's expense, of course. He's one of Dr Ayadi's old classmates – His Majesty's Special Physician, you know. But then he got transferred to Headquarters of the Army Health and Medicals, and after that into the Army Commissariat Headquarters.'

'You mean into thieving.' I have finally finished tying my shoelaces.

'I wish he were merely a thief. He's a panty-raid rat, too.' She gets up and starts straightening her skirt and readjusting her scarf.

'Shall we go down?'

She tugs at my sleeve. 'Don't you want to kiss me?'

'No.'

She makes a face. 'Well, I don't blame you.'

'Don't be silly. There's a time and place for everything.'

'You know what kind of an offer the General Doctor Qu'em Maqami's made me?'

'No.'

'Do you want to know why he's been mooning around after me?'

'No.' I pick up my jacket and switch off the radio, which has been left on and is now giving out financial and stock market news, the Dow Jones Index, the current rate of exchange, and the increases in the price of gold in New York, London and Hong Kong.

'He's offered to give me fifty thousand dollars to send a little message on Radio Vatan. Have you ever heard the term, "Prostituée Politique"?'

'No!'

'Couldn't you use fifty thousand dollars. How much would that be in French francs?'

'Leila! You're talking like some silly schoolgirl! For God's sake, don't talk like this!'

'What did I say?'

'What's the matter with you?'

'Okay, okay, I'll shut up. Don't get upset, please.'

'Let's go.'

'Please don't get *upset*.'

'Let's go . . .'

'It was a *joke*. I just meant it to joke around a bit. I swear to God.'

'All right.' I turn out the light, and we leave the room together. We take the lift downstairs.

I see the enormous figure of the General Doctor in a corner of the diminutive, half-dark lobby. Next to him there is a smallish man, with full, closely cropped hair. Side by side, they look exactly like Laurel and Hardy. They are standing in front of a city-map of Paris, complete with a plan of the Metro network. The delicate mimosa plant beside Quem Maqami's bulk is dwarfed to a thistle. The General Doctor is wobbly on his legs. We have met before. Leila introduces the smaller man as *Jenab Aqaye* Abbas Hakimian, apparently a carpet dealer in Frankfurt and Vienna. We do not shake hands. He has a heavy Lurestani accent – or more like mixed Lurestani–Isfahani. The General Doctor laughs and makes some pleasantries.

'Come, Leila, my dear,' he says. 'Let's all go for a spin in my car. You can have your little chat there.'

'Good idea.'

'As your friend pleases, of course.' He looks at me, grinning wolfishly.

'All right.' I say. All I want is to get them out of the damned dingy hotel, without waking everybody up.

The General Doctor's car is a Mercedes Benz 350-SEL limousine, parked a little farther up the one-way Avenue Monsieur le Prince, across from the hotel. The chauffeur sees us coming. He leaps out and opens the doors. The General Doctor sits in front. Leila Azadeh, the Lurestani dealer and I sit in the back. I am perched cozily in the middle, with Leila on one side and Hakimian on the other; three peas in a pod. I still have not managed to figure what use Hakimian could be to me.

Since we left the hotel, Hakimian has had his hand tucked under my elbow. '*Aqaye* Engineer,' he says. 'I should tell you I am ready at your service, sir.'

He has granted me this 'Engineer' title having heard of my working in the Oil Company I presume.

The General Doctor says, 'Hurry up and settle your money affairs, then we'll go home for some carousing!'

'At once, General,' says Hakimian, 'I am your willing and obedient servant, sir, if I may say so. And also that of Madame Azadeh here, too. I have already said I am absolutely at the gentleman's service, anything from one rial to a million dollars

... The gentleman needs only to say the word ... How much were you planning to transfer?' He flourishes his cheque books. 'I have accounts here at the Credit Lyon, also at Barclay's Paris branch.'

'I'm not sure,' I say.

'Anyway, I am at your service.'

The limousine turns northward, across the river. Apparently we are heading for the more opulent homes in the Clichy area. It is one of those nights when the Paris air is crispy cold but fresh, yet you somehow wished you could be almost anywhere else.

'Why do you say you are not sure, *Aqaye* Engineer?' says Hakimian. 'Aren't you in need of a money transfer here?'

Leila speaks up. '*Aqaye* Aryan's sister in Tehran has sold some of her things to pay her daughter's hospital expenses here, and then have her taken back home. They need money for this, and you know the Islamic government doesn't allow any private money to be sent out of the country.'

'Forget the Islamic government. Since *Khanum* Azadeh wishes it, I will gladly make out a cheque for as much as you would care to mention. In French francs, or in American dollars, in Deutschmarks, in English sterling pounds, whichever currency you prefer. Nothing to it. Absolutely nothing to it. And as for the repayment in rials – I'll give you a phone number in Tehran, your sister can deliver the money in cash there. If she hasn't got the money – well, don't worry! Consider it a gift, sir. Consider it as a gift, for the sake of the lovely *Khanum* Azadeh, and of the General Doctor, who is dearer to me than the apple of my own eye, than my own life. Now ... How much shall it be?'

I do not want to discuss smuggling currency in front of all these people. Also I feel cross with Leila for putting me in such a spot, suddenly tonight – even though she has taken on the duty of being my official spokesman. Hakimian and the General Doctor sense my half-heartedness. But I cannot let them think of me as a timid greenhorn.

'It won't be much,' I say, 'Only a mere hundred and fifty thousand francs.'

'Oh, that's no problem,' Hakimian rushes in. 'Honestly. We bring out money like drinking water. Why, this very morning, I got eleven million out for a pro-Shah Doctor, a former professor from the University of Isfahan. He himself sneaked out and came over, via Pakistan. Yesterday, we bought up a loanshark's goldstuffs and furniture in Tehran for twenty-three million, gave him the money here in dollars. We bought an Armenian's house from him in Tehran right here too, for one and a half million. We've sent a couple of thousand dollars for this automobile dealer's kids in Los Angeles, and he paid us right back there in Tehran.'

'If you should decide to sell the twin bronze lions in front of Tehran's National Bank in Ferdousi Street,' says the General Doctor, '*Jenab* Hakimian will give you a cheque for it, right away.' He has put a cassette by Delkash on the car stereo. The lady sings:

> I give my heart to no one but *you*.
> Oh, my flower
> I will give my heart only to *you*.

The General adds: 'For *you* Hakimian! As Delkash knows, too, *you* is nothing but hard dough!'

Hakimian laughs, artificially. 'Well, what else is there to do, in this dreadful situation?'

'You think it's bad, *Jenab* Hakimian?' Leila asks.

'Well, yes, it is. Isn't it? By God! See for yourself what they've done to our poor country? What good days we had. Peace, throughout the country. No war. Everywhere safe. Security. Freedom. People lived their lives. All sorts of comfort. All sorts of goods on the markets. Now see what they've done to the poor people!'

I stare at him. Then I turn to look at Leila. She looks indifferent, as though she has heard all this before, too often. With a careless smile, she says, 'Well, Monsieur Hakimian – things certainly haven't turned so badly for you! You said yourself just now, that you've made about forty million profit in two days – selling dollars at five times the official exchange rate!'

'We are but your humble servants, *Khanum* Azadeh.'

We have now stopped in front of the huge iron gates of a mansion. The chauffeur opens the gates and drives in, then he gets out, carefully closing and locking the gates. In front of the house a wide tree-lined drive winds through the garden. Leila tells me the mansion is a remnant of Louis XV's era, of Regency style. She has been here before, and informs me that the General Doctor bought this house in the winter of '78. He, himself, is now giving us a run-down on the history of the building, which dates back to the years before the French Revolution. The house was built over two hundred years ago, in the style of the Petit Trianon at Versailles, designed and built by Louis XV's very own personal architect, Jacques Ange Gabriel! At the entrance, the chauffeur stops the car and opens the doors for us to step out. Before following us inside, he opens the boot and brings out two ice-buckets with the silver heads of champagne bottles ensconced therein. Prior to his entrance, Abbas Hakimian pauses on top of the three steps to the threshold of the latticed, ancient door, with its intricate metal-work, to empty out one nostril after the other, by pressing a thumb against the side of his nose, shooting into the darkness of the historic garden. I only hope Jacques Ange Gabriel is not revolving too violently in his grave.

The rest of that night's adventures are not too clear in my memory. Briefly, we spend the first half hour in the Post-Renaissance, rococco-styled hall of the General Doctor's house, listening to the 'true' Iranian music of Abolvahab Shahidi and the goodly voice of Banan, of whom the General Doctor is most fond. We watch the revelling, and Doctor Qa'em-Maqami's flirting with Leila Azadeh, and the vagrant clan soak themselves in champagne. Meanwhile, the General Doctor gives us a lecture on the procedure of making of champagne. (In his best French diction, he pronounces champagne as 'shompany'.) Champagne, we are gratified to hear, is a bubbly wine, the special and exclusive product of an old French province of the same name. The white grapes for it are grown in lime-rich soil. The corks on the bottles must have wire stoppers, or else they will jump in the air! Next, the General Doctor discourses on brandy and cognac. Brandy is the finest *liqueur* obtained from distilled wine. Brandy must be taken *sec*, that is, it must never, ever be diluted with anything, save the saliva in one's mouth. All the brandies in the world are brandy, except the brandy produced in the French area of Cognac, France, whereupon this brandy is no longer brandy, but cognac. Of course, it is still brandy, only it is cognac. From this oration, the General Doctor enters upon the topic of Art, which has been his *dearest* life-long 'hobby', and tells us of his three '*magnifique*' collections. First, his collection of Paul Cezanne, whose works hang in the General Doctor's *boudoir*; secondly, of Pierre August Renoir, the Impressionist painter whose works adorn the library: and finishing with a talk on Francois Millet, whose paintings can be seen in the Hall of Mirrors, upstairs. Most of these paintings have been collected by the General Doctor during the past thirty years of his obsession with the culture and art of France. (I wonder when the old sod ever found time for the Army's cows and mules?)

It is almost three in the morning when I get up and say I must get back to the hotel. As for the exchange of money, I announce that I cannot make any definite decision until I call Tehran the next evening. Leila, who has been drinking with the General Doctor and Hakimian and the chauffeur, is beginning to shine brighter than ever and is talkative and vivacious. The General Doctor's chauffeur is a youngish man with keen eyes, and extremely well mannered, and they call him *Aqaye* Biglari. But he has uttered hardly more than ten words all evening. So, it's not hard to guess he's a tongue-tied member of the old SAVAK. The Moslem and bazari-looking Hakimian, who earlier said he used never to touch 'intoxicating beverages' now plasters himself with drink, since he has now by God 'lost his faith and everything', altogether. In between, with immense speed, he devours the fruit set on the table.

After gulping down a couple of cups of hot coffee and lighting himself a thin More, Biglari drives Leila and me back to town. Leila chatters all the way to Port d'Italie, and she tells me things about herself and London and Abbas Hekmat that I swear I am too far gone to understand. I ask Biglari to drop *Khanum* Azadeh off first. It is idiotic but I don't dare leave Leila alone at this hour – and in such a state – with Biglari who is getting more 007-ish by the minute. He takes us first to the Port d'Italie, and drops Leila off. I get out, too, see Leila into her flat, then come back and get in the front seat with Biglari. He chain smokes American filter cigars, and listens to the English news on his radio. He stops the car in front of the Palma, in the middle of the deserted Avenue Monsieur le Prince, and says, 'At your service!' I thank him. He asks, 'Will your honour be returning to Iran soon, *Jenab* Aryan?'

'In time, yes.'

'To the Oil Company?'

'I'm still on the staff. As for future years, I'll have to see.'

'Which department were you in?'

'Training, Technical Training Department, in general.'

His searching, keen eyes look fresh, his face handsome and understanding. 'I am ready at your service, *Aqaye* Aryan,' he says. 'I will give you a number to contact. Anything you need. Anything you need at all, at any time.'

'Thanks.' He hands me a visiting card with a telephone number.

'Please get in touch. I'll be glad.'

I don't understand what the devil he means by this, now, but it doesn't matter. If it turned out he was SAVAK's General Nasiri's second cousin twice removed, or even if he were CIA's Richard Helms' son-in-law, it wouldn't surprise me. Even if he turned out to be one of Sir James Manson's boys, arrived this afternoon straight from Zangaroo, I still wouldn't be surprised. Nothing could surprise me any more tonight.

'Thank you, *Aqaye* Biglari.'

'God be with you, *Aqaye* Aryan.'

The youth at the reception desk is still awake, and has almost reached the last page of his novel. I pick up my key again, and upstairs in bed, this time, I need neither pills nor cigarettes. I close my eyes. Thoughts of Leila and thoughts of Sorraya float through each other over the layers of my mind, like flashes in the dark.

. . . In the night, looking out of the hospital windows, we could see the flash of flying shells and artillery in the city skies. Frightened dogs howled incessantly. Whenever they started shelling the area, we used to stay awake the whole night, trying to guess where they hit. Shots fired towards Iraq from Abadan positions were heard first. Then we counted to twenty, till we heard the impact making contact across the water. The *Khamseh-Khamseh* mortar shells fired over from the Iraqi positions came over the northern palm tree plantations from Fav, then crashed down on to Abadan. Now, the shattering sound came a-grrrumping somewhere, followed by the long, rat-tat-tat-tat of shattering shrapnel flying out in all directions, hitting trees, doors, windows, cars, anything and everything. Sometimes the sounds were so close that we could actually tell exactly where it had fallen. And one always wondered where the *next* one would fall!

They had told us to sleep along the walls of our room, because the walls were less likely to collapse than the ceiling. The room was in total darkness after sunset, unless someone happened to have a flashlight, or candles. In the glow of the exchange of fire overhead, against the black skies, sometimes you could see the remains of the city water tank, still on its huge metal stand, but broken, crooked and bent at almost 45 degrees, waiting to fall.

Davud Keshavarz, a student who was hit by a shell while driving a Land-rover and had been hospitalized, had asthma, among other things, and now he was afraid of dying. He was terrified. The sound of his breath, whistling through his wide chest and huge nostrils, all night long, was pitiful. We had oxygen on hand, but he wanted to be transferred to Mah-Shahr. These days, the last week of October, were the worst days of the war in Abadan, yet. We were completely blockaded by the invading enemy.

At night, close by, we also heard sudden bursts of machine-gun fire from the Revolutionary Guards barracks behind Razi High School, not far from the hospital. 'The Iraqis are here!' we thought. Before the Revolution, these barracks were the SAVAK centre in Abadan. Now, several Iraqi spies and political prisoners were kept there. At times, we could not tell whether they were firing at the Iraqis, or executing the prisoners.

13

In the morning, it is sunny and fine, but a cold wind blows from the river. After breakfast I leave the hotel, walking up to the Boulevard Saint Michel, where a few newspaper kiosks are clustered. It is a holiday, and the streets are less crowded. To my surprise, in one of the news-stands I see copies of the Iranian papers, *Kayhan, Etela'at, Mizan, The Islamic Revolution*, all very recent issues only three or four days old. I buy a *Kayhan* dated two days after my departure from Tehran. There are other Persian language papers as well, printed in London, Paris, New York, or Los Angeles; *Iranian News, The Voice of Iran, The Cry of Iran, The Iran Post*, etc., etc.

Walking back towards the Rue Saint Jacques and the hospital, I see Hamid Khodabandeh, a young man from Abadan, who tells me he is studying here. He has a load of books under his arm, and his nose, under heavy metal-framed glasses, is red with the cold. He is happy to see me, we shake hands.

'When did you arrive, *Aqa*?' he asks.

I tell him, briefly mentioning my reasons, too.

'Things are bad in Abadan, eh?'

'Yes, very bad.'

'Khorram-Shahr's gone, too . . .'

'Well, at the moment, yes . . .'

'And they've renamed it Khunin-Shahr . . .'

'Well, sorry to say, yes. How are you?'

'Broke . . . but surviving . . .'

I give him the hotel's address, telling him I shall be there for some time, and would like him to come for a drink and a chat.

'*Aqa*,' he says, 'Come to the Sorbonne Amphitheatre this evening – Dr Ahmad Reza Kuhsar is lecturing, giving his manifesto . . .'

'I saw him last night.'

'You did?'

'In an assembly of his friends, so-to-speak.'

'You seem not to approve?'

'I don't know, I don't feel what they are doing here is any great cure to Iran's problems.'

'I know what you mean, *Aqa*.'

'Still, they're not all the same.'

'No . . . They're all kinds. One is the group who were in France before the Revolution, then there's those who fled the Revolution. And then, the ones who escaped over here after the war. There's plenty of them all over. The last two are the shakings of the bag.'

I laugh. 'I'll say!'

'There's all kinds of trash among them.'

'Well, for the time being, they're here.'

'The first type aren't too bad.'

'. . . They each have their own special formula. Well, *au revoir*. You will come and see me?'

'Yes, *Aqa* – of course.'

At the hospital, I find that Sorraya has been taken to the Radiology and ECG Departments. Nurse Georgette Jardin informs me that my niece has been taken for her twice-weekly brain scanning graphs. May I wait and see her? I ask. Yes, of course. While I am waiting, I search out a phone booth and call the number Leila Azadeh gave me. No answer.

I linger around the ward for a while, then come out into the small gardens. When I go back upstairs to the ward, Sorraya is back, but no change. I stand at her bedside for a while, stroking her face and hair. On her forehead and temples, the little marks left by the wires and attachments of the machines are still visible. I try to ask the nurse about Sorraya's condition, but she tells me we must wait for Dr Martin to see the results of the graphs. I'd better wait and speak with him tomorrow. There is nothing else to be done in the hospital. I leave, and walk back towards the hotel.

Around two o'clock, I arrive at the Restaurant Luxembourg,

on a corner of Jardin du Luxembourg, where I have an appointment with Nader Parsi. I must talk to him about money. Inside, there is a huge dining room, but I cannot see Nader anywhere, though spotting Nader's now famous head should not be too difficult, with his giant egg skull on which a child has doodled eyes, nose, mouth, glasses, and a little goatee.

On a stool at the bar, by the windows, at the far end of the front hall, I see a familiar face ... Hossein Abpak, sociologist, poet, TV announcer and commentator. I remember him from when he worked for the Oil Company at the Public Relations Department, but I do not break a leg now to go and greet him. For one thing, he seems deeply absorbed in his beer and the book he is reading. And this is how I see Hossein Abpak all the while I am in Paris on this trip; with his books, his beer, in a corner, alone, lost, sulking. At this very moment, there are seven or eight empty beer glasses in front of him, and he is reading the French version of *L'Etat Confisque – The Confiscated Government*; with a picture of a fist coming out of a USSR-labelled box, on the cover.

I sit at a window table, order coffee, and start reading the *Kayhan*. I am just lighting my second cigarette when an old man, who has been staring at me from the opposite table, asks, 'Are you Persian, Monsieur?'

Nodding with a smile, I blow out the smoke from my lungs. He himself is nursing a pipe. He has a dried-out, thin face but a huge, white moustache, like that of Clemenceau, Like me, he begins to nod his head sheepishly. 'Yes, of course.'

'You guessed?' I ask. 'The newspaper?' I point at the *Kayhan*. 'You are disturbed?' he asks. I do not know what he really means.

'In a way I am,' I agree.

'I was over there, once,' he says. 'Thirty-five years ago.'

'Lucky you!'

He is a very old man, about eighty, with pinkish eyes like owls of Brittany. He holds his pipe on the table with both hands, as if to keep it from slipping away. His suit and tie are worn and shiny.

'What was it like there, in those days?' I ask, just to be polite, smiling.

'What did you say?'

102

'What was Iran like in the years gone by?' I make a slight sweep with my hand.

'Cold and wet out, isn't it?' he says, looking out through the window. Then he says: 'I was in Isfahan.'

'Were you there long?' This time I try to speak very grammatically.

'I was in Shiraz, too,' he says.

This is good, I say to myself. Raising my voice, I ask, 'Was your stay in Iran a lengthy one?'

'I was in Isfahan,' he says. 'I was in Tehran, too. And in Shiraz. And in Tabriz. My wife was with me, too. My wife was an anthropologist.' He pronounces the cities' names correctly, except all the 'r's are rolled as in the French.

'Were you in trade?' I ask.

'Where are you from?' he asks smiling.

'Tehran,' I reply. But I am sure he is deaf, or perhaps living in Iran has liquified and evaporated his once glorious French brain, rendering him senseless.

'I was a merchant,' he says. 'I was in Kerman, too. Then I went to Mashhad. I had just married, in those days. My wife was an anthropologist. She was very good, too. She died in 1973.'

'God rest her soul,' I say.

'Can I buy you a drink?' he asks.

'No,' I decline, pointing to my coffee. '*Merci mille fois.*'

Then Nader Parsi arrives, finds me, and I am rescued.

'How are you, Jalal, old boy?' he says. I get up, and we shake hands.

'Salaam. I'm fine, thanks.' The deaf Clemenceau is now puffing on his cold pipe.

'How's everything?' Nader asks.

'Bad,' I say. 'They've done another ECG on her brain today. But there doesn't appear to be anything promising.'

'Where did you and Leila go off to last night?' He does not meet my eyes.

'We came back to the Sanction, but you had already left . . . I said goodbye and went back to the hotel. Leila left with a Doctor General Qa'em Maqami Fard, and a certain Abbas *Aqa* Hakimian, who was apparently one of his long lost back-water relatives . . .' I skip the rest, and the scene at the Doctor General's mansion.

'Jalal, let's go to London,' says Nader.

'What?'

'For a few days – you and me and this uncle of mine who's the last of the big spenders. He wants to go to London and have good times and fun ...'

'Why don't we go to Pamplona, intead, and see the bull-fights and have fun at the fiesta!?'

'No – London's fine.'

'*God*! Are you joking?'

'No, honestly. Come on, it'll be good for you, too.'

'What is all this? I'm here for this kid's sake, I can't just leave. There's the problem of the hundred and fifty or sixty thousand bloody francs I have to raise, that's not been settled yet, either.'

'In the first place,' he says, 'your niece is in good hands. You said yourself she's unconscious, in a coma. In the second place, you could do with some fun, yourself. I, for one, am simply dying for a bit of free love.'

I look at him, shaking my head hopelessly. I cannot tell whether he is the deafer and crazier, or Clemenceau, or *me*.

'No!' I say.

The *garçon* arrives; Parsi orders a double Courvoisier. My own cup is still half full.

'You're absolutely, seriously thinking of going back to Iran, now?' he asks.

'Well ...'

'To that ungodly place? Without wine, women and song? You're ready to waste the best years of your life?'

'There *are* other things.'

'For example?'

'For example, my sister. She's my whole family.'

'Do you love her that much?'

'I don't have many people who love me. When one of them does turn to me, I can't brush her aside.'

He lowers his head, allowing this crazy discourse to rest in silence. Then he says: 'Have you had lunch?'

'No. And I don't think I want any. I had a big breakfast.'

'Come on,' he says. 'Let's have a proper lunch. I haven't bought you a dinner for a long time.' He turns to a *garçon*. 'Menu, *s'il vous plait*.'

'*Oui*, Monsieur,'

'Would you like it better if we took Leila with us instead. Just the three of us?'

'The three of us? Where to?'

'London, stupid!'

I get it. It is Leila he has been hankering for all this time. 'No!'

'Great *God*, come on.'

'No.'

'How is she?'

'Fine. She appeared to be pretty cheerful and lively last night.'

The *garçon* brings the menu, and we give our orders. The restaurant is getting crowded. Hossein Abpak is still sitting alone, with his book and his beer. Clemenceau is still busy with his pipe, his glass of red wine, and his silence. Parsi is talking about his rich uncle, who used to run four public baths in uptown Tehran. Apparently, uncle would now like to go to Los Angeles as soon as his visa comes through. He is going to buy a sauna parlour, or a gas station. The *garçon* begins manoeuvring with our food, which includes soup, salad, *bifsteck*, potatoes and *petits pois*, sweet peas. 'Didn't she tell you what her illness was?' Nader asks.

'Who?'

'Leila.'

'Why don't you ask her yourself?'

'How are *your* relations with her, Jalal?'

'Zero.'

'Really? Honestly?'

'Cross my heart . . .'

'What about in the past? If it's not my business, just hit me over the head. Tell me to shut my mouth, if it's not my business.'

'Nader, for *God*'s sake! What has come over you people? Don't you ever stop and think there may be other things going on, too?'

'I've been . . . *worried* about Leila Azadeh,' he says. 'I want to know if she's all right. Ever since she's been unable to write, she's been going to pieces. Oh, I know she can always sit down and *write* something, for *God*'s sake, if she really wants to. But

105

just writing isn't enough. It's got to be printed, and published. She's a very fine and a very sensitive person. She writes when she is affected, and here, her creative soul is affected by nothing, not any more. At least not the way it was before, back in Iran. She produced lovely short stories, which she can't do now. How is she?'

'Nader, Leila's just been divorced from her – I don't know – fourth, or fifth husband. I think she's recently got engaged to the fat-n-famous Abbas Hekmat.'

'Abbas Hekmat? He's in London, In England?'

'Well, you're improving at geography. As far as I know, Leila's going to London to work with Hekmat.'

'Leila's going to London to work with Hekmat? But he works for an Asiatic Advertising and Publications Organization – which any damn fool will tell you, is under the British Foreign Office and the Intelligence Service.'

'I don't know a thing about that.'

'Leila wants to work with Hekmat?'

'She was saying something about it last night, but she was high and my head was so fogged up by those confounded cigarettes of yours, I couldn't exactly make out what she was saying. I think she said she was going to London in February, to stay for a few years.'

'A few years?'

'That's what I think she was saying.'

'I don't believe it.'

'Suit yourself . . .'

The *bifsteck* and potatoes are awful. I play around with mine for a while, and then we finally get around to discussing my money problem. Parsi himself wants very much to help out, but he says he is rather short of hard cash himself at the moment. His French ex-wife has filed a suit against him claiming the only house he's got in Paris as alimony. I tell him I didn't mean to borrow the money from him – I meant to contact a reliable person through him, someone who could loan me the money here, and whom I could repay in rials back in Tehran. Parsi tells me his uncle might be able to help out, but he is a bargaining rascal, and with him business is business, and he himself is still on another wave-length. 'What's she going to do with that lovely apartment of hers?' he asks.

'Leila?'

'Yes.'

'You'll have to ask her yourself.'

We are now finishing our desserts and coffee, but Nader is still hungry, and orders the *garçon* to fetch him a steak sandwich, *bien cuit*. Well cooked.

'I had heard about her relationship with Abbas Hekmat,' he says. 'But I didn't know they were getting *engaged*. Are you sure about this?'

'No.'

'Then why did you say it?'

'I just wanted to fool you.'

'Jalal! ... I really never can tell when you're kidding and when you're serious. Like last night . . .'

The *garçon* is refilling our coffee cups, when I say to Parsi, 'Don't look now, but guess who's just walking up behind you?'

'Leila?'

'No, stupid! Your dear wifey.'

'Oh, *God*, I forgot to tell her I wasn't coming home for lunch. She's probably furious.'

Parsi's wife and sister-in-law, both dressed to kill, come and find us. Neither one of them is the least bit furious.

'I knew I'd catch you here,' says Parsi's wife, good-naturedly. '*Salaam*!' She is the daughter of an Iranian big-time Company owner, and I can't imagine what she has seen in Nader Parsi to make her marry him – except perhaps his literary genius and his acting in stage and cinema. Or perhaps Nader Parsi has some other accomplishments and knows other tricks in other places that I don't know about. Nader gets to his feet, drawing up chairs for the ladies, Sara and Simin, and they sit down. 'How are you?' Parsi's wife asks me.

'Well, thanks. You?'

'Very well, thank you.' She looks at me, as Nader and I are both goggling at Simin, who has taken off her coat. Her breasts are literally falling out of her low-cut neckline.

'What did you eat?' Parsi's wife asks. 'The food here is rubbish.'

'We had a little something, in *Aqaye* Aryan's pleasant company, Sara.' Nader says. He looks at me seeking help in conversation.

107

'They served us with a bit of old rubber, passing as steak.'

'Sussan and Javad Alavi are coming here at three,' Sara tells Nader. 'Simin and I came a little early.'

'That's fine,' Nader says.

Then, suddenly, her tone changes. 'Nader! Next time you aren't coming home for lunch, at least call me!'

'All right. Yes, dear. I apologise. My fault.'

'The cook made a whole load of food which I had to tell him to throw away.'

'I completely forgot! You were asleep this morning, when I left, and I went over to my lawyer's house and we got so engrossed in ...'

'Forgetting is one thing ... not caring is another. You're going too far.'

I look up at Parsi. In the presence of his wife, he has suddenly begun to shrink. Like a hen-pecked old rooster, he lowers his head.

'I said I was sorry,' he says.

To change the subject, I look at Parsi and ask, 'Does any one want to come to London for Christmas with me and Leila Azadeh and Abbas Hekmat?'

'London?' says Parsi's wife.

'London?' echoes Parsi's sister-in-law.

Someone gives me such a kick under the table it bruises my shin.

'Jalal's joking again,' says Parsi.

'Over there, sitting at the bar,' I say. 'Isn't that Hossein Abpak, the TV personality?'

'Yes, it is,' says Sara.

'He's always there, pan-handling beer off people,' Parsi says.

'Invite him over one day, let's ask him how he is getting on,' Sara says.

'Let him alone, he's got no class, he's a bum.'

'Don't say that about the poor fellow – it's shameful.'

'The poor fellow?! It wasn't shameful when he went round, organizing strikes and sit-ins in the Television and Radio Iran, brewing up anti-Shah demonstrations? It wasn't shameful when they were all full of Maoist fervour, going on strikes, picketing, and street rioting? When they leapt bare-assed into the love rivers of the Islamic Revolution it wasn't shameful then?'

'Everyone was doing it then. You did it yourself!'

'I was a damned fool!'

'You think everyone except yourself is a bum!'

I get up. 'If you'll excuse me, I have to be getting back to my hotel. The husband of one of my niece's friends is coming to see me.'

Parsi gets up too, and shakes hands with me. 'Phone me tomorrow,' he says.

I stop by the bar on the way out and buy a couple of packets of cigarettes. I turn round for a last look at Parsi and company. The three of them are still sitting there, looking chic, dignified and distinguished, drinking coffee and brandy. Parsi's wife is still talking at him, as if only this can keep her intact and happy and contented. Parsi is listening, as though this is the only thing that can keep him intact and happy and contented, too. They are ideally suited. The deaf Clemenceau is now having his lunch and reading his paper. Hossein Abpak is drinking his nth beer and reading his book. The restaurant is getting crowded and no one pays any attention to anyone else. Everyone is the same, each one thinking of his own, and this is probably what keeps them intact, happy and contented.

It is like the day when I am just outside Abadan's Bahmanshir Station, under the bombing and heavy shelling of *Khamseh-Khamseh*. I have come to send Matrud and his boy to *Aqa* Jari. Beyond the Bahmanshir Bridge there is all hell-broken-loose chaos. The scene is truly unimaginable. Far off, in the distance, the giant Refinery chimneys are still stuck-up in the air in the smoke and flames. Every moving vehicle on this side of the river is nose-to-tail for kilometres on end. Arabs and Iranians, swarming dazedly in their thousands, are running for dear life. People cling to any moving object, anything – from pick-up trucks to lorries, orange taxis and motorcycles. They are fleeing into the desert highway, in long lines. One cannot see where they begin, or where they end. In the back of the pick-ups, even on the back of motorcycles, men and women, young and old, are packed like dried figs in a box. Some are leaving on foot, moving along the sides of the road with their cows, goats or sheep, or what they have of livestock. The roaring of the fighter bombers blasts overhead, and the firing of heavy guns and the exploding *Khamseh-Khamsehs* throw the crowd into an ever-increasing panic ... Fear, the trembling bodies, the shattered nerves, and that dreadful feeling – the feeling that the unthinkable is happening and can't be stopped ... And it's the same for everyone ...

After a certain amount of pain and panic, or of happiness and security, people become the same. They lose the ability to judge accurately. They cannot distinguish between the good and the bad because there is no contrast.

I come out of the restaurant and walk back to the hotel.

14

When I get back to the hotel, there is a note for me. 'Mademoiselle Azadeh called to see you. She will probably return again around five.' This is the time when the Charnauts are coming. I say to myself this can go quite well; they can all meet each other. Leila Azadeh has a passion for being sociable and Christienne and Philipe Charnaut will probably be glad to meet a young Iranian woman author, translator, and poet, a self-exiled artist from the Iranian Pahlavi era.

There is still an hour before they arrive, so I give Farangis' phone number in Tehran to Sumunju, asking her to make the connection for me. I will take it in my room. It is now early evening in Tehran, just about the hour I told Farangis I would call.

After five or six minutes, the call comes through. I hear the voice and the click-click of the operator in Tehran, and then immediately Farangis' voice, as if she has been sitting by the phone waiting.

'*Allo*, Jalal?'

'Yes – *Salaam*, Feri.'

'How is she?' she pleads.

"The same. She's all right . . .'

'Has she come to yet? Has she *come to*?'

'No, not yet. But they're working on her.'

'Listen, Jalal – let me say this first, before anything happens and we get cut off. I have five or six hundred thousand tomans, ready to deliver to whoever you say, whenever it's needed . . . I've sold some of my jewellery.'

'God! Where are you keeping the money? In the house?'

'I've got some of it here with me, yes, just in case.'

'Put it all in the bank, immediately, Feri. Keep it there, till I tell you. The banks are safer. It's not right to keep any large amount in the house . . .'

'All right, all right. Just tell me, who do I give it to?'

'For the moment, keep it in the bank. There's no hurry, Feri. I'm trying to find out what's the best way to do this.'

'Tell me about my child, Jalal.'

I spend two or three minutes telling her about Sorraya's condition, and the treatments, and about the ECGs. I cannot tell whether all this is any comfort to her, or worries her more.

'It was my own stupid fault,' she says, 'Sending my child out there with my own hands, to waste away like this.'

'Feri! What are you saying? For God's sake! How were you to know?'

'My poor child! She didn't want to go back to France after Khosro was killed. It was *me* who made her go! It was *me* who sent her to that blasted place. *I* sent her by force, to her death –'

'Farangis! Why are you talking gibberish? Why do you torture yourself like this, for nothing? What death? . . . Besides, how were you to know such a thing was going to happen? Thousands and thousands of people come to France, or send their kids to France, and they have a damn good life. You made a logical and intelligent choice. It's better than when she was there. They had killed her husband. They took away her government job from her because she is a *woman*. You wanted her to come out here and carry on with her studies. You yourself were left alone. Not every mother would make such a sacrifice. You were courageous. This was just our fate . . . So, for the love of God, don't talk like that . . .'

'I don't know . . . Whatever it was, I can't help thinking it's *me* who's to blame . . .'

'No,' I say. Then in the hope of distracting her from the subject of Sorraya's misery, I ask, 'What's going on in Tehran? Any more air-raids?'

'No, oh, no. Nothing goes on here. But they keep hitting Abadan and Ahvaz and Dezful, and those places . . .'

'How about yourself? How are you?'

112

'I'm all right.'

'How's the old leg?'

'It's nothing. I'm all right.'

I know she is lying. 'Are you still alone?'

'No. Dr Mohammadi's wife and two children are here with me. They're refugees, you know. From Abadan.'

'Is the doctor hmself there, too?'

'No. He comes and goes back to Abadan. Oh, Jalal, take care.'

'Sure, I will. And you take it easy.'

We talk for a few minutes then say goodbye.

At five o'clock, I shave, wash, change, and go downstairs. I sit reading in a corner of the small lobby. Madame and Monsieur Charnaut come at a couple of minutes past five, along with their two children. Charnaut is a short but good-looking man, very jovial and good-humoured. His wife is wearing a not-too new, pinkish coat with a matching hat. Charnaut shakes my hand firmly, introducing his two children as Jean-Louis, four, and Paulette Françoise, three. They both deliver a polite '*Enchanté*, Monsieur'. Altogether, they form a warm, cheerful group. I ask if they would mind sitting down for a few minutes, and have some tea and cakes before we leave. I explain that a friend has left a note, promising to call again at around five; I am not *sure* that she will come, but she might. I tell them briefly about Leila.

But Leila Azadeh does not show up, not even by five-thirty. So I leave her a note, explaining where I am going, and adding that I shall probably call her in the morning. We leave the hotel.

Phillipe has a brand new Renault, and we first drive over to the hospital. Christienne Charnaut and I go upstairs, while Phillipe stays in the car with the kids. Sorraya's condition seems unchanged. The nurse on duty tells us that two other friends of Sorraya's have also called. Christienne Charnaut tells me this is the usual pattern; her friends come, and there are many of them – but because they cannot speak to Sorraya, they never stay long; they leave sad and depressed.

It is dark by the time we head for Saint Remy, in south west

Paris. Phillipe Charnaut and I sit in front, with the household in the back seat. He drives conservatively, down the Rue René Coty, we pass through the Rue de Cité Université, where Christienne Charnaut shows me the building where Sorraya used to live. The building stands alive, and lit up, like many others. It is dark over Paris now, and the Sunday evening traffic is heavy. It seems as if people from all directions of the world are pouring into Paris. For many, Paris is the end of the line. The tired, the helpless, the outcast, wherever they may be, they all turn up here. No one with any sense would ever leave Paris. Who said that? Only me, the odd one out, is leaving it in the twilight. I wish Leila Azadeh were with us.

It begins to rain again. Phillipe drives into a clean residential area, where there is no sign of the city, of the autoroute, or the traffic. Just modern apartment buildings and town houses. But you get a feeling you are entering the largest and most modern beehive system, on some other planet. Christienne Charnaut is still busy chattering, at the same time quieting, reprimanding and loving the children. Through the Renault's windscreen I see the glowing of the lights and the lamp-posts, and the wind shaking the trees, and the windscreen wipers washing away the rain-drops.

I remember little of any significance that evening, except that the Charnauts' house is very modern, very clean, and that they are very fond of art, of reading, of wine, and are also very thoughtful, and that everything about them – at least to a confused, war-stricken outsider like myself – seems very orderly and intimate. The children have supper with their nurse, and go to bed at the appointed hour. Christienne Charnaut's mother, *Grand-mére*, is also with us tonight. She helps prepare the dinner and look after the children. Before dinner, *Vin Rosé* is served with the *hors d'oeuvres*. I abstain. With the meal – mushroom soup, shrimp garlic soufflé and grilled trout – a *vin blanc* is served. Afterwards, coffee and some liqueur, the name of which I do not catch, are taken with dessert. Madame and Monsieur Charnaut and *Grand-mére* Labourge make love to the food and wine almost reverently, as though the only logical means to salvation, in this transient life, was through deep contemplation of food and wine. *Grand-mére* Labourge looks the same age as Farangis; she works in the local library, is deputy of the Saint Remy Girl Guides. She is a plump, round, healthy woman, a jolly soul, and never interferes in her daughter and son-in-law's debates, or anything. She just eats, drinks, and laughs. She sits beside me, and has the top two buttons of her blouse generously open across her white bosom. Christienne Charnaut and her husband have different opinions about wine and food and education and child psychology and politics.

Charnaut is a moderate Gaullist. He has twice visited America, and very much likes the '*Etats Unis*'. Christienne is a Social Democrat – but not a 'reckless Communist'. Charnaut believes Jean Piaget has brought about a great revolution in the annals of human thinking during the latter half of this century. Christienne is a traditional Freudian. She thinks excess liberties, in the American style, followed by clinical therapy for children, is a load of trash – children must be disciplined at home, and occasionally given a 'good' spanking. She does not look at her mother while saying this, but *Grand-mére* Labourge turns to me with a hearty laught. 'Oh, I never hit *my* children, Monsieur. I always *explained* everything to them . . .'

Charnaut is fond of beer, but Christienne prefers a light Dubonnet or a Saint Raphael. It is 'absolutely horrifying' the way some French families now are beginning to serve *beer* with *hors d'oeuvres*! 'My God . . .' she says. 'What is the world coming to!' They have their little differences, but they also know where to draw the line, and close the discussion, with a kiss, and God knows how many times they do the one-two slap-dash kissing and agreeing the whole evening. Their views about the situation in Iran are different too, and sadly off-beat. They have no clear opinions about the philosophy of Monsieur Khomeini's Islamic Revolution, because they say they do not 'grasp' it. They do, however, understand the French-educated Iranian 'Liberals'!

They are what one would call honest, *thoughtful* people, too. Christienne shows me Sorraya's possessions she is looking after. Among them is a good deal of her gold jewellery – her wedding rings, a watch, a large 'Allah' pendant, a necklace, a couple of bracelets – all the things Farangis had told me Sorraya had brought with her. I cannot very well take any of Sorraya's things with me that night, not just out of any modesty or bashful reserve. Apparently, Phillipe Charnaut does not mind keeping the jewellery as some sort of collateral in lieu of his having signed the guarantee on the hospital fee. I understand. I ask them to keep the jewellery there for the time being, until Sorraya recovers and can collect it herself. 'In any case,' says Charnaut, 'it is safer here than in the hotel.'

After supper, we sit by the fire, drinking coffee. Christienne tells me of her long friendship with Sorraya, whom she has known for seven or eight years, both from their former days at the University together, and during the past years, since Sorraya's return. She genuinely loves and respects her.

'Tell me about the day of her accident,' I say. 'She was here that day, was she not?'

Christienne Charnaut sighs. 'Oh, yes, she was here. It was a Sunday. Oh, how I remember. We had roast beef – with Russian salad, cheesed potatoes, and ice cream. After lunch, she played with the children for a while. Phillipe was watching some football match on television. Sorraya and I sat and talked for a while. Right here. She sat on the same chair you're sitting on now. She said she was going to call her mother that evening; that she was going to have a serious talk with her, and get her permission to start back to Iran by land. You know, the airports in Iran were closed, weren't they?'

'Yes.'

'She wanted very much to go back. Those last days, she came here often. She had packed up almost all her belongings. Her jewellery had been left in my keeping for a long time. There was a lot of pilfering going on in the dormitory, you see – no security.'

'What time did she leave here?'

'Oh, not late. Around four o'clock. It was still daylight. She liked getting about by bike. She was a very careful cyclist, though.'

'She wasn't ill?'

'No, no! Not at all.'

'Fever? Headache?'

'No, no, no. Absolutely. She was in the excellent health, perfect. If I'd thought there was anything wrong I would never have let her cycle back. There was never the slightest sign that she was unwell, or even upset. In fact, before she left, she gave each of the children a ride around the garden and played and laughed with them.'

116

'Then what?'

'Then she said good-bye, kissed the kids, and rode off, slowly. It started raining just after she'd gone.'

'What time were you notified?'

'About a quarter to nine. No . . . It wasn't her fault, poor thing. I don't think it was any driver's fault, either. No one was to blame.'

'She simply swerved at a corner and had a fall,' says Phillipe. '*C'est la vie*! That's life.'

'It isn't fair.'

'No, it's not. But that's the way the dice fall, sometimes.'

Charnaut drives me to the Saint Remy Metro at about nine o'clock, and I return to Paris alone. There has been nothing further from Leila Azadeh. I reclaim the note I have left for her, tear it up, and then take the lift to my room.

I arrive just in time to hear Radio Tehran's midnight news, but there is only more war news, and all bad. 'Saddam Hossein Aflaqi's invading forces' have completed the blockade of Abadan and are now besieging Dezful and Ahvaz. The defenceless towns are being shelled and bombed, and innocent, 'martyr-breeding people' are killed. Hundreds of thousands of refugees are leaving their homes. (After Radio Iran news broadcasts, I also listen to the French and British stations' news and filter out some shade of truth from the combinations – and the contradictions.) The Supreme Commander of the Iranian Armed Forces, President Dr Abolhassan Bani-Sadr, has announced in a radio interview, that while *he* is alive, the Iraqis shall never succeed in capturing Dezful, the crucial artery in the country's economic survival – the oil pipeline system! He says he will fight in Khuzestan to his very last drop of blood!

The foreign broadcasts say more or less the same things, only they sound more alarming for Iran. In a BBC radio interview, Bani-Sadr lays all the blame on the 'fanatic fractions', foreseeing 'bad days' ahead for Iran!

As my eyelids grow heavy with sleep, I try to think of Sorraya. Alone there, in her silent agony. I try and imagine her on her good healthy days, but all that comes to my mind is a rainy afternoon and she is cycling alone on Saint Remy Road. Oh, bad days!

The village headman once gathered his tribe together, and said '*Aye* people! I have good news and bad news for you. The bad news first is that this winter we have nothing but cow and donkey dung. But the good news is that we have all the dung you want.'

15

Despite our initial hopes, the results of the dialysis, the ECGs, the SSRs and other tests on Sorraya during the third week of December are not very promising. Yet, medications, sero-therapies and the analyses of her tests continue, and Dr Martin and the two other doctors looking after her are not disappointed. I pay another ten thousand francs to the hospital but we still owe one hundred and thirty-nine thousand francs, and the good hospital shows patience. Of course, it would be unchristian and uncivil to throw a comatose patient out – not to mention the Charnauts' signed guarantee form, resting in the hospital's office, and not to mention that the Charnauts have Sorraya's belongings and jewellery in their keeping. Well, let's not be cynical.

In the Hotel Palma, I move to a smaller, cheaper room – with a view – on the top floor, beneath the attic. My new room has a private bath, which is bigger than a phone booth. It also has a pretty little crescent-shaped balcony, overlooking the church and its small graveyard. If you got bored indoors, you could sit on the balcony, and freeze to death.

Bad news still pours out of Iran. The Iraqi advance has been somewhat halted, but 'Saddam's infidel forces' have captured Qasr-e-Shirin, Naft-e-Shahr, several other border towns in the west, and many towns in Kermanshah, Ilam, and Khuzestan, including all of Khorram-Shahr. Unable to capture Abadan, they are now systematically shelling and firing on the city from the north, south and west. The Iranian government, apparently desperate to obtain foreign currency to pay the heavy costs of the war, is negotiating with the help of the Algerian government, for the return of its foreign assets through the release of the 'Spies Nest' hostages.

I do not see Leila Azadeh during the last ten days of December and the Christmas festivities. She has gone to Marseilles with her younger brother and his fiancée, who is the daughter of an ex-University of Tehran professor. The night before Leila leaves, she comes with me to the hospital to visit Sorraya. Then, she insists that we go to her home in Porte d'Italie for dinner. I don't really want to go – I don't want to be alone with her. She probably senses it too, so she says her father is with her in Paris that night – don't I want to meet her father, and get to know old, famous Professor Azadeh? We are standing outside the hospital, waiting for a taxi, as she is saying this.

'I thought your father was in Marseilles?'

'Yes, my father is in Marseilles. But he's come to Paris for his medical check-up.'

'I see.'

'I see ... and tomorrow we're going to Marseilles and thereabouts ... and I won't see you again till after January.'

'Well, so what else is new! How is your dear father?'

'Stop being a tease, now. Are you coming or aren't you? I promised Papa I'd bring you home. I've told him a great deal about you.'

'About me?'

'About this Jalal Aryan ... My faithful, long-lost love, who's just come over from Iran ... I've told him lots of things.'

'All bad, I hope.'

'All good.'

'Okay, twist my arm a little more.'

'It's *Shab-e-Yalda* tonight, the longest night in the year.'

'So?'

'We will be traditional and sit and eat *Shab-Cherah*, crack nuts, stuff ourselves with *ranginak*, and chatter away. Papa loves these old traditions.'

I look at her over the top of my glasses. It is one of those empty looks into which almost anything can be read.

'Come on. How much must I beg?'

'I don't feel like it.' I turn, and look up at the window of Sorraya's room. 'You saw her ...'

'Yes, I saw her. And I'm sorry. But come on. It'll be good for you, distract you. Have you got the medicine you have to take at night, with you?'

I put my hand to my pocket; it is there.

'Come on, then. I want to show you something, really.'

'Then let's go!'

She laughs. 'Aren't you going to ask what it is?'

'Whatever it is, it's better than goddamned nuts and *ranginak!*'

We take a taxi to the Porte d'Italie. Leila's flat is what they call a duplex in one of those *Batiment neufs*. Her apartment consists of two half-storeys, the first with a hall, dining room and boudoir. Stylish curved steps lead down to the bedrooms, etc. Inside the apartment, there are about a million plants and flowers, all over the floors, the windowsills, and crawling all over the walls, or suspended from the ceilings; cared for by a creature called Genevieve, Leila's aged housemaid. In the taxi Leila warns that her father has lost his voice as a result of a larynginal disease, and speaks through a voice synthesizer. So he must not talk too much.

Dr Abdol-Ali Azadeh is a tall, exquisite looking, extremely dignified and diplomatic-mannered gentlemen, with white, brush-like moustaches and eyebrows, and thick, wavy, white hair, like half a kilo of hydrofoil cotton. He wears a pair of heavy black-framed spectacles with thick lenses which we used to call 'beer-bottle bottoms'. The Professor habitually holds his head stiff but tilted, his handshake is limp, almost neutral, probably the result of his long years in universities and as Cultural Attaché. In his left hand, he holds an American-made 'voice-synthesizer'. The Professor places it on his windpipe, from the outside, and 'voice' comes out of it. The other end of its wire leads to one of his waistcoat pockets, which presumably conceals the rest of the gadget, and its batteries. The sound which emanates from the synthesizer's little amplifier is smooth but vibrant and metallic; making the Professor sound a bit like R2-D2 in *Star Wars*. Over his waistcoat, starched shirt, and tie, the Professor wears something like a chic *jellaba*, or kimono, which gives him an extraordinary, rather mystical appearance. He is extremely modest and courteous. After handshakes and greetings he offers me the best armchair – in order, I suppose, that if I, who had come from Abadan battle front after a stroke and a leg injury, were to drop dead, I may at least do it in comfort.

On black leather armchairs we sit around a stylish table of white marble and blue crystal. On another table, with fine wooden inlaid work, there are several crystal and china plates full of Iranian mixed nuts, neatly sliced watermelons and musk melons, *ranginak*, dried watermelon seeds roasted with marjoram , *baqlava* from Yazd, rice pastries, and some decanters of wine; these mut be the *Shab-e-Yalda* refreshments. Leila tells her father why I am in France, where we were earlier in the evening, and whom we had gone to see. The old man listens attentively, with his head inclined, his eyes lowered, only occasionally looking up at me. Then he puts the synthesizer to his throat, and says, 'I wish I was younger, and had the courage that you have, and could be in Iran and participate in the events you have. The very name of Iran makes my pulse beat faster.' The vibrant, electronic voice issuing forth does not match with his words.

'The poet Ouhadi Maragheh'i says: "We are drunk, and this drunkenness is of love./The day I die at the threshold of love, my first history will be that of love." Love of one's country and motherland – and its traditions – is the dearest ever love.'

'You're not referring to me I hope?'

'You were in Abadan – and the war is there.'

'I *happened* to be there, entirely by accident. I was a government employee, in hospital at the time . . . A spectator, at the very most.'

'Is that why you stayed in Iran?'

'I didn't stay in Iran. I've been living in Iran.'

'Let's please not spend this precious night quarrelling like Sa'adi and the Challenger,' he says. 'Leila esteems you very highly. She has spoken much of you.'

'Leila *Khanum* has a dreamy, imaginative character.'

'Papa,' says Leila, 'Don't listen to the things Jalal says. If you keep on, he will even deny he's sitting here.'

'Yes, so I see,' says the Professor. 'And what a virtue that is, my girl. Mowlana says; "Total shape emerges from total shapeless-ness" . . .'

I have eaten nothing since breakfast. I can hear my stomach rumble, and hope supper shows up soon. But Leila's house-maid is just bringing a trayful of drinks and coffee. Pernod-and-lemonade for Leila, Irish coffee for the Professor, and plain coffee for me. Each served in its own special container.

'Perhaps *Aqaye* Aryan won't object to an Irish coffee this evening,' Professor Azadeh suggests. Leila replies, 'Papa, Jalal is on doctor's orders, so we must excuse him.' And she looks to me.

I remain silent.

'I understand, my son . . .' The Professor says. And goes on to explain to me that Irish coffee is a traditional beverage from Ireland, and that he himself picked up the habit twenty-five years earlier during his first diplomatic service mission in Dublin. Irish coffee was an '*interessant*' blend of hot and cold natures, and agreeable to the Professor's taste. Of course we are speaking in Persian this evening, but the Professor's modern Persian is tinged with various French and English phrases – languages of which the professor has complete command.

'And tell me, *Aqaye* Aryan,' he then says, 'have you met any others of the immigrant clan here in Paris, besides Leila?'

'Yes, a few.'

'Jalal has been literally camping in the Val du Grace hospital.' Leila has filled two plates with *ranginak* and mixed nuts and places them in front of me.

'There are herds of them here,' says Professor Azadeh.

'Yes . . .'

'What do you think of them, *Aqaye* Aryan? Please, help yourself with the *Shab-e-Yalda*.'

'As one of the students said, we have all types and sorts here.'

'Oh, every type and sort,' he agrees. and God knows, we Iranians are traditionally on the up and down trail, and have had every type and sort in our country. You know we are all, traditionally, good hands at migrating and nomadic wanderings.'

'Not all of them, Papa,' interrupts Leila.

I pick up my plate of nuts, and start with the pistachios and almonds.

'Of course not . . .' agrees the Professor. 'And by migrations I didn't just mean finding new pastures for the sheep and the horses, as in our primitive Aryan tribes . . . I mean for the political, the social and the vital needs of our civilization, which have been with us since pre-Ashkanian times, in the form of migrations. This is still with us today . . .'

'For the rich, of course, Papa,' says Leila again defiantly, setting down her glass. Then she excuses herself, winking at me, and disappears into one of the rooms downstairs. I watch her pretty figure as she walks, but not so avidly that her father will clout me over the head.

Professor Azadeh feigns not to have heard his daughter's remark, which is probably an old father–daughter antagonism. He turns to me, and in a rather ambiguous tone, says 'Professor Omstead, in his book *A History of the Achaemaian Shahs*, gives us proof that even in the Achaemanian period, a number – and often even classes – of Aryan peoples left their homes and lands for various reasons, or because of political and social turmoil, and emigrated to the west, or the east – east, at that period meant the towns of present day Afghanistan or India, and by the west we mean Mesopotamia, Syria and the Antioch.' He looks to me, as if waiting for my confirmation.

'Yes,' I say.

'After the Arab invasion and the domination of Islam in Iran in around 600 AD groups of Zoroastrian high priests and the higher classes of society migrated to India, both by land and by sea, through the Persian Gulf and the Sea of Oman, and most of them gathered in Gujerat, near Bombay, to form the largest Parsi community, where they still speak the old Pahlavi language, or as they now call it *Gujerati*.'

For someone who has lost his vocal chords and larynx the Professor is holding forth at length. Good, I think, and this is the traditional *Shab-e-Yalda* – the longest night. The tradition is complete.

Just before I left Tehran, I attended the *Khatm* ceremony of old man Jalili – a relative of Farangis' husband's – who had died of cancer. (The martyr-breeding people of Iran still died of such causes, among other things.) I sit on the carpeted floor of the Mosque beside my old friend and childhood neighbour, Bahman Azari, and say a *fatehah*. The women sit in a separate room. This too, is complete tradition. The men all sit around in the drowsy-looking main chamber of Dabbagh-Khaneh Mosque, cross-legged, with our backs to the wall. Our shoes are paired in neat rows outside. People enter, shake hands with the head mourners, offer their condolences, deposit their shoes and tip-toe quietly in, half-bowing here and there, one hand to their hearts, and then seat themselves in a corner. A Mosque attendant hands us each a pamphlet, which we kiss and press to our foreheads, and start reading its few verses of the Holy Qoran. We sip hot tea with lumps of sugar. We smoke *Oshnu Vizhe* cigarettes. The mullah preaches from his pulpit. The loudspeaker rustles with static, from time to time. I see familiar faces from the past, from the family and from the neighbourhood. Bahman Azari explains to me who so-and-so is, and what such-and-such is doing now. That one serving tea is the late Jalili's nephew, a third year University of Science and Industry student, before the Revolution, now he drives a taxi. The one with the white hair is Dr Torabzadeh, who has been kicked out and retired. That one with the holes in his socks is Mohammad *Aqa* Javadi, who used to be a Court Judge, and now deals in real estate. The one with the tie is Mas'ud *Aqa* Hosseini, who used to be in the Computer Department of the Plan Organization before the Revolution, he now sells smuggled video sets and tapes. '*Fateheh!*' the Mosque attendant wails mournfully, and we all say another *fateheh*.

'Mind you,' continues Professor Azadeh, 'Naser Khosro, too, who spent most of his life gathering knowledge and serving the rulers of his time, indulged in pleasures of life and debauchery, as well as accumulating riches and bettering his social position. But when he came under persecution he emigrated and went to Turkestan, and then to Indus, and India, and associated and exchanged ideas with the leaders of various religious bodies... It is said in the *Javamé-al-Tavaritch* and in the *Dabastan-al-Mazaheb* that he went from there to seek refuge in Yamkan, and spent the last twenty years of his life in that territory ...'

I let the Professor's voice fade in and out of my ears. '... And above all we have *Hakim* Abolqassem Ferdousi himself, as you know, after finishing his legendary *Shahnameh*, or *Book of Kings*, seeing that the Samanid empire had been toppled, sought refuge in the west of Iran, in the court of the Buyid Sultans, and went from ...'

I glance towards the door behind which Leila has vanished. I don't know whether she is organizing supper, changing her clothes, taking a bath, or what.

'... Of course,' the Professor was still going on, 'history shows us that such events have happened – and still happen – in all countries and societies, throughout the world. Also, in our own

Iran, the reverse of course, has been known to happen. The great historian Plutarch tells us that in the year 529 AD . . .'

I continue to wonder what Leila is doing.

The Professor pours himself more Irish coffee, and begins talking of Sheikh Sa'adi Shirazi, who journeyed to Syria, Aleppo and Ba'albek. We have got to the part where Sa'adi, upon returning to his homeland, writes: 'As I returned, I found the land at ease/The tigers put away their beastliness', when I see Matrud and his retarded boy, Idris, back in Abadan. Their home, in the rooms at the back of my garden in Breim are being shelled day and night but I cannot force them out to *Aqa* Jari for a few days. And I see the old man with the overturned onion pick-up. He is still there by the petrol station on the road to Karaj, a few kilometres from the bus terminal, wondering what to do. But not contemplating emigrating.

Leila's ascending the stairs brings me back to Paris. The waiting is well worth it. She is now attired in a light dress of thin black and white silk, which suddenly turns the old duplex in Porte d'Italie into Masnavi's mythical Enchanting Castle.

'Supper at nine,' Leila announces.

Professor Azadeh now rises and disappears into another room – for his evening prayers; at least so Leila tells me. Every evening, before dinner, even if he had been drinking alcohol, he would wash out his mouth with water three times, perform the ritual ablutions, and say his prayers for *Maqreb* and *Asha*; a habit from his youth in his father's house in Shiraz. His absence tonight is much longer than the normal time needed for these prayers. But probably he is prostrated in deeper prayer, conversing with his Creator; or perhaps having a nap. After all, he is a retired old gentleman, belonging to a retired regime.

What Leila wanted to show me turns out to be a video film. She brings a video cassette, and puts it on. It is an American feature film, by the name of '*Coma*'! This is for me to see! Leila, in her own happy, exciting world, has probably supposed seeing this film, under the present circumstances, will be 'interesting' for me. She has taken a 'lot of trouble' to get hold of this tape for the evening.

This film, among other things, of course, is one of these hospital stories – Hollywood shock-mystery stuff. It has a capitalist fraud theme: the authorities of a large hospital happily send the occasional 'emergency' patients into a coma, while announcing the unfortunate patient 'deceased'. The body is then kept in the morgue. Later, the various organs, eyes, kidneys, etc., will be sold. I accept it is an idiotic, nonsensical story, but its macabre resemblance to Sorraya's situation makes me feel sick, and I get cramps in my stomach. When the doctors begin sending a new patient into a coma, I emigrate to the bathroom. When I come out my face must have been some very pretty colour indeed.

'Oh, God forgive me!' Leila says. 'It was my damn fault. This stupid film upset you.'

'It's nothing . . .'

'You've gone white as plaster!'

'This is my natural good looks!'

'No . . . let me get you something.'

'Just sit down by me . . . Talk to me. Did they take her into the morgue?'

'To hell with that! I'll turn it off.'

'All right.'

'A milk-coffee?'

'Fine.'

'Blast me and my film-choosing! . . . Stupid girl! What sort of a film was that for this poor man?'

'Shsh – it is Hollywood.'

She stops the film just at the point where Mike Douglas is running after the bad guys and discovering the morgue where the comatose bodies are stored. Then she brings milk and coffee from the kitchen. 'First Papa bored you to death, with his gibbering about the decrepit history and culture of the land of the rose and the nightingale, and then me with my stupid American nonsense . . .'

'Could you hear him down there?'

'Papa's voice can drive one crazy!'

I laugh, and she laughs with me.

'How are you really feeling?' She lays a hand on my forehead. Her skin against mine is hot, almost burning.

'Fine,' I say. 'Fine.'

'How's your pressure?'

'What pressure?'

'. . . Your blood pressure, silly!'

'Don't worry about it.'

'What happened in there, anyway?'

'Nothing, I just erupted a bit.'

I drink some of the milk-coffee down with a handful of my pills. A feeling of calm returns to my head and chest. Leila puts on a video of Iranian music. 'That beautiful concert singer,' she says, 'is one of Papa's loves.' Then she comes and sits by me. 'Your head isn't hurting?'

'No.'

'Did your *eruption* hurt?'

'No – but the only thing left inside must be my spare pancreas.'

'When you came out of that door, looking so pale, *I* was practically going into a coma, myself!'

'Poor thing ... I must have scared you.'

She looks into my eyes, the way she used to, long ago.

For a moment, for the first time on this trip, I feel I have come to a good point, where I want to be, where a good life could exist for me. But at this moment Genevieve announces supper.

Soon the Professor joins us.

Supper consists of special, Olivier mixed salad as hors d'oeuvre, mushroom soup, roast chicken, a sort of partridge dish, white rice and curry – served in that order, with a *Chateau d'Yquem*. Dessert and fruit follow. The Professor does not talk much over dinner, probably because he can't use the voice synthesizer and manipulate his knife and fork at the same time. First, he eats quickly, then sits back, drinking *Chateau d'Yquem* and toying with this and that, speaking and lecturing eloquently – that is, he enters once again into the discussion of the emigrations of cultured and intellectual Iranians throughout ancient history. In view of his past career it is surprising that he makes no mention of the hostage-taking affair in Tehran – the hottest political issue in the world at this time. He moves in his own world, and in the world of *emigré* Iranians.

'... In contemporary history, too,' he says, 'although conditions have improved somewhat, and the society enjoyed more freedom and progress, the migration of the elite – the open-minded politicians, intellectuals, thinkers, writers and poets – has been as natural an act as ever. Even among the Iranian clergy ...' I try to tune out the Professor's voice ... '... And today, as you know, cities like London, Paris, New York and Los Angeles are swimming with dissident Persian language newspapers.'

The Professor is now fully warmed up by the large quantities of *Chateau d'Yquem* he has absorbed. He is plucking out bits of partridge, chicken and rice from his teeth and flicking them to one side.

'. . . And even in our present times, we have many cases to show almost all our writers, thinkers and poets have pulled out of Iran, because the society's mentality hasn't accorded with their creative nature, or has disagreed with them, or they have found a chance to breathe and to create something outside Iran, which they would not have found back home. The most famous was, of course, the late Sadeq Hedayat. Also, we have *Aqaye* Mohammad Ali Jamal-Zadeh, in Switzerland. We have *Aqaye* Bozorg Alavi in Germany, we have *Aqaye* Sadegh Chubak in London, *Aqaye* Abbas Hekmat in Oxford, *Khanum* Mahshid Amirshahi in Paris, and many others who left *after* the fall of the Pahlavi dynasty. Take, for instance, my very own daughter, sitting here –' 'Papa,' Leila interrupts. 'In the first place, don't mix *me* up with them.'

'Why shouldn't I? It is a literary historical fact, my girl.'

'In the second place, I think we've given *Aqaye* Aryan more than enough headache for one evening.'

'Not at all,' I say. 'It's been a pleasant evening.'

'Very well,' says the Professor. 'But these things are facts.'

'I wouldn't be so sure,' Leila says. 'They all have their own *potpourri* of personal reasons for coming here. You can't generalize like that, nor can you say that they left their dear homeland because they suffered hardship, and were persecuted by the ruling regime. Besides, many have also stayed right there all their lives, and some are still there. Ali Akbar Dehkhoda stayed on in his beat-up house, in poverty, and in humiliation until, I've heard, they even cut off his water and electricity, because he hadn't paid . . .'

'All right,' the Professor says simply, smiling and filling Leila's glass. 'All right . . .' He shakes his head, as if mourning the loss of greater things. He says: 'Plutarch summarizes the fall of the Roman Empire – as "*Sic transit gloria mondi*" . . . thus passed the glory of the world . . .' and he empties his glass in one gulp, as if these were the last drops of *Chateau d'Yquem* in the world. Then, he adds, 'May I quote Emad Khorasani, who once said, "My heart is sad, sad, sad;/I'm a stranger, stranger, stranger to myself." '

He winks at Leila and me. I cannot make out what he means by this wink, or by the verse. But it doesn't really matter. I don't imagine the Professor himself quite knows what he means. Perhaps he is under the impression – or rather, Leila has given him the impression – that Leila and I, after years, have found each other again in Paris – and that the gifts of joyous matrimony are in store for us. We are now eating *ranginak*, with a sort of pineapple ice cream. As a nightcap, the Professor asks Genevieve to bring him a glass of his favourite, special cognac, and she brings it in, on a gold tray, as if it has just been taken from the vaults in the French Central Bank. The Professor raises the glass towards his daughter and me: 'The cup of life mut be drunk full to the brim, my children.' he says.

> Happy time and happy spirit for lovers,
> For, without their binding love,
> The world is but a legend.

'Let's not get *too* sentimental, please, Papa,' says Leila.

'All right. Very well . . .'

'And don't forget to call mother before you go to bed. She's expecting you to. And also, we're starting out early tomorrow morning.'

'Very well, very well.'

After which, the Professor points to the video, saying, 'I like this song very much . . . It's a delicate sonata.'

The emigré singer is now performing a melancholy, heart-wrenching song about Iran. I don't recall her name, Susik, or Susa, or Sucker, or something. She is all done up to the nines, with what there is of a décolleté dress. The lyrics and tune are done by a pair of immigrants, too. The lyrics endings go something like this . . .

> Whenever you go, the sky is blue,
> But the sky of my heart, is grey.
> My pulse beats for Iran,
> My tears are my epitaph.
> Halalai lalalai halalai . . .

130

The Professor, glass in hand, keeps almost dozing off. He drums softly on the table with the fingers of his other hand, saying, 'Sing it, *Khanum*. Sing, pretty *Khanum* . . . Sing until morning dawns after *Shab-e-Yalda*.'

It is around eleven thirty when I take my leave. On the whole, it is a merciful evening; especially the later hours. Well, there is Leila.

She drives me back to the hotel at about midnight. She does not come inside.

I have, anyway, enough Leila-remedy to see me through till January.

16

I see Nader Parsi two or three times in the week before Christmas – whenever he can manage to get away from his wife and his sexy sister-in-law. He comes to the hospital with me to visit Sorraya once, but he does not invite me home, thank God. His world is different from the aristocratic, luxurious world of Professor Azadeh. As Ahmad Safavi had said, Nader Parsi's little circle in Paris that year were a sad lot.

The old literary crowd at the Tehran Riviera Restaurant were a far cry from the likes of General Doctor Qa'em Maqami Fard, Dr Majidi, Colonel Javad Alavi, Dr Qassem Khatibi and Dr Kazem Makaremi and Farhad Biglari, who were all political escapees, ex-Freemasons, or outright swindlers. They had their fun and games, and then promptly disappeared. These fellows were involved in hard core political rackets; shadows, who, in the last hours of the night, ended up in the houses of ex-leaders from the past regime – around the opium brazier. People like Nader Parsi, and Dr Ardakan, and Veisi and Homa Ala'i, too, might turn up around the brazier from time to time but this would be for kicks, never for more serious 'ideals'. The night when Leila and I were at the General Doctor's 18th-Century mansion, while the fat vet was wooing Leila Azadeh, from upstairs there were noises that sounded like a flock of spies and mercenaries in full action – a few of them possibly from James Manson's outfit, and very likely, James Manson himself!

It is the last week of December and I have not straightened out the money angle yet, because I don't really want to draw Farangis' money out of Iran to deliver it into the hands of these parasites. Secondly, I have taken some bureaucratic steps to try to have the hospital fees covered by government insurance.

These days there are biting winds, and it freezes every night. After leaving the hospital, I take long walks, sometimes dropping in at the Saint Sulpice Public Library. One evening, Ahmad Safavi turns up at my hotel. I had seen Ahmad Safavi once or twice at the Oil Company's Management Training Seminars. Among his other accomplishments, Safavi has been one of the better literary translators in recent years. I quite liked him; he was an Isfahani, and very sharp. Unlike the members of Nader Parsi's 'Screwed-up-Generation', or the politicists' clan, Ahmad Safavi was an independent soul, a European–Iranian, a German resident. He still made trips to and from Iran, collecting his pension, and the royalties on the reprints of his books.

On the afternoon that Safavi comes to see me, he first telephones. He explains that he arrived in Paris two or three days earlier, and had heard from Nader Parsi that I was here. When he arrives, he is in the best of spirits, all smiles. He tells me that Stuttgart is a wonderful city, its people are wonderful, and very disciplined, it fills one with delight. The people in Hamburg are wonderful too, he says, the weather there is exceptionally fine, it fills one with delight. Stuttgart is a very clean town. Anyone caught littering the streets of Stuttgart with so much as a cigarette stub, will be fined by the police. What's more, Persian carpets have a very good market in both Hamburg and Stuttgart, it is there that the civilized world truly appreciates the real value of this real, Persian artwork. Ahmad Safavi is well contented with life in general. He and his wife own a villa in Stuttgart. He says he has just returned from one of his numerous trips to Iran. In spite of all the troubles and irregularities, he says, things are now absolutely splendid in Iran. In fact, things are very very much better than before. No more drinking, no more *bi-hejabi*, no more pointless wasting of money and extravagance. In short, things are splendid.

It is dusk when we leave the hotel together and stroll towards the café on Saint Michel, which is a sort of a hang-out for many Iranian immigrants, and which Safavi knows well. We take our seats by huge glass walls, looking on to the side walk. I have coffee and Safavi lemon tea – he tells me he never touches spirits. He says he has made his Creator a promise to deliver a healthy liver unto the hands of Israel, the Angel of Death.

'How come? Israel need a liver transplant?' I ask.

He laughs. 'No, *Jenab*. It seems to me all your thoughts are centred around illness, hospitals, operations and death and dying ... Tell me, then. What's good news?'

'Your health!'

'Thank you.'

'You seem to have enjoyed your short stay in Iran?'

'Things are fine, the people here grumble for no reason.'

'And how do you justify the war?'

'The war will be ended very soon, too, God willing. War has its positive aspects, too. You know it has, and plenty of them. Brings the country into unity, into innovations and actions. Gets the national blood boiling.'

'Did you travel all through Iran?'

'Yes,' he says. 'Why, I was a born Isfahani. You've heard the saying: "Isfahan, half the world" – how can one resist going there? What water! Isfahan water is still the best in God's world. I swear. Whenever I go to Isfahan, no matter what ills – God preserve you from them – I may take with me, three days of Isfahan's water and my entire body and spirit is purified. Believe me, *Jenab* Aryan.'

'Did you come back by bus?'

'Yes. Huh, what fun! Not bad at all.'

'It's quite a trip. Did you come all the way to Istanbul?'

'I caught a plane from Erzerum.'

'Do you have to go back to Iran?'

'Ah – if I don't, my retirement pension will be cut off. You know, the buggers have a limit on absence from the country. We'd be ruined! I have a thousand other problems, besides. A whole lot of properties, and valuables and land we've still got there, left to us by my mother, who died two years ago – rest in peace. The estate is still in Isfahan, in the hands of my fellow heirs ... that needs to be checked up on, every once in a while. What about you, *Jenab* Aryan?'

I told him briefly of the reasons for my trip.

'I heard you were in need of a bit of money?'

I laugh.

'Look, I'm at your service, which is my duty, of course.'

134

'Thank you, *Aqaye* Safavi.'

'No matter how much you need, just mention the amount, dear Aryan. Easy, straight and simple. If we, in this dog-eat-dog world, don't help each other, who will? Humanity, and the moral duty to help an honest compatriot like you, binds me. Especially as you are caught in this delicate predicament. I understand.'

'Thank you indeed, *Aqaye* Safavi. I'm embarrassed by your kindness.'

'Why should you be embarrassed? You need money, and I happen to have a few pennies stashed away for rainy day. Take it. Whenever you can, you pay it back, pay through my brother-in-law in Tehran. If you couldn't pay back, you're welcome to it as a gift.'

'It's not as easy as that.'

'It's even easier and simpler than you think.'

'We aren't schoolboys.'

'Well, I've said my bit, my share of compassion. Parsi told me you were here and in need of money, I almost flew over.'

'Thanks, *Jenab* Safavi.'

'It was my duty, *Jenab* Aryan. I came, I saw, I offered my service.'

'I came, I saw, I conquered – who said that?'

'Julius Caesar said it. But to hell with Julius Caesar – I am at your disposal, *Jenab* Aryan. Just doing my duty, that's all. Bahman Qaraguzlu's BMW and furniture were damned nearly lost in Tehran, poor devil. I rescued them for him, he sold them to my nephew in Tehran and I gave him the money right into the palm of his hands, right here.'

'He paid you in rials in Tehran?'

'I gave him an account number, he deposited it into that account. Will be just as simple in your case, too. In fact, *you* will be doing my family a favour. We can do with as many rials at home as I can get, in Tehran, that is. I can use rials to send out government foreign exchange tuition for my children.'

'Are they studying in France?'

'In Stuttgart. We must prepare the young generation for our dear Iran's future.'

'How much foreign exchange does the government allow for each student per month, these days?'

'They're supposed to be given a thousand dollars a month – but the buggers keep fiddling around.'

I do a little mental arithmetic. He sends out a thousand dollars a month for each of his three children. That makes thirty-six thousand dollars a year (from the budget of a nation at war) that can be put into German, Danish or American banks, at 16.5% interest rate per annum ... I hope Safavi with his keen mind and intelligence has not read my thoughts, but he is shrewder than I have even imagined.

'When I said I am pleased with the state of affairs in Iran,' he says, 'naturally, I did not mean the present generation of Iranians. The present generation, especially the young, will suffer. But, to quote Pandit Jawahar Lal Nehru, "One must look forward to future possibilities and expectations." Like the revolution of the people of India against British colonialism, we in Iran have been fighting against world imperialism and the domination of the West. We must show the world, we must prove to them, that there are not just *two* superpower ideologies, two opposite poles of East and West in the world – that is, capitalism or capitalist democracy on one side, and communism or communist submission on the other. There is a third answer, yes. This system will work for Iran. A government which will join together the best techniques from both blocks, but resist becoming attached to either, instead present something in proportion with its own history and philosophy. Well, sir, what about you? Do you have any particular opinions?'

'Well,' I smile at him. 'If you asked me which I preferred rice-and-kabab or frog-legs, I'd say rice-and-kabab ...'

'Surely you're joking ...'

We both burst out laughing.

He asks: 'Did you bring a carpet or a little rug with you?'

'No. They don't let you, do they?'

'They do, they allow one small one, as a prayer-rug. I bring one back with me every time I go there – as a "prayer-rug".'

'Are you a praying man?'

'No, I'm *smart*!'

We both burst out laughing again. Even in Abadan, not every one who stayed defending the island was free of dastardly intentions. Rats came up through the sewage pipes, Saddam's dogs of war dropped shells from all sides, and thieves – whom we had named 'war hyenas' or 'war vultures' – came through the door. Even in the hardest days of the siege – the island completely blockaded, under constant gunfire – the war hyenas were there, scavenging houses and the shops. Sometimes they sneaked in with shopping bags, and took jewellery, small electronic gadgets and cameras. Sometimes they brought jeeps, taking carpets, television sets, etc; sometimes they came in a truck, and simply cleaned out the entire house. Lately, they were even dismantling the air conditioning. A Mohammad Reza Nikfarjam in West Breim made several trips to and from Abadan, gradually transferring his possessions to Shiraz, each time taking several cardboard boxes and suitcases with him. The war hyenas had broken into his house so often that finally he left a sign on his front door 'Please take note: This house has already been burglarized twice, only heavy furniture such as tables and beds are now available!' Even in the hospital, it was rumoured, somebody in the emergency ward pinched wrist-watches, rings, and money from the wounded and the dead.

'How did you come to meet Parsi?' I ask Safavi. 'You weren't into things like modern writing and plays and TV and cinema, were you? Before the revolution?'

'You wouldn't catch me dead in those set-ups! Nader Parsi's present wife happens to be my cousin. Abbas Barzegar's daughter. You might have heard of him – he's my younger uncle. He used to own the Barzegar Imports Company. Now he's living in Los Angeles. Between you and me, though, Parsi himself is a real jerk.'

'He's all right. I've never seen any harm in Nader.'

'Oh, he's friendly all right. He's talented, I'll grant you that . . . But he's witless and confused. He had a fine French wife. He divorced her two years ago. You know, I hear, now she's planning to get the house from him. And he's trying to double-cross her.'

'Not really. I'd heard there was something there.'

'Aren't you hungry?' Safavi asks. 'I usually have dinner at seven.'

'All right. Let's eat' I say.

We go into a large, pleasant self-service restaurant at the corner of Saint Michel and Saint Germain. The food there is not bad, the atmosphere is free of arrogance, and there are window-seats overlooking the busy street. I take my medicines before eating.

Safavi is a really pleasant meal-time companion. He is well-travelled, and widely informed on the general history of the world, especially on nationalism. He thinks of himself not only as a nationalist, but an internationalist. *Nationalism the Great Fountainhead of History*, was one of his most famous translations. He dedicated it to Dr Mohammad Mossadeq (in the last years of the ex-National Front Leader's life, in exile in Ahmadabad), who wrote a thank-you letter to Ahmad Safavi in his own handwriting. Durng the early days of the Iranian Revolution – when the Nationalists were in their heyday – Safavi had printed a copy of the letter in a new edition of his book, which resulted in several further reprints. Safavi, however, lived in Stuttgart since even before the National Front came to power in Iran, in the 1950s. As he puts it, nevertheless, he has kept 'in touch with the soil' of homeland and has cherished 'Nationalistic Iranian feelings', though he tends to discuss nationalism theoretically, rather than actually being a part of the grassroot, to shed blood, to sweat, or to weep. Still, he analyses everything very well, and exchanges opinions freely about everything and anything – from the National Socialist theories of Pandit Jawahar Lal Nehru to the vitamin and calorie content of the persimmons that grow in his inherited Isfahan orchards. He is a walking *Encyclopaedia Britannica*, and highly entertaining, at that. Over coffee, he returns to the subject of literature and books in Iran. Clearly, in the History of Persian Literature, based on Gospel according to Safavi, nobody, save Ferdowski, Khayyam and Hafez, is anybody, or even has the right to be alive! He is especially incensed by Nader Parsi's type, with their criticisms, their discourses, their new short stories, their modern poetry and modern drama and modern 'extraction'ists.

Outside the café night has fallen. We sit warmly at our table by the window, drinking coffee. Safavi accepts one of my cigarettes. He says he allows himself one, each night.

'Have you read any of Nader Parsi's works?' he asks.

'Some of them, I tried to!'

Safavi laughs. 'I couldn't understand a word of them either, no matter how many times I tried. There's apparently "form" and there's "structure" – but contents, zero. He copies his forms

138

and structures from foreign writers such as Genet, Brecht, and Beckett. But there's no meaningful content. Either because he and the likes haven't understood it themselves, or else they haven't been able to communicate anything significant to the Iranian reader. Also perhaps, because the Iranian reader isn't yet ready to accept such concepts. Don't you agree?'

'The ones gathered *here* seem happy enough.'

'No – deep inside, they are all both sad and saddening. . . I've seen plenty of them, so I know their type. Nader Parsi and Bahman Qaraguzlu, Dr Ahmad Reza Kuhsar, Jilla Varasteh, Bijan Karimpur, Sudabeh Barzegar and so on, are the nucleus of a group of refugee poets, writers and artists who ran away from the Islamic Revolution. This is the Parsi 'set'. There are other groups as well. God knows how many groups there are in London. As for Los Angeles, New York and other clans in the US – there are oceans of them. The Islamic regime has clogged up their fountainhead of inspiration! In Iran they can't write their new prose and verse and plays, with wine and women in plenty, tossing their artistic impulses to performances on Channel Two and the Iran–American Society's Culture and Art Centre. I swear no one will harm them if they go back to Iran, and live quietly, of course, but they prefer to stay on, in Paris, London, New York, where the booze flows freely, and there's music and free love. So they sit round and tell each other, "I'm being hunted. If I set foot in Iran, I'll be thrown into Evin and lined up against the wall". If they acted this way in Iran, the Islamic Guards would kick them in the jaw. They'd be made to queue for hours for milk and chicken and Kleenex tissues. Some of them here who can speak French, like Daryush Ardakan, may string together a book, an article, or essays about the Revolution and get them printed by some *avant-gard* Paris publisher. But the rest have fizzled out. Nader Parsi himself is always on about "the great novel" he has put together about the Iranian Revolution, or is still "working" on. He said he was stuck in it, though, because he hasn't yet found a publisher for it. He told us this the other night when he was pretty well-oiled with courvoisier, and had begun opening his little homesick heart to us. One mustn't stamp out the creative impulses, he said, for they are "the breath beneath immortality". He said the Nader Parsis in Iran today are wretched, down-trodden souls, the way the "Ferdowsis and Mansur Hallajes and Farrokhi Yazdis were wretched and down-trodden. I apologize, I'm paraphrasing Parsi's own terminologies, I assure you. "I am a contemporary Iranian antagonist–realist, a truthful observer of the Revolution in his homeland. I cannot remain silent. I feel myself obliged to write," he said. He said if he didn't write, he would betray his own integrity, his ideals, his people, and his country. Ferdowsi was a committed man. Naser Khosro was a committed man. Mirzadeh Eshqi was a committed man. Likewise Trotsky. José Marti, Farrokhi Yazdi, and Mozhfeq Kazemi. Dr Daryush Ardakan is a committed man. We are all committed, even if we are in wretched positions ... Only immediately after uttering these words, Parsi ordered the waiter to bring him another double courvoisier, and stuffed another forkful of *filet mignon* spiced with Dijon mustard into his mouth. The waiter brought him his courvoisier in a round, big-bottomed glass, Nader gulped it down, to the "Immortality of Iran", and to better days in future. Then I told him Parsi, my dear, don't forget Mowlavi's story about the prayer and the prayer-hole. Or in our case, more like incantation and not prayer. Incantations are not bad in Paris but the hole is very much mistaken, I told him. Parsi just laughed, thinking I had meant Dr Ardakan's literary attempts, and I let it pass. Then, of course, *Jenab* Aryan, Paris is Paris and all sorts of the discontented and the disheartened and the desolate of all countries have always come to Paris – Paris has always been the historical and traditional haven of the discontented. But, now I am not sure about one thing. The Iranian writer and author who bears no great message for the world, belongs mostly back home in Iran, not in the Café de la Sanction . . . Don't you agree?'

Nor in Stuttgart, perhaps, would be the ideal answer to his question. Instead, I say, 'I agree,' which for one thing amounts to the same thing, and secondly because, apart from all the gibberish, he is – as I said before – pleasant company. He pauses. I feel he wants to talk about money exchange again. But, instead, he asks, 'Would you like to come to Versailles tomorrow?'

'I usually go to the hospital every morning.'

'Well, then, we can go in the afternoon. I shall have the

honour of your company. It's an hour's journey by train. I haven't seen le Chateau Versailles myself for ages. Agreed?'

'My pleasure.'

Finishing our coffee, we leave the table. Ahmad Safavi carefully wraps his scarf round his neck, puts on his hat, adjusts it before the mirror, puts on his overcoat, then we leave the restaurant.

It is cold and dry outside, but Paris looks alive with the crowds of Christmas shoppers and the dazzle of lights. We walk up to the Metro station at the top of Saint Michel.

'I hope your niece recovers soon.'

'I hope so, too.'

'Make a *nazr*.'

'We have!'

'It's in the Good Lord's hands, then. You know, *Jenab* Aryan, whatever is His will, it will come to pass. I sincerely believe this.' He finally manages to bring up the subject of money, 'Take this as an example: around late 1978, when the Iranian Revolution was boiling, I had a complex of flats in Tehran, in Mirdamad Avenue. One day, it was as if Good Lord through a divine inspiration shafted me right smack in the back of the head: "Safavi, sell out those flats ..." That very same day, I sold them all, for eight million tomans – much less than their actual market value, of course. I exchanged the money into a million dollars, and transferred it here ... It would have been gone to the wind, otherwise. So you see, my good sir, it is all as the Good Lord wills it.'

'Good-night, *Aqaye* Safavi.'

'Good-bye, *Jenab* Aryan.'

He goes into the Metro and I walk up to the riverside on my way to the hotel, strolling about for a while. I walk down the Rue Bonaparte to Saint Sulpice, and make a macabre, paranoid circumambulation around Hopital du Val de Grace. I then come back up the Rue Saint Jacques into the Boulevard Saint Michel, and arrive at the hotel in time for the midnight Tehran news.

When I am undressing for my shower, before going to bed, I find a pair of new holes in my socks. I feel a smacking at the back of the head as if the Good Lord was shafting: 'Aryan, toss out those socks!' But I toss them into the laundry bag instead, which Sumunju takes to the laundramat for me. I have implicit faith in Sumunju, who is the source of many strange and secret blessings for me this crazy winter.

17

On the Khorram-Shahr Road, along the Breim palm tree plantations. I am driving towards Alfi square, to buy some books. Suddenly, the Islamic Guards have blocked the road. Turn back, brother, this is a war zone. I try to turn back, but as I make a U-turn, a sound like the stripping off of a huge sticking plaster rips out from behind the Parvaneh Kindergarten. Another explosion blasts in the area; then the crack-crack of *Khamseh-Khamseh* shells falling all around. Another explosion, a brilliant white light flashes out, turning to scarlet and then to black. Choking, I throw myself into the gutter. When I raise my head to see if I am still there, I see Matrud's boy, Idris, coming this way, singing out merrily, selling Winston cigarettes. The sky is now brown and purple from the thick clouds of smoke billowing from the Refinery, and the air is full of the stink of sulphur and gunpowder. I yell at Matrud's boy, telling him to lie down and hide. The sound of a bomber helicopter, flying fast and low, shakes the very belly and bowels of the Road, and successive, new explosions roar; bursts of anti-aircraft fire follow the helicopter. Lying under the hedgerows along the border of the pavement I see Matrud's boy in flames, along with the hedges. By the time I get myself to the sidewalk, he is so charred I can no longer tell who or what he is ... The bomber helicopter comes roaring back, and I toss myself into the gutter again; this time they hit the water tank a few houses above the kindergarten, and I see the huge metal structure collapsing from its stilts down on top of me ...

When I wake, my mouth is dry and stale. The room feels cold. The radio and the bedside light are still on, and a strange insect is fluttering around under the claret-covered lightshade, banging itself around the lamp, warming itself. I go to the sink, turn on the cold water tap full blast, fill a glass and drink it. The cold water makes my jaws ache, it also brings back my recent nightmare. On the radio, softly, Christmas carols are being sung. I stand by the window. Outside the Avenue le Prince is peaceful with its Christmas lights. Only the quiet hum of the white garbage truck, parked in front of the hotel, can be heard. The city, lit by countless Christmas lights, together with the music of carols, has a joyous, almost ethereal quality.

I cannot sleep, or even lie down, or read. I feel empty and shivering inside, and I am badly worried about Sorraya, too. I turn back, wash, shave, dress and go out. It's too early for the hotel breakfast, and besides, I don't feel like eating or talking to old man Duval, or even Sumunju.

It is still dark as I walk up the Monsieur le Prince and through the Saint Germain, and cross into the Boulevard Saint Michel. The smart buildings, the banks, the bookstores, the wineshops, clothes *boutiques* and toyshops are clean and white under the glow of the lights. Several of the cafés, bars and restaurants are open, with people inside, eating and drinking. The Café Domingo is the loudest and most crowded of all. A grey-haired man is playing pin-ball with a very thin, golden-haired woman. They are very happy, the woman keeps nudging him, in peals of laughter. I wonder what they have been up to all night.

I see the Cathedral across the river, and walk towards it. The Cathedral is lit beautifully, abundantly. The first time I saw it, I thought only of Victor Hugo's miserable Quasimodo. Now, I rather like it. I enter through the tiny, open door. Inside it is also magnificently illuminated. A group of priests are singing; someone is playing the organ. The side aisles are quieter and dimmer. I walk along one of the aisles and stand in a corner, leaning against a pillar, a little apart from where hundreds of alms candles are lit. The music and singing stop. A priest begins a Communion. His voice, amplified by several loudspeakers, is firm and clear. I don't understand all he says. Apparently he is talking about direct communication with God, of attaining peace of mind and tranquillity of thought – which is beyond my intelligence. He speaks of a sort of connection and unity: between the human brain and the whole of existence. He speaks repeatedly of a micro- and macro-universe. Micro-universe . . . macro-universe . . . I close my eyes and try to think of the macro-universe, on the transistor of the Notre Dame. I have not seen much good from the *micro*-universe.

In the days when my grandmother Khanjun had a monthly *ruzeh* at our house, on the first day of every lunar month, we had a good mullah (*ruzeh* singer), whom we children called *Aqa* Qeliyuni because he was the only *Aqa* who smoked a *Qeliyuni* (water-pipe) before he sat on the chair for the *ruzeh*; we liked him a lot. *Aqa* Qeliyuni knew us all, and always chatted with everyone, asked after everyone's health. Before singing the *ruzeh*, about the martyrdom of Imam Hossein in the Karbala disaster, he always preached a little. What we children then knew of God and Man, the earth and the universe, and dying and the end of mortal man and the everlasting, originated from *Aqa* Qeliyuni. He said that if the earth was clean and dry, and had no visible signs of impurity, that is, of blood, urine or faeces, it was pure and one could say one's daily prayer on it. About the universe, he said that blessed, exalted Allah had created the skies, the sun, moon, and stars, only for the sake of the Holy Five, so we must love the universe the way we love them. About dying, *Aqa* Qeliyuni said . . .

The sound of organ music and the voice of the French priest bring me back to the Notre Dame de Paris and the micro- and macro-universes. In addition to all Farangis' alms and prayers, back in Tehran, appealing to the Amir-al-Mo'menin, Imam Ali, and his holy daughter Fatimeh Zahra, I, too, try now to concentrate my thoughts on that point, at the Super Centre of it all, in the middle of all the skies and galaxies, which the French priest says one can think of, and towards which one can reach out. Eyes closed, I try to tune my brain into the frequency of the macro-universe.

I pray. All my life, I have never asked God for anything – perhaps with one exception – the night when my wife lay dying. Tonight, too, I ask nothing for myself. Dear God – let this child live. Let her wake up from this sleep.

A nun, lighting candles, motions to me to step forward. She wants me to light a candle. She has a fat, full-moon-shaped face,

145

and looks like a mother about to put a breast to her baby's mouth. But her long, black robe and starched, white cuffs give her a metallic, almost an iron-clad appearance. I walk forward, accept and light the two candles she is holding towards me. I think she says I needn't put any money in the box for the candles – because they are a church gift, or some charity. I thank her, then leave.

When I arrive back at the hotel, I have a hearty breakfast with fair Sumunju before setting out for the hospital, It is a very bright and fine morning. The air, after the all-night rain, is clean, fresh, almost fragile. With the feeling instilled in me by the good French breakfast and my communications with the macro-universe, via the special grace of the Notre Dame my morale is a bit improved. But then, in the hospital courtyard, by the Emergency entrance, I see a group of men and women dressed in black, stand in mourning by two cars. A hearse, too, stands by with its rear door open. Who could die on such a fine morning? I ask myself.

I see Nurse Jardin, with her scarlet cape over her white uniform. She is coming out of the building apparently heading towards the exit gates. Even she seems younger and more lively in the bright morning air. She sees me, and comes towards me.

'Bonjour, Monsieur Aryan. *Joyeux Noël.*'

'Bonjour, Mademoiselle Jardin, thank you. The same to you.'

'It is lovely weather, no?'

'Yes. Lovely weather. And how is my niece? Better I hope?'

'I wish I could give you some really good news . . . but no. She is . . . you know, the same.'

'No change at all?'

'Her temperature is a bit less today.'

'Is that a good sign?'

'Yes, it is a good sign. She is more peaceful since the dialysis.'

In spite of her fresh, ham-pink, smiling face, and cheerful words, I feel she is lying. Without saying goodbye, she walks towards the mourning group by the hearse. It is still too early for me to see Sorraya. I sit on a bench in the sun, at the other end of the courtyard, and open my newspaper. At nine-thirty a body is brought out and put into the hearse and the mourners get into their cars and drive off after it, quietly.

I have gone to Tehran to attend the mourning ceremony commemorating the year's death of Lieutenant Kamran Naqipur.

It is a Thursday morning in early August, and Farangis and I are in Tehran's Behesht Zahra Cemetery. The sun, past the twin minarets, gleams down over the tops of the dusty cypresses and elms. A little further on, unused lots, with their bleached, dry soil, look parched even in the morning coolness. At the end of the empty lots, a few crooked firs and withered birches lean sickly against each other. Sparrows and crows flit from tree to tree, vexed and frightened. Shafts of sunlight set the spiders' webs between the tree-branches glittering. The earth is littered with trash – rotten fruit, crumpled tissues, torn plastic bags, and the shrubs and thistles are decorated with scraps of paper blown by the wind.

Only the wailings at the gravesides break the silence of the vast cemetery. Our group is somewhat quieter than most of the others. The women shriek and moan, the men slap their foreheads, and the Qoran reader chants.

Further on, a meek family of six or seven are gathered around a fresh grave. They all wear black, even the tiny children. It is 'Friday's eve'. They have come to say *afateheh* for their martyred son. The man, evidently the head of the family, keeps saying 'Thank God, Thank God', over and over again, shaking his head. His wife, hidden in her black *chador*, can only moan 'Oh God, Oh God'. Their son's portrait is set in a frame at the head of the gravestone. Curly hair. Thick black moustache. Young face, full of life. He is wearing a sports shirt.

Beyond them there is the loud, painful wailing of the 7th day mourning of a young couple, killed in a car accident on their honeymoon. These cries even override those at the graves of several martyrs.

The air is filled with shrieks of pain, cries and wails, sobs, entreaties, weeping, moaning and lamenting ... I am holding Farangis' hands, to stop her shaking.

147

It is almost ten o'clock when I catch sight of Dr Martin, coming out of the building, going towards his car. I walk up to him, and say hello.

'*Ah, bon! Cher Monsieur Aryan!* You have had a pleasant Noël in Paris – *non*?'

I don't know what to answer. I like the way he is a born jolly good-timer.

'*Merci*, Doctor,' I say. 'You are most kind. How is our Sorraya *comatosée* today?' I ask.

He grins, raises his head with a penetrating, philosophical look. 'Ah . . .' he says. 'Sorraya *comatosée* . . . The combination has a chimera-stirring quality, did you know that?'

I stare at him.

'What does the word Sorraya mean in Persian, Monsieur Aryan? Tell me.'

'I don't really know, Doctor. I'm not sure.'

'It doesn't have any connotations with Iran, or the world?'

'I don't know. It doesn't have any particular connotation with Iran as a country, or with the world as such.'

'What about the universe?'

I had heard that when doctors have nothing definite to say about their patients, they start talking about pie in the sky.

'I think it's the name of a part of the Moon, and the Pleiades.'

'Ha . . . This becomes even more dreamlike. Almost symbolic. Sorraya *comatosée*,' he repeats looking away.

'How is she, Doctor?' I ask. I try to bring him back to earth, to the asphalted parking lot in front of the hospital.

'Well. Not bad.' Then, he adds, 'Ha. I was just going to have some coffee. Would you care to join me?'

'With pleasure.'

He takes something from his car, relocks the door, and we leave together.

'You are married, Monsieur Aryan – *non*?'

'I was married once . . . Not now.'

'Ha! Then you must take the full advantage of your liberty. Full advantage, you understand?'

'Of course,' I say, lightly.

We enter one of the countless round-the-corner Paris cafés. We sit on the high stools, at the bar. It is mid-morning, but there

is a good crowd. '*Cherchez la femme*,' says Dr Martin to me.
'Look for the woman ... That is our motto.' I smile, too, saying
'*Cherchez la femme*.'

'Are you?' he asks. 'At the moment? ...'

'Yes and no.'

'Is she on good terms with you?'

'She is ill. She's had an operation.'

'How sad ... She will recover, of course, *non*?'

'Yes. Of course.'

The barman comes, and exchanges greetings with the doctor,
shaking hands. Because I am with the doctor, and bigger than
he is, he shakes hands with me too, and says *Ça va*? Dr Martin
orders an Expresso, and a drink whose name I don't understand, which the barman brings him after quickly mixing up
sloshes from several bottles. I just have an Expresso.

'And where is she now?' The doctor asks me.

'Who?'

'Your wounded canary,' I think is what he says.

'Oh. She's ... gone to Marseilles, with her father,' I reply.

'And when she returns ... She will fly right back into your
arms – *non*?'

'It's probable that she will fly right into the arms of a fat-
necked Persian novelist in London.'

'Ah! *C'est beau l'amour* ... This is beautiful love. Have
courage, my friend.' He picks up his drink. 'This may be a game
... Fight for me, she is saying. The eternal triangle of love, you
know ... Well, your health.' He drinks from his glass.

'My niece, Doctor ...' I say. 'How is she?'

He shoves his glass aside, and pulls his coffee cup forward.
Whatever he drank must have been strong, because it changed
his mood.

'Well. She is getting along,' he says. 'You ought not to worry
too much, Monsieur Aryan. She will recover, in future. One
hundred percent.'

'Thank God, I hear this. Is there any evident change? I want
something definite to tell her mother. The poor woman is
waiting in agony.'

The doctor gives a deep sigh, which, for a thinking
Frenchman, entails pushing forward the chest and pulling
downward one side of the mouth. 'Coma,' he says, 'at this stage,

149

that is to say, after five weeks, enters a critical stage.'

I ask Dr Martin to continue our conversation in English, because I am more fluent in that language. He accepts, happily, but lowers his voice. His English is perfect, with a heavy French accent, of course. He has done a six-month specialization course on something in Boston. 'In this stage of coma, our duty is to keep the comatose patient in a stable condition – and to stop him or her from gradually "sinking deeper", as they say.'

'Is Sorraya gradually sinking deeper?'

He does not give a direct answer. 'In the initial stages, the important and vital task – to prevent irremediable damage from being inflicted on the brain – the patient's immediate need, is for us to prevent any disorders in the respiration and circulatory system, while carrying out the laboratory tests and other investigations. Fortunately, in Sorraya's case, this has been done successfully. A patient in a fixed state of coma is naturally insensitive to stimuli – that is, stimuli which disturb a normal, deep sleep – loud noise, intense light, or pinpricks – although the patient may show involuntary, muscular reactions to extreme stimuli. For instance, she may move her hand slightly as a result of a painful pinprick.'

'Sorraya shows no response to painful stimuli?' I ask impatiently.

Dr Martin picks up his coffee cup, and drinks. He shows signs of pondering and of concern.

'No,' he says. 'She did show some response in the first week. But the point that somewhat worries me is that Sorraya's recent EEGs have been rather unsatisfactory – that is to my expectations. In a deep, hypoxic coma, such as this, an isoelectric state, or in simpler words, an unresponsiveness towards a voltage or two to three waves per second, is a sign of further deepening.'

'Has Sorraya become unresponsive to two to three voltages?' I ask.

'No . . . no . . . I said her graphs have not come up to my expectations.' He sighs deeply. 'Unfortunately, the state of coma itself gives us no indication of its degree of seriousness, and appears like a calm sleep. Only by studying the test results, can we learn how serious this "calm sleep' really is. It is philosophical, *n'est-ce pas?*'

I know he is trying to comfort me.

'She doesn't respond to mental or drug-induced stimuli, right?'

'Well, we have evidence that she is unresponsive to mental stimuli. When you came, and held her hand and talked to her of her mother – that could have caused a great spiritual stimulus, but Sorraya's response was negative.'

'What does this prove, Doctor? That there is no hope?'

'No. That is not so. Absolutely not. We think this simply gives us more evidence of the damage. The damage inflicted on the cerebral cortex has spread to the central parts of the brain. But it is still too early to say that this damage is irreparable and irreversible. We know a good deal about the brain's motor operations. But little is known of the complex nature of "being conscious". Evidence so far suggests that the centre of awareness of consciousness is in the inner brain, the cerebellum, but we still don't know about its connections with the functions of the cerebral cortex, which controls all the senses. So... in this situation, like my professional ancestors, I must say "it is in God's hand" ... We are not in control of everything in this world. Things happen. That's life. But as I said, there have been cases when a patient, in far more advanced comatose conditions than Sorraya's, have recovered.'

'A patient whose coma has been caused by *brain* damage?'

'Ah ... Well, yes – of course, I understand what you mean. A patient whose coma has been caused by a physical blow to the brain is clinically different from one who is in a coma as a result of other internal malfunctions. Apart from things like head wounds, lesions and internal bleeding, any sort of blood clotting in the brain, or capillary lesions, or a sudden, serious decrease of the blood pressure can cause coma. A serious decrease in the blood-sugar level, or malfunctioning kidneys or liver poisoning, or severe narcotic or alcohol intake, can induce coma. But with a comatose patient whose condition has been caused by a blow to the brain it can take longer for the injured tissues to be renewed, and for recovery to take place. And we now just ... I don't know – hope.' He looks at his watch, 'Mon Dieu! I must hurry back! Excuse me, please.'

We go outside and I walk back to the hospital with him, where I look in on Sorraya, lying there in her room silent and motionless on the bed. That is life.

151

I stroll back towards the hotel. The sunny, cheerful feeling I had in the morning is gone. I don't feel like having lunch; nor going to the library, nor to the cinema. I don't feel like going back to the Notre Dame for a renewed contact with the macro-universe. All the same, I stop by a Chinese shop near the hotel, and after taking my pills, I fill myself up with a plateful of fried rice, after which I go to my room and lie down. I smoke two of Nader Parsi's cigarettes, and drag what's left of my brains between the eight and the ninth chapter of *The Dogs of War*, waiting for Ahmad Safavi.

But Ahmad Safavi does not show up. I suppose he has lost faith in me buying foreign currency from him. But he phones at three o'clock, to say that he is sorry, he cannot come. He has an appointment to see the contemporary French historian, Jean Fourget, whom he plans to present with a copy of his book which Safavi has translated into Persian. 'So,' he then says, 'I'll phone tomorrow.'

'Please do.'

'You really must forgive me, *Jenab* Aryan. I apologise deeply for having spoilt your plans for this afternoon.'

'Don't worry, my friend. I didn't have any great plans, anyway!'

'Well, good-bye then.' But the day does not turn out a complete loss, after all. Near sunset, a long letter arrives from Leila, by Special Delivery, which warms me up for a part of the night.

Jalal:
Your face is before me as I write this to you: sitting there, tall and thin, in your black sweater, knitted by your sister, over a white, open-necked shirt. You are worried, I know. But you are not sad. You are never sad. Only worried. And when you are *really* worried, your eyes look hollow, and I then know you are even more sensitive and sincere ... Don't get cross. I'll talk about myself, now. In fact, that's why I am writing this to you. I need you. I know you're probably needing someone, too.

Tonight, if I remain conscious, I'll take this down the road, and have it sent off to you, Special Delivery. That way, it should get to you by tomorrow evening. I can see you as you return from the hospital, stretched out on the bed, with a cigarette, reading these delirious ramblings. How lucky it is, this letter. I wish it was me you were reading there, in your bed, two or three times. But how can anyone read a torn letter? Beside, I am dying of other wounds. A wound that bleeds does not kill.

It is Christmas Eve. Ho, ho. Everyone is drunk. My whole damned family is drunk. *Joyeux Noel*! I'm sitting up here in my boudoir, by the window, not far from the sea. I'm playing a tape of Gugush's slow songs. 'My heart is nostalgic,/My heart is nostalgic for crying./Where is it, mother?/Where is my cradle?' My cradle is still in Shiraz, rotten, lying in an attic in my old aunt's house. Only where my *grave* is, I don't know. Or where my self *respect* is, I don't know either.

The sea is stormy, tonight. But we are drunker than the sea. We are drunk with life. My brother, Ferri, has drunk so much champagne that he's hiccupping non-stop. His fiancée, Jilla, is hiccupping, non-stop. Mama isn't hiccupping. Papa is burping. I want to! The good, simple French life. The cradle and the grave of knowledge and literature. Father gave champagne. Mama gave caviar. Tomorrow, which is Friday, we are going to Bordeaux. We're going to live until we die. In your Abadan, the kids die until they live. All right, all right! I'll shut up! These things can be said by a woman who is pure, virtuous, innocent. What about me? Who am I? I've been so bad that sometimes I want someone to beat me up. Which is probably just what Nosrat Zamani did to me. Served me right!

This afternoon I dreamt I was back in Shiraz, my little sister had just been born. It was *Eid* [Iranian New Year's Day]. Did you know, my grandfather was one of these pure *Ali-Allahi*s? I loved him so much. White beard and moustaches. White skullcap. Beautiful, camels' hair *abba*. How lovely it felt when I tumbled into his lap. I still remember the faint smell of opium and alcohol from under his moustaches when he kissed me. Those childhood scents are still in my soul's senses ... But that *Eid*, as we sat around the *Haft-sin*, Grandmother had a heart attack – the final one. We all cried. My baby sister, Pari, never stopped crying. Then, when summer came, Grandfather got cancer of the prostate, and he died. And that autumn was hardly through when my wet-nurse, Agha-Tavus, died of a cancer in her womb. How much sweet milk I had drunk from her breast ...

If I were a poet, I would write a poem about the prostate and cancer of the womb. Let them go *Joli Noël, joli Noël* till they fart. I stop thinking about prostates, and swellings under the breasts and malignant wombs. And slit bellies. And brains in a coma. And the whole damned malignant and infected world.

We will be in Bordeaux for three days; we are coming to Paris for New Year's Eve. At present, the national motto is this: if there is no Paris, we will die. That night – at the New Year Eve that is – Abbas Hekmat has a lecture, a Manifesto, at the Sorbonne. I know you never pass within a mile of these gatherings. But come – just for laughs. Have you ever thought, that it is absolute wretchedness that drives us to these things? You don't know how I long for a women's *Khatm*. An *Om-ol-banin sofreh* party. *Ashura* night, and lighting candles and giving food to the poor in the Mosque. The night before *Ashura*, cooking *sholezard*. The night Bahman Qaraguzlu heard his brother had been executed by the Islamic Guards, he drank so much he had a stroke. They say if an Iranian woman is artistic, these days, she is miserable. What about the *ordinary* Iranian woman? What about the ordinary Iranian man? What if he hasn't got his life in his hands, ready to give it for God? What is the Iranian man to do if he is a simpleton? But this is all just talk. We are worms, that need to squirm in certain slimy water – otherwise, we shrivel up. On a wider spectrum, a misfortune and disaster has eaten into our destiny, and there is no cause and effect. What had your Sorraya done, to deserve such a fate? What about you? What had you done, for such a thing to happen to your life?

Oh, Jalal. When I see you again, I shall tell you how happy I am that you're here. The last time I was back *there*, I was frightened. Jalal, I was really frightened – the way one is when standing in a tomb, surrounded by the ghosts and spirits of his ancestors. And I was afraid of a scream, choked within my chest, and I was afraid of the dark. But now, here, I am afraid of other things, in other ways, and I despair the decay and tearings within me . . .

18

Her letter is very long; she seems to have a lot on her mind. I read it over twice, that night. Towards the end of the second reading, I can hardly keep my eyes open. I put everything aside, turn off the light, and try to sleep. After reading her letter, I feel somehow warm and secure. For the moment, I have a feeling, that perhaps, just perhaps, everything may somehow, possibly, turn out all right. Perhaps Sorraya will get well again ... Perhaps too, something intimate and lasting might take root between the injured Canary and myself.

Like a child anticipating Christmas night, I feel ...

... I have come up to Tehran from the southern oil-fields. It is a Thursday afternoon, in the year nineteen hundred and sixty-something ... Only this Thursday afternoon is different from all other Thursday afternoons, in fact it is a fantastic Thursday afternoon, though not as magnificent as the autumn of five years before ... And on this Thursday afternoon, I am returning in a chauffeured Company car, from the Seminar on the Management Courses. I arrive at the Riviera Restaurant. In the Riviera Restaurant I have a luncheon date with Leila Azadeh ... It is a quarter past one, when I enter the restaurant. She sees me, rises from her surrounding cluster of friends and admirers, Tehran's finest artistic and literary clan. She leaves them and drifts towards me. When she walks, her pink jersey and her long, coiffed black hair seem to ripple. She greets me, and says she is fed up with everything and everybody, even herself, and would love to come to where I am staying. I forget whether she was between her first and second or second and third husbands.

We take Leila's maroon-coloured Ford Tanus up towards Sa'i Park. She drives along Pahlavi Road with the birches arching high overhead, with the breeze and the sunshine in her hair, the distant vista of snow-covered mountains, people stroll round the park, Homyera's voice, warm and fine, coming from the car radio, the talk of new travels, of new films, the turquoise blue of the endless skies, the freedom, the variety of life, charmed by the thrill of love ... All of these are parts of the history of this beautiful afternoon.

'How is Masjed-Suleiman?' she wants to know.

'It's fine.'

'Still there dormant among the hills and mountains?'

'Still there.'

'How are you managing after the troubles we gave you?'

'I'm glad you came.'

She glances at me.

'I didn't think you'd come today,' she says.

'Sure ... I thought of you quite often.' And that is a lie, because I have thought of nothing else. God knows how much I loved her. 'Finished your film?'

'Yeh.'

'When's it coming out?'

'They're going to start on the dubbing soon. Or as they advertise, Soon.'

She had written the screen-play for a film, and some of the scenes had been shot at Lali, near Masjed-Suleiman. We met at the Masjed-Suleiman Naft Club. That was where she made the Riviera Restaurant luncheon date with me.

'Do you still have that little flat in the hills?'

'Yes.'

'119, Camp Crescent.'

'You have remembered! ...'

'I haven't forgotten ... because everything was so simple and so good. So are you. Simple. And good. Maybe someday I'll write something and put you and Masjed-Suleiman in it.'

'You won't put *everything* in it?'

'No!' She laughs. 'Isn't it tiring for you down there?'

'I haven't been there long. It's all right.'

'But – you didn't seem very happy.'

'I'm happy now.'

156

'I'm glad you came . . .'

'I bought your new book. *The Cage*. It's fine.'

'I think it's the best thing I've ever written. It's about the one person I love best in the whole world. My mother.'

'There is a sort of antagonism between the husband and the wife in the story. Aren't they good together?' I do not mean her own parents.

'Well, yes, my mother puts up with him. Papa's knowledgeable and wise – full of politics, history, literature and pomp and Europeanism.'

'Where are they now?'

'In France. Papa's going to buy a chateau. Mother spends twelve months a year shuttling between here and there.'

'Your friends weren't too happy to see you leaving them.'

'Which friends?'

'Back in the Riviera.'

'Oh,' she shrugged, 'That is their eternal hang-out. They'll be there tomorrow and I'll be there tomorrow. The chatters and the jabbers are eternal too. They're forever sitting there, rating Veal Escalopes, drinking *Majidieh* beer, and babbling ideologies and schools. You know what we were babbling about today?'

'What?'

'Did you know – who wrote the first stanza of the first ghazal of Hafez – "*Ala ya Ayyoh-al-Saqi adar k'asan wa navelha*"?'

'Hafez?'

'No!' she laughs.

'Well then, who?'

'It's by Yazid . . .'

'Who?'

'Yazid the son of Mo'aviyeh.'

'No!'

She laughs again. 'The way you said no! It sounded as if I'd accused you!'

'Please, Miss – it wasn't me, I swear!'

We laugh.'I didn't even know Yazid was such a brilliant bastard.'

'He was a brilliant bastard all right.'

'What did Mo'aviyeh do for a living?' I ask.

'He probably wrote movie screen plays and short stories,' she laughs.

'No. He was a born leader in the Management Seminars and Conferences.'

We both laugh again.

She quotes, '*Ala ya ayyoh-al-saqi . . . Adar Kasan wa navelha.*'

'What does it mean?'

'It means: "Come, oh Saqi, fill a bowl and drink it".'

'Yazid? – the Moslem Caliph?'

'Uh–huh.'

'So – Yazid, too, eh.'

'Very much so.'

'Forgive oh Allah their sins –'

'And what moral ending do we good students deduce from this lesson?'

'That Yazid did it, too . . .'

'No.' She looks at me, and cites the second stanza: 'That love seemed easy at first, but, oh, problems did befall.'

Now, what could be better, than Hafez of Shiraz and the poems of Hafez? That is obvious: Leila Azadeh in autumn sunshine, in room 1033 Hilton, where she reads *The Cage* to you, in bed. Her voice is warm, and full of feeling. Through the wide tenth floor windows, the Alborz mountains are in view, the sun glitters on the snows. On the wall by the bed is an oil-painting, a composition in deep, clear colours. A cluster of grapes in an olive green dish; cream-coloured plate of cheese; a glittering crystal goblet; a golden straw-covered wine bottle. All on a tray beside a window. The wind rustles the curtains. The wind rustles the curtains in room 1033, and Leila reads. The characters in the story are gradually taking shape, centred about the parrot. The inner conflict is that of a simple girl in Shiraz, who marries and goes to make a home with her husband. She takes her pet parrot with her. In the new home, they buy a new Italian cage for the parrot, a thing with mirrors, creepers, trellis and so forth. But day by day the parrot becomes more melancholy. She stops talking. She becomes ill. She degenerates and is almost dying – like her mistress in her pretty, new, husband's house . . .

Leila stops reading. 'My lips are tired.'

'Take a break.'

'Kiss me.'

The sun is setting on the mountains now. The wind blows the curtains aside. It has grown cold, and Leila huddles beside me.

'It's fantastic.'

'The best season of the year.'

'Wouldn't it be hell if right now we were in the middle of town?' I ask.

'Town's nice, too. I love people. Don't you love people?'

I look at her. 'Yes.'

'I was wondering who is going to win the First Prize tomorrow night,' she says brushing back her hair.

'Which prize?'

'Bah ... Tomorrow, it's the last night of the best Children's Films Festival from the Third World countries. Where have you been?'

'Empress Farah herself's giving out the prizes.'

'Your film's not in the Festival, is it?'

'No, but a friend of mine's is. It's great.'

'You have been invited?'

'Well, I have an invitation, yes.'

I was afraid of that. Usually when the subject of films and work came up, it meant she couldn't see me. 'Well,' I say. Right now the mountains and the autumn trees are beautiful.'

'I don't mind pottering about in bookshops and cafes.'

'That's all right, too. I suppose.'

'What else have you been reading? Tell me.'

'Just your book. That's all.'

'Which story did you like best?'

'This one. The one you're reading.'

'You are simple.' She touches the tip of my nose.

'That goes without saying.'

'This is a *woman's* story, what does it have that you would like?'

'You.'

She laughs. 'Simone de Beauvoir wrote "All lovers are crazy/ Except me and you ..." But I sometimes wonder even about you ...'

'Read.'

'Shan't we take another rest?'

Afterwards we both light cigarettes, and Leila continues. By now I am feeling light and a little drowsy. She reads on, and the characters become more and more alive. The young woman's entrapment in her new cage becomes obvious, and the meaning and the message angles are resolved. But in between sentences, I think I hear the distant roar of a fighter jet, and by and by, it is as if an explosion, not too far away, shatters and causes the ground to tremble, and Leila's voice takes on a sluggish tone.

> Outside it was windy. The woman shut the window, but remained standing there and looking out at the seashore. Her husband was still sitting motionless on the round, white chair.
> He was holding the *Newsweek* magazine. He seemed even farther away than usual. The waves were now coming up higher. The woman took a long breath, and turned her head to look round. The house was silent. She thought the parrot had made a sound. She stared at the cage, but the big, orange beak was still clamped tightly shut. Its neck, too, seemed to have sunk deeper down in its body.

I am now feeling a cold draught through the air and the cigarette smoke twists and turns. The wail of an ambulance sounds from far off. An explosion closer by shakes the room, and from outside the window the rattle of G-3 machine-guns is plainly heard, answered by bursts of shelling. The shouting and screaming of people running echoes from behind the water tank, and I hear the sound of Iraqi helicopter gun-boats hitting the palm trees ...

19

I wake at dawn with a bitter taste in my mouth and an empty feeling in my whole body. After reading Leila's letter through once more, I listen to the seven o'clock news from Tehran. The reception is awful, and the news of the war worse than before. The 'Infidel Saddami Ba'athists' have now bombarded the cities of Ahvaz and Dezful with rockets and cannons, and the newly formed corps called 'Mobilization of the Meek' has moved the two million or so war refugees to the deserts around Lorestan and Shiraz, housing them in makeshift tents, in the middle of the waste-lands. The 'Swift-winged, dauntless pilots of the Islamic Air Force' are busy destroying Iraq's military bases, oil terminals, oil refineries and petrochemical plants, with their 'lightning attacks'. Only the number of those claimed to be killed on the enemy side is mentioned and this – even accounting for exaggerations – is grossly inflated; or so it seems to me this early dawn.

It is still too early to go down for breakfast. I am still drowsy and numb. I stay in bed, half-awake, reading *The Dogs of War*. I keep reading the same two pages over and over again, unable to concentrate. From Sir James Manson's office in London, orders are given by phone to mercenary Cat Shannon, of the Zangaroo Mission. They are to receive American guns from a dealer in a Communist country, delivering the money in Holland, and the payment to be in pounds sterling. The guns must be delivered to a group of mercenaries on an island off the coast of Zangaroo, so that they can topple the Republic's President, Jan Kimbnam with a *coup d'etat*. I don't exactly remember ... Perhaps they were Russian guns, bought in a Western European country, with the payment to be made in

161

England, in Dutch florins . . . I don't want to shut the book and turn the light off. I know the instant I closed my eyes, Sorraya's image, or Leila's, or Annabel's, or even memories of old Darkhungah will swarm back into my mind, thoughts, dead and drowned in blood, will start precipitating around on my brain . . . So long as the light is on and my eyes are on the pages, dead thoughts cannot gather.

At last I fall asleep again, and when I reawake at seven thirty, the light is still on, the book still open at my side, and Leila's letter lying on the floor by the bed. I get up, put the letter inside the book and the book away in a corner. I shower, change, and go down to breakfast.

It is still early when I come out of the hotel, walking round the corner of the Jardin du Luxemburg and towards the hospital. I hear someone calling my name. At first glance, I don't recognize him, but then I realize it is Ahmad Safavi, loping along in a red-and-white jumpsuit, jogging up towards me. He has obviously been exercising hard, because he is now panting. He comes up and shakes my hand, unties a thicker sweatshirt from around his neck and puts it on.

'*Salaam*, there, my good sir Aryan. Good morning.'

'*Salaam*.'

'What splendid air! Lovely weather!'

'I didn't know you were such a sportsman?'

'Sure. Every day . . . In any part of the world, this is my regular physical exercise. Sound in body, sound in mind, you know. Especially as we were out last night, and ran to excess a little bit . . .'

'Well, don't let me stop you –'

'Not at all. I'm through my daily hour. Do join me for breakfast. I had a little something to discuss with you, anyway.'

'I've already had breakfast, thanks.'

'In that case, a coffee.'

'A coffee's fine.'

'You know, Aristotle tells his disciples to try and maintain "physical unity" in their sculptures, for when this is achieved, "spiritual unity" will follow.'

'Hooray for Aristotle.'

We enter the Danton Restaurant. Ahmad Safavi orders two

162

kinds of fruit juice, half a grapefruit, two soft-boiled eggs, toast without butter and Roquefort cheese. I order the Expresso.

'I have recently been given an extremely interesting and valuable little book by a friend of mine, a scientist and a philanthropist,' he says. 'It is about weight-watching and body-watching with the aid of running, or – as the Americans call it – "jogging". One must "jog" every morning . . . I am, by the way, translating it into Persian. I feel this book is sadly missed in the "Iranian Literary Society" of today.'

'I see.'

His sumptuous breakfast keeps coming, and as I am free until ten o'clock, I stay and keep him company.

'Well, *Jenab* Aryan,' he says. 'What news? Do you listen to the Tehran radio?'

'I listened to it just this morning.'

'Have they freed them?'

'Freed who?'

'The American hostages.'

'Oh, that. Not yet. They're still haggling.'

He coughs and says: 'Yes . . . Since the government is badly in need of funds, they will all be freed, so the Americans unfreeze Iranian assets kept in American banks,' he says. 'But those dastardly Americans will manage to keep most of the money. They won't give more than six or seven billion, at the most, of the twenty-odd billion dollars which we have in their hands.'

'You seem to have an inside tip or something?'

'No. But I know this Democrat Administration and I know the Carter clan, and I read the papers. They are in a tight spot. They want to get the problem solved, somehow, by the 20 January when the new Administration takes over, so the Democrats won't lose too much face. Our mullahs are smart too, by God, mark my words. I think they'll keep dilly-dallying and clicking their rosary beads, until the last minute, making a royal fool out of Carter, and tormenting him for supporting the Shah on the last days just before Ayatollah Khomeini took over.'

He has carefully lopped off the tops of both his boiled eggs, and is gently mixing the whites and the yolks together, with a dainty little gold spoon, adding a dash of salt.

His full moustaches and his bony hands remind me of a

163

revolutionary student of mine back in the Oil Company Technology Institute. After graduation he spent a couple of years in the Abadan Refinery, where he had become a political-religious leader of the Revolution . . . Since the outbreak of the war, he spent so many nights and days in the trenches on the Front line, without proper food and care, that finally they dragged him out on a stretcher unconscious, with stomach ulcers and gastric haemorrhage. He came back to the front after a couple of weeks.

Safavi spreads Roquefort on his crisp toast. With infinite care, he smooths the cheese in an even layer, covering all the corners. 'It took about half a century,' he says. 'Including the events in Vietnam, Iran, and Nicaragua, to bring Uncle Sam to his senses. Since the beginning of the second half of this century, American imperialism has been following exactly the same path as Great Britain's when she was at the most glorious point of her Empire. The pattern is fixed: political intervention, or neo-colonialism, imposed on a country usually by controlling its ruling body. England did it for decades. The United States has been doing it for a quarter of a century or more. In other words, today, the United States is still using the small, ruling party – like Kao-Ki, the Shah, or Somoza – to do her work. But this sort of business is done by the use of an iron-fisted dictator and a military force. This, of course, fundamentally and inevitably upsets the people – and then what do we get? Revolution, and war, and Death to the US . . . We had it in the Far East. Now we have it in the Middle East, and in Latin America.'

I scratch the back of my head. 'You mean the United States of America has now woken up, and is rubbing the sleep from her eyes, feeling remorse, and wishing only to serve the Middle East and the Latin American people?'

'No, no! But she is rubbing the sleep from her eyes, by God . . . All those kicks in the face have finally had an effect. I must say I like the way Iran has given them such a kick in the pants as to bring them to their knees, making them remember it, I hope, for years to come. It will also have ramifications in the entire Middle East. We must resist. The national integrity and the self-respect of the country must be preserved.'

He has now made neat, geometric little cuts in his grapefruit, dividing and dissecting the little segments, and is busy sprinkling sugar on top. Like his words, his actions seem simple, logical, and wholesome.

'You are physically well preserved, *Aqaye* Safavi,' I say. 'Still youthful, fit, fresh.'

'I shall be sixty-two years old on the 24 of this coming February!'

'You've kept your health perfectly. Slim, agile, healthy.'

He chuckles with glee and pride. 'Well, to tell the truth, I must either eat out, or not at all. You see, the Lord, in his wisdom, saw fit to bestow upon me a wife who's truly stupid. Almost thirty years abroad, and still cooks with animal fat! Fried food, and rice-and-*khoresh*, fried *couscous*, fried meat-cakes, fried potatoes ... and melted animal fat poured all over everything. She doesn't believe in cholesterol or arterio-sclerosis. If there isn't a finger's width of fat floating on top of our stewed eggplants, the family's reputation will go to pot. Every time I come back from Iran, or she makes a round-trip, two drums of Kermanshahi fat must travel back with us. However many times I tell her – first she is offended, then we argue, then it's back to square one again.'

I shake my head, glancing outside.

'Well,' he asks, changing the subject. 'How is your niece?'

'The same. I'm afraid, maybe even worse.'

'Have you done anything, eh – about money?'

'No. Not yet.'

'Are you in need?'

'I sold a ring – that got me fifteen-or-so thousand francs. We're managing.'

'Don't you want that hundred and fifty thousand francs – to be repaid in Tehran, in rials?'

'Of course,' I said. 'But nothing's been decided yet. You see, I've taken some steps through the University Health Insurance and the Local Municipal Authorities.'

'In any case, I am at your service, dear friend.'

'Thank you.'

'By the way, I must return to Stuttgart by 21 January for my dental appointment.'

'You said there was something you wanted to discuss, *Aqaye* Safavi.'

165

'That was it. If there is any way I can be of service financially ... I should be delighted to help out, until that date.'

'Thank you.'

He is finishing the last little triangles of cheese-covered toast, washing it down with coffee. 'Have you seen our friend, Nader Parsi, lately?' he asks.

'No ...' I yawn, looking for an opportunity to make my exit.

'He's busy playing at Christmas and the New Year.'

'Among other games.'

'Will you join us at the Louvre this afternoon? I know you spend your mornings and evenings at the hospital.'

'Very well. And now, with your permission, I'll be leaving ...'

'See you in the afternoon, then. Ah ... And here comes our dear Dr Majidnia ...'

Dr Majidnia, also attired in a tracksuit and running shoes, joins us. I decide to stay a few moments longer. Safavi, on a full stomach, is in an even better, jollier humour. 'Professor, we must mark you late! Good to see you!'

We exchange greetings. Majidnia used to be a Melli University Professor of sociology, specializing in Iranian and Third World societies. 'I put in an extra half hour today,' he says. He is patting his stomach. 'I put a bit too much in here, last night. I thought if I were to put some more *in* this morning, I should have to take something *out* the top, first! Ha ha!'

'Professor,' Safavi says, 'May I recommend a splendid book to you. If you can't find it here, I shall be glad to send you a copy from Stuttgart.'

'What book is that?' He sits himself at the table.

'*Jogging, the Key to a Healthy Life*. With an appendix including a list of the basic natural foods with their respective calorie content, and a series of recipes, made from the very best of them. You can have three splendid meals a day – all for less than 2,000 calories. That means you lose weight as well ... But with an hour's jogging, every day!'

'No, I haven't seen it,' Majidnia says.

'Then I will send you a copy.'

'Thank you. Have you gentlemen had breakfast?'

'Yes. You go ahead, Professor.'

In Darkhungah, on Thursday nights, the men gather together

in the *tekyeh* behind the Mosque with the lights off. They would stand in a huge circle, beating their breasts for Imam Hossein. The children are inside the ring, the men around them. Sometimes they would warble, moaning *Karb-o-bala* Hossein, Hossein!' *'Karb-o-bala*, Hossein, Hossein!', so loud, and strike themselves on the head and chest so violently, that a number of them would actually fall to the floor, unconscious.

Dr Majidnia orders himself a mixture of apple and carrot juice, a half a grapefruit, an *Omelette aux fines herbs avec Champignons*, croissants, butter, jam, an extra plate *du bacon* and Fontainebleau cheese.

'*Jenab* Majidnia,' says Safavi, 'Have you ever tried Roblachon cheese?'

'Yes. It's superb, but it's got to be eaten while it's absolutely fresh. But better than that, is Roquefort.'

'Which, in your absence, was just consumed!' cries Safavi victoriously.

'Good for you! It has blue veins and is prepared with ewe's milk and fresh herbs, in the mountains – and is often consumed with white Bordeaux!'

'Which I never touch! So we have it for breakfast!'

Then, as though struck by a sudden flash of inspiration from above, Majidnia asks, 'I say, have you heard the new recording of Eugene Ormandy conducting Beethoven's symphonies? – with the Philadelphia Philharmonic Orchestra? It's absolutely marvellous!'

'I heard the Fifth last night, at our friend's house – *Jenab* Dr Rahnema.'

'It's brilliant, sir ... A true genius masterpiece from a genius conductor who has finally succeeded in giving new life to Beethoven.'

'I think,' Safavi remarks, 'the best performance of Beethoven's symphonies, up to now, were Toscanini's, put out in the 1950s by the American RCA Victor Record Company. That was and still is a most profound masterpiece, renowned as a classic all over the world.'

'As a matter of fact, I happen to have the complete set of that production!' Majidnia says, 'all nine of them, which Toscanini made with the NBC Philharmonic Orchestra, which was one of the very best. But this work of Eugene Ormandy is the very ultimate of all masterpieces. This very Fifth in C minor, Opus 67 ... The first movement, with its allegro beginning, simply rises above human technique and artistic mastery, you are unearthed, transported to the very transcendental heights of Beethoven's genius.'

'Have you heard his interpretation of *Le Sacre du Printemps* by Igor Stravinsky?'

'Yes,' Majidnia says.

'That has breathtaking orchestration.'

'Beethoven's Fifth is even better than that.'

'*Le Sacre du Printemps* was a classical breakthrough in classical music tradition!'

'Stravinsky himself is the indisputable tradition-breaker of classical music.'

'By the way...' says Dr Majidnia, changing the subject, 'have you heard the latest news from the US?'

'No – what news?' Safavi drains the last drop of his fruit juice.

'What news?' I ask, thinking he means news of the hostages.

'Carter has haemorrhoids, or something,' Dr Majidnia announces.

'No!' Safavi says, almost laughing.

'So the White House Medical Report said.'

'No wonder the decisions are so lousy! Heh heh! But is it serious?'

'It was in *Newsweek*.'

Safavi laughs again. 'Well, that's men. Men are vulnerable, mortal creatures – even the President of the World's Greatest Power!'

I get up. 'Well, gentlemen. I must be going.'

Safavi and Dr Majidnia both rise, and shake hands with extreme courtesy.

'Then I shall call in this afternoon, Aryan, my dear sir,' says Safavi. 'Two o'clock?'

'I should be at the hotel by then.'

'Thank you, for the pleasure of your company. Goodbye, *Aqaye* Aryan.'

'Goodbye, my friend', says Majidnia.

I leave them chatting away about the world of jogging, superior nourishment, the importance of calorie-consciousness and the beauties of symphonic orchestration. I start walking towards the hospital.

All is silent in the ward where Sorraya is kept. Nurse Jardin, in her starched uniform, is, as always, busily supervising things. The woman at the information desk is writing in her notebook. The janitor is polishing the corridor floors. A nurse's aide with a medicine trolley emerges from one room and disappears into another. Doors are opened and closed noiselessly. The second hand on the wall clock moves silently. Sorraya is lying there still – in her hushed, speechless, nightmarish sleep . . . The silence is unbroken and no one can tell whether this is the end or just a passing phase. Is there hope for her, hidden within the silence, or is *rigor mortis* already setting in? Is everything dead or dying in her, and is she in Isthmus, or is it all just a 'sleep-like' unconsciousness?

20

The next two or three days pass pretty much the same way. On the evening of a rainy, late December day, in the salle 3 of the Hospital du Val de Grace, Qassem Yazdani flashes across the horizon of my journey to Paris. I have had a meeting with Dr Martin, and am about to look in on Sorraya once more before returning to the hotel, when I find Qassem Yazdani there in the doorway, looking in at Sorraya's bed. I have seen him several times before, both alone and in the company of other student visitors, and have even said hello to him but without paying much attention. He is quiet and well-mannered, with fine, even beautiful features. His skin is very soft, his complexion fair. His eyebrows are fine, and his blond beard and moustches are thin and almost exquisite. His honey-coloured eyes are calm, and reliable.

'What news, brother?' he asks. '*Salaam-aleikum.*'

I smile at him. '*Salaam*. Political news ... Or news of Sorraya?'

'Of Miss Sorraya ...'

'The same. *La même condition*, as they say.'

'No tangible changes?'

'No, I'm afraid not.'

'I'm Qassem Yazdani. My pleasure.'

I give my name, and we shake hands. There is a bunch of tall-stemmed narcissi, that had not been there when I had looked in earlier this afternoon.

'You are Miss Sorraya's uncle, right?'

'Yes.'

'Pleased to have met you. You are in good health? *Insha' Allah.*'

'Eh ... Yes, thank you.'

'How is Miss Sorraya's mother?'

'She is worried, of course, and a bit troubled by sciatica ... But well on the whole, thanks.' I explain briefly about Sorraya's late father, and that she is the only child.

'*Insha' Allah*, things will turn out well, soon.'

'You are the one who brought these lovely flowers; who often brings them – aren't you? Thank you.'

'I and the other kids, together.'

'But our Sorraya is in a coma, and can neither appreciate these flowers, nor your kindness, I'm afraid.'

'If Sorraya cannot see, God can ...The Lord in his wisdom is here.'

'Well, I'd like to thank you.'

'Shouldn't we get to know each other better? We can have some tea, or a fruit juice somewhere. If there's any way in which I can be of any service, please don't hesitate to mention.'

'With pleasure.' I have nothing special to do, and he has aroused my curiosity; so I agree. 'I'd like that.'

'Were you leaving?'

'Yes, there's nothing to be done here.'

We walk down the stairway at the end of the corridor. 'Were you well acquainted with Sorraya?' I ask.

'No, not very. She didn't socialize very much. I saw her only a few times, with a married couple of students, mutual acquaintances.'

'Did Sorraya participate in the demonstrations here against the regime and the War?'

'Oh, no – she was quite scared of them.'

'You know, her husband Khosro Iman was killed in the September '78 demonstrations, in Tehran.'

'Yes – I've heard.'

We come out of the hospital building, and walk towards the Metro.

'Would you like to come up to the "Cité", and see how we students live?' Qassem Yazdani asks. I say I would.

'You'll be doing us an honour.'

'Do we walk? Or shall we take the Metro?'

'It's not far. But it seems you have a bad leg.'

'No, it's nothing. Let's walk.'

171

He knows a short cut to the University. A steady drizzle is falling, and neither of us has an umbrella. The only piece of information I can get out of *him*, is that he is studying for a doctorate in chemistry, and that because he came first in his class at Tehran University, his father sent him to France to complete his studies – 'Because Islam is not opposed to science, it is only opposed to decadence and immorality.' He says little about his life in Paris, but judging by his bony face, sunken chest and stomach, I can see that a good, healthy meal would do him no harm. I would like to buy him one and find out what he really thinks, but since he has invited me first, politeness demands that I wait. 'Let me guess,' I say, 'Aren't you from the Holy city of Mashhad, or thereabouts?'

He laughs. 'You were pretty close! I'm a Torbat Heidariyeh boy, how did you guess?'

'I'm not sure, myself. There's just something spiritual and Khorasan province about you that is rather pleasant.'

'You yourself are an Abadani, isn't that so? Madame Charnaut said you had arrived here all the way from Abadan.'

'No. I'm actually a Tehrani.'

'Really Tehrani, or once-provincial Tehrani?'

'Born and bred in the Darkhungah Bazaar and the old Shahpur street.'

'But you have the southerners' warmth and generosity.'

The wind is cold, and I feel my head is about to start acting up again. It would not have been such a bad idea to take the Metro, I think.

'Brother,' he asks, 'What was your aim in staying in Abadan? After the outbreak of the war, that is?'

'I had no particular *aim*.'

'None at all?'

'No, I was in hospital.'

He asks about my famous stroke, I confirm it.

'You've never married?' he then inquires.

I look at him, and smile. At least, I think, we are getting close to the subject. 'Once,' I say. 'Years ago ...'

He shakes his head. But it is not in sympathy for the loss of my wife. He does not ask how. That is not important. The head-shaking is more because I did not take another wife.

'How is it you never remarried?' he asks. 'A man must take wives!' There is a humorous note in his voice.

I laugh, allowing this to pass unanswered. But he does not. 'You didn't answer . . .' From the tone of his voice, and his way of speaking, it is clear he cherishes no great credence in my type and cast; but he is behaving courteously and with kindness, all the same.

'Well,' I say, 'The one person I would have wanted to marry, had other things and other people on her mind. Maybe I'm still on her list, I don't know. What about you, *Aqaye* Yazdani? You aren't married?'

'No. But as soon as I finish here I shall get to it.'

'I know – a man must take wives!'

He offers me a simple smile.

'Have you anyone in particular in mind?' I am making no special reference to Sorraya, but he understands.

'No. If you were referring to Sorraya Khanom, I must humbly explain that it is only since the accident that I have become interested in her. Sorraya didn't mix, and was mostly seen with Madame Charnaut, a former classmate. I think you have already met her.'

'Yes.' I feel a bit of fever and sore throat, and the cold and rain is no help. I am thinking that once we get to Brother Qassem Yazdani's flat, hot tea will be fine. We enter a narrow, dirty alley, ending in a narrow and dirty dead end. The building we go into is an old ruin, about to collapse within the hour. After opening the ramshackle door Qassem Yazdani leads the way to a tiny, attic room. We go in, removing our shoes. He offers me the only chair, and while he is fiddling about with the gas ring, I look around. Apart from a bed, the two-ringed gas burner, a sink, a few pieces of crockery, a table, this one chair, a clean woollen rug, and an untidy pile of books, the other contents of the room could adequately be transferred into an eye-dropper. A print of an ancient painting of a Paris scene hangs crookedly on one wall – as if dangling thus for ages. On the wall opposite the doorway, Qassem Yasdani has put up a vivid, blood-red paper cut-out of a dome and minarets. The room is chilly, one windowpane is broken and covered with paper. I take off my raincoat and sit down. Even my own room at the Hotel Palma was a hundred times better than this hole. 'Is this entirely yours?' I ask, shivering.

By now, he has lit the gas, and put the kettle on. He laughs, 'It's funny that you should ask that. Officially, yes, but there's a Morteza Khomami, who hasn't had any money from home for two or three months. He camps out here for the night in a corner. I've bundled his bedsheets and blankets under the bed so the concierge won't see.'

'I see!'

He perches on the side of his bed, looking around his room as if for the first time.

'At least you can live here in peace and quiet. In Abadan there is nothing but bombing, bloodshed, killing, day and night.'

'We will go on fighting until impiety and blasphemy are wiped from the Earth.'

I am not quite sure what he means by this, or if he does either. But I say 'I'm sure you will be a credit to any university when you go back to Iran.'

'But not like universities here . . . The centres of corruption.'

I want to change the subject.

'*Aqaye* Yazdani,' I say, 'Tell me, what is your opinion about our Sorraya's illness? You think she will recover?'

'*Insh 'Allah*. God willing.'

'Do you have no other, more precise view?'

'What do you mean?'

'You've been here longer than I have, you have a more scientific outlook, and your French is far better than mine . . .'

He nods.

'Did you see her from the very beginning?'

'Well, yes. Since the third or fourth day, when we found out what had happened.'

'How was she then? Was she better or worse than now?'

'She was better, I think – though of course I didn't see her every day. This is just my personal opinion, of course. But I think she did show some reactions, then. She was different just after the accident. She had life.'

'That's what Dr Martin told me.'

He raises his eyebrows. 'You must leave everything in God's hands, you know,' he says.

I sigh, leaning back in the creaky wooden chair. 'In the present situation – what the hell can we do, *but* that?'

The kettle is boiling; Brother Qassem Yazdani sets about the business of getting the tea ready. Beside the gas rings and next to the tiny sink, is a saucer, with a used tea-bag, complete with its string and Lipton label, ready for more action. But my host drops a fresh tea-bag into the kettle, and leaves it to brew, while he comes and sits down again.

'I want to know everything I can, about this poor girl's condition. Her mother is anxious for news, too.'

Qassem Yazdani rubs one hand over his eyes and eyebrows, and then over his soft beard, and draws a deep breath.

'I don't know very much about coma,' he says. 'I don't think the doctors or even the specialists know enough about it either. The exact damage to the brain cannot even be estimated, because the exact functions of the various parts of the brain are not yet known. And besides, the matter does not end with the complete study of the human brain. Other things are involved.'

'Oh? What other things?'

'The secret of the creation and resurrection of man by God.'

'I see.'

'We must realise that man is made of two parts; one part consists of his body or *corpus*, made up of matter. This finally comes to the end of its cycle, and begins to decay and decompose – but its vital organic elements do not change. Like this water just boiled in the kettle, turned to steam and vanished into the air, where it will stay till it returns to earth again. It is always there; preserved. But another part of man is his soul, his *spirit*, his self. Having no material form, it remains always the same. This part, the soul and the secret of life, cuts off its communication with the corpse after death, and exists in the world of spirits and souls. I've heard there are parallels to this notion in the Zoroastrian myths. The soul then lives on, until one day, when God commands, the vital components for the creation of the body to gather together, and the spirit returns into the physical body.'

'But this is terrible, *Aqaye* Yazdani!'

'What's terrible?'

'... I don't want Sorraya to die today, so that she can be reborn in maybe a billion years from now. Hell. I want Sorraya to get well now, I'm talking about tomorrow or next week. I want Sorraya to return to *this* life, so that I can take her home to her mother. This poor girl is just twenty-three years old. She's seen little happiness in her life, it's not fair ...'

'No ...'

'So you agree that it's not fair?'

'But what can we do if it is God's will?'

'I don't think God would do such an unfair thing.'

'Think of it this way, the Lord often put his subjects to the test.'

I shake my head, with a sigh. 'Yes.'

'Yes, indeed, and this is where we must pay attention to what I called the human soul, and to man's faith. In this society, when you see the cafés, bars, and even the thousands of bookshops, you can see that everyone is abetting decadence, materialism, and worship of the body. Says Hafez "They headed for the tavern because they couldn't see the truth." Let me bring the tea. I'm afraid I have nothing else to offer you!' He grins. I doubt if he is referring to booze, but I let it pass.

He only has one teacup, so he drinks from a glass. He takes the tea-bag out of the kettle, and puts it aside. At least the tea is good and hot. He also sets an old, half-empty box of Isfahan *gaz*, before me. He sits cross-legged, on his bed.

'There is a story about faith in the Holy Qoran,' he says. 'It goes like this: One day, during his prayers and his conversations with the Lord, Abraham calls oh, Lord, show me how thou bringest the dead back to life? Do you not believe? asks the Lord. I believe, says Abraham, but I want to see it, so that my heart may grow calm. The Lord tells him to take four birds and kill them (this is not written in the Holy Book, but it is interpreted) pound up their flesh, and mix it together. Then divide it into four parts, take each part, set it on a hill, then call to those birds. They shall come flying back to you, that you may become aware that the Lord has power over all things, and knows all the mysteries of the world. So Abraham does all this, and when he calls the birds unto him, lo! each lump of flesh becomes a bird, and takes flight ... This, of course, is only a meagre example of the mysteries of creation and resurrection, but it is the basis of faith in the day of resurrection, and the re-establishment of divine justice ...'

'Yes ...'

'You said it wasn't fair for Sorraya to have to experience death at twenty-three. Of course it isn't. But the very essence of this discourse is faith, which is the final and greatest truth. Only the Enlightened Eye can see this truth, and those who do not see it exist in an eternal coma, cut off from everything, from existence itself.'

I start sneezing for no reason. 'Hooray,' I say to myself, 'a bloody cold on top of everything else.' As I let him go on talking, I picture him as a bright-eyed three-year old, in Torbat-Heidariye, sitting in a corner, on the carpet, beside a cushion, listening to the good *mullah*. It was then that he heard these principles, recorded them, and has since expanded them to all-encompassing universal dimensions. Now, in his mid-twenties, about to get his bio-chemistry doctorate at one of Europe's largest universities, the essence of these principles is still unshaken, or he makes it sound that way.

'You seem to have caught a cold, Brother Aryan. Have some aspirin?'

'It's all right, I'm a drugstore on feet, myself.' I lay a hand on my breast pocket, and we both laugh.

Compared to people like Safavi, Majidnia, Parsi and Abdol-Ali Azadeh, even Qassem Yazdani is a sort of gift . . . The only thing about him I don't get is the economic philosophy behind the used tea-bags for himself, and the narcissi for Sorraya. It can't have been a prearranged act for my benefit, because how could he have known he would be bringing me here today?

We chat for a further half-hour, mostly him talking about the one-Allah, the philosophy of the resurrection, the creation of the earth and its ending; about mankind from the Islam viewpoint, death and the isthmian passage between the firmaments, about explosions within the earth, caused by earthquakes, and man's astonished questions as to what makes this happen, and of the Sarat Bridge, which is thinner than a hair's breadth, and sharper than a sword's edge, and how, in the hereafter, each person will be rewarded for their every act of good and punished for every bad act . . .

Since it has stopped raining, I suggest we go out for a bite to eat. He thanks me, and tells me he has to say his prayers, and then finish writing up a report. Usually, he says, he has a small supper at home. As he has no refrigerator, and I can see no cupboard or shelf, I cannot imagine what this small supper consists of – perhaps he brews the dried tea-bag, and has tea-

and-*gaz*? I could not imagine he'd call for dinner to be brought in from Maxim's.

The following afternoon, I go to the Louvre with Safavi. He is a walking encyclopaedia; he knows more about each painting, statue or artefact than the museum curators. The next day, at noon, Parsi arrives at the hotel in a new Citroen with his wife and sister-in-law – the fair Simin – to take me to Fontainbleau. We wait for Safavi to arrive, and then we all set off. Parsi wants to know whether Leila Azadeh is back yet? I tell him she is not back, as far as I know. He says Abbas Hekmat is going to give a lecture at the Sorbonne on New Year's Eve. I say I have heard that, too.

The weather is fine. Simin is seated next to me in the car, and she smells good, too. Fontainbleau is not bad, either. Safavi says he knows a café where they serve excellent Spanish food. He says it is run by an old fortune-telling woman, from the Alps.

We go to the Spanish restaurant. Safavi's information turns out to be correct. After a lengthy meal, when most people are a little bemused, the old fortune-teller comes, and both Parsi's wife and Simin have their fortunes told. The sly old lulu, having sized up each one of us, tells Simin a man with hazel eyes and greying hair will give her great pleasures and some suffering. Nader Parsi, who can't keep his eyes off his sister-in-law, says jokingly, 'Jalal, don't torture her,' and we all laugh. After leaving the restaurant, we walk about for a while; then Safavi, and Parsi and his wife go into this ancient cathedral, while Simin stays with me, in the car.

Her large reddish-brown eyes remind me of Laleh Ahmadi, the wife of Farangis' brother-in-law.

Laleh Ahmadi was arrested one spring evening in Tehran, as she stood outside Tehran University's main entrance, with a group of boys and girls. Laleh was twenty-one years old at the time – a third-year sociology student. She had recently been married, and was four months pregnant. Laleh and the others were bundled into several Peikans, taken and held, for distributing illegal pamphlets. During the first night, in the *Kommiteh*, Laleh 'faints'. When she comes to at dawn, she has severe pains.

178

She tries to stop the bleeding with her torn clothes, but she loses her child. The following day, she is transferred to the Qasr prison, and held there with a hundred and fifty other women. Seven months later, Laleh is released without a trial or even a case file. But by then Laleh's husband has committed suicide, and been buried in the Behesht Zahra cemetery for four months. Lieutenant Kamran had put his Colt 45 into his mouth and shot himself through the palate, in his bathroom. His brain had been splattered all over the shower walls.

Simin and I talk about Michigan. She says she lives in a dorm in Michigan State University, in East Lansing; boys and girls live 'kind of mixed', and have no sex discriminations.

Idris, Matrud's retarded son in Abadan, had only one dream. After he was no longer able to sell Winston cigarettes, he dreamed of being accepted into the Mobilization of the Meek outfit, to join the lines of the 'Martyrs of the Path of Hossein', and hasten to the Vision of Allah. And, on the day when I went with old Feizpur, an Oil Company colleague, to help him move some furniture from his house, twenty girl students from the Relief *Kommiteh* were there. They had taken over the house, with friendly intentions. These 'Sisters' in *chadors*, headscarves, blue jeans and tennis shoes, armed with U-Z machine-guns, had made the house their headquarters, and were serving with the 'Brothers', who were stationed in Abadan International Hotel building, not far away.

East Lansing was not bad, Simin Barzegar says, but she thinks Paris is better – although the one place she *really* loves, is Switzerland. I compare her with Sumunju of Hotel Palma, who is Swiss. They would look almost identical, made of the same mould. Only Sumunju is shaped like a doll made of Swiss cheese, with a face so open that it seems almost ageless – she could be anything from thirty-five and sixty-five. Wereas Simin Barzegar is not even twenty-five, made of milk and honey, plus all the Christian Dior products. When the others rejoin us, and I ask what kept them so long, Safavi jokingly replies 'Our Parsi went to see the Father Confessor, and his Grace was so shocked that he swooned clean away.'

Outside the town square in Behbehan, by the Vali-Asr Mosque, they are about to carry the corpses of two 'martyrs'. A crowd of about twenty thousand mourners are standing around, ready for the procession to the graveyard. The shrouded bodies are laid in the small coffins, and covered with shawls, *termeh* cloth, and tulips. Small children walk in front of the mourners. They are beating their breasts, crying Death to Saddam, Death to America, Death to Israel, and Death to the Soviet Union. Behind them, a group of *hezbollahi* sisters, in their black *chadors* and bearing G-3 machine-guns, are ready for the march. Then come the coffins, on Toyota Ambulances. The men – of all different types, armed and unarmed – follow. Everyone is repeating slogans barked by the mullah into the loudspeaker. At the very end, behind all these people, is a small group, weeping in silence, perhaps the families of the dead. Their weeping almost makes me weep, too.

Outside the town, the driver, *Aqa* Seyyed Reza, stops at a dusty orchard belonging to a member of his family, and here we have tea, and a little rest. The orchard is forsaken, silent and bare. An old shack built a few hundred years ago, and then frozen in time, stands in a far corner. But the owner of the orchard, Valiollah Khan, is a fine man, and brings us tea and dates. In another corner of the orchard, near the shack, is a large cage, where a retarded, and apparently dangerous, thirteen- or fourteen-year old girl is kept. When we walk past the cage the girl claws at me. Her mouth opens in a rectagular sneer, and a strangled, inhuman cry comes from her throat.

21

The next two or three days at last the weather is good. It rains overnight, but each day the sky is blue, warm and sunny with bits of white cloud scattered around, giving Paris a not too unpleasant appearance.

One evening Nader Parsi takes me together with his household to Bijan Karimpur's place, which is next to his school. Among other things Karimpur is a socialist, a humanist, a discreet refugee resident and a very fine poet. Being an Iranian communist has made him taciturn and tight-lipped. He enrols penniless, Iranian refugee kids in his school for free. I get to like him.

I also spend a really boring evening in Parsi's own flashy apartment, watching his super-8 home movie and the 'art' slides he has proudly shot of the bazaars and old mosques and shabby crumbling ruins of 'Persia'. Only Simin's presence somehow saves the evening.

Sorraya's condition is the same, if not worse. I spend next to the last night of the year alone at the hotel, reading, waiting for Farangis' telephone call. She now calls twice a week. I do not feel well. I have taken my medicine regularly, but I feel heavy and dizzy, the worst I've felt since I've been here. A sensation of weakness and yet like a heavy weight bearing down in my forehead and at the back of my neck. I think of going to the hospital and having the situation examined but I don't feel like seeing a doctor. I wish Leila were in town!

By the time Farangis' call comes through I am practically unconscious. Talking to her revives my spirit a little, but my aching head worsens.

Late that night, I have a really terrific idea. I'll write a will! I think of writing a list of formal instructions and telling everyone what to do in case I expired in the middle of the night here in Hotel Palma, Paris. Then I think what nonsense! What if I did write it? What will they do? Nothing! They would move my corpse to the morgue – everything, my bags, dirty clothes and all. I remember Leila Azadeh saying that Sadeq Hedayat died in a room like this, not far from here, some thirty years earlier. Turn on the gas in the little room, lie down and wait, wait for *rigor mortis*. For God's sake, but he was *somebody*! What about me? What will they do with me? Even the Good Samaritan Paris gendarmerie will be reluctant to handle me. They will report it to the Prefect of Police, somebody will contact the non-residents' bureau. Somebody will report it to Consulate at L'Ambassade de la Republic Islamic d'Iran in Paris. The good 'brother' at the Consulate will courteously take notice and notify the next of kin in Tehran. No! Farangis couldn't take that! What about Sorraya? Come on, you stupid slob! Pull yourself together!

I put aside the thoughts of dying and writing a will. I am not going to die for the moment. I promise myself to call a doctor if things get any worse. I have come here to help out not to pass out! That is what I will do. To hell with *rigor mortis*!

I get up and take a whole extra batch of pills – which is not such a brilliant thing to do, I admit. I lie down, close my eyes. I try to slip away into my own very special dream world – something which was not so hard to do when I was young. The spaceship in the Cloudlands. I try to put the vessel of life into reverse gear and down the Tunnel of Time. I bring Annabel into the spaceship with me. We travel back to the night we met at that beach in the early hours of morning. The sea shore at Fisherman's Wharf is quiet. In the distance we see lights. Then it is another night. I want you to make love to me. Through the window we can hear the ocean not far away. The house is quiet. The world is calm.

Suddenly, there are no cloudlands or spaceships. There is no Annabel. The house is not quiet and the world not calm. Just lunatics at war, with mortar shells zooming in the tunnel of death. We are coming down the Bahmanshir River along the Abadan shores in the dark in a beat-up motor dinghy – heading for Mah-Shahr. I and this Mr Fesharaky and a few other employees. Black waters of Bahmanshir in the moonlight, as we drift down towards the tip of the Gulf. The wooden dinghy groans and seems to list under Mr Fesharaky's heap of Italian furniture from his Bavardeh house. A smaller dinghy pulls alongside us as we slow down because of low tide. She is carrying four cows picked up at Cho-ebdeh. We are stopped at a pier in a quay. We have to wait for the high tide.

We wait, and wait, until the glorious sun rises from the direction of the Iraqi palm plantations and over the mouth of the Gulf. Saddam Hossein's Russian-made helicopter gun-boats also rise. They move to the top of the Abadan Island where the action is. Above our heads we also watch the Islamic Republic Air Force's American-made Phantom 5 fighter bombers, tearing on to destroy the enemy's oil installations. The cows in the little dinghy have glued their heads into the pile of hay in front of them. One of them lifts its head and stares at me, shreds of hay still dangling from its mouth. In the background, the huge, gold sun also rises above the legendary Persian Gulf. The cow's eyes are beautiful, but stupid and puzzled. I think of my ancestor Sinbad the Sailor. The cow's eyes seem to be asking me a question. What's happening to you? Why are you not eating? We have nothing to eat. The cows are better off.

I want to return from nightmare gun-boat to the old dreamship, to the quiet and the calm of the beach at Fisherman's Wharf, to the Christmas Eve of 1960 – I can't. Road closed. No Exit. I have only two roads, both behind me. One leads to the hospital where Annabel died after giving birth to our dead child, that night, twenty years ago. My private, eternal nightmare. Another road is back to Abadan. The rest is free fall, into oblivion. Or free float into mudlands. Motor-dinghies in low tide, and the burnt banks of the Bahmanshir River. Abadan, Abadan! Happy days will be here again!

Sorraya and Khosro came to stay with me for three days. It was their honeymoon. When was that? I picked them up at the Abadan International Airport, and took them to my lonely, quiet house in the Breim, the exlusive residential area, not far from Golestan Club – the club of the Garden of Roses. Sorraya and Khosro had lovely times. That was another Abadan, in another time, in another world. They stayed for two or three weeks after their wedding in Tehran. What a wedding! Sorraya loved the palm-lined streets and turnabouts. Khosro loved the silent shores of the vast Arvand River gently creeping into the mouth of the Gulf. They went for endless strolls. We had dinner at the Golestan Club or at the Boat Club, by the water. On Friday afternoons, they sailed down the river and round Minu Island, in Dr Nurisa's pleasure skiff. They would take hundreds of photos. Later, they would stroll down the Khorram-Shahr Road to Alfi and to Hassan Arab International Bookshops to buy books and magazines. At night, they slept in one of my rooms opening to the garden where Matrud had something blooming all year round. They were in love. They were happy. The house was quiet and the world was calm. That was autumn 1977. In winter 1978 Khosro was killed in street rioting in Tehran, and the following spring, when the storm of the Revolution was at its height, Farangis sent Sorraya to Paris, to be away from it all. Poor Farangis!

I do not know what time it is, but the dizziness in my skull lessens. With eyes closed I think of Farangis, alone in Tehran. The tiny portable radio by my bedside is still on short-wave, sliding from one European station to the next, as if leading a rambling life of its own. Somewhere, a woman is singing a melancholy song in a lonely, far-off voice. The words have something to do with bonds, the bonds of life in this world. Who has counted the bonds of life? When is life ever free from bonds? First we are bonded to mother's womb to feed through her blood. Then born into the bonds of childhood helplessness. Who will pick me up? Who will feed me? The school year's bonds are hard indeed. The teachers' jeers, the punishments for misbehaviour, the painful bonds of adolescence . . . Then the bonds of love, and the bitterness, for we are grown up now. The bonds of securing jobs and business obligations are the most painstaking, and the most exhausting of all. Next is the bond of marriage, a different chain on the soul and the body. The bond of children is abiding, for they inherit our entire resources of life and spirit. And at last, bonds of old age and frailty, of sickness and pains, and of gradually sinking into ashes of what is left of life . . . Yet, all this is only the start. The world is uncertain, the future dark. Nothing is ever guaranteed. No one knows where the road will lead us. But then again . . . In one way or another, little man, somehow, somehow, through all these bonds . . . survives!

That night, in any case, I must have gone to sleep fairly early which would be thanks to Gavarine Rx, Adalat, and Nitro-lingual, and Comadine. In the morning, I don't remember having heard the Tehran midnight news.

22

On the morning of 31 December, Sorraya is transferred to the Intensive Care Unit. When I arrive at the hospital at around ten o'clock, Nurse Jardin takes me to see Dr Martin. The doctor explains that Sorraya has been having some breathing difficulty and needs to have a respiration regulatory treatment. They have also put her on a dialysis machine. There is no immediate alarm. However, very politely – they forbid me to go in and see the patient.

Around midday, when I am still reluctant to leave the hospital, Christienne Charnaut hurries in. She, too, has heard of the change. She makes me wait while she goes upstairs to have a look at Sorraya and have 'a word or two with Mademoiselle Jardin'. Apparently she has no great faith in my French. When she returns, her usual lively, chatter-box manner is missing. She looks a little concerned.

'Well,' she asks me. 'How is she?'

'You tell me.'

'Sorraya has been in Intensive Care before, too.'

'When?'

'When she was first brought here.'

'Why have they moved her back now?'

'I don't really know. Problems. Complications. But, don't worry. She'll get better.'

'I hope so.'

'Yes. Well, and how about yourself? How are you?'

'Still alive.'

'Don't talk that way. The world hasn't come to an end, you know. You have given so much help since you came. One must never lose hope. Of course, things *could* have turned out better.'

'Yes, they could.'

'So, now don't go thinking things have taken a turn for the worse. You did the best you could.'

She uses the past tense, as if Sorraya is in a much worse condition than I had thought. I get to thinking she probably knows more than I have been able to understand.

'But – you said she would get better.'

'I absolutely hope she does,' Christienne Charnaut replies.

I look into her small blue eyes. Though they are always honest and kind, I don't know why I feel I could not trust in them.

We walk along the corridor and downstairs together.

'Come to our house this evening,' she says. 'We're having a little party. It's New Year's Eve you know.'

'Thanks, but I . . . have something planned,' I lie.

'Oh? What?'

'I'm going to a lecture.'

'What lecture?' She certainly doesn't give up easily.

'By an Iranian writer, who's coming over from London.'

'Oh, Sorraya and I used to go to all these lectures. Where is this one?'

'In the Amphitheatre des Beaux Arts, at the Sorbonne.'

'Who's the writer?'

'Abbas Hekmat.'

Christienne Charnaut repeats Abbas Hekmat's name several times, softly.

'Isn't he the one who wrote a novel about a man and his singular, private rebellion . . .?'

'I think he is the one.'

'Sorraya used to say this was one of the few good books that helped bring about the Iranian Revolution. What does he do now?'

'Who?'

'Monsieur Hekmat. I expect he is one of the leaders of the Cultural Revolution now, *non*?'

'As far as I know, Monsieur Hekmat is in London – and has been living in London for quite a long time.'

'Didn't he even return after the Revolution?'

'He left after the Revolution.'

'Why?'

'I don't know ...'

'Why, really?'

'Well, probably, because there was no more beer!'

She giggles. 'Is he a beer drinker then?'

'So I've heard.'

'You start off a Revolution and then run. You light the fuse, and then, when the flame starts to burn, you cry out. Yes?' She smiles.

'No. One can't generalize.'

'No, perhaps not. One cannot generalize. The bit about the beer made me laugh, though.'

But it is not funny. Nothing seems funny this morning. I just want to be alone.

'I suppose Abbas Hekmat has nothing on the "Martyrdom" theme?'

'Not as far as I know.'

'The theory of "Martyrdom" is the ideal of the new Islamic regime, isn't it?'

'*Comme ci, comme ça*. In a way, yes.'

We are out on the steps, leading to the gardens. My head is feeling heavy again, but I walk with her to her car.

'Did you know Sorraya wrote poetry?'

'No ... I didn't.' I turn and look at her. 'I didn't know. Of course she paints well.'

'She paints beautifully. She wrote very little ... But very touching, very well. Sometimes she read some of them to me. Next time you come over, I will show you her little notebook, with her poems and some of her notes in it.'

'*Merci.*'

We are outside and she scrutinises me more carefully, now.

'You look paler, out in the sunlight,' she says. 'And a bit unwell. Are you all right?'

'You should see me at night!'

She laughs. 'Don't lose hope. You know, Sorraya always has absolute hope. She had suffered much pain, but she never lost hope. There was a certain Iranian poetess whom she loved very much. I forget her name now ... Forukh ... Farkheh ... Zadeh?'

'Forugh Farrokh-Zad?'

188

'Yes, yes, yes. Sorraya once translated one of her poems for me. It goes like this: "I plant my hands in the garden,/They will grow,/And swallows shall lay their eggs,/Among my inky fingers".'

We are now standing by her car. I look into her eyes.

'Sorraya was very perceptive about symbols. "Planting", "growing", "laying eggs". These are serious symbols.'

I scratch my head.

'You can come as late as you like this evening. I can show you Sorraya's notebook.'

'I'll come sometime during the week.'

'. . . These sorts of parties don't usually get going until about midnight. I do wish you could come. I'd like you to read her poems and translate them for me.'

She pouts her lips, as though for a kiss Her small, bead-like eyes seem to emit new messages, maybe.

'Do come if you can.'

I have lunch at a nearby restaurant, and read the *New York Herald* over coffee. When I get back to the hotel at two, I feel a bit relaxed as if the initial shock of Sorraya's transfer has worn off, a little. There have been several letters – one from Farangis. There is also a note from Leila Azadeh. Sumunju hands them to me, telling me that Mademoiselle was here and wrote the note herself. 'She was very beautiful,' she says, looking me in the eye. I wink at her and read the note in the lift. Leila has simply written that Abbas Hekmat's lecture begins at eight o'clock, wanting me to be sure to be there. She came, she says, to take me along, sorry to have missed me. She adds: The 'government' people have already condemned the meeting, because of its 'political undertones!'

From my room, I give Sumunju Farangis' number, asking her to connect me when the call comes. While I wait, I write two letters – one to Farangis, and another to a friend in the Oil Company who had written to me. I had asked him to extend my 'leave-without-pay', and today he has written that thanks to the seventeen thousand or so Abadan Oil Company employee refugees . . . who had been stranded all over Iran, my request had been granted with pleasure. He had ended with best wishes for my niece and my own well-being in Paris. Apparently a copy of his note has been filed in my personnel file, and the permission of leave is semi-official. Both letters I wrote turn out rotten, because I am expecting the phone to ring any minute. They cannot get a connection, though I know at this moment Farangis is waiting for my call. I pick up the phone, and ask Sumunju to check and see how my Tehran connection is coming on. She tells me it's New Year Eve, and all international lines seem to be in use. So I light another cigarette, and keep waiting. After ten minutes, the call to Farangis finally comes through. I describe the latest change in Sorraya's condition. Farangis gets very upset, I think she begins to cry. I try to cheer her up, telling her things are still not so bad – I tell her Sorraya's friend Madame Charnaut was there too, and that she had told me Sorraya had been in Intensive Care before, in the first days of her illness. And after a while, I think she begins to calm down, especially when I ask how things are in Iran. She says there are mass funerals, every day, for the casualties, the 'martyred', in groups of ten, twenty, thirty at a time. Millions of people mourn in the streets and they show it on the television. The suffering, she says, is no longer ours alone, nor for just a few families – it is a communal plague. I promise to keep phoning regularly, unless I have some urgent news, in which case I should call at once. Farangis tells me to take care, and asks how I have been, I tell her I am fine, and hang up after saying goodbye.

It is dusk, and I am shaving, getting ready to go out for some supper, when the phone rings again. I pick up the receiver, and hear Sumunju's voice saying, 'Monsieur Aryan, a call for you from the Hopital du Val de Grace.'

My stomach churns with fear. 'All right, put it through, please.'

'Hold on. It's a Dr Monet.'

A voice comes through: 'Monsieur Aryan?'

'Yes – this is Monsieur Aryan.'

'I am Dr Monet,' says the voice, 'from the Val de Grace, about Mademoiselle Sorraya.'

'Yes? Yes?'

'I'm Dr Martin's assistant. Could you come over to the hospital? There is a form which you must sign.'

Oh, hell's bells! I say to myself. Heaven help us.

'Yes, of course. What form will that be, Doctor?'

'It turns out we may have to perform a simple electrotherapy on Sorraya's heart. We must have your permission.'

'Of course. I'll be right there.'

'Thank you very much.'

'Has something happened, Doctor?'

'No, Monsieur – not yet – simple hospital routine.'

'I'll be there in less than five minutes.'

'*Bien, merci,* Monsieur.'

I throw on a raincoat and get myself to the hospital in a taxi. Dr Monet, Dr Martin's assistant, is a very young, fair-skinned man of small build, but with a relatively large head and face, and an impressive head of oiled wavy hair, combed back with a wide, white parting on one side. He is in Dr Martin's room, sitting behind his desk, chatting with Nurse Georgette Jardin, two other nurses, and a lady doctor. He rises, shakes hands with me, smiling and exchanging pleasantries. Others present also greet me kindly and enquire about my health. They even offer me a glass of Bordeaux, which I decline with thanks.

It turns out that there is no urgency for the electrotherapy treatment that night. They just want the permission form for the treatment signed, for an emergency situation. This is now explained to me. It is a special treatment in which the patient's heart is gently stimulated by means of *electro-cystolique*. The procedure is to have the form in the patient's file, in case of an emergency, in the middle of the night, etc, etc.

'What time will Dr Martin be in?' I ask.

'Dr Martin has gone on his annual holiday,' Nurse Jardin smiles.

'I see.'

'Happy New Year, Monsieur Aryan.'

'Thank you, and Happy New Year, ladies and gentlemen.' May God rest your merry fathers and ancestors, I whisper under my breath.

When I come out of the hospital, it is past six and dark. Outside the main entrance, I meet Qassem Yazdani – Sorraya's faithful visitor – with another boy and girl, all worried about Sorraya. I tell them briefly about the situation. They are saddened even more, especially Qassem Hazdani. I say good-bye and leave them there. My own nerve indicator, which has

191

been oscillating since the morning, is leaping around again. I don't feel like going to hear Abbas Hekmat's lecture. The film of *The Dogs of War* is at the cinemas; I decide to see it and kill a couple of hours. The plot which had seemed so interesting in the book, becomes a watered-down parody of international espionage acrobatics in the film. The wam-bam, zip-zap games of the West: international cloak-and-daggter, arms smuggling, machine gun firing, bombing, and chucking presidents of small republics out of the window like cigarette stubs. Even Sir James Manson, the great exploitationist, is phonier than his character in the novel. Of course, the Big British merchant's dogs of war succeed in throwing out the ruling President of the legendary Zangaroo and setting up their own puppet leader in his stead.

After the film I have supper in a Chinese restaurant, a fried rice concoction, and green tea. Whle bending over my plate, I feel like the old goat in that Hollywood joke, eating a roll of discarded film in a studio garbage lot, saying, 'The book was better.' It is still early evening when I get back to the hotel.

23

But the night is not over as simply as that. I have just come up to my room when the phone rings again. This time it is Leila Azadeh herself, calling from some place with the background of music. Sounds of jazz reverberate down the line.

'*Salaam*, Jalal.'

'*Salaam*. Did you call to cheer me up?'

'Yes. I called to cheer you up.'

'Cheer away, then.'

'I missed you!'

'It's good to hear *your* voice again, believe me.'

'You know where I'm calling from.'

'The bloody background music's coming over, anyway.'

'The scene: Café de la Sanction.'

'Fun and games?'

'I want you to come and join us.'

'Nah.'

'I knew I'd find you there. No matter where you go, you always come back to the hotel for your sister's call at night. I can count on you.'

'You can do lots of things with me.'

'Yes, I can. Now come on over, I want to see you. Or else I'll come there myself.'

'All right.'

'Would you like me to come over there?'

'You know the answer to that, yourself.'

'Come on ... How much do I have to plead with you?'

'How was the manifesto?'

'Manifesto was magnificent ... There must have been a thousand or so enthusiasts over there. All very serious. Very broadminded, so to say. But don't change the subject. Come on, get up and come over here. It's New Year's Eve. Everyone's here. The candle and the rose and the butterfly and the nightingale.'

'All you need is a Darkhungah beetle.'

'Are you coming, or shall I come over there?'

'All right.'

When I get there, it turns out all Leila wanted was to complete her little collection. She was telling the truth when she said everyone was there. Evidently, after the lecture, or the manifesto, the nucleus of that group of pious pilgrims migrated from the amphitheatre at the Beaux Arts to the Café de la Sanction. Those present in the Café this evening are mostly from the bookish, literary circles, plus a few odd-balls. In addition to the one-and-only Abbas Hekmat, is Leila Azadeh with her young, lovely sister, Pari; Nader Parsi, Professor Moghazzez, Bijan Karimpur, Ahmad Safavi, Doctor Ahmad Reza Kuhsar, Bahman Qaraguzlu, Dr Khatibi, Dr Siasat, Dr Ardakan, Dr Majidi, plus Ahmad Qandi and several others – including, this evening, Hossein Abpak, the television personality, and Dariush Farhad, the film maker – mostly with their wives and mistresses.

There is also a Frenchman by the name of Jean Edmond, who knows Persian and, as it later turns out, used to be the cultural attaché in the French Embassy in Tehran, and who is now apparently doing a series of translations of Persian short stories by the Iranian writers of the last half of this century. Actually he looks more like a Viking than a French man of letters. He is tall, and as pink and white-skinned and bright-eyed as Dr Qassem Khatibi – only where Dr Khatibi's skull is covered with shining pink, Jean Edmond has wavy, blond hair, falling on to his forehead.

They have occupied a secluded corner of the café. exclusively. On a long table, presumably reserved for dinner, are as many drinks and as much food as you could wish for – together with New Year's Eve decorations. Several bottles of Bordeaux and Burgundy, two bottles of Pernod, two or three bottles of Johnny Walker, a bottle of Courvoisier, one of Rémy Martin, several ice buckets of champagne, and beer bottles aplenty, along with hot and cold foods. Leila Azadeh is on top form. She chatters, smiles and glitters non-stop. But it is obvious that the illustrious star of the evening is Abbas Hekmat. I had seen him once or twice before. His Freud-like, whiskered face is just as it was in his portrait on all his books, before the Revolution. By the time I arrive, everyone is already pretty well-oiled. I sit somewhere near the end of the long table, between Safavi and Ahmad Qandi and his infernal, portable radio-cassette. Leila comes quickly over to say *salaam*, and looks after me for a bit, winking as she says, 'Man is noble . . .' I soon learn that she is hinting at the group's current joke about Ahmad Qandi, my neighbour, about whom Hekmat – paraphrasing a poem by Sa'adi said: 'Man is noble according to his mind/ Clothes won't make Man.'

At that moment, Abbas Hekmat and Dr Kuhsar, evidently old chums and friends from way back, are talking loudly in *Zargari*. I think they are making fun of Jean Edmond and Nader Parsi, who, at the other end of the gable are having an apparently heated argument. Abbas Hekmat wears an old suit in black, white and pink checks, with a beautiful lemon-yellow shirt, a tartan tie, and a handkerchief folded in his top pocket. But his waistcoat bulges over his stomach, one of its buttons has popped off, exposing a quantity of yellow shirt and even undervest. His teeth are brown and crooked, and his almost lashless eyelids are dry with eczema. His complexion is still smooth and white thanks to daily ministrations of lotions and loving care. He is saying to Dr Kuhsar, in *Zargari*,

'Ahmad, tell Parsi . .'

'What?'

'Tell him the fellow won't put out!'

'Tell him yourself!'

'Tell him he's good-looking, but won't put out!'

'You tell him yourself!'

Almost everyone is laughing, with the exception of Jean Edmond, who undoubtedly does not understand *Zargari*, and Nader Parsi, who is probably too angry to pay attention, or probably has heard nothing at all, being at the far end of the table.

'Were you at the lecture?' Safavi asks me.

'No.'

'You were at the hospital?'

'I was there early this evening.'

'How is she?'

'Not well. They've taken her to the IC unit.'

'Ach! I'm sorry.'

I light a fresh cigarette. Leila is seated next to Hekmat, but she has been listening to us; 'Why've they taken her to the IC unit?' she asks.

'Her heart, her respiration . . .'

'Oh, poor dear!'

Parsi's voice rises, as he talks to Jean Edmond.

'What's up?' I ask Safavi.

He smiles wrily. 'Monsieur Jean Edmond's publishing an anthology – of contemporary Iranian short stories.'

'And there isn't one of Parsi in it?'

'Right! And that's what the hullaballoo's about. *Jenab* Parsi claims that this is a shameful stain on the *skirt* of the History of Persian Prose Literature in the eyes of the world, and neither one of them is ready to give quarter. What do you think – you know Nader well?'

'Can't they just drop the whole thing?' I ask, simply.

'You mean drop the Contemporary Prose's skirt?'

I smile. 'Well, they can add one of Parsi's works into Monsieur's anthology.'

'They can always give the skirt to the cleaners afterwards,' suggests Parsi's wife, who is sitting some distance away from her husband.

'Please Madame –' says Safavi. 'This sort of stain does not just wash out at the cleaner's!'

'Kindly remove your hands from the skirt of contemporary Persian literature,' advises Dr Ardakan. 'The whole issue is developing a sexual overtone.'

This time everyone on this side of the table bursts out laughing.

And this is how things go during my one hour at de la Sanction on New Year's Eve, 1981. Leila Azadeh remains mostly by Hekmat, but her eyes roam sometimes on to me but mostly on to Jean Edmond. Dr Ardakan gets up and dances with his wife. Bahman Qaraguzlu keeps going to the juke-box and puts on American Rock songs. Dariush Farhad dances with Pari Azadeh, continually. They are intimate. Or at least they're intimate this evening. Dr Khatibi, seeing Parsi pre-occupied, sneaks up and dances with Simin – who is a whole head taller than the rolypoly Khatibi, and whose blouse is ever more generously open this evening.

Hossein Abpak, sitting at the corner of the table, between me and Ahmad Qandi, is on his seventieth beer. He is telling me that he is still enchanted by Hekmat's books. He is explaining to me how Hekmat's first short stories were really 'genuine' and 'original', and had undertones of Sadeq Hedayat's own works. These stories had been actually influenced by Hedayat. The late Hedayat himself had read and *edited* them! Hedayat was the giant of them all. Then came Al-e-Ahmad, and then Hekmat. Hekmat had written with devotion. His writings always reflected the suffering of the poor and lower classes, the social diseases; poverty, the filth of society, the ignorance of the masses; the stupidity and misery of the masses. Hekmat's prosaic style was simple, as clear as a mirror – and unpretentious – without obstacles and obstructions. No one who read *The Candle in the Mosque* was left with any doubt of Hekmat's devotion in describing and explaining the pains of the deprived and miserable people of his country, especially the South. Hekmat was born in the province of Fars, and educated in Tehran. First he had worked in the British Embassy. Then he had gone into the Oil Company and worked there for some twenty years or so, becoming Chief of Staff. Hekmat had travelled to London, Moscow and New York, and spent several years abroad. He was a resident author in these cities. He had taught two courses in the University of London. Abbas Hekmat was now the crusader for Iranian Literature in the Free World. His wife had died last year. Now, apparently, he had some job with the British government, in a branch of the Foreign Office, or the BBC, or something. He was a literature and language consultant in the University of London. Hekmat was a literary personality in Europe. Or at least, Hossein Abpak thought so.

'Did you know, he has a unique sense of humour, too?'

'No, I didn't know.'

'Oh, he has. Some years ago, he wrote a critical review on a short play of Parsi's, *The Cane*. The name of the article was: "Mr Nader Parsi's Entire Knowledge"!'

'No!'

'Believe me! And another thing. Two years ago, the University of London sent him, as a "Guest Professor", a questionnaire. When he tells of it himself, it's hilariously funny. When he's filling out the questionnaire, for the item "Religion", he writes "Horhori". Religion: *Horhori*. When the University yearbook came out, in the Who's Who section of foreign guest professors, there were so many Christians, so many Muslims, Buddhists, Jews, etc., ... and one *Horhori*!' The way he himself tells it, it's just killingly funny.'

Abbas Hekmat raps on the table with a finger. 'Listen, friends.'

'Listen, everybody!' Leila relays. 'Listen!'

'At the beginning of this evening,' Hekmat says, 'I bored you all stiff.'

'No! ...'

'No, master! We were enlightened.'

'Listen – and so now, I want to bring you back to life, just a bit!'

'Hurrah!'

'There was once a rebellious *dervish*,' Hekmat says. 'Professor Purdavud quotes a certain poem from this rebellious *dervish*. This poem expresses, I think, our position in the world today, or the way *we* all feel this evening. It's a lively poem. I shall sing it for you. It's rhythmical. Now, I want you all to tap on the table, or snap your fingers, to its beat, and get into its rhythm ...'

Everyone suddenly comes alive, enthusiastically.

'Everyone ready!' Leila calls.

'One more thing. You must all repeat two lines in chorus after me – "Oh, Lord, save us! *Mowla* [Master; Imam Ali], see us!" ' He repeats it. 'Ready?'

'Yes.'

'Oh, Lord, save us! *Mowla*, see us! Come on. Oh, Lord, save us! *Mowla*, see us!' Everyone strikes up the chant, 'Oh, Lord, save us! *Mowla*, see us!'

Abbas Hekmat, whose voice and intonation is really like that of the best *dervishs*, begins chanting rhythmically:

'What's the reason for our misery?
We're down and under, dismal, weary,
Driven homeless, callous, jittery,
No one's ever seen desolates like us.'

He lowers his hand, and everyone joins in the chorus:

'Oh Lord, save us! *Mowla*, see us!
Oh, Lord, save us! *Mowla*, see us!'

Hekmat raises his hand.

'Look at Iran, ruined and sad!
Love of the homeland a myth we had!
People everywhere, all gone mad!
It's how a nation's demolished, and thus!
Oh, Lord, save us! *Mowla*, see us!
Oh Lord, save us! *Mowla*, see us!

Henceforth, we'll march the path to glory!
Seek out the cure for homeland's worry!
Cry out Iran, Iran, Iran, victory!
Day and night, in our prayers!
Oh Lord, save us! *Mowla*, see us!
Oh Lord, save us! *Mowla*, see us!

Beside me, Ahmad Qandi turns up the volume on his transistor. It is broadcasting the midnight news from Tehran. He brings the radio close to his ear, not far from my own. He, too, is evidently worried about the news from Iran, and the release of the hostages, because Carter has forbidden the entry of Iranians to American soil, and Ahmad Qandi, with his Green Card, and his anxious heart, anticipates the day when he can be granted his visa and be united with his money, stored in American banks. In the midst of Hekmat's recitation, the news from Iran has its usual 'War against the Blasphemy' message. The voice of the current realities of Iran, from the Islamic Republic of Iran, is a far cry from what goes on in the Café de la Sanction. The news theme tune, with its rhythmic but foreign Arabic words, played before the news broadcasts – and now almost halfway through – clashes with Hekmat's Persian song and dance ensemble and vehement Iran-worship.

Vahdahu vahdahu vahdahu vahdah
Vahdahu vahdahu vahdahu vahdah
(*He's one, He's one, He's one*)

199

Lasharik lasharik lasharik lah
Lasharik lasharik lasharik lah
(*No partner, no partner, no partner*)

Anjazah anjazah anjazah va'dah.
Anjazah anjazah anjazah va'dah
(*He's faithful, He's faithful, He's faithful*)

Nassara nassara nassara abdah
Nassara nassara nassara abdah
Anjazah va'dah va nassara abdah . . .
(*He helps, He helps, He helps his servants*)

In the news headlines, the one hundred and third Military Communiqué from the Army of the Islamic Republic, published this evening, states that the 'Forces of Islam', under the 'blood-coloured flag of the Islamic Republic of Iran', with the magnanimous efforts of the 'self-sacrificing' battlers, the Islamic Revolutionary Guards, the volunteers of the 'Mobilization of the Meek', the 'self-giving' soldiers of the Army of the Islamic Republic of Iran, the 'valiant personnel' of the Gendarmerie of the Islamic Republic of Iran, the 'fearless, sharp-flying' pilots of the Islamic Republic Air Forces, various tribesmen and the common people of the 'Islamic *ommat*' [followers of an Imam], have managed to deal 'crushing blows' to the invading, 'infidel, Ba'athist enemies' . . . The miserable, vanquished, evil enemy, realizing its inability to advance against and defeat the Muslim *ommat*, has shown further evidence of its 'helpless impotence' by bombarding the residential areas of Dezful, Ahvaz, Kut-abdullah, Hoveizeh, Bostan, Abadan, and Khuninshahr, killing, wounding and rendering homeless hundreds of women, children and innocent persons . . .

Hekmat recites;

Blasted! Blasted! We are drunken!
Doped and drowsy, feeble, shrunken!
We're delirious, we are sunken!
We're not conscious of things that pass!
Oh, Lord, save us! *Mowla*, see us!
Oh, Lord, save us! *Mowla*, see us!

(We'll) Fight for the homeland, to the last breath!
Be decorated by the Lord of Death!
Drink from the poison of bottomless depth!
Till the mouth of the motherland sweetens thus!
Oh, Lord, save us! *Mowla*, see us!
Oh, Lord, save us! *Mowla*, see us!

Like an old *dervish*, Hekmat kisses his hand, places it against his forehead, and extends it towards the gathered party. Everyone applauds loudly, Hekmat raises his glass, toasts their health, and drinks. Even in the old Riviera Cafe, in the Qavam-el-Saltaneh, the crowd weren't *this* lively.

But Hekmat does not speak continually of himself, as does Parsi, and unlike most of them, does not speak every other word in French; neither does he think Persian writers are dishcloths, as Safavi does. In his character, there are still stains from the gutters of the alleyways of the small towns in Fars – especially, when he has had a pint or two. You wouldn't think he was a long-time Iranian resident author in London, and an employee of the British Government. His Persian is still pure and mellifluous. He actually talks like Rafsanjan doughmakers.

At about eleven-thirty, I rise and excuse myself. Hekmat is unaware of my existence, and is busy telling of the house he has bought in the King's Road, London, and how he has been hassling the councillors over the right to have a Persian-style lavatory installed in his house. I try to catch Leila's attention but she is engrossed with Jean Edmond. She is laughing and chatting away with him. So much for my great expectations for the New Year's Eve. Hekmat is apparently sleeping in Leila's apartment this evening. Leila is going to sleep at her sister Pari's place – or at least, that's what is on the agenda. As for Pari, she is still dancing with Dariush Farhad. Parsi, seeing his wife otherwise occupied, is flirting with his sister-in-law, again. Parsi's and Safavi's stupid wives are having a heart to heart chat, but I doubt if it is about 'world nationalism'. Leila's engagement to Hekmat the Great is a foregone conclusion. Leila is going to London in February. As I get up and walk away, they are all sitting there, with the bottles and the glasses and the dishes of food, fruits, sweets, chatting and laughing.

I am walking out of the door, when Nader Parsi comes up and

calls me, he grabs me by the shoulder from behind.

'Where are you off to so early, Jalal?'

'The hotel.'

'I haven't seen you. It's so damn noisy in here, I didn't get to speak two words to you.'

He is dead drunk.

'Why the hell so soon? All the fun, the noise and the kissing starts at twelve o'clock!'

'Yep!'

He laughs. 'So, stay.'

'I'm really sleepy.'

'Who's this bastard?'

'Who's which bastard?'

'This bastard, Jean Edmond . . . The one Leila's been making eyes at?'

At that very moment Leila and Jean Edmond have gone to a corner bar, but Parsi, standing with his back to them, does not see them.

'How the hell do I know?'

'You really don't know him?'

'You're the one who's been talking to him all evening.'

'He talks a load of crap! Since when has Iranian literature been in need of a caretaker and publicity agent? Do you know what's going on between him and Leila?'

'No – honestly. I haven't seen Leila for two or three weeks, before this evening. And this is the first time I've been privileged to a glimpse of Monsieur's noble countenance.'

'Did you see the way she looked at that bastard?'

'Who looked at who?'

'Leila, idiot – at that bastard.'

'Leila looks at half the world's population, that way. Besides, she and Hekmat are practically walking up the aisle for holy matrimony.'

'Leila said that?'

'Look, I'm off – good night!'

He is stoned.

'Have you done anything about the money yet?'

'No.'

'No.'

'How much do you need, now?'

'About a hundred and forty or fifty thousand.'

'Listen, Jalal. I spoke with my uncle. He can give it to you. The

French franc is forty-two rials on the market. He's willing to give you forty!'

'All right.'

'You want me to tell him to come to the hotel tomorrow morning?'

'No, I haven't decided yet.'

'Then don't get it from anyone else. All right?'

'All right.'

'Come to our place for the night, Jalal. Come on, don't be a party-pooper.'

'No. Thanks, really.'

'Then keep in touch.'

'All right.'

He walks back to the table. On my way out, I turn and look at him. He makes his way through the tipsy, crazy crowd and sits opposite Leila, who is also back at the table, in the place I had just vacated. Two garçons are busy clearing the empty plates and placing fresh bottles on the table. Abbas Hekmat says something and the whole table bursts into laughter. Everyone is sky-high. They are waiting for the twelve o'clock midnight, the advent of the New Year, with its kissings and huggings and singing and dancing.

There is a cold, biting wind on the Rue Saint Jacques, but the sky is still clear. It is like the evening when the Iraqis attacked the Zulfaqari through the Abadan Cemetery. That night, we slept in a trench in North Bavardeh, in front of the Abadan Institute of Technology. One of the students was stung by a scorpion, on his leg. I made a cut above the wound with a knife, but we could not leave the trench until daylight. He spent the whole night waiting to die.

At the junction of the Boulevard Saint Michel and the Rue Vaugirard I hear a noise that sounds like the chariot of destiny, in full gallop, with busted exhaust pipe beating a Death March on the asphalt.

I look round; it is an Audi 200, the latest model, with a German licence-plate. The driver pulls up and the noise dies down. A thick-moustached fellow calls, 'Moosiou ...'

Something blares out that he is Iranian. 'Yes?' I reply in Persian.

'Ah – God bless you! Are you Iranian, then, *Aqa*?'

'Yes, I am. What can I do for you? *Salaam-aleikom*.'

'Where's this Eiffel Tower, brother?' The wife, and several children are ensconced in the back seat. He is a smallish man, in a grey suit, with a pleasant, Northern face and curly hair.

'The Eiffel Tower is some way from here,' I tell him.

'We've just got to find this Eiffel, Meiffel – whatever-it-is Tower, this evening,' he says. His speech is something.

'What do you want with the Eiffel Tower, at this late hour of the night?'

'Like they speak it; if we'd had a bit of luck, we'd have been a horseshoe. We wanted to go to this nephew of mine's house, which is supposed to be in a street opposite the Eiffel Tower, you see. But we're some bit lost, tonight.'

'Well, the Eiffel Tower's pretty far from here.'

'He'd told us there'd be a boulevard thingy, running straight up to the Eiffel,' he says with some puzzlement. 'We've just arrived from Germany, you know. Wish you were there! But at the corner of this street, a Peugeot tried to undertake us, he knocked us over into the paveway and our exhaust-pipe popped off. These foreigners, *Aqa*, they're even worse than we are, by God! Give me the Ismal Bazzaz alley in Tehran any day, I swear to your life! Give me Ismal Bazzaz.'

'With this exhaust pipe and all that racket, you're liable to get a ticket from the police. Let me tie it up for you with a wire or something. Do you have a piece of wire or anything?'

He comes out and shakes hands with me, saying his name is Abbas Mir-Mohammadi.

'Wire, shmire! Where would we get a piece of wire from, at this time of the night – luckless idiots, that we are, *Aqa*! If I'd had a bit of luck, I'd have been a horseshoe, not Abbas Mir-Mohammadi.'

Inside the car, one of the chidren is crying, and the wife is shouting at him.

I take off my belt, and start tying the disconnected exhaust pipe to the rear fender.

'Do you have your nephew's phone number?' I ask. 'You could call and have them come and pick you up.'

'We've got our nephew's number – but we don't have the code number.'

'You don't need any code number if they live here in Paris.'

'Yes, well, you see, we've lost the number. It was on a piece of paper inside the Missus' passport. We sent the Missus' passport to have "Islamic photo" inscribed in it. They lost the paper with the phone number ... *Aqa*, you've no idea what trials and trimbulations we've been through! All the money we'd brought with us, was spent up, in Hamburg. So then we thought we'd come and look up this nephew of ours ...'

'I can get you a room for the night, where I'm staying.' I offer. 'The kids can have a rest, and tomorrow you can start looking for your nephew.'

'No, God bless you, *Aqa*, thank you ... We've got to find this nephew of ours. The Missus is ill, too, and we can't find her blood type easy. It's a very rare group, you see – "O linus" or "O minus", or something, yes. Our nephew is a doctor, you see. He can find it.'

'Well,' I say. 'If he's a doctor, I can find his number for you ... What's his name?'

'No, really, *Aqa*, you're too kind. We wouldn't want to give you any more bother. Why, oh, *Aqa*, we had a decent living for ourselves, back home. We lived in comfort. You see, we had a dealer's shop and an agency in Bandar Pahlavi. We also had a few hectares of property in Tehran. I don't know what happened, by God! What came over these people?! Like they speak, it's as if people've all been brain scrubbed. Yes *Aqa* ... The ones who've stayed in Iran are real wretches, by Allah!'

I finish tying up his exhaust pipe, and test it with one hand. It is not loose and dangling any more, at least. I get to my feet, and give him directions, showing him how to get to the square in front of the *Tour Eiffel* area – but by the way he stuffs the scrap of paper into his pocket it is clear that he can't even read latin letters. I send him in the general direction of the Eiffel Tower anyway.

'Right, *Aqa*, thank you very kindly.'

We shake hands, and kiss each other on the cheek, something we all did in Abadan everytime we said good-bye, during the war. He sits behind the wheel again, and – less noisily this time – drives on in the direction I had indicated, or towards the rest of his destiny, disappearing down the Saint Michel. Maybe I should have sent him to Café de la Sanction. I want to shout out after him, 'Man, what did you have to go and leave for?' But when I get to thinking, he's no less than any of the others here. Perhaps he really did come because of his wife's illness, poor fellow. After all, she has 'O Linus' type blood.

24

New Year's day is dull and cloudy. Even the Hotel Palma seems too hung over to stir before noon. It is still very cold and looks like rain, and I catch sight of Qassem Azdani's tall figure, standing outside as if undecided whether or not to enter. He comes in, I say *salaam*, and we shake hands; he has two thick books under his arm. He has come to ask after Sorraya. I thank him, and we walk toward the Boulevard Saint Michel together. Somewhere, I stop to buy a paper, and post a letter. Then we head for the hospital. As well as concern, there is a sort of innocent pleading in Brother Yazdani's eyes, though not like *Aqaye* Mir-Mohammadi's with his busted exhaust pipe. He has become more interested in Sorraya's coma, though to my mind his interest is personal, perhaps to do with marriage. His unpretentious, naive character is attractive, and in contrast to the types centred round Leila Azadeh. You want to believe him even when he says that at a prayer gathering he had attended two nights ago he felt much better and *lighter* afterwards. A café is open in the middle of the Rue Gay-Lussac and it is still too early to go to the hospital.

'What would you say to a cup of milk-coffee, *Aqaye* Yazdani?' I ask.

'With pleasure, but my treat.'

'Even if we took turns over it, it was you who hosted last time. Besides, I invited you *first*.'

'Yes, but since Sorraya Khanum's accident, your financial affairs are ...'

'My financial affairs are fine.'

'One hundred and fifty thousand francs is no joke.'

'No – but we'll be fine.'

Inside the café we seat ourselves in a corner. He puts his books on the table, blows into his bony hands, rubbing them together to warm them. We order our *cafés-au-lait*. 'I've heard you were thinking of sending money from Iran,' Yazdani says.

'I can assure you that idea has now been put out of my mind.'

'Then how are you going to pay the hospital bills?'

'We'll pay them right here, somehow.'

'I could help out,' he declares seriously.

I look at him. Apart from his noble eyes, the rest of his worldly means could very well amount to a couple of hundred francs.

'Thank you, brother Yazdani,' I say. 'This problem is mine, my sister's, and Sorraya's, and I will somehow solve it. I'm sure you have problems of your own. Everyone has. I hope you aren't offended. In any case, I'm very grateful to you.'

Our *cafés-au-lait* arrive.

'Madame Charnaut said you had sold your ring.'

'It was getting too loose,' I laugh. 'Let's not go into that, if you don't mind.'

He smiles. 'Yes, of course . . . But why?'

'I admire your offer, and I like you a great deal, as well. And one never talks money with someone he likes and admires . . . Besides, we have made a request to the Welfare Office at Sorraya's university to cover the hospital fees with their insurance benefits . . .'

He stirs his coffee.

'Madame Charnaut said there had also been some problems with Miss Sorraya's visa and that her student's insurance had expired.'

'It does have its complications. But we'll get it sorted out. I'm sure.'

'*Insha-Allah* . . .God-willing . . .'

To get him off the subject of money, I ask, 'What are you reading? University stuff?' I point to the books.

'No . . . This one –' he picks up one of the thick volumes '– is in English. I had it sent from America. *Brain: The Structure and the Functions.*'

'Has it got anything on "coma"?'

'Yes. Three or four chapters in the parts where the consciousness is being discussed.'

'After my own stroke,' I say, 'I borrowed a smaller book on this subject from one of the doctors. I was reading it in hospital when the war broke out. What's the other one?'

Yazdani lifts up the other book. 'This one's in French. *Psychologie Mystique*. I had lent it to one of the brothers, and went to pick it up this morning.'

'What's it about? Gnostic psychology, or what?'

'Yes. I think that's the closest description.'

'What's in it?'

'Lots of things, including Cognisance of Meaning and Man's Essence ... It's an extraordinarily large field, hardly known here in the West. But in the East, we have a great deal on the subject, from Mowlana, Attar, Hafez, and many others.'

'I see. Nothing on the brain, though?'

He laughs. 'No ... The science of the brain's structure and its functions and all that, is a part of modern knowledge and technology ... But today it is slowly being realized that there is a connection between an entity called "the man's brain" and an entity called "the universe" ... 18th Century scientists compared the human brain with the gears and wheels of a clock. Then, in the 19th, they likened it to the working of an electrical system. Today, they think of it as a huge and extremely complex computer that operates on electricity and chemistry. God knows what they will compare it with in the 21st Century. But the question is: Will man ever advance to the point where he sees "nothing but God"?'

'Go on, Brother Yazdani ...'

'You should naturally be interested in these sorts of problems.'

'You always surprise me.'

'Is that good or bad?'

'Good ... Have you taken up studying about the human brain and psychology etc., for Sorraya's sake?'

'Miss Sorraya has been the cause of it ...' He smiles.

'What are your feelings towards Sorraya, may I ask?'

He suddenly blushes as red as a strawberry. He raises his cup to his lips, takes a sip, then breathes in. I take out my cigarettes, pick one out, and offer one to him. He makes use of this as a chance to delay before speaking. finally, he just says, 'Miss Sorraya's accident can imply . . . and signify . . . many symbolic things, for all of us.'

'Oh? Imply and signify what?'

'You know,' he takes a deeper breath, 'the centre of thinking and of consciousness is in the brain. And of course this power of thinking, and this recognition of meaning, varies continually. But the enormity of the brain lies not just in its biological structure and its enormous capacities in various functions. Just as one cannot appreciate the significance of the Sistine Chapel in Florence in terms of the number of bricks, or the amount of plaster and lime used in its construction. What the scientists have so far been able to establish, is that there exists a sort of a nerve code and the brain records external concepts in millisecond sparks and milligrams of chemical substances . . .' He stopped, frowning thoughtfully. 'Let's put it this way – an average human brain contains a quadrillion complete and complex computers . . .'

I give a whistle.

'But, remember, that even the most complex computers, capable of taking on infinite data calculation, processing different sets of information simultaneously, and even of decision-making, cannot have *feelings*, or logic, or be aroused spiritually. They have no creative powers or motives, or other such things. But most important of all, they cannot have *faith* . . . Whereas man's brain – in addition to its astronomical numbers of mini-computers, has all these things as well.'

I whistled again.

'And now, we come to the two main points: Firstly, what is the ultimate knowledge this brain can achieve? The answer, in my opinion is the study of the universe, and divinity. In other words, we have all the answers in here.' He taps the corner of one eyebrow. 'We–just–have–to–decode–it!' He falls silent, allowing the enormity of this revelation to percolate into my brain.

I take a deep drag on my cigarette. 'Well, what's the second point?' I ask.

'The second main point is, why is consciousness sometimes suddenly cut off, as in Sorraya Khanum's case? The simple, *biological* cause, of course, is that a *physical* obstacle in the

210

actual brain is causing a disorder in the organ's normal functions.'

'Isn't this what the problem is?'

'I said the *simple, biological* cause could be this.'

'Dr Martin said they are almost sure that it's a small, but vital part of Sorraya's brain – I think he called it the *nucleus basalis* – that has been damaged.'

'Yes. But there could be other explanations.'

'What other explanations?'

'Another explanation could be that the brain has cut off its communications with the outside world under an Almighty will –'

'Wait a minute now . . . You mean . . . Sorraya's brain received an order from God Almighty for her to fall off the bicycle? Or, after she fell off the bicycle, she got the order to cut herself off from the outside world – and now she is carrying out this command?'

'Exactly, or something like it.' He smiles.

I smile too, and look at my watch. It is almost ten. 'My dear brother Yazdani,' I say, 'instead of just a meagre quadrillion neuronic connections, I need a hundred thousand quadrillion of them to try and absorb these heaven-to-earth joint operations . . . Would you like another *café-au-lait*?'

'No, thank you . . . But you see, this is where we enter the realm of mystical psychology, and the divine secrets and mysteries that exist between God and man – and it takes a certain power to be able to fathom these mysteries.'

'Yes . . . *faith*.'

'Exactly. And when the brain is possessed with the power of faith, God alone knows what capabilities it can have!' He still hasn't answered my question of what are his feelings about Sorraya, but I know.

'Well,' I say, 'may it be God's will for Sorraya to get well again so that we can all head back for Tehran. I'm sure that when my sister sees how you have given every help you can, and even brought flowers every day while Sorraya was in a coma – she will be more than impressed and grateful for your extraordinary gentlemanly behaviour.'

'My scant services have been for God's sake. By the way, how is the problem of getting University insurance for the hospital fee going?'

'We've made out a request, and the University authorities have agreed. Now I've sent it to the aliens office, and – like they say – "it's being *processed*". There's just one problem. Sorraya had finished her studies months ago – and, because of the war, and the closing down of the airports, she stayed on here after her visa expired – and didn't have it extended.'

'They are being strict on these matters as far as the Iranians are concerned, now.'

'But I've promised myself not to bring any money from my sister out of Tehran . . . There is some of Sorraya's gold jewellery here, from her marriage – I can sell that and pay the hospital fees, if we have to.'

'I can raise however much money you need from the kids at the Islamic Centre here, with just one word,' Qassem Yazdani offers.

'Come on. Most of the poor kids here haven't a penny to their names. But thank you, seriously.'

'These very kids are the real self-sacrificers.'

'Oh, I'm sure . . . Thank you, *Aqaye* Azdani.'

In the hospital, Sorraya is still in the Intensive Care Unit. Qassem Yazdani and I are not allowed in. I try to find one of the hospital workers to ask whether the treatment has been given to Sorraya yet, but I don't find anyone I know. I am told that Dr Martin has not been in this morning, but that Dr Monet saw the patient at eight o'clock, and will be back at twelve-thirty. We start saying goodbye at the entrance doors.

'You know,' Qassem Yazdani says, 'Ayatollah Taleqani once said that anything – absolutely anything – is possible, where there is *faith*.'

'That's something I see very little of, here.'

'Have faith, and everything will be well.'

'I'm sure you say that in complete faith, yourself.'

'Well, goodbye. You will be back this evening?'

'I should be around here somewhere.'

'Go with God.'

25

Someone's waving to me from a red car parked outside the iron gates of the hospital's eastern entrance. Her face is pale behind large, dark sunglasses and under a black beret, pulled down over one ear. She is also wearing a black leather jacket. It is Leila.

'Miss Azadeh!'

'Say *bonjour*, and I'll scream!'

'What's happened?'

'*Selles*!' She is in a hell of a temper, all right.

'What are you doing here?'

'My head . . . It's killing me.' Her enormous dark glasses are weird. In the centre of each lens is a little square of plain, colourless glass. She is like some science fiction creature from another galaxy.

'Haven't you slept since last night?' I ask.

'Why? My eyes show it?'

'You're still wearing that printed yellow dress under your _'

'*Viens ici*!' she orders, opening the door on my side. 'Come here!'

I get into the car. There is an urgency in her voice that is frightening.

'You scared me, there! . . .'

'How's Sorraya?'

'Still in the IC Unit.'

'Who was that you were talking to? The bearded one with the paramilitary jacket?'

'Sorraya's friend. He's a good kid. We were talking about *Psychologie Mystique*.'

'Jalal!'

'You asked who I was talking to.'

'Where are you going now?'

'Me? No place special.' Then I add, 'I have to be back here by twelve.'

'My head,' she says again. I wonder if she might have taken something, or done something to herself, and is now looking for help.

'Do you want to go a little further up and park somewhere on Rue d'Ulm? We can go somewhere and have a coffee.'

'No – I can't!'

'Why?'

'I want to die!'

'Leila, please.'

'Close that door!'

I slam the damn door shut. She turns the ignition key without having her foot on the clutch pedal. The engine is in gear and the car leaps forward with a jolt, and chokes. The keys fall from her hand to the floor of the car. 'Ah – damn it!' Her hands are shaking. I pick up the key ring and hand it to her. With my face close to hers, I can smell the fumes of tobacco and alcohol. The gay, laughing, talkative – almost feverish – mood of the night before, is gone. In its place, a bitter, manic-depressive, hopeless state – or maybe something even more dangerous.

'Did you go to the hotel?' I ask, trying to keep up a conversation.

'I called. They said you were out. I came here.'

'Good. Where are we going?'

'Let's go to Pari's house.'

'All right.'

'Thank you. *Fou* . . .'

'Well, and what's going on there?'

'*Selles*!' This was a part of Mademoiselle Adèle Françoise Mitterand's language. Leila changes gear, and turns the ignition key again. This time the engine doesn't start at all. She tries several times, but it is useless.

'Jalal, can you get this jalopy going?' she asks.

'Sure.'

I get out and cross to the driver's side, Leila scrambles over. I get into the driver's seat and using the choke get the car started. I let the motor run for a while, then release the hand brake. There is an old, long-expired International Driver's Licence at the bottom of one of my packets somewhere, but I do not care about that today. 'I've got an International Driver's Licence,' I say to reassure her. 'Dating from some years BC.'

'Oh, who gives a damn!'

'Where do we go?'

'Passy-No. 37. Turn into Boulevard Raspail here, and go across the Pont de Concorde. I'll tell you where to go after that.'

'Good girl! You be my co-pilot. And I'll be Charles Lindbergh.'

The fuel tank indicator is standing at Empty. The engine is not tuned, it knocks, and the timing is wrong. I get out and raise the bonnet. I take a look at the water in the radiator, and the oil. There is very little oil, the cylinder heads are leaking; the radiator tank is nearly empty, spark-plugs dirty, dynamo and starter need cleaning and the fan-belt is slack, also the battery needs charging. I get back into the car.

'How does it look?' Leila asks.

'It's fine!'

'It's in terrible shape!'

'How the devil did you drive this thing here, girl?'

'It's that bad?'

'You need petrol, oil and water. The spark plugs don't spark. The generator doesn't generate. The radiator doesn't radiate. The carburettor doesn't carburett, and the battery doesn't batt. Otherwise, everything's fine!'

She chuckles. 'Let's leave the thing here and go by taxi. I'll send a mechanic along for it tomorrow.'

'Shsh! Have faith! We'll get it fixed up at the nearest petrol station.'

I manage to get the car going, somehow.

'You had a hell of a good time last night, it seems.'

'The end was nauseating.'

'Hekmat went to your place?'

'Yes, he's still there.'

'How long did everyone stay at the gala gathering?'

'Jean Edmond left early. The rest stayed till three, three-thirty.' She is silent for a while. Then she says, 'You know, I've lived here for years and I never knew people had switch-phones in their houses.'

'And just what is a switch-phone?'

'I've been having a row with the blasted French telephone system since four in the morning. *"Bonjour, Madame! Bonjour, Madame! Un moment, Madame! Je regrette, Madame. Bonjour, Madame!"* I mean, I didn't know people could switch off their damned phone, so it wouldn't ring.'

'And how did you make this grand and glorious discovery?'

'I rang, and rang, and after the thousandth call, I asked the operator to please connect me, and they said the number you're dialling is in order, but it has been switched off.'

'Aha – here's a petrol station – *Esso Station Service* ... and there's hardly a car in it!'

We pull in. 'Let me do it,' says Leila, starting to get out.

'You sit tight. Just tell me which is the key to the petrol tank.'

'Only if you pay from my purse. Do you understand?'

There are about ten or twelve petrol pumps, and a small garage where the oil is changed, and there are compressed air pumps. A young lad in clean white overalls comes to help. First we fill up the tank, and then get the rest sorted out. I pay him three hundred and twenty francs out of Leila's purse, which contains some seventeen or eighteen thousand francs in cash, and three or four different credit cards.

Leila has gone to sleep when I get back into the car. Half asleep she purrs and clings to my arm and breathes a sigh of relief.

'How easy everything is with you.'

'I'm easy. Do we keep going to the end of Raspail?'

'Yes. But sometimes you are not so easy.'

'I'm easy.'

She sighs deeply again, and retreats within herself. Her manic-depressive manner is gone and her voice is calmer. We drive on in silence, for a while.

'Why don't you want to stay here and make an eternal wife out of me, as they say?' she asks.

I look into her face, in silence.

'Well, why not, hm?'

'All right.'

'Why not?'

216

'Leila – you know how I feel about you.'

'You don't *want* to?'

'We had this discussion years ago. You know *you* didn't want to.'

'That was years ago.'

'With people, things never change.'

'Why don't you want to?'

'I never said I didn't.'

'You said all right.'

'Don't you want Hekmat to make "an eternal wife" out of you, now?'

'It's only his halo of fame that attracted me to him.'

'Oh? And what do I have?'

'You're just something else. You really need a wife and family, Jalal.'

'Like you?'

'Like any wife and family.'

'Right now, I need a wife and family the way someone addicted to antibiotics needs a disease.'

She laughs. 'It's not that bad.'

'No ... It's worse!'

The sun is now shining through the clouds hanging over the river. It is bitter cold, though. The wind shakes the naked tree branches. Leila Azadeh remains quiet for a while but she still seems ill and removed from reality.

'You're right,' she says. 'If you'd married me, I wouldn't have loved you like this, today.'

The way she says this is like saying if I'd bought that pair of red shoes, it wouldn't have matched my new hand-bag.

'Is this the Pont de la Concorde?'

'Yes, but make a turn here – go left.'

'You said *cross* over at Concorde.'

'No, don't cross the bridge! I've changed my mind. Turn left here, and keep going along the bank. Go across the Pont de l'Alma.'

'You're sure?'

'Yes, once we're across, turn right. Sorry left.'

'Left again?'

'Yes, the Avenue de New York. Further on it becomes the Avenue de President Kennedy.'

'Then turn left at the first crossing.'

'Left at the first crossing.'

'Ah ... Stop being a tease!'

'All right.'

'You see that tall building? It's the Radio France Building. Jean Edmond's house is just further on, in the Avenue de Victor Hugo.'

'I see. Good for him.' Damn Jean Edmond.

Leila says, 'Here ... This is the place.'

The place is a multi-storeyed, cylindrical building, ultra-modern. At first sight, it resembles a 12th Century tower or fortress made of reinforced concrete, with steel doors – quite incredible. But it is Paris, where nothing is incredible.

Leila Azadeh is now in a somewhat better mood.

'Is this Pari's house?' I ask.

'Only a flat on the third floor!'

'Do you park right out in the front here?'

'Yes, anywhere.' Then, 'Come in,' she adds, no longer commanding, just pleading now.

'Shall I?'

'Yes. Come in, it's all right. Thanks for bringing a crazy, mixed-up girl home. You must come in for a coffee. I insist!'

It is eleven-thirty by the clock over the dashboard. 'All right.'

'Come on, Mr All Right. You can take the car to the hospital, which means you'll have to come back to me this evening. I want to see you and keep you till I'm tired of you. I'm fine now – in every way.'

'Don't you have to see Hekmat?'

'Genevieve is there, she'll look after him. Besides, Hekmat's got a date with Dr Kuhsar for lunch – they're going to Fontainebleau.'

She manages to get the entrance door open with some key, and we take the lift. She opens the door, leading the way into a large, ultra-modern decorated apartment.

'Where's the hostess?' I ask.

'Oh, Pari and Dariush Farhad left for the Riviera at three o'clock this morning.'

'The Riviera!'

'Yes, the sneaks. Anyway, I'm going to fix that coffee. Unless you want something else?'

'Coffee's fine.'

'I ought to have a bath, but I can't be bothered. I can't be bothered to do anything.'

'That doesn't include coffee, I hope?'

'Of course not. How do you like your coffee?'

'Raw!'

She laughs, for the first time today. 'Have you started the New Year off on that foot, too?'

Like a lost ghost, she wanders off in the direction of the kitchen, I think. I take off my raincoat, and toss it over one of the stools at the bar-buffet. There is a vast array of coloured liqueur and wine bottles – with a collection of glasses, mugs and decanters and other decorative odds and ends. I sit down by the telephone – which is ashen and orange colour, to tone with the room's general colour scheme. It has digital numbers, you need only touch each number lightly, and it 'beeps' quietly in reply. On the top page of the notepad beside the phone, is written 'Jean-Edmond–Paris–123-7654, No. 194 Ave de Victor Hugo-near the Rue de Longchamps-Ap. 9-C.' First, I dial the Charnaut's number; and I wish them a Happy New Year. They are planning to go to the hospital this afternoon at two o'clock. I tell them I will be there then, too. I am just about to call the hospital, when Leila comes in with a tray of coffee, cake, and a green bottle of Pernod.

I arrive at the hospital at about one-thirty. Qassem Yazdani is there, with two other boys and two girls, all friends of Sorraya's. The girls are wearing scarves, and one of the boys is almost like Yazdani – clean, but ragged looking.

Charnaut and his wife arrive at two o'clock, and we speak with Dr Monet for a while. The *cardiaque electro-cystolique* has not yet been necessary, despite the signs of further weakness in Sorraya's cardiograms, blood pressure and respiration. Dr Monet says this mild shock treatment has been successful in recent years in the US hospitals, in cases like Sorraya's. With Dr Martin's departure and the coming to power of Dr Monet, changes are taking place in the ward. Martin used to say "Wait", but Monet believes one must take new, decisive steps. In his opinion, the hospital must not keep a patient in a state of limbo. He demands positive action.

I stay at the hospital with the others until four-thirty or five o'clock, then, as there is nothing to be done, and everyone else is gone, I also leave. I am worried about Leila, and I still have to return her car.

It is getting dark when I drive back to Passy. Leila does not answer the intercom. I sort through the keys for the one that opens the front door, and finally let myself in.

Leila is nowhere to be seen. It is dusk, everywhere is silent. Calling her name, I search everywhere – except behind the locked door of what must be the bathroom. 'Leila!' I call. There is no answer, but I can then hear what sounds like a throaty breathing, or a quiet snoring. 'Leila!' I call in a louder voice, 'Are you there?'

Then I hear a noise, like someone tumbling in a tub full of water.

26

'Leila ...'

There is still no answer. I rap hard on the door with my knuckles.

'For God's sake, Leila! You in there?'

There is a 'Mmm ...', then, Leila's voice comes, 'Yes, yes ... I'm here.'

'Are you all right?'

'Yes ... I ... I fell asleep.'

'Leila – get out, put some clothes on and come out here. I want to see you.'

'I'm all right ... Don't worry.'

I swear at myself, tossing the keys on the table. I am almost about to leave.

'The keys are on the table,' I say.

'Wait, wait!'

'I'm still here.'

'It's dark in here ... dark as hell.'

'Turn the light on, for *God's* sake! The switch is inside.'

'Oh, yes ...'

'Turn on the light and open the door.'

It is a very long time before Leila opens the door and comes out. A towel is wrapped around her hair. She is wearing a bathrobe and a pair of trousers. She leans against the door-frame. Her face is blank, and her eyes look even more sunken than before, like a scared, beaten child. I don't know if it because she is drunk, drugged, or both.

'Oh, Jalal. If you hadn't come in,' she says, 'I'd've been dead by now.'

'Oh, God!'

'It's ... crazy, isn't it?' She also looks as if she's been crying. It is a side of Leila I never did understand.

'What happened anyway?'

'Nothing; I went to have a bath – I stretched out in the warm water, had a drink, and a few cigarettes, and then fell aleep.'

I breathe a sigh of relief, shaking my head. 'Are you all right now?'

'Oh, yes ... What an ass I am! I wanted to make myself pretty for when you got back. Now look at me. What a hideous sight! And you have to come in here and find me in the tub, snoring and drowning. But, I'm fine, you know ... in every way. Come.'

'You're still asleep.'

She moves to the bar, I go near her, I guess to catch her when she falls.

'How was your patient?' she says, 'Sorraya.'

'Weaker. They moved her to the Cardiac Care Unit today, for *electro-cystolique* stimulation, or whatever it is.'

'Oh, the poor thing! How long has she been in a coma, now?' She fumbles with the bottles.

'Nearly four months.'

Leila draws a deep breath, that breaks into a sob. 'And it's four years for *me* since *I* picked up a pen!'

'You can pick up a pen and create a masterpiece at any moment, Leila ... If you put your mind to it.'

'Don't try to push me back into that mirage, my love. Didn't you see what a shape I was in, this morning. Or a little while ago?'

'Well, what really happened a little while ago?'

'Did I give you a fright?'

'I've seen worse!'

'It wasn't any stupid suicide business, I swear! That's one thing I hate. I'm not too crazy about a lot of the things I do but I hate suicide. If I have to die, let it be sudden. Not bit by bit. I'll never welcome death. I'll die hard.'

'Come and sit down, oh Leila. Have a smoke and try to be logical for a minute. For the love of the God of your ancestors! What more could you want here? What's wrong? You are one of the luckiest people I know. Here, free, do what you want. Everything to your pleasure. Everyone loves you.'

'Don't tease me.'

'I'm not . . . think about it.'

She comes to me and sits on a soft chair, one leg dangling limply. She accepts the cigarette I offer her from the inlaid wooden cigarette box. I sit facing her.

'I'm so lucky I'm going to puke. I'm degenerating and rotting away . . . Who loves me?' She asks with a smile.

"Nader Parsi!'

'Devil take him! I just as soon have a frog. Don't tease me!' She laughs.

'What did you do with Hekmat?'

'I called . . . He said he was going to Dijon with Kuhsar and his wife – and Jean Edmond!'

'With Jean Edmond?'

'With Jean Edmond.'

She says this as though they had kidnapped darling Jean Edmond and they were going to molest him.

'Well, they'll be back,' I say. 'What the hell is supposed to be going on in Dijon?'

'There's a Professor Tabataba'i in Dijon who's got tons of opium.

'Good! When are they coming back?'

'I don't know. I don't know what to do.'

'Worry! But they'll be back, dead or alive.'

'Dead, I hope!'

The phone rings. I pick up the receiver and hand it to Leila. She tries to put it to her ear, and drops it. I pick it up again, and hand it to her again.

'*Allo*,' she says. 'Oh, *Salaam*, Pari . . . Yes, I'm still here . . . No. I'm fine . . . No, he's gone to Dijon with Dr Kuhsar. I came over to have a bath, and I'm still here . . . I'm fine, really . . . Guess who's here now? . . . No, he's gone to Dijon with Hekmat and Kuhsar . . . I'll tell you later . . . So tell me, what have you been doing? . . . No! . . .' She listens for a while, and I can see that she is almost fainting again. She listens for about a minute longer, just barely sitting up. Then she says, 'Pari . . . give me your hotel number, I'll call you back later . . .' She repeats a number, then a room number. I jot them down on the pad for her, under Jean Edmond's number and address, and add 'Sissy' underneath. She puts down the receiver and looks at me bleary-eyed.

'Leila,' I say. 'Get dressed and we'll go out for a walk.'

223

'Oh, hell!' She stubs out her almost untouched cigarette. 'I can hardly sit up, let alone go walking.'

'The cold air will do you good. So will a nice long walk.'

'You know what would go down well now?'

'The *ascenseur*!'

'No, silly. A dozen of those hash cigarettes Nader Parsi gave us, that night.'

'The Cloudland things? . . .'

'Do you have any with you?'

'No.'

'I've got some but they're not so good.'

'Better than nothing. Where are they?'

She produces a packet from her dressing-gown pocket.

'So these are what you knocked out yourself with?'

'These . . . and other things.'

'What other things?'

She gets up, and goes into the bathroom, returning with the half-full bottle of Pernod. She unscrews the top, and pours herself a slug. 'You still on doctor's orders?'

'This cigarette is fine.'

She looks at me, and draws a deep breath. Her pretty forehead, her slender eyebrows and puffy, drawn eyelids have been made up like an American film star. 'So it's just Nader Parsi who loves me, eh?'

'He's rickety about you.'

'Stuff him. He can't even sleep with his own wife.'

'And where did you get that sex intelligence, may I ask?'

'I've heard it here and there, from people who are well acquainted with the Parsis' personal lives. You want to hear?'

'No!'

'His wife won't sleep with him. They've spent one hundred and eighty thousand francs doing up the bedroom with a complete set of Louis XV furniture, mind you. But Sara takes a blanket and sleeps in a corner of the living room, rather than be with Parsi.'

'Nothing wrong with that.'

'Or with her sister.'

'Go on.'

Leila laughs. 'You've seen how they behave in front of

company. She just needs an audience, and she's off; making a jackass of Parsi, playing the "See what an ass he is" game.' She giggles again.

After two or three drags on the cigarette, I'm beginning to feel better myself. I feel more light-headed.

'I've heard Safavi's wife's a marvel.'

'*Khanom* Nosrat Safavi is a lulu!'

'Safavi himself told me his wife was an ass.'

'I'll tell you something that'll make you burst your sides, Jalal. Last year – ugh! These things make my mouth taste bitter – last year, I went to Stuttgart with Abbas Hekmat and Pari and this Doctor Sussan Kargar. There was a Conference or something there, on Persian poetry. We went to Safavi's house for dinner one night. His wife had made a *khoresh-fesenjun* for us. His wife is from Qomsheh, somewhere near Isfahan. There was also *ash-sholeqalamkar*, with about three inches of sheep-fat and fried onions floating on the top. There was *beriyuni* and tomato kabab and on flat Turkish bread, all covered in at least a finger's width of fat – supposedly, as an "*hors d'oeuvres*". When we were all seated round the table, his wife suddenly jumps and cries, "Oh my gosh, I forgot the paper napkins!" And off she runs and brings a roll of toilet paper, which she plonks smack in the middle of the table for everyone to use ... Pari and I were practically dying with laughter!'

I drag deeper on my cigarette.

'Why don't you laugh? Wasn't it funny?'

'Today is the first day of the New Year, girl. Think positively of goodwill to all men in the future world.'

'Don't you think it was *funny*?'

'I'm not sure whether it was funny or tragic.' I take another puff of the cigarette. 'This damn thing isn't so bad, after all.'

'Safavi seems to be making plans already for the hundred and fifty thousand or so francs you're planning to send from Iran.'

'Guess so.'

'Has he offered or said anything definite?'

'He said he can use rials in Iran – to send government-rate exchange for his kids' college tuition in Germany.'

'Kids my foot! Old racoons! They're all in their late twenties and thirties ... How's your cigarette?'

'About as bad as Cloudland 2000 . . . Nader Parsi was making plans, too. He said his uncle can sell me francs at two rials cheaper than the current black market rate.'

'I'll bet. It's his own money.'

'He himself wants to swap his own house for a publishing outfit in Tehran. His house is in danger of being confiscated. Then he'd easily sell the publishing outfit and transfer the money out here. Then he's got his house here. If he doesn't sell his house by February 20th, his French ex-wife may get a court order and claim it from him. He wants to sell out.'

'Bugger him!'

'Aren't you hungry?'

'Yes.'

'Let me fix you something.'

'No, thanks. Really.'

'You scared I'll blow up the kitchen?'

'Yes!'

She giggles. 'Let me telephone and have something brought up.'

'I could go out and scrounge a couple of sandwiches.'

'Hand me that phone, and stop being silly! This is Paris, France!'

'I never said it was Bangladesh.'

She drains her umpteenth glass, and sets it down on the table.

I pick up the telephone. Before handing it to her, though, I first dial the number of the Hotel Palma. Sumunju herself answers. I give her the apartment's telephone number, and ask her to call me here if something important comes up. Then I hand the telephone over to Leila.

She is gradually coming out of her manic-depressive mood and is swaying into the manic-talkative-energetic phase. She dials a number; her French is impeccable, and she now exchanges biddy-buddy pleasantries with a creature by the name of Jean-Jacques, as though she were back in Shiraz back-alleys, saying a how-d-ye-do to Mash Mohammad Ali the local butcher.

'I want you to send some things over, Jean-Jacques. Oh, yes, it was good, *merci*. Very well, *merci*. You too. I have company . . . yes. Special, of course.' Then she listens, for a while. 'What, what do you have, that is really good tonight, eh? Yes, we'll start with an appetizer, yes, some of your own special hors d'oeuvres, for, make it three or four people, yes. She goes on, ordering enough for a full-scale banquet. Fish? Let me see . . . caviare, salmon; and turkey breast, no duck, a little partridge, and . . . yes, small mushrooms, cauliflower . . . of course some lamb, some beef . . . some *Roquefort*, yes. No, we've got plenty of drinks . . . thank you, Jean-Jacques. And there's no hurry!'

She covers the receiver with one hand, turning to me. 'What about beer? Can you drink that?' I shake my head.

'The only thing we haven't got here is beer; I can have Jean-Jacques bring some over if you'd like –'

'No.'

'Are you sure? . . ."Come fill the cup to the brim" . . .'

'Later.'

Leila thanks Jean-Jacques again, says *au revoir*, and hangs up. Then she says, 'There's a Hossein Abpak here . . . you might have seen him. He used to work for Iran TV back in the good old days, in Tehran. Writes poetry too. And he translates. You've seen him, haven't you?'

'He was filling me in on Hekmat's biography last night.'

'He migrated from Iran for the love of beer. Without at least twenty cans per day Hossein Abpak drops dead.'

'Have you counted?'

'It's gospel truth, believe me! In Tehran, his navel cord was tied to Shams Beer Brewery. Everyone swore to that. He'd stop off on his way to work every morning, for a hot dog and some beer.'

'No gossip, Leila. Please!'

She laughs. 'All right.'

Before dinner arrives, Leila disappears into one of the rooms and reappears in a pair of black Japanese or Philippino pyjamas, which gives her eyes and face an even more alien, more remote look. She comes up close to me. 'I'm fine now, in every sense. Know what I mean?'

At about eight o'clock, Jean-Jacques emerges with the supper extravaganza. He's little but swift, the bow tie balanced on his adam's apple, and a white towel draped over one wrist.

In Station No. 12, Ahmadabad, in the trenches, the kids had two things to eat; tinned baked beans and tinned compote pears. At noon, they opened the tin of beans and ate them cold. In the evening they had the pears in the same way. When they were really famished, they would empty the compote on top of the beans on a plate, and eat the whole lot at once. It did not taste so bad, either.

Jean-Jacques himself brings the trays in, and arranges the food on the table in a fine, elegant manner. There is just enough to feed an entire hungry battalion, and still have some left over. Leila signs the chit, and Jean-Jacques, with his tip and his hearty thanks, vanishes into the Paris night.

Leila eats nothing, only toying with this and that; but she hardly sets down her glass or the cigarettes for a minute, and occasionally complains of dizziness, feeling faint, and of sudden, gripping chest pains.

I take my pills before dinner, and then give the old stomach a royal treat. Leila, along with her chattering about this book and that writer, points out the name of each delicacy as I eat it, like the guide on a tour of the Museum of Epicurean History – in case I were to mistake the partridge for turkey or – heaven forbid! – spread mayonnaise on my sweet corn instead of on the chicken supreme. I eat, allowing Leila, meanwhile, to play zithers on my eardrums with her words. She talks about *emigré* writers, poets, and translators, dissidents, hopping from one subject to the next, like a grasshopper.

After dissecting Parsi, Safavi and Hossein Abpak, she goes on to tell me of the life and work of Bijan Karimpur, the once-famous modern poet, who has opened a school here in Paris. Apart from making his living teaching Persian to the children of dissident Iranians, Karimpur tries to promulgate the schools of Marxism and Socialism. But he is really a great fellow, an absolute traditionalist. At the crack of dawn, he brews himself a pot of Darjeeling tea, and studies for several hours. It's got to be Darjeeling, nothing else will do. Now, only after an argument with his wife, when he is sulking, does he write anything. Or he takes a whack at painting a surrealistic or even impressionistic picture. Admiring fans purchase his paintings believing that, some day, they will become immortal keepsakes. Here, in Paris, Karimpur is almost something of an undeclared leader-in-exile, a source of inspiration. He has written a long poem about a white-bearded old man who returns to his homeland after years of exile. Only it is not quite clear whether it is meant to be Vladimir Ilych Lenin, returning to Petrograd from Germany by a sealed train, or Master Bijan Karimpur, returning to Tehran from Paris, in a chartered 727 Air France Boeing! Anyway, Leila goes on hashing and rehashing this one's wife, and that one's husband; shredding and discarding them, one by one. From time to time, she stops to ask, 'Jalal, oh, you don't think I'm ruining myself with this sort of talk, do you?' And I assure her I think nothing of the sort.

At nine-thirty in the evening, when it is time for the Midnight News from Tehran, I bring the small transistor radio and set it on shortwave, and tune in. I put the radio on the table, next to Leila's bottle of Pernod, so that she can have it close at hand, and listen if she likes. As usual, there is nothing but talk of bloodshed and martyrdom and bombs and the killing – together with the usual war propaganda – the unfair and 'imposed war' on the 'martyr-breeding nation'. Leila Azadeh gets upset again after listening to such words – which I think she must be hearing for the first time. Her talkative, vivacious mood gives way once again to depression. She begins to feel bad, and even gets the gripes. After ten-thirty, though, once she has called Pari again, and chatted to her sister – because she is very fond of her – about clothes, pills, cosmetics, and what each one is doing, right now, Leila begins to cheer up and feel better once more. Later, she starts chattering about the wonderful, artistic Persian films of Dariush Farhad, Pari's lover. Farhad made films only to win *festivals*, not for any other purpose. Farhad had a wife, whom he had left in San Francisco. Then he had married a rich American widow, in Paris, who had 'kicked the bucket' in an automobile accident. He is a truly wonderful creature though, fantastic, this Dariush Farhad.

We spend the next thirty-six hours in more or less the same way.

I hoped now that I was beginning to feel better myself, maybe Sorraya's condition, too, will somehow begin to change for the better. I hoped, as Christienne Charnaut once said, the symbolistic portents in 'planting', 'growing' and 'egg-laying', might come true.

27

But on the 4 January, at two p.m., Sorraya is taken to the Cardiac Care Unit for *electro-cystolique*. Although the therapy has a positive effect that night, there is no overall change in Sorraya's general condition, and her charts and graphs continue their usual downward fall for the rest of the week. On the evening of the 6th, the therapy is repeated, again with the same results. Or the same lack of results.

I telephone Farangis and tell her the news. I call her once on the evening of the 4th, and the next evening, at around nine o'clock, she herself calls from Tehran. I can imagine how she sits there waiting by the phone, till eleven thirty, waiting to hear whatever small, hopeful news she can get from Paris, while sciatic pain burns her leg – although she never speaks or complains about it.

In Iran, the grim course of the war and the Iraqis' savage attacks on the southern and western cities, towns and villages, continue. Now, at the beginning of 1981, the Iraqis have taken over a large section of Kermanshah Province, near Qasr-e-Shirin, a large section of the Province of Ilam, including the Dasht-e-Abbas area, the whole western strip of Khuzestan, including the towns of Dehloran, Susangerd, Bostan and Hamidieh, the Hamid Sentry Post, and the territories within ten kilometres of Ahvaz and 25 kilometres of Dezful. Khorram-Shahr is the only large city under complete Iraqi occupation. After giving up all hope of being able to capture Abadan, the Iraqis are now destroying it, systematically, day and night. Bigger news in Tehran, these days, is of the negotiations for the release of the American Embassy hostages.

In Paris, the not-so-carefree lives of the Iranian *emigrés* and refugees continue. After her depressed, suicidal behaviour during the week-end, and our brief time together, I see Leila only once or twice, during all of the following week, once on Monday evening when she comes to the hospital. Then, I don't see her again until the second weekend in January. Nader Parsi and his uncle turn up at the hotel once or twice to talk about money. I ask them to give me another week, because I had taken steps through the University, the Prefect of Police, the Passport Office and the Iranian Consulate, the results of which were yet to come. Safavi has gone to Vienna, but is coming back. Hekmat is back from Dijon, and is still living in Leila's apartment, so I hear. Leila and her sister, Pari, who has just returned from the Riviera, are still apparently on loving terms. I see Leila, Hekmat and Pari in the Café Danton, with their friend, General Dr Qa'em Maqami Fard and the inevitable Jean Edmond. The talk is still of Leila accompanying Hekmat when he returns to London in early February. Pari Azadeh thinks a change of climate and scenery will do dear Leila a world of good. Hekmat believes Leila's presence in London will be of inestimable help in the 'Translation of the great Persian Classic texts' which he has undertaken. Leila now looks more towards Jean Edmond than towards Hekmat.

I have no count of how many times I walk down the decrepit Monsieur le Prince into the vast Luxembourg Square, these days, down the damned Guy Lussac, along the bastard Rue Saint Jacques, to the *Hôpital* du Val de Grace, in this bride of all the world's cities. One day I go to the Iranian Islamic Republic Consulate in Avenue George V, to the Passport Renewal Section. Not only has Sorraya no valid French residence permit, her own passport has long expired.

The doors and windows of the Consulate building are covered with posters of *Imam* Khomeini and various Islamic Revolution slogans and propaganda. Somewhere, on the closed door, is a notice, typed in Persian, announcing that passport renewals are dealt with *only* when documents are *sent by post*. A renewal procedure takes a *minimum* of three weeks. After passing a mob of applicants, several policemen and guards, I manage to ring some doorbell – Sorraya's case is an emergency, an exception, and I have with me a letter from the hospital, in which her condition is specified, I explain to the guards. I wish to speak to the 'brother' in charge of the passport renewals, about urgent business. They accept. All right, wait.

A bearded brother comes out and listens benevolently to my explanations. He examines Sorraya Naqavi's passport and other papers. He examines my own passport and other papers, too. He then lets me go in after a not-so-thorough bodysearch. In the reception hall, he asks another brother to show me to brother Parastu'i's room.

Brother Parastu'i's office is a tiny room on the ground floor – behind a very large room in which fifteen or sixteen brothers and 'Islamically' clad and concealed sisters squirm around attending to mounds of passports and files piled on the floor. There is not a spot on the walls which is not covered by posters and propaganda slogans. The brother guiding me sends me into the large room amidst the brothers and sisters working on the floor. I start searching for Brother Parastu'i. A young fellow stands up. 'Can I help you, brother?' he asks. 'Are you Brother Parastu'i?' I ask. He does not deny it. 'Can I help you?' Again, I introduce myself explaining Sorraya's case. He has fair skin, a short, reddish-blond beard and moustaches, and fine, gentle, hazel eyes, like Qassem Yazdani. His grey shirt is well-worn, and he wears baggy, paramilitary, khaki trousers and slippers. He, too, listens to what I have to say good-naturedly. He has 'heard' something of Sorraya and says he is sorry for her. He leads me into his little office, which is as messy and confused as the front room. He examines Sorraya's documents thoroughly. He inspects my own passport and papers thoroughly. He inspects everything thoroughly. He looks me over. I still have with me the note from the Brother Deputy Oil Minister in Tehran, commending my emergency trip to the Home Office Passport authorities; I show it to Parastu'i. From then on, everything works presto. He gives me a request form to fill out. Also, it is necessary to write out a memo describing the situation and the reason for delay. I do so. Brother Parastu'i takes a scrap of paper, and after inscribing a '*Besmehe Ta'ala*' (In his Name the Almighty) at the top, writes a few words to another fellow, Brother Mohseni, requesting him to take immediate action. 'Have you two photos of Sorraya and 50 francs with you, *Aqaye* Aryan?' I have. 'Clip those on, too, and be gracious enough to take them along to Brother Mohseni. He will see to it at once,

Insha'Allah.' Thus, something which would normally take a minimum three weeks is accomplished within fifteen minutes. With just a small catch, that while I am waiting in Brother Mohseni's office for the passport to be stamped and signed, the time for noon-time prayers, *Namaz*, and lunchbreak arrives. Everyone suddenly drops whatever they are doing, and goes to the prayer-room, on the third floor, from where the sound of *ezan* is heard, through loudspeakers. I am told to come back at two-thirty, or tomorrow. Or I can wait in the front hall.

It is pouring outside, and I don't really want to leave Sorraya's papers here with no receipt or anything. The brothers and sisters try to work with honest intention, but still, you don't feel safe about leaving unregistered documents here in these jumbled rooms. I have no particular business anyway. I wait in the front hall.

The front hall contains a few comfortable armchairs and two or three low tables. The room is warm and pleasant. Several magazines are scattered on the tables. I pick up a copy of the new women's magazine *Mahjubeh* (the *Veiled*), and sit under a poster of the *Fajr* (Dawn) of the Iranian Islamic Revolution. It is near the 11th February, the Anniversary of the Islamic Revolution victory in Iran, and the Consulate is practically crawling with commemorative posters. In a corner, an armed French policeman with a walkie-talkie sits with a smart, uniformed doorman, also French. They talk, paying no attention to me. I don't look the type to tear down the posters and rip them up or eat them. I am just waiting.

I leaf through the pages of the *Mahjubeh*. On the cover, there is a picture of a five or six year old girl, wearing a *chador*, holding a G-3 machine-gun bigger than herself. The first four or five pages are taken up by the news on the War, pictures of the battle scenes, and of the sisters' dedication and presence on the battle-fields. One page bears an article on the question of money (settled before a wedding) the groom must pay the wife if he divorces her, the 'bad problem' of traditional marriages. The next page is about the theological differences between 'international communism' and the 'European Communism' ... which I cannot make head or tail of, no matter how many times I try to read it. But the magazine's centre pages are taken up by a short story; and it is something to ponder, too. It is today's story of the people and the system. I wonder whether Hekmat and Parsi and the Clan in their Screwed-up-Generation read this – which may be a 'New Chapter' in the History of Persian Literature opening up. 'Twenty-four Hours in the Life of Fatemeh *Khanom*'. A short story by D.A. Shafaq. A precis of the story: Fatemeh *Khanom*, mother of fourteen children, is a cleaning woman on the staff of the Hotel Revolution in Ayatollah Taleqani Avenue, Tehran. She has to work, since her husband and her eldest son have been 'martyred'; they live in the south of Tehran, in a tiny two-room rented house. Fatemeh *Khanom* wakes everyone up every morning before dawn to perform the ritual ablutions and say their prayers to the call of the local Mosque's loudspeaker *ezan*. Then they say the Thursday prayers, because it is Thursday. She then drops the last seven or eight tea-leaves into the kettle, and they drink it with their breakfast of cheese and three hot *taftun* loaves. They eat listening to the 'Revolution Self-sacrificers Programme', broadcast daily on the radio, before the morning news. Two of Fatemeh *Khanom's* sons are at the war fronts. Another son, aged twelve, is also going to the front today, joining the 'Mobilization of the Meek'. Before going out to work, Fatemeh *Khanom* makes him pass under the Holy *Qoran* (a Persian custom to ensure the safety of one going on a journey), praying, wishing that he may be martyred and go to heaven. She loves them, but is *willing* to give them for Islam. Two of her daughters, who are thirteen and fourteen respectively, have left school and enrolled in the local Mosque Mobilization unit and in the Holy *Qoran* interpretation classes. Today, they also plan to enrol themselves in the local Mosque *Kommiteh* of Islamic Guards, as volunteers to marry the invalids listed with the Martyr Organization. Fatemeh *Khanom* has already given her approval for this; for their *deed*, if not as blessed as being martyred, is no less consecrated. It is midday, and Fatemeh *Khanom* is scrubbing bedsheets. When the letter arrives, her heart 'trembles with happiness'. 'With commiserations and congratulations', the letter informs her, 'another of your pure sons has reached the divine high valour of being martyred at the war fronts'. She prays to God and to Imam Hossein. She pleads that this sacrifice may be accepted. And she prays that Islam may win victory over Blasphemy

234

throughout the world. With that, she goes on with her work. In the evening, before going home, Fatemeh *Khanom* goes to the 'Literacy Movement' classes; because the Holy *Qoran* has said: 'To seek knowledge is to be faithful'. At nightfall, she returns home to her ten remaining children, and before supper (as it is a Thursday) they go to the Mosque for *Komeil* Prayers, and give devout thanks for the bounties they have received that day . . . (By God, I say to myself; Fatemeh *Khanom* is better off than my poor sister, Farangis.) There is also a 'novel' in the magazine – printed in instalments – about the holy prophet Abraham. In this week's issue, Abraham 'dumbfounds and astonishes Nimrod, the Idol of his time, in the royal Court of Oppression'! All the angels in the Heavens and the cherubim and seraphim, and the attendants of the Eternal Gardens are seething with righteous anger, for only *one* man – Abraham – on all the Earth, worships the One-God, and he is to be thrown into the flames! 'But Abraham, upright and firm as ever, without fear or fright, without even a whimper, his face unchanged . . . gives his very life for God and walks towards and into the fire with a joyous expression, his lips forming the words, '*Ya Allah, ya wahed, ya ahad, ya samad* . . .'

The fire has just turned to flowers and Nimrod has been humiliated, when I notice Brother Mohseni emerging down the stairs from the top floor of the Iranian Consulate in Paris. I follow him into his office, where Sorraya's passport renewal rigmarole is finished in six or seven minutes.

The next day is a holiday. In the afternoon Charnaut, his wife and I sit for hours on a bench in the hospital gardens, talking. Qassem Yazdani is with us, too. The children play in the sunshine. Christienne Charnaut and Qassem Yazdani discuss logic in religion, and the powers of faith versus the power of science. Qassem Yazdani avoids looking directly into Christienne Charnaut's face. Charnaut himself occasionally joins in the discussion, but not as heatedly as his wife, because he has to look after the children. Christienne Charnaut has also brought with her a little notebook belonging to Sorraya; a sort of calendar-diary, in which Sorraya has written down notes and occasional poems. I read out a couple of her poems for Christienne Charnaut at her insistence, translating them with the help of Qassem Yazdani. Christienne Charnaut, too, has started speaking of prayers and supplications, and hoping for miracles now. I, who have been taking her for a socialist, am not surprised to hear her talking this way. She tells me she says three 'Our Fathers' and three 'Hail Marys' for Sorraya before going to sleep every night. I thank her. Who cares if Christienne Charnaut is a Christian Socialist or a reckless Communist? Or if her husband is a Gaullist or a Christian Democrat? He may pray, too. I am ready to walk through Nimrod's bloody fires myself, if it saves Sorraya. I want Sorraya to recover so that I can take her home to my Farangis.

Next day we are into the second week of January and during the week I spend several really empty, lonely days. I do not even see Parsi as often as I used to. Simin Barzegar has gone back to America, and Parsi spends most of his time in court, running after his lawyer, and his ex-wife's lawyers, and trying to somehow get his house sold. There is no sign or news of Leila, and as it later turns out she has gone to Zurich with some old schoolfriends. Her sister Pari tells me this on the phone, making me *promise* not to tell Hekmat, because Leila has told Hekmat she is going to Marseilles to see her parents. I assure Pari Azadeh that Hekmat will never hear such news from me, as I never see Hekmat, and even if I did, Hekmat never condescends to speak to me anyway.

I see a few old movies in the little cinema at the top of the Monsieur le Prince. Sometimes I sit and smoke in the hotel's tiny lobby, and chat away with Sumunju or old man Duval. Duval swigs glass after glass of red wine, and Sumunju sips lemon tea. I am sure she slips a dash or two of something into it, for she gradually becomes livelier and her eyes more sympathetic. Old man Duval, like Ahmad Safavi, has all the answers and all the news, all the time. But I have seen no harm from either of them – especially not from Sumunju!

The most important social discourse in France these days centres around the ever-increasing rise of the Socialists and the gradual decline of Giscard d'Estaing and the Gaullists. The hottest item of world news is still that of the release of the American Embassy 'Nest of Spies' hostages in Tehran. Even the dirty, violent war with Iraq has not been overshadowed in Iran by the news of the hostages' release and the handing over of

Iran's foreign frozen assets.

The matter of payment for Sorraya's hospital bills, which the University authorities reported to the government by a letter, has been referred to a commission in the local council's office, which, in turn, have sent a letter to the Ministry of Justice and the Foreign Residents Bureau, asking for advice. The situation is a little less complicated than that of the American hostages and the Iranian frozen assets!

The hopeless situation of the remaining members of the Aryan family, that is Farangis, me, and Sorraya, in this world, is summarized in a paragraph in one of Farangis' letters. '. . . I sent my poor child away from this chaos and war, after her husband's death. I sent her to a school, far, far away, in a city which is the centre of peace and quiet. So that she may *live*. So that she should no longer throw herself under a shower of bullets and bombs. Then she has to fall from her bicycle and be lost to me, and now you can't even bring her home dead. Why?'

If there is a why, and an answer to it, somewhere, I do not know. It is beyond my ken.

I swear it.

Lines scribbled on pages of Sorraya's diary:

> From the skies of Iran,
> A world-catching resonance
> Goes Westward.
> Where am *I* going . . .?

> Whatever misery,
> Take it not hard upon your heart.
> Dormant tiger, lying in the sun,
> Chin on his paws.
> I love him;

> What is my share?
>   In this world . . .
>   In this house . . .
> In this hateful flooding?

> I build a dream-castle,
> Of you.
> And at dusk,

As waves wash away my dreams,
I do not cry.

The sky is so clear today,
That I see it all.
Frozen dreams,
In a shattered world.
And we wanted no madhouse here.

Loneliness is human.
The day dies
The dark comes.
And the year passes crab-like.

A woman with no hope:
She dies.
She walks in the alley, she dies.
Nothing is left, except what was before.
Whatever . . .
I'll return to the familiar soil
The sour wine, the empty book
I'll return to the familiar soil.

28

Early in the morning of the 20 January 1981 I wake with a start. Outside it looks colder than the last few days, and it is cloudy.

It is still too early for breakfast and I lie back in bed, light a cigarette and turn on the radio to the news of the mad, mad world that turns and turns. Iran is top of the world news, at the moment. The probability of the American hostages' release overshadows the entire Western news scene, including the new US President's inauguration. Top in Iran, however, is news of the propaganda of the war against 'Saddam Hossein's infidel Ba'athists'. The 'Mercenary Ba'athist Army' has attempted to open a new front at Sumar but has been defeated and crushed; the corpses of 57 epic-forming 'martyrs' have been flown to Tehran from the southern fronts; the resistant, dauntless cities of Abadan, Dezful and Ahvaz have again come under the merciless, inhuman attack of rockets, cannons and other heavy artillery. The government has justified the recent rise in the price of petrol and announced that forgers of counterfeit petrol coupons will be dealt with according to Wartime Regulations. From the Trade Services Organization a council has been appointed, responsible for the provision of meat, chicken, milk, butter and other essential needs. The problem of restarting work at the nationalised factories has been discussed in the Cabinet. The Deputy Minister of the Interior has issued an explanation about the armed robberies recently carried out by the Afghan refugees.

Two new statements have been issued by the Islamic Prohibitions Office. On the world news scene, it seems possible that the hostages will be released on the terms of the Algiers

Treaty. The government of the Democratic Republic of Algeria has published an official statement on the signing of a three-way treaty by representatives of Iran, Algeria and the American Deputy State Secretary. Dr Henry Kissinger and President Anwar Sadat meet in Egypt. Sadat's army have 'massacred' hundreds of revolutionary Islamic *mojahedin* and burned their corpses. In France, the socialists have accused Giscard d'Estaing's imperialist government of ruling the country in a monarchist fashion. Monsoon floods in India have taken almost seventy or eighty thousand lives . . . And today, at twelve noon, Washington DC time, the 'shame-faced and defeated' Jimmy Carter, previously a Georgian 'peanut farmer', will hand over the Presidency of the United States of America, to Ronald Reagan, 'a second-rate' former Hollywood movie-actor. For the past 48 hours, two Algerian passenger planes, plus another plane for doctors and reporters, have been waiting in Tehran for the completion of the transfer of Iran's frozen assets from America – so that the US Embassy hostages can be flown out of Iran. The news agencies talk endlessly about the 11.1 billion dollars worth of Iranian frozen assets America has agreed to release on the condition that the hostages are released. The Bank of England will be in charge of the transfer of these assets. Most Western broadcasts, even Radio France, are making it seem that this is no easy undertaking; that this money cannot be handed over to Iran 'just like that', despite the USA's 'best and most sincere attempt'. First, $3.7 billion must be returned to the US banks, as repayment of past loans to Iran. $1.4 billion must be kept in a new account, for repayment of loans which, as yet, have not been clarified. And $3.7 billion must be kept in yet another account, for the purpose of settling various American companies' claims. Only $2.8 billion – to be paid into an account in the Algerian Bank – will actually be handed over to Iran, and today, as yet, this sum has not been transferred into the Algerian Bank, and so the planes bearing the hostages are still waiting on the runway in Tehran's Mehrabad Airport.

I dress and go downstairs for breakfast at about usual time. Sumunju, with her ever-tranquil face and her eternal spectacles, is sitting behind the counter, reading.

'*Bonjour*. Tea or coffee?'

'Coffee, please. *Bonjour*.'

When she brings the tray, she is smiling.

She comes through the tiny door, which leads to the small room behind the counter, which doubles as a kitchen.

'I have done a foolish thing.'

'Oh? What have you done?'

'I was still half asleep this morning, and put the lid of the strawberry jam on the black cherry jam jar – and vice versa! Then I looked down at the muddle and I asked myself, now, what has happened here?'

'What a catastrophe!'

Sumunju laughs again. 'Well, and how are you this morning, *cher* Monsieur?'

'Well, thank you.'

'Have the hostages been flown out yet?'

'No, they're still in captivity.'

'Now about an egg? Would you like me to put an egg on for you or I have some good honey ... just came in. You like?'

'Another day, perhaps. This is fine.'

As I am raising my last cupful of coffee, Sumunju comes back with the news: 'Telephone for you. Behind there.'

It is Leila Azadeh.

'*Salaam* ... Are you well, Jalal?'

'*Salaam*. Yes, I'm fine.'

'Jalal, I need your help. I want you to come and do some fibbing for me. Can you do that?'

'All right. I'll come fibbing.'

'I'm not being silly, I swear. I'm really in a spot.'

'What sort of a spot?'

'When you come and see Hekmat today, I want you to say Leila's been in hospital with my niece for the past two or three days! I don't want him to find out I've been out of town.'

'Am I going to see Hekmat today?' I ask.

'Yes, we're going to Versailles together.'

'No!'

'Absolutely. You have to, Jalal! Don't you want to see me?'

'All right.'

'How's your head?'

'Which head?'

'The one you said you thought was still stuck to your body.'

I laugh. 'Not bad ... Where did you go, anyway?'

'Oh, here and there. Were you worried?'

'Yes.'

'Then come and let me see you.'

'I'm going to the hospital at ten.'

'That's fine. We're not going till noon. We're all meeting in the Café Quarantain. From there, we'll go to Versailles, it won't take more than a couple of hours. Then we'll all have lunch. I'm buying.'

'Who is everybody?'

'Hekmat and Dr Kuhsar, and I think, Parsi, Qaraguzlu and Safavi are coming too.'

'Safavi's back from Vienna?'

'I didn't even know he had *gone* to Vienna! But I do know that Qaraguzlu has just returned from Strasbourg, in the company of Doctor Ala'i – you in the picture?'

'Well, Leila – tell me, what exactly is it that I'm supposed to do?'

'I'll pick you up at the hospital at eleven.'

'All right.'

'Remember now, you must come to my rescue.'

'What rescue?'

'Bah! ... You haven't forgotten already, Jalal?'

'Oh ... The grand fib.'

'That's right. For God's sake, my love, save my honour!'

'Eleven o'clock then, outside the hospital.'

'Right where I pick you up the other day.'

'Yipes!'

'What does that mean?'

'Nothing ...'

I replace the receiver. That conversation seems unreal, like a dream. In fact nothing seems real; like Sumunju's putting the wrong lids on the jam-jars. I go upstairs, for my gloves and overcoat. I glance at my reflection in the mirror. My eyebrows, nose, moustaches, mouth, and chin, and the cleft in the chin, seem to be in line. Downstairs, and out of the hotel, I trek my usual route to the hospital. I pass by the same bars, cafés and bookstores. I buy the same newspaper, or so it seems. I see the same faces. The same old effervescence and bubbliness of life in France.

At the hospital, I look in on Sorraya through the glass of the closed doors. She is still stretched out on her bed — just as I had first seen her, two months ago. There is no one with her. Her face looks more drawn and colourless than ever. I do not know why my heart suddenly seems to tremble, with no reason. Sleeping, her face looks very much as it did in a picture of her which Farangis sent me, when she was just born – a miniature little human being, aleep, between birth and death, or vice versa. 'Loneliness is human.'

Outside the hospital doors, I feel lost and lonely myself – the way I felt the morning we moved through the frozen steppes of Azerbaijan. Or the night we were in the motor-dinghy, in the Gulf, waiting for low tide. I stand beside the huge, iron gate. I do up the top button of my overcoat. There is no sign of Leila, or of Leila's red Ford, anywhere. I light a cigarette, and wait. Maybe she won't show up. I'll wait until eleven fifteen, I tell myself, and that's it. What hope for anything to exist between her and me? But I hope to God she will keep her word, today. She might well have forgotten. Leila Azadeh is Leila Azadeh. How does it go? When she is good, she is good, and when she is bad she is terrible. When she is left by herself there is nothing she might not do. What can you expect from the granddaughter of a Shirazi virtuous Moslem *dervish* who came to Paris, was converted a Christian, yet still believes that Zoroaster was the greatest prophet on earth, and the creator of the great myth of the old Persia.

I am just about to give up, and leave, when Leila appears in a Citroën taxi. She opens the door for me to get in.

'*Salaam*! Did you freeze waiting for me?'

'Not much.'

'My damn car wouldn't start. Come on, we'll take this thing to the Saint Michel Station, and then go by train.'

I get in beside her and close the door. The taxi moves on.

'I'm miserable, Jalal.'

'What?'

'I don't know why, but I've got a terrible, disturbing feeling in my heart.' I don't think she is being serious.

'Where's the one I'm supposed to fib to?' I ask.

'Who, Hekmat?'

'Don't tell me he's not the only one!'

'I was at Pari's house. I was going to pick up Hekmat, but

when I phoned I was told Hekmat had left a message that he had gone with Ahmad Safavi in Dr Kuhsar's car.'

I ask no further questions, but let her talk for the rest of the journey.

At the station, Leila buys two tickets; on the platform she shows me the little electronic signboards where the names and times of the trains flash before the trains themselves arrive. 'They are run by computer,' she says. We board our train, and it is new, shining and smart, and sit facing each other, alone in a *coupé*. The train rattles along, Leila talks, and the outskirts of Paris becomes less and less congested. I find myself slipping back into thoughts of Sorraya, and what she was like when she was born, and later, and Farangis, and Abadan ...

'What is it?' Leila says. 'You're like a ghost fading away, Jalal.'

'I'm here. I think.'

'Something happened?'

'No.'

'You are taking your pills and things?'

'Of course.'

'If you want, we can just skip this whole Versailles shit. Do you want to? To hell with Louis XIV and XV and the lot!'

'Don't foul up your arrangements. It won't take very long, will it?'

'Two hours, at the most.'

'That's not bad.'

'We can start back whenever we feel like it.'

The train is moving more rapidly, now. We pass through a region which is very green, full of trees, yet also of houses and residential areas. Leila explains to me how this place was once one of Louis XIV's hunting grounds, and so on and so forth.

'Are you planning to go to London with Hekmat?' I ask her.

She smiles sadly with her mouth closed. Her smile, too, seems unreal today, like Sumunju's laugh. Her face has the drawn, washed-out look of Sorraya's face.

She shrugs her shoulders. 'I don't know.'

'What do you mean, you don't know?!'

'I'll have to see.'

'You kept repeating Hekmat this Hekmat that, today on the phone.'

'Now don't start teasing today, Jalal. I beg. I haven't seen Hekmat for seven or eight days. I only returned to Paris late last night.'

I do not ask where from.

'By the way, have you done anything about the money?'

'I think the University Insurance Scheme will probably pay for it.'

'Oh? It is all fixed, then?'

'They said a letter is going to be written. The fellow in charge said apparently everyone has agreed to it. Unless they back out at the last minute. All that's left now is for the Court Commission paperwork to be finished.'

'What if this doesn't work out, though?'

'If this doesn't work out, we'll have to sell a few pieces of Sorraya's jewellery.

'The National Gold Reserves . . .?'

'Frozen in the Charnauts' banks!'

We laugh.

29

It is raining when we reach the station at Versailles. Outside the station we quickly walk the short distance to the café. In the rainy, out-of-season day, the Café Quarantain looks more like a large, deserted tea-room, nothing like the crowded, tumultuous cafés in Paris. Inside, our friends are seated at a large table, in the midst of many empty ones. Abbas Hekmat is there, with Dr Ahmad Reza Kuhsar, Ahmad Safavi, Dr Barzegar's wife, Doctor Ala'i, and Nader Parsi plus his fat uncle. Only Qaraguzlu is missing. As Leila and I approach, everyone – including the ladies – get up to shake hands with us. The ladies of the party kiss Leila. Nader Parsi embraces me, but he is obviously in a rotten mood, and it is not hard to guess that he has had another argument with Abbas Hekmat. On the table are empty bottles, cups, and glasses of various liquids. There is a collection of empty beer bottles in front of Hekmat, something disgraceful to Parsi, who cannot stand *artistic* people who drink beer. He think artists should never touch anything less than Courvoisier, or at least a three-star cognac, or Bordeaux, and ladies should *always* order Bordeaux, Chianti or Pernod.

No one asks why Leila is late, or where has she been. She sits beside Hekmat. I turn to Hekmat and remark that Leila has been to the hospital several times this week, and has been most concerned about my niece. In the present company, somehow this does not seem unrealistic or foolish. Nothing does in this gathering.

'How is your niece?' Hekmat asks.

'Not very well, I'm afraid.' I say. 'The same.' Hekmat simply says, 'It's in God's hands. I hope she'll get well again, soon.' And I thank him.

But the running conversation is about music. Evidently they had been talking about Aminullah Hossein and Chopin and Tchaikovsky before we came in.

'If not better than them, Hossein is by no means less than them, either,' Parsi says.

'Comparing Hossein with Tchaikovsky and Chopin is absurd.' Hekmat says.

'If not better than them. Hossein is by no means less than them, either,' repeats Parsi. 'So now we're absurd? Eh?'

'I didn't say Aminullah Hossein's works were absurd. Or that you were – heaven forbid! I simply said comparing him with Chopin and Tchaikovsky was absurd.'

'Then you might as well say that comparing your excellency's *Dust of the Tavern Door* with Tolstoy's *War and Peace* or Kafka's *Metamorphosis* is also absurd!'

'It may be absurd or it may be clever,' Hekmat replies.

Hekmat is wearing a smart, dark-grey gabardine suit, a pearl-grey shirt and tie to match. He has an Irish tweed, casual overcoat over his shoulders, with a red silk scarf. Nader Parsi is wearing his black leather jacket, a black turtleneck sweater, with black trousers and brown American boots. Hekmat looks like a diplomat; Parsi could pass for a Bohemian film director defected from Czechoslovakia.

'That's a ridiculous comparison,' he says.

'Come now. That's not a subtle thing to say, *Jenab* Parsi.' Hekmat says. 'And an unintelligent remark.'

'Why don't we end this discussion right here, friends?' Safavi suggests.

'Hear, hear!' says *Khanom* Ala'i.

'Now that *Khanom* Leila Azadeh is here, why don't we start?'

'Yes,' says Safavi. 'Let's have lunch somewhere, and then go and have a look at *le Château*.'

'Really now, *Jenab* Safavi!' says Dr Kuhsar 'We've all had breakfast only an hour ago! Let's see *le Château* first, then lunch.'

'That's an idea.'

'What would the ladies prefer?'

The ladies have no objections to anything at all; ladies do not participate in Hekmat and Parsi's discussions. The atmosphere around the table is none too jolly due to the Parsi– Hekmat dispute.

Parsi says, 'The day has yet to come when our dear master Hekmat agrees with a single word that I say.'

'I'll agree.' Hekmat smiles.

'What do I have to do to make that honourable feat happen? Work for the Intelligence Service?'

'No – but you could stop smuggling out money of Iran with your devious ways. Iran needs her money.'

'What I do isn't anyone's damned business.'

Hekmat laughs, and turns to Dr Kuhsar. 'Some people are smartening themselves up these days.' He is obviously referring to the trendy, expensive way Parsi is dressed.

Parsi begins to drum on the table with his fingers.

'Is it me?' Hekmat mimics. 'Am I the one?'

'My dear *Jenab* Hekmat,' says Safavi. 'We are all at your service.'

Hekmat guffaws, looking at me. I don't know what he means by that, except that he could suppose that Safavi, Parsi, or his uncle, or even the three of them, are smuggling dollars out of Tehran, with my sister's money.

Safavi calls the waiter and asks for the bill. When it arrives, there is a scramble, as everyone offers to pay. Hekmat pays.

There are nine of us, and we drive to *le Château* in two cars – Dr Kuhsa's Mercedes Benz, and Parsi's Citroen. The uncle is telling us the life-story of his brother, a construction iron dealer in the Tehran Bazaar, who has now gone to America and has bought a supermarket in Los Angeles. He is making five thousand dollars a day! As soon as the restrictions against Iranians entering the US are lifted, Parsi's uncle himself is going to Los Angeles to buy a petrol station.

We arrive in front of the *Château* Versailles, and stroll slowly, in groups over the cobbled courtyard, towards a small entrance door. We are at a comfortable distance from Hekmat and company. I am not sure, I think this is probably Safavi's tactic to keep Parsi away from Hekmat and his group. He is busy talking with Parsi now.

The old but overwhelming stone palaces are in front of us. Even the very cobbles of the vast courtyard seem impressive, antique, and historical!

'Have you done anything about the houses *Jenab* Parsi?' asks Safavi.

'What house?'

'Your own place, here – which you wanted to give our General Qa'em Maqami Fard's brother, in return for the "Maktab Publishing House" in Tehran, from his cousin?'

'Yes – that's all done,' Parsi says. 'They sent the deed over here from Tehran, I signed it.'

'Is that a fact! My, you are a clever operator!'

'We were lucky.'

'Did you know the notary public people, beforehand?'

'Friends helped us out ... It was done.'

'You really are a smooth one! Congratulations.'

'Thank you.'

'Have you taken care of the handing over of the house here, too?'

'Yes – yesterday.'

'Well, bravo!'

'Thank you.'

'What are you going to do with the publishing house?'

'My brother's found a couple of really good buyers for it in Tehran.'

Leila has already bought nine entrance tickets, and is asking, 'Chambers of the King and Queen, anyone?'

I don't understand.

'Yes ...' Safavi says. 'One mustn't miss that.'

Doctors Ala'i and Barzegar agree.

'Jalal?' Leila asks me.

'No.' I say. 'I don't know.'

'How many shall I get?'

'Why put yourself to trouble, Leila dear?' Parsi says. 'Allow me.'

But Leila has gone into the ticket queue, and won't give up her place.

'You need one ticket to enter the *Château* itself,' Safavi explains. 'And a separate one to see the Chambers of the King and Queen.'

Hekmat, Kuhsar, the ladies and Parsi's uncle, want entrance tickets for the Chambers of the King and Queen to be bought for them.

Safavi is telling us about Louis XIII and Louis XIV, who built and completed *le Château* in the 17th Century. He is explaining the castle's essential role in the history of art and architecture in France, and commenting on the grandeur of court life in the good Louis' regime, when Leila and Parsi rejoin us.

We are barely in the *Salon de Hercules* when Hekmat and Parsi start off again. Leila moves away from them and joins Safavi and me. Several times, I am tempted to leave, but decide to stick around because of Leila.

'Really,' Safavi says. 'It's quite deplorable.'

'Just like schoolboys. They keep squabbling and fighting over the most petty things,' says Leila.

Are they still arguing about money, or is it art now, or what?'

'Oh, everything.'

'There was a dispute between them – but that was fourteen or fifteen years ago.'

'What dispute?' I ask.

'Nothing important. There was a literary magazine; Hekmat was the chief editor and owner. At one time, it published an article about Parsi's plays. It said all Mr Parsi's plays are meaningless, slavish imitations of European structure and form ... Parsi has been on bad terms with Hekmat ever since. But really ... that should have all been forgotten by now.'

'Yes, I remember,' Leila says. 'But that was ages ago. Besides, Hekmat had nothing at all to do with that article. He was abroad at the time. His assistants put that crap out then.'

But they are on the wrong track. Any man who so much as *looked* at Leila, Parsi would want to chop his head off. I remembered how he had leapt at Jean Edmond in the Café de la Sanction, on New Year's Eve.

We pass into *La Gallerie des Glaces*. I cannot hear Parsi and Hekmat now because they are behind us. In *La Gallerie des Glaces* everything is grand, yet peaceful and serene, filled with lights, artefacts, paintings and sculptures ... Through the full-length windows, the rays of the sun, which has just come out, pour in on to the golden floor. The curved ceiling is painted, and as well as colourful busts of various Roman Emperors, there are some life-size statues of Greek deities. We have seen almost all of the gallery, and are standing in front of the statue of Venus, when suddenly, a resounding smack echoes through the gallery, as the rustling of a fist fight breaks out at the other end! I turn around, and there, between the statue of *la Pudicité* and a pair of candlebra-bearing maidens, Abbas Hekmat and Nader Parsi are flying at each other's throats – seriously. Actually, it is more Parsi who is thrashing out at Hekmat's head and face, hitting him in the mouth, nose and ear. Hekmat's scarf is flying, Parsi's feathered hat has fallen off. Hekmat's scant white hair is sticking up on end, and Parsi's pink, shiny pate bobs up and down like an angry bantam cock.

'Oh, good God!' Leila cries.

'Oh, capital!' says Safavi. 'What a disgrace.'

'Oh, Jalal, go pull them apart!' Leila says.

I make no haste.

'Better leave them,' Safavi says. 'Let's get out of here, *Khanom*. If we join in, it'll make it worse.'

'No ... Oh, dear! We must stop them ... Come on, Jalal!'

Leila and Safavi hurry towards the battlefield. I follow up rather slowly. But by the time we have crossed the length of the gallery Parsi's uncle and Dr Kuhsar have already separated the contenders, and are taking Hekmat out; Leila follows them, as does Ahmad Safavi. The incident has only attracted a few, startled tourists.

When I reach Nader Parsi, he is as green as a leaf, and his hands are shaking. There is no one left but his uncle, standing in front of the Julius Caesar and the nude, *la Pudicité*. The uncle is advising Nader to cool off, something he has probably done ever since Nader was two.

I don't really know what in hell to do. I'm not sure I want to go and pat Nader on the shoulder. He may fly at me, too! But we grew up together in the back-alley slums of Tehran, and I don't want to just leave him there.

'Come on, let's go have something, Nader,' I say.

'All right,' he mutters.

'So much for *le Château* Versailles!'

'No, why? We'll go upstairs.'

'I think we'd better go. Come on, let's get a drink. You blew your damned top there.'

'Let's go.'

Back in the entrance hall there is a café and bar, in one

corner. Thank God there's no sign of Hekmat, Leila or the others. They've probably taken Hekmat out. Perhaps he was hurt, even bleeding.

I order coffee, Parsi orders a double Courvoisier, and the uncle, using fingers, eyes, and eyebrows, signals for the same. The uncle is still whispering soothing things in Parsi's ear. Parsi nods, and puffs on his cigarette. His hands are still shaking, as are his knees – as if his entire nervous system has gone haywire. He orders another double Courvoisier. He himself looks more defeated and broken than the one he has just beaten up.

After a while, I say, 'I have to be going back, Nader.'

'We're hopeless,' he says. 'We're all dead!'

'Do you need me, for anything?'

'We're all dead!' he says again. 'We're all really miserable. We're all making fools of ourselves. What do we know about art and civilization? We should just eat *abgusht* [a weak, watery broth] and sit belching in a corner, and be beaten on the head. Eat. Sleep. And die.'

'Good-bye, Nader.'

'Wait a minute – I'll drive you back myself.'

'No. I'll see you later.'

'You think I can't manage it?'

'I'll see you later.' I don't know why I feel sorry for him.

'The son of a bitch says I fled the country illegally, so all my property can be confiscated. He says I'd better just pray no one ever informs them what I've got over there. As if everyone was a double-faced bastard like him – in the pay of the BBC.'

'Nader,' I say. 'Good-bye.'

'I said I'd drive you back, man!'

'No, you stay. Till you cool off.'

He laughs. 'I didn't blow my top much, heh, heh. Honestly! Just beat the bastard up!'

'I'll say!'

'I'd been wanting to smash his face for years.'

'Good-bye, Nader.'

I leave the bar, and go out of the *Château*. I walk across the cobbled yard and out of the heavy iron gates. There is no sign of Kuhsar's blue Mercedes. I start walking back to the station in the drizzle that is starting again. It is not very far, just along a boulevard, and then to the right. In front of the station café, I notice Kuhsar's car. Leila, Safavi and Kuhsar are sitting inside, but not Abbas Hekmat. The two other ladies seem to have vanished somewhere.

Leila sees me, and calls to me, so I go inside. This time, they are sitting at a smaller table. Safavi and Dr Kuhsar have ordered lunch. Leila has only a Pernod before her, and is smoking. I sit next to her. I don't want anything; I want to get back to Paris, I tell her.

'Stay a bit and have a smoke then, before you go,' says Leila.

I sit back and take out a cigarette. She is watching me. She doesn't look too disturbed or even concerned.

'The Great Historical Fist-fight!' she says.

'Um-hm.'

'You all right?'

'Yeah.' I say. 'I'm taking the first train back to Paris.'

'Why?'

'I don't know. I'm going, that's all. I'm going to the hospital.'

'Sit for five minutes, at least. Tell me, what was Parsi doing back there?'

'Forget him.'

'Well, all right.'

Dr Kuhsar and Safavi are whispering together.

Leila lights a fresh cigarette. 'I'm sorry for Parsi,' she says, looking at me.

'Don't be. He's been doing this sort of thing since he was a kid in back-alleys and in school.'

'Did you see him?'

'He was at the bar.'

'How was he?'

'Nothing damaged except his nerves.'

'What was he doing?'

'Sitting there, drinking double Courvoisier.'

'He shouldn't have done what he did.'

'Don't keep talking about it.'

'We're all in a coma, by God!'

'Leila!'

'Guess where Hekmat's gone to?'

'Call in the cops.'

'No. He's gone to the telephone office. It's just behind the station.'

'Forget about them, I said.'

'He's gone to phone Tehran.'

'What the hell for?'

'He knows some fellow in the Central *Kommiteh* of the Revolutionary Guards. He's gone to phone him, to say that Nader Parsi has recently bought the Maktab Publishing House in some sort of an illegal racket transaction. He's going to give them the address and everything – including the information that Nader Parsi is planning to swap the place.'

'Forget them, Leila.'

'I feel sorry for Hekmat. He got a real beating up!'

'Don't talk about it any more.'

In an unusual and uncharacteristic mood, Ahmad Safavi turns to Kuhsar, saying, '*Jenab* Doctor Khayyam says:

For in and out, above, about, below,

Tis nothing but a Magic Shadow show.

Play'd in the Box whose candle is the Sun,

Round which we Phantom Figures come and go.'

Kuhsar inclines his head in concurrence. Then, although he is not drunk, he turns to Leila. With the gesture of a man who has just solved the most intricate problems in the history of mankind and civilization, he asks, 'My very dear Mademoiselle Leila Azadeh ... I am having another double Hennessy ... What would you say to another double Pernod and lemonade?'

'*Merci*.'

'Good. *Jenab* Safavi?'

'This mineral water is just fine, thank you.'

'Our dear friend, *Jenab* Aryan?'

'*Merci*, nothing now.'

'Then it's a double Hennessy, a double Pernod, and a double *merci*.' He guffaws in false laughter, and beckons to the *garçon*.

'*Jenab* Aryan, did you hear what *Jenab* Doctor Kuhsar said?' Safavi asks.

What did he say?'

'He says Mehrabad Airport has been reopened! There are three or four Iran Air flights from Tehran to Europe and back, each week!'

I don't answer. I suppose I should have said 'Hooray!'
I sit for another minute in silence, while they talk.

Behind the ammunitions depot at Ahmadabad Station 12, both sides were answering each other's shelling and heavy gun-fire. Fesharaki and I were sitting in a trench, waiting for the jeep to come and take us to the Maintenance Centre on Petrochemical Plant Road. Several young 'Revolutionary Guard' youths had just finished their morning prayers. They were now busy running and exercising. They hopped around freshening their morals with loud rhythmic cries of 'One-two-three-Martyr! One-two-three-Martyr!' Then a *Khamseh-Khamseh* came down and activated within twenty metres of us. I ducked my head further down into the trench, but looking overhead, I saw an amputated arm come sailing down to fall on the back of Fesharaki's neck.

When the *garçon* arrives with the drinks, I get up. Leila wants to walk to the station with me, but I thank her. There is too much rain. I say goodbye and leave. I walk back to the station alone, in the pouring rain.

The rain is heavier in Paris, and it is getting dark when I come up the stairways of the Odeon Metro Station. I skip going to the hotel, to take an umbrella, and instead walk right down the Rue Saint Jacques, and enter the hospital with the rain-water dripping down my face.
I will never forget that damned night.

30

Sorraya is not on her bed.

I start looking for Nurse Georgette Jardin, and find her in old Dr Martin's room. I see her through the glass panel. There is another woman there, sitting opposite her. I enter the office. The woman sitting with her back to the door is Christienne Charnaut. She is seated on the edge of a fibreglass chair, leaning forward, with her legs crossed, supporting her chin on one hand, with her elbow resting on her knee. At that moment, they are not speaking. Christienne Charnaut is smoking – something I had never seen her do in the hospital before. I feel as though something is exploding inside my own heart.

'Where is Sorraya?' I ask.

'*Bonsoir*, Monsieur Aryan,' the nurse says.

'*Bonsoir*, where is Sorraya?'

Christienne Charnaut does not get up to shake my hand as she usually does, but she does remove her chin from her hand.

'Sit down, Monsieur Aryan. Why don't you?'

I look at the nurse. 'Where is Sorraya, Mademoiselle?'

'Sorraya is not to be disturbed.'

'Well?' I turn back and look at Christienne Charnaut again.

'She is not well.'

'Has something happened?'

Nurse Georgette Jardin says, '... Her general condition and her vital life signs have been weakening gradually. The doctor wanted me to tell you this.'

They had never treated me this way before, I am terrified by this medical jargon 'general condition and life signs gradually weakening'. Christienne Charnaut is dabbing the corners of her eyes with a handkerchief. I get a feeling there are things I have yet to know.

'Can I see her?'

'There is no visiting allowed in that unit, Monsieur.' the nurse says.

'When is Doctor coming in?'

'Dr Monet is here; he is in a conference.'

'Does that mean I cannot see him?'

'There is a proverb,' Nurse Jardin says. 'We must always hope for the best and prepare for the worst.' With that, she leaves the room.

'We had better sit down, my dear Monsieur Aryan,' says Christienne Charnaut again. '*I* have spoken with Dr Monet. In the EEG taken yesterday evening, Sorraya showed no reactions to a voltage of four waves per second.'

'My God.'

'Yes.'

'What about her blood pressure?'

'He said it was not more than two, at the very most. With an extremely rapid pulse.'

'*Two*?'

'More frightening than that at the moment, is that Sorraya has caught bronchopneumonia today – something absolutely terrible in her weakened condition.'

'How in the world did she catch this pneumonia?'

'Frailty ... but this hasn't alarmed them as much as yesterday's EEG. Sorraya's brain has become unresponsive even towards the highest human-endurance voltages.'

I remember Dr Martin's fearing the possible isoelectrification of the brain, as far back as late December.

'What are they doing now?'

'Their best struggle is to maintain these life signals going ... however weak they might be.'

'She's not in any pain, is she?'

'Oh, I don't think so ...' She sighs. 'As Monet puts it, Sorraya has entered the state which is known in medical terminology as "The brain death syndrome".'

'The brain death syndrome ...'

Christienne Charnaut sighs.

'*Mon cher* Monsieur Aryan, I think the end is near.'

I lean back against the wall, bringing my hands up in front of my face. I do not want her to see my tears. After a while, I sit down on a chair Christienne Charnaut has pulled up for me. I accept the cigarette she holds out to me. Something sounds within my throat.

'What can I tell her mother?' I say in Persian.

'What did you say, Monsieur?'

I look at her face, so remote and meaningless.

'Her mother ... I am thinking of her mother.'

'Yes ... one must tell her. Although it is not yet definite. By the way, that friend of hers was here, too.'

'What friend?'

'That thin student – the bearded one. Qassem.'

I say nothing.

'He seemed very upset, too ... I think he went to your hotel ...'

I only nod.

Another minute passes in silence.

'After all this time ...' I say.

'And all this trouble ... and this waiting ...'

'I just don't know.'

'*C'est la vie.*'

'Perhaps.'

'It could have happened to anyone.'

'But it's happening to our Sorraya, now.'

'It usually happens to the best.'

'It's not fair.'

'*Mon Dieu*, non!'

I do not remember how long I stay at the Val de Grace that night. There is no definite answer from anywhere. Dr Monet does not come to the ward, either. He goes from the conference to another operating room. Once, Christienne Charnaut and I creep silently into the Intensive Care Unit at the end of the ward, and catch a glimpse of Sorraya from behind the thick glass door. She is lying under a sort of plastic covering, among a number of wires and plastic pipes. Her face, almost invisible under the mask, seems smaller than ever. The sheets have been pulled up to her chin, as though she is wrapped up and put aside already.

Christienne Charnaut wants to take me to their home, for the night. I thank her, no. I want to be alone. I tell her I must phone my sister. She drops me off at the top of the Avenue Monsieur le Prince.

I head towards the hotel, walking in the pouring rain. I look all around the hotel and into the lobby. There is no sign of Qassem Yazdani, or anyone else. I don't feel like going upstairs. I come out and go back up along the Boulevard Saint Michel, and walk up to the river. I pull my hat down over my eyes.

I cross over the Pont Neuf, and on to the Ile de la Cité. Everywhere is deserted and silent, except for the sound of the rain. I walk along the riverbank, towards the tip of the island – the same route Leila and I took that second night after my arrival in Paris. But that was a century ago – another island, another river; another planet. I would not mind now walking on like this, right into the water. To sink down in the river. Under the waves. To the river bed. Under the mud. Don't be an idiot, Monsieur Aryan! *Bonsoir*, Monsieur Aryan.

The western tip of the Ile de la Cité is covered with grass and bordered with tall, iron railings. The soaking asphalt of the narrow pavement squelches under my feet. Every square millimetre of the footpath sends its own separate shocks and messages, up my spine. This is the exact spot where Sorraya sat one spring day last April, and wrote a long letter to me, in Abadan:'My dear, lovely Uncle Jalal – you've no idea how happy I am, as I write these lines to tell you how much I love you. It is a fine spring day, towards the end of April, and I am sitting at the farthest tip on the western side of the Ile de la Cité . . .' I look to my right, and left. Huge masses of buildings stick up in a complex of light and darkness, grim and absolute. Before my eyes, the river, black as night, now and then lit by passing boats, ripples away like a stumbling drunkard. The strange river of time, and of life, and of hope, in motion. It is light and it is dark. And drunk. Like Leila's love. But it might just as well be the Karun. Or it could have been the Arvandrud, embracing Abadan, where Sorraya and Khosro went sailing that Friday afternoon. Or it could have been the Bahmanshir, on which I sailed, among the flames of war, down into the Gulf. Or it could be the Nile, where they mummified the last Shah of Iran. Or the Volga. Or the Missouri. Or the Amazon. Or the Ab Mangol in old Tehran. I sit in a corner,

259

under a shelter meant for the streetsweepers' dustbins. It stinks foul and rotten. I light a cigarette. What a day!

I have come here, in the middle of one of the most crucial upheavals ever to happen in the destiny of my people and my family. I am sitting in this corner, in this darkness, under this terrible rain, by this drunken river, next to this garbage dump, and cry in *Arabic*! Persian is of no use to me, and I do not know anything else. I am in Zangaroo, and I am speaking Swahili. I am at the centre of a storm of reality, for which no language has yet been invented. And no one cares! Geographically, I am in Paris, in France. According to the Christian Calendar, I am somewhere at the end of the 20th Century. But I am in ancient Zangaroo . . . In the era of 'What the hell do we do now?' And in Zangaroo, maps are drawn on the sands at the seashore, and history is written with dead men's saliva. In Zangaroo, the calendars and clocks are numbered backwards. In Zangaroo, after a change of regime, university professors are cab drivers, cab drivers are glassblowers, glassblowers are public prosecutors, public prosecutors are tobacco planters, tobacco planters are policemen, policemen are yoghurt-makers, yoghurt-makers are factory engineers, factory engineers cook sheep's head and feet, sheep's head and feet cooks are higher education authorities, higher education authorities are hubcap swipers, hubcap swipers are mat-weavers, mat-weavers are spiritual leaders, spiritual leaders are bulldozer drivers, bulldozer drivers are bean-sellers, bean-sellers are senators, senators are dentists, dentists are religious singers, religious singers are pineapple distributors, pineapple distributors are bookbinders, book-binders are helicopter pilots, and the pilots are all grave-diggers, because the grave-diggers have fled to seek political asylum in neighbouring country. In Zangaroo now babies are born from the grave. Infants have hair and beards, then they anti-grow, and enter the other life-stages. After the years of youth, of power and motion, they gradually forget how to walk, they crumble and degenerate, and begin to crawl on all fours. At the end of their life, they are placed in their mother's womb, which is watered from the sewers.. . .

Walking back towards the hotel, I begin to sense that the things about this trip are coming to a head. It is still pouring and I am soaked to the skin. I walk slowly, now, feeling sicker by the second, as if my brain is about to ooze out of it's clownish, grey box. The Boulevard Saint Michel is exactly as it was on that first evening, when I arrived at the end of my long trip from home. The rain, too, seems to be the same rain. The same wind. The same muddy gutter. There is a Café Danton, where Safavi, or Parsi and I chatted aimlessly. There is the Rue des Ecoles, where I met Mademoiselle Adèle Françoise Mitterand, and where she had a hot dog; it was good mustard but a bit hot. *Un peu trop fort,* ça. There is the curve, which leads to the Rue Saint Jacques, and the Café de la Sanction. That is where Leila and I walked up the Ile de la Cité. Here, at the corner of the Vaugirard, is where the exhaust pipe of Mr Mir Mohammadi's Audi went rattling on the asphalt. Here, at the corner of the Avenue Monsieur le Prince, is where Leila dropped me off, that good evening before Christmas, and sent me back into dreams and hopes, again. But nowhere on this street do I have a single memory, or remembrance of Sorraya – though I am sure she must have walked this way hundreds of times. It's as though she had died before I got here.

It is still drizzling by the time I get back at the hotel. Sumunju, with her hat and her handbag, stands at the reception counter, glancing at a newspaper. The youth on the night shift is busy talking on the phone. The little woman is startled to see me in this shape. I mumble a *Bonsoir*, only stopping to take my key before going towards the lift.

'Monsieur Aryan ... How are you feeling?' Sumunju says.

'Oh ... I don't know. *Merci.*'

'Two of your friends were here.'

'Did they leave a message?'

'No ... How are things at the hospital?'

I shrug my shoulders.

'I hope nothing bad has happened ...'

'We don't know yet.'

'Your friends told me things are not too well.'

'No, Mademoiselle.'

'Oh, Monsieur Aryan ...'

'You are leaving?'

'No ... I'm not in any particular rush.'

'Thank you...'

I go upstairs. Without even turning on the light, I take off only my hat, raincoat and shoes, and lie on the bed. The telephone is by my head. I decide not to tell Farangis that night. Tonight is neither mine nor her turn to call. I will call her first thing in the morning, I tell myself. I don't want her to hear of Sorraya's condition from any other source.

I pick up the receiver, and ask the night clerk to dial Leila Azadeh's number for me. He tries twice, but there is no answer.

Someone knocks on the door. It is Sumunju – with a tray of coffee, cake, and sympathy. But what I need tonight is not coffee, cake, or sympathy. Sumunju knows it. She takes off her hat, and sits down.

In the night there are explosions, and everything is shattered in a stagnated world where gobs of slimy, black, burning mud are suspended from the bloodied horizon. It is immediately after the last night-attack of Ardeshir's on the Worm, and even now, in my sleep, I know for certain that when the bells of fair fortune next chime out over the Iranian satellites, the only wretched finger not on the buttons of the Master Computer of Luck will be mine. Then, the first *mujahed* to fall before my eyes, hits against the nightingale. And the nightingale hits the candle. And the candle hits the sheep. And the sheep hits the donkey. And the donkey hits Majnun. And Majnun hits the tin of petrol. And all of them topple over one by one in the wind, like raw bricks laid out in a row, under the sun. And the sun shall set for the last time ... In the soft, slackening darkness ... I return to Tehran with Sorraya's body in a 747 Jumbo Jet ...

It is still quite dark outside when I get up and wash my face. I sit on the edge of the bed, pick up the receiver and ask the young man on night duty to get Farangis' number for me. My whole body aches ... I must have caught a chill in every muscle and bone last night. It is near nine a.m., Tehran time, now, and Farangis herself answers the phone at once.

After saying *salaam* and the usual greeting remarks, I ask, 'What were you doing, Feri?'

'I was just getting ready to go to the milk queue ...'

'Milk queue?'

'Yes ... We need some.' I remember she has company.

'Have they contacted you from the Company, for me?'

'No.'

'So, you were going out to the milk queue, then?'

'Yes, I was all dressed, holding my cane in the other hand, and my basket and Mosque-issued ration booklet in the other. Why are you up so early? Don't tell me you have to go to queue for bread and milk, too.'

'No. I . . . I couldn't sleep. Sit down, Feri. I don't want you to get tired.'

Farangis gives a long sigh. Then: 'Very well, I'm sitting down.'

'How's your head? You said it felt dizzy the other day.'

'I don't know,' she says. 'It's still the same.'

'Why?'

'How should I know? It keeps spinning. Keeps on spinning, spinning. I don't know what's wrong with me.'

'Are you alone in the house?'

'No . . . *Khanom* Mohammadi is in the room with me . . . Her child is ill. And she's not well herself. They're both down with a nasty flu.'

'Give my regards.'

'How are things there?' she asks.

'The weather's terrible. Cold, rainy, windy – sleet, too . . . and other things.'

'It's snowed pretty badly here, too . . . Everyone's been having trouble with it. There's no fuel, either.'

'Oh, Feri, Feri . . .'

'I had a bad dream last night, Jalal . . .'

I gasp. I do not know why I get a feeling that she already knows, as if she has sensed that Sorraya is dying. 'Feri,' I say. 'It looks as if it's not a dream, any more.'

'What?'

'I said it looks like it's not a dream . . . You know, you said yourself life is in God's hands.'

'Good God! Has anything happened?'

'No, no.'

'Tell me the truth, for God's sake!' I hear a thumping noise, and I know she is pounding her fist against her chest. 'Jalal, tell me. Tell me. Has something happened?'

'No, no, no.'

'I swear to you, on the *Qoran*! Whatever's happened, tell me.'

'I said, no! That's the truth. Didn't we promise each other we'd tell each other everything the minute it happened? Didn't you want me to give you all the news, immediately? Well, they tell me her general condition is weakening. That's all. But she isn't in any pain. And there's still no definite news ... Madame Charnaut was there, too. Of course she was upset, a little.'

'Have the Doctors given her up?'

'Feri! Don't say that. No, I don't know. Like her nurse said, we have to hope for the best and prepare for the worst.'

'Mother, mother, mother!'

'Feri, let's control ourselves – for each other's sakes.'

'What about money? Shall I send it? What shall I do?'

'No. No way.'

'Sell her jewellery, if you need to.'

'Don't worry about those things – I'll look after that here.'

'How?'

'You don't have to worry; there's money for the hospital, and transportation, and everything here.'

'I ...' Again I hear the 'thump! thump!' of her fist beating against her chest.

31

It is still dark; there is nothing I can do. I haven't the courage to phone the hospital. The thought of hearing it on the phone . . . I light a cigarette and sit by the window. I wait for daybreak. Or for death. From the balcony, I look down the length of the Avenue Monsieur le Prince, as far as to the junction with the Saint Germain.

The narrow, tight, historical avenue is empty, but clean and freshly swept. Steam rises out of the unlidded drainage hole of the sidewalk. The garbage lorry is parked at the end of the Monsieur le Prince. Across the street, a garbage collector is sweeping the litter off the sidewalk, into a little gutter that empties into the sewage grind. The news-stand kiosk is still closed, but several bundles of papers have been dumped in front of it. Two black Latin-American looking tourists, complete with bags and cameras, pass at the crossing of the Saint Germain. They are gazing at the buildings, the earth and the sky . . . discovering the experience of Paris! In the shadowy light of the dawn, and the empty moments of the street, their faces look like skeletal skulls. On the other side of the Saint Germain, a waiter in a red frock-coat and white apron is bringing chairs and tiny tables and setting them out on the sidewalk. His face, too, is a skull.

I close the window, come inside, and stub out my cigarette end, lying back on the bed. I turn the radio on, and tune into the news, somewhere.

. . . Old man Duval is behind the reception counter downstairs. He asks the eternal question. 'Tea or coffee, Monsieur?' He brings the breakfast tray. This morning, he has a skull-face, too. There is no one in the room but him and me. My face is a skull, too. He knows that Sorraya is dying. Or dead.

I stir my coffee-and-milk. I spread butter on my *croissant*. The sour-cherry jam is coagulated blood. Old man Duval comes and sits in a corner. He's got his pipe and ashtray with him. I watch him as he comes through the kitchen door and sits on a chair, by the worn curtains. He puts his pipe in his gaping, skeletal mouth.

'So today everything is finished, yes?'

'Yes, it's all over.' I imagine he means the American hostages.

'I am sorry, Monsieur,' he says. 'It is a terrible tragedy for you and your sister.'

'Oh . . .'

'Please accept our deepest condolences. If there is anything –'

'*Merci*, no.'

'Will you be leaving here?'

I am a customer. Check Out time is 2 p.m.

'Not yet.'

'Of course. What will you do now?'

'About what?'

'About the body . . .'

'I don't know. Her mother wants the body to be returned to Tehran.'

'Returned?'

'But I'll speak to her again this afternoon. Perhaps I can get her to agree otherwise.'

'For the funeral arrangements to be made here?'

'It might be easier.'

'It will be infinitely easier.'

I don't know what else to say to the skeleton.

'But, yes. Naturally,' he says.

I take out my cigarette case.

He nods. 'She wants to see her daughter. Poor woman! God grant patience.'

I lower my head, and light my cigarette.

'*Psychologically*,' Duval continues, 'she is not able to accept this death. Something in her subconscious prevents her from accepting that such a thing has happened. It is quite natural.'

He is still talking, but I do not hear him any more. He is only a skeleton. I just smoke, and look in his direction. I want no more of their help, and explanation, and brains, and knowledge.

When I wake up again and come back downstairs, there is an envelope delivered for me to the hotel desk, in the morning post. The envelope contains an official letter, bearing the stamps of the Prefect of Police, and the heading of the Bureau of Foreign Residents. Enclosed, among other things, is a typed note from the Hospital du Val de Grace, stamped Urgent across the top. My heart trembles with fear. My hands are shaking as I read the note.

Dear Monsieur:
The director and the members of the Commission investigating the problem of Mademoiselle Sorraya Naqavi's medical expenses at Hospital du Val de Grace, hereby notify you that due to the expiration of her official student stay permit and the violation of Aliens Residents laws in France, the above mentioned is not eligible for government medical insurance coverage.
Respects: M. Antoine Macadam

Several sheets of hospital bills are pinned to the letters. Some of them are computer printouts, others are printed forms, or typed on stationery bearing the letterheads of various wards of the hospital. It would take a Messiah to decipher all the cryptic gibberish there. But I get the gist of the message. Sorraya's total debts, minus the payments I had made, and the initial payment, made by Charnaut, using Sorraya's own money, apparently comes to something like 110,486 francs. 24,000 francs of this is for the hospital room; 22,000 francs for medicine; 10,500 francs charge for the radiograms, ECGs, SSRs, X-rays, etc.; 55,000 francs for the visits of doctors and specialists; and something in the region of 5,000 francs for miscellaneous expenses – all of which, with several changes, and corrections, have been accounted for in detail. This is up till the end of 20 January, 1981. In closing, it is requested that the payments be settled as quickly as possible. I take a deep breath ...

So much for the clemency of the hospital of the Valley of Grace. And this is no longer a dream. Like the rest of the events of this swinish day, it is a bitter, absolute reality. Qassem Yazdani spoke the truth when he said French government officials are strict, even cruel, with Iranians. To hell with them. A couple of pieces of Sorraya's jewellery will shut their mouth.

At about nine-thirty, I enter the hospital, my mouth dry with whatever. I enter the Ward. My whole body aches. I walk down the corridor, looking around. I manage to get hold of Nurse Georgette Jardin in front of the doctor's office. I can hear my heartbeats within my chest. We exchange *Bonjour, ça va.*

'How is she, Mademoiselle Jardin?'

She shrugs her shoulders.

'Weaker ...'

'No pain?'

'She feels nothing at all.'

She walks away, awkwardly, as if maybe in tears, leaving me there.

Hoping to see the doctor I go and sit inside the office, by a desk. There are several files, on the desk with reports clipped on them. I look out through the window. There is nothing but the tips of barren trees. So. This is how it ends.

I sit around for half-an-hour, waiting for any news of Sorraya. But the doctor does not come, neither does the nurse return.

I use the office telephone to call Christienne Charnaut. I tell her how things are. I talk about the expenses too. She tells me not to worry about the money. Philippe knows of a good jeweller, in the Boulevard Van Heusen, who will give us a fair bargain, if we come to that. I thank her. In fact they would like to buy the gold themselves, but the prices must first be ascertained by the Van Heusen jewellery experts. And so we arrange to meet in front of the hospital at three o'clock tomorrow afternoon, because Philippe has a bicycle race this afternoon.

After a while, I get up and come out of the office. I walk to the Special Care Unit at the end of the corridor. No one stops me. Quietly, I open the double-glass doors and go near Sorraya's bed. At first I cannot see her. The ward lights are turned off during the day. Then I see her, almost hidden under the sheets, as she was last night. The upper half of her face looks yellow, and there are brownish circles under her eyes. The nurse, who had been sitting by another patient's bed, gets up and comes towards me. She puts her finger to her lips, but does not frown or scold. She simply takes me out of the room. She knows me.

'How is our little angel?'

She too shrugs, shaking her head. '*Non*, Monsieur,' she says, smiling. 'You must not be in here.'

'How is she?'

'She has had a bad night.'

I look at her.

'I thought they said she wasn't in any pain.'

'No, no. But her general condition is worsening. The doctor has done the best he can.'

'Will she –'

'Go to the office, Monsieur.'

'Mademoiselle –'

'Goodbye, Monsieur ...'

There is nothing I can do. I come back through the corridor, down the stairs, and out of the hospital. Somehwere in the crowded vicinity of the Avenue Monsieur le Prince, and Saint Germain Boulevard, I enter a Russian restaurant. Inside it is crowded as always, even the long tables and benches down the middle are full. I don't feel hungry, I don't know what's wrong with me. I've eaten nothing since the night before. The pains in my body are growing steadily worse. Maybe I would feel better if I ate something warm. One of the old waiters who knows me by now beckons me to a tiny table in a far corner by a window, under a Charlie Chaplin poster. A drunk is seated across the tiny table, eating cheese and pickled cabbage. A half-full *demi-tasse* is in front of him. The waiter himself is an almost senile, very old Russian *emigré*. His long moustaches stick out of his face like twin brushes. As usual, his ancient medallions, badges, and decorations, from the Tsarist days, are pinned on the front of his red *garçon's* jacket. They say he was an actor before the Revolution, and had fled Petrograd to Paris.

'What is today's menu, dear Monsieur?' I ask.

'*Cote d'Agneau*, Monsieur ...' It is a sort of mutton dish – their best meal.

'Bring me some, please.'

'But it's all gone, Monsieur!' And he laughs.

'A *borscht*, then, and a roast.'

'And *Salade Russe*? Agreed?'

'Agreed.'

'The wine list?'

'Just mineral water, today.'

'A glass of vodka, perhaps? Eh? Vodka!'

'Not right now.'

'As monsieur wishes.'

He sings *The Volga Boatmen* out loud in French, heading towards the kitchen.

First, I swallow down my pills with mineral water. The *Salade Russe* consists simply of two boiled eggs, covered with mayonnaise, some olives, and slices of tomato. I eat part of it while the *borscht* cools off. They serve plenty of French bread in a little basket, covered with a red-and-white checked cloth, and the bread is good. Suddenly, I am very hungry, and I pay no attention to the French drunk's ramblings. I can't concentrate, for one thing; for another, I'm in pain, and the image of Sorraya's yellowed face stares up at me from under the sheets, and will not go away. I see Farangis, in her headscarf and Islamic robe, sitting beside the phone, her cane, shopping basket and ration-booklet fallen to the floor. She is beating her fist against her chest. I cannot bring Leila's image to my mind's vision. The French drunk orders another *demi-tasse*. He thinks we are on warm and friendly terms, and he is breathing senseless words into my face. His hot breath smells vile. He orders a liqueur, too, which he swirls round in its glass before gulping it down. I barely manage to keep from pouring the damn *borscht* over his head. He looks a bit like Monsieur Macadam, with the same thick, grey, dingy moustaches.

After lunch I return to the hotel. A heavy fog has by now settled outside the window, making everything seem even more unreal than it already is. I call Leila fom my room. Her maid, Genevieve, answers the phone. Apparently, Leila is not in. And Genevieve jabbers too fast, and with such a provincial accent, that I can never understand what she is saying.

I call Leila's sister's apartment. Pari Azadeh is at home. She tells me Leila has gone to Le Havre. Le Havre is a port on the Channel. I ask her to give my regards to Leila when she gets back, and ask her to get in touch with me at the Hotel Palma. Something important has come up, I say. Leila's sister does not ask what it is, but she says she does not think Leila would be back before the weekend. She has taken two suitcases. I ask how is she doing and the family. They are all well. Then sensing my restlessness, she asks me if I would like the number of the hotel where they are staying in Le Havre. They? I ask whether she has gone with Papa or Mother? No, she replies, Leila's gone with Jean Edmond. I say no more, nor do I ask for the telephone number. But I ask her to give Leila my message whenever she returns, anyway. This completes the plot, I say to myself.

I replace the receiver, and go on to the balcony and look out towards the street and the city. The fog, whch settled down after the heavy noon-time rain, has now grown thicker – wrapping around the city like a cold, grey shroud, strangling its arteries – a city in a coma.

When I move from the balcony, the pains I'd had all day get worse. Maybe I shouln't have spent all that time last night pottering around on the Ile de la Cité in the rain. When I sneeze, it feels like my whole body is exploding. I try to lie down, but a burning knife is being twisted around in my chest.

I get up, and go out of the hotel towards the hospital, but the pains are worse; my breathing is all wrong somehow. I have to sit down. I lean my head against the wall and close my eyes.

I must have fallen asleep or passed out because next I hear someone saying, 'Monsieur! Monsieur! Are you all right?'

I open my eyes, and move my head. A young woman, her lips thickly coated with lipstick, is smiling at me in the fog.

'Are you okay?' she asks. 'Are you all right?'

I lower my head. 'Yes. *Merci*, it is nothing.'

'Anything I can do, Monsieur?'

'*Merci*, no.'

She realises I am a foreigner. Now, in English, she says, 'Can I give you a hand?'

'Thanks, no ... It's nothing.' I answer.

'Is it your heart?'

I look down; my hand is still clasped against the left side of my chest.

'I don't know.'

'Where, exactly, does it hurt, honey?'

I smile. 'Exactly all over.'

She laughs.

'Where're you from, honey?'

'Islamic Republic of Iran!' I reply.

She grins. 'You a resident here? Or just visiting?'

'Just visiting!'

'Alone?'

'Yes.'

A new stab of pain twists. I close my eyes.

'Can you get up? There's a clinic near here; I'll take you.'

'No . . . go on, girl. Leave me alone.'

'But it's right near here.'

'It's nothing. I'll be all right in a minute.'

'Have you had these pains before?'

'Yes.' I lie.

'Chest pains?'

'Not like this.'

'I think you ought to let them have a look at you, at this clinic. Come on, up you get, honey. Give me your hand.'

I try to take a deep breath, but the pain, whatever it is, thinks otherwise.

The girl now sits by me. 'I've lived in this crazy city almost all my life,' she says. 'Paris . . . it can be cruel, like a bad dream. Us lonely folks have to help each other out.'

'Thanks. You're very sweet. But . . . It's really nothing.'

'You're in pain, man!'

'I'll be fine. I'm really all right. Go on.'

But she doesn't move; she's quiet for a bit, then she says, 'It's a rotten, mixed-up, lunatic world.'

'Yes.'

'Life here can be a beautiful, but God-forsaken nightmare.'

I nod, agreeing. 'It can be a nightmare, all right.'

'Feeling low?'

'Yeah, I'm low.'

'Here, have one of these.'

'What?'

'Drugs . . . lifts up the spirits!'

'No, thanks.'

She take a box of pink pills from her bag, and holds it out to me. She picks one out herself, popping it like a jelly bean under her tongue.

'What is it?' I ask. 'LSD? Grass?'

'Neither. It's one of these *modern* things. In Brooklyn they're called "Floss".'

'Floss?'

272

'It's just a narcotic, no side-effects. I've had three already, since morning.'

What the hell, here goes, I think, and pop a 'Floss' under my tongue. It can't be worse than the pains.

'What about coming to this clinic for a little check-up, honey?' she says. 'It won't cost more than a few francs. I don't suppose you've got any medical insurance, right?'

'No ... I mean, yes. You're right.'

'A simple check-up don't cost much. If you don't have any money on you, I've maybe got enough. It'd be my good deed for the day. Know what I mean?'

'I've got some money,' I say.

'How much?'

'Thirteen or fourteen hundred.'

'Dollars? Or francs?'

'Francs ...'

'That's fine.'

I remain silent.

She says her name is J.C. – it's the name her father gave her. Just J.C. It doesn't stand for anything – just J.C. She came over here with her father when she was just three years old, and has grown up like a wild plant. My chest pains are not so bad now, and thinking of Sorraya makes me decide to get up. But the instant I try to stand up, the pains come back.

'How d'you feel now?' J.C. asks.

'Like hell.'

'Have another Floss.'

'No ...'

'Then come on, let's go see the doc. I know the way – been there myself. They don't charge much. OK?'

I don't answer, but J.C. takes this as an agreement, and helps me get up. I see no harm in going for a simple visit, to a private doctor – these damn chest pains are unusual. Within a couple of minutes we're entering the wide door of the clinic. The pains are fantastic now.

J.C. sits me down on one of the chairs, while she goes to the information desk. It looks more like a ticket office. J.C. starts talking to the young, and extremely beautiful receptionist. Her French is perfect. I lean back in my seat and watch.

'Monsieur would like to see a heart specialist,' J.C. says.

'Immediately!'

'I'm sorry,' the girl replies. 'We have no heart specialist in the clinic, at the moment.'

'Monsieur is in great pain.' She raises her voice.

'What are his symptoms?'

'He is in pain.'

'Where?'

'Everywhere.'

'*Partout* ?' Her eyes widen, as if to say 'I knew you were crazy.'

'This is what the Monsieur says.'

'Please be more specific!' she snaps.

'Mainly chest-pains, I think.'

'Is Monsieur a "cardiaque" patient?'

'No – he says. He's not had heart trouble before.'

'Are you Monsieur's wife?'

'No, just a friend. Please do what you can. Anything.'

'Dr Grabo will be here in about half an hour. There is a strike on, you know. We only work on emergencies. I can give you the address of another doctor . . . But I'm not certain whether he'll be there or not.'

'If your own doctor – what was his name?'

'Dr Grabo –'

'Well, if Dr Grabo will be here in half an hour – Monsieur can wait.'

'As you please.'

'Please tell us as soon as he arrives.'

'Yes.'

J.C. now comes back and sits next to me. 'A bunch of crazy wine-and-garlic guzzlers! But it doesn't matter. We can wait half an hour.

It's funny, but the more they talk about my pains, the fainter they seem to get. Or maybe it is the effect of J.C.'s Floss! Other people are waiting too – J.C. talks about her life . . . her eyes are soft as she talks. But now, suddenly, Idris, Matrud's boy, is sitting next to me . . . telling me that Matrud had gone to Kofeisheh in old Ahmadabad to buy rope and nylon binding, to tie up Engineer Nurbakhsh's belongings, and he was hit by *Khamseh-Khamseh* shells. Matrud is in Taleqani Hospital now, where his leg has been amputated. Idris wants to go to the war-front, and become a *martyr*. He says he has written his will already, that he wishes to be *martyred*, and has sent it to the *Kayhan Daily*, to be published *after* his death. He says he wants to give up selling cigarettes, and go to war, instead ...

The receptionist calls J.C., pointing to a man and saying that's Dr Grabo. Dr Grabo is tall and very fat, with thin, sparse hair, drooping moustaches and a goatee, and when he speaks, one side of his mouth hangs down. He has small, penetrating eyes. J.C. gets to her feet, but when I try to do the same, a new wave of pain starts. The doctor stands in front of us, like a wall of flesh.

'*Qu'est que ne va pas?*' What seems to be the trouble?

J.C. starts to tell him, but after the first few words, and a hasty glance at me, he says, 'Take Monsieur to Room No. 13 for a cardiograph. Then I will see him.'

J.C. and I find Room No. 13 empty. After a while, an old nurse enters. She, too, is in a hurry. She begins writing out a receipt for three hundred francs. One hundred francs for the doctor's visit, and two hundred for the cardiograph, she explains.

'It's goddam highway robbery,' J.C. says to me in English.

'It's all right,' I whisper. 'I can afford it.' I reach into my raincoat inside pocket.

'Do I pay here?' I ask the nurse.

'For this, you pay here.'

I take out the thin wad of notes, extract three hundred francs, silently bid them farewell, and hand them over. I put the odd thousand francs or so back into my pocket and zip it closed. J.C. watches.

The nurse speaks into a phone, and then turns to me. 'Second floor, Cardiography,' she says.

The second floor is calm and quiet – like a church. The room we enter is full of equipment, and a younger nurse is waiting for me. She is small, with black hair, a broad face and sensitive, rouged lips, but dominating manners and movements. She sends J.C. out of the room. J.C. says it's all right, she'll wait outside. She wishes me luck! The nurse doesn't ask me about anything; she simply takes the form I am holding.

'Behind that *paravent*, please. Take off your clothes.'

'Everything?'

'Everything. Even your wristwatch.'

She gives me a small, green plastic nightshirt. 'Then put this on. Tie it in front.'

I am still not finished with the plastic thing, when she slips in, bringing some equipment with her.

'Ah, Monsieur. Are you ready?' She smiles.

'Almost.'

'You are very tall.' But she is not looking at my height.

'What shall I do now?'

'Lie on the bed, on your back.'

I obey meekly. She quickly begins sticking the machine's wires and buttons on to my body. Two on my ankles. Two on my wrists. Several on my chest, and under my arm. Lying there, all naked under her wires and connections, I begin to feel foolish. She moves me this and that way, and I get a feeling she is bending over me too much, more than she needs to, really, doing whatever she pleases. Oh, well, let her do it. It doesn't matter. It's just a test. *C'est la vie*! Let her mess around; everybody's messed around with me. Life has been messing around with me for some time. Even the damned rats in Abadan. This Mademoiselle on top of it all. So what? To hell with the three hundred francs. I can be out of here in half an hour. I'll go to the Hospital du Val de Grace, to see Sorraya. Then all this foolish scene is over.

Now she's rubbing around my heart and the left side of my chest with a medicine-soaked pad of cotton. Her painted lips are so close I can smell lipstick. Her uniform is generously open above her breasts. She wears a smart, black, rectangular badge: *Nourice* Michelle Gabriel. She places the machine's watchuma-callit on my chest. 'Don't breathe,' and then, 'Breathe.' 'Don't breathe.' 'Breathe now.' I hear the clicks and whirrs of the machine, starting and stopping. I feel her soft hands, working on my chest and I see her face, coming down over mine. She speaks all the time, saying things which I mostly do not understand. She has become very friendly, now. When she rubs the moist cotton pad under my left nipple, she laughs. '*Ètes vous chatouilleux?*'

'Pardon?' I am feeling anxious about the result of the graph. The machine is doing a lot of clicking.

'How do you say it –' she says, in broken English. 'When someone touches you, and you feel – you feel, funny, and you laugh?'

'Ticklish?'

'Yes . . . Are you ticklish?'

I like her sense of timing.

'Not there.'

'Many people are. I had a patient, two days before yesterday, who was absolutely ticklish . . .' Her English is not quite as good as Mademoiselle Adèle Françoise Mitterand's.

'Then he wasn't a heart patient!'

'But he was *very* sick, Monsieur.'

When she has finished with me, she tells me to get dressed. I am fastening my belt when Dr Grabo shows up. The nurse pushes the *paravent* aside. Grabo examines the tape. He clears his throat, leaning against the cardiography machine. 'Have you had any previous heart trouble?'

'No.'

'Any sort of chest pains? Shortness of breath? Heartburn, sweating? Anything like that, that you have been hospitalized for?'

'No.'

All this is obviously a preface to what he wants to say next.

'What do you think, doctor?'

'I think you had better stay here for three days, so that we can run some tests.' I suppose he thinks I'm a Latin American money bag.

'Is something wrong?'

'I'm suspicious.' But his off-hand, light way of replying makes *me* suspicious.

'You want me to stay here for three days while you run some tests?'

'Common sense demands it.'

'I can't spend three days here, doctor. I have other, very urgent things to do. Can't you give me something?'

'No. Of course, the decision is up to you. You could leave now and nothing may happen to you. On the other hand, where the heart is concerned, problems of this sort must be dealt with immediately – as I'm sure you know.'

But before I can say another word, he leaves the room, stopping only to give the nurse some instructions. The nurse picks up the phone and gives a few off-hand orders to the

Receptionist, downstairs – to the effect, I think, that Dr Grabo's new patient can be hospitalized, if he decides. After this the nurse, too, forgets my existence, and goes about her work.

When I leave the Cardiography Room, I am even sicker and more confused than before. J.C. is still standing there, smoking stealthily.

'Did you have a cardiogram done?'

'Yes.'

'Did the doctor see it? What did he say?'

'He wants me to stay here for three days. For tests.'

'You better do it,' she says at once.

'I can't.'

I hand my raincoat to J.C. while I do up my shoelaces. I feel a new weakness and anxiety. We walk towards the lifts; she is already holding my arm, supportingly.

'I suppose he must've seen something nasty in your tape, honey.'

'I didn't find out ... with that nurse of his!'

'What was she doing. I peeked in. Looked like she was eating you up!'

'French touch!'

'Here's the reception desk. Let's see about you being hospitalized.'

'No – I'm getting out of here.'

'Why? ...'

'Lots of reasons. I don't have the money, for one thing.'

J.C. stares at me. 'But you've got a thousand or so, that might be enough for a start?'

'No! ...'

'Anyway, let's ask. There's no harm in that. For God's sake! You a sick man, honey. It's not the end of the world! You want to go out in the street and have a heart attack? You can't help nobody then, and nobody can help you!'

'I have to go, really.'

We are now standing at the clinic's reception desk. 'Wait a minute,' says J.C. Then to the receptionist: 'Monsieur is to be hospitalized here for three days. What is the charge per night?'

'Monsieur is not insured?'

'No –'

'Five hundred francs a night.'

'And how much does Monsieur pay in advance?'

'The person on duty will tell you.'

'Can you give us an estimate of how much is usually needed? For three days with Dr Grabo.'

'Usually fifteen thousand francs.'

'Fifteen thousand francs for a three-day check-up?'

'You will find our prices very fair, compared to other clinics.'

J.C. turns and looks at me. 'Fair ... my ass.' By now I am backing quietly towards the exit doors.

'Leave it,' I say to J.C. 'Come on.'

'You need care!' she says.

'Not here. Let's go. It's over.'

'Is there nowhere you can get some money?'

'I'd rather lie in the gutter and wait for the angel of death.'

'A bunch of damn capitalists!'

'I don't care. Come on.'

She is still holding my hat and raincoat.

'Sit down a minute,' she says. 'Have a rest.'

'No – I'm going into the washroom. I'll just splash my face with cold water, and then we can go.'

'Yeah – go cool off, man.'

'You'll wait till I come back?'

'Sure ...'

'I'll be back in just one minute.'

'Look honey, I can get a couple of francs together.'

'No! Absolutely not. Thanks.'

'You want another Floss?'

'Yeah!'

'Don't worry, man,' She hands me a Floss. 'Take it nice'n easy. Don't get angry or anything. Keep calm and cool.'

In the tiny washroom I splash cold water on my face, run a hand over my hair and look at myself in the mirror. There are brownish hollows under my eyes, and my cheeks are a sickly yellow. I'm breathing heavily but my old heart is still pumping away. There's a pain, down at the bottom of it. Or a new disease. All right. All right, so much for the check-up! It was an experience. Over and out. Have to get going, somehow. I have to go out of here, for a start ... I have to go to the Val de Grace. I straighten my collar and tie. I do up my coat buttons. Don't get angry, or anything, man. A bunch of capitalists! Want another

Floss? All right, let's go. I must get back to J.C., my angel of mercy.

But when I come outside, my angel of mercy is gone. My hat and raincoat are still there. The clinic waiting room is the same, only there is no sign of J.C. In a millisecond the message flashes across on the computer viewer of my brain. I reach into my raincoat, the pocket is unzipped and it is full of nice, memorable Paris air ... Wonderful! So much for that.

I try not to laugh, it makes the pain worse. Anyway, I sort of liked J.C. She worked clean. I knew she must have wanted something. They all want something. But she had better public relations methods, and was superb at establishing human relations – far better than Dr Grabo and Nurse Michelle Gabriel.

I leave the clinic, and start for the Val de Grace. By the time I get there, the old hospital is enveloped in the darkness and silence of the dusk. Tonight, the place has also a sudden new glum look, and a new biting fear. I think of Dr Grabo, of Nurse Michelle Gabriel, and of J.C. Clinical angels of mercy. I say hello to a nurse whom I see coming down the stairs. I ask after Sorraya. She shakes her head, no definite news, but she is in no pain. I thank her.

Pain! I hear nothing but pain tonight. There is no talk of health. Only pain. Pain everywhere. Even the Cross at the entrance of the Val de Grace must have been incurably contracting it for nineteen hundred and eighty odd years. Iran has been bitten through by it in her belly, for thousands of years. Myself, I suffer from the cancer of calamities. Paris has syphilis of the brain ...

And the rest of that damned week passes in the same way.

Sorraya's condition worsens. I am lonelier, orbiting painfully between the poles of the hotel and the hospital. There is no sign of Leila Azadeh. There is no answer at Nader Parsi's number. I see no more of Safavi either; he has probably gone to Stuttgart, as he had said, for his dentist's appointment on the 20th. I don't see Qassem Yazdani any more, either.

Sorraya, Farangis and her guest, Dr Hosseini's wife, together, are on the other side of the world – only the three of them have turned into crabs. I tremble with horror and pain. Everyone around them is a crab, too. Like crustaceans they walk, scuttling from side to side. They enter the cold. pre-ice age, into stony lands. They secrete a viscous, foul-smelling fluid, like bloody froth. Dr Hosseini's wife, and Farangis, and Sorraya edge silently across the ground. They are not permitted to make a sound. Every morning, they stand head-to-tail, queueing up to suck seaweed sap. Sometimes they fall asleep as they wait.

32

Now, the nights seem endless, and endlessly bad. I start awake several times, my mouth dry and bitter. Sometimes I can't sleep at all – thinking of Farangis, of Sorraya, and me, and what will all happen in the end. I think about this journey, from its beginning to its end. I think of the war and all, of all of us, and the state we are in. Farangis, with her pains and troubles there, Sorraya in her sleep of death here, and me in between, their go-between, the bearer of their broken destinies.

I pick up my travel papers and my bag from the shell-blasted, rat-infested house in Breim. Matrud and Idris are staying there. I return to the hospital, to the Personnel Office, to get my documents to leave. In the evening, we start out. With two others I get a Landrover, and head for the only exit from Abadan Island. We drive down Bavardeh, through Khosrobad, to the southernmost point of the island, and to Cho-ebdeh, on the bank of the Bahmanshir . . . The island is in the enemy's grip – bruised and agonized. Silent but struggling . . . Bavardeh, with its Company houses, burnt hedges and broken trees, is in a coma. At the south end of Bavardeh, on the banks of the Arvandrud, the huge oil tanks are shattered and blackened by the explosions, scattered, chaotic. The captured, looted and devastated areas are just stubble now. Houses have collapsed on women and children. Bazaars and shops have crumbled into drunken heaps. The lawns are parched reed-beds. The streets are graveyards of crippled vehicles and dead animals. The people are either dead or homeless. Schools and colleges are shut. Factories are closed, farms are empty, wells dry. Desperate and weary, the men, women and children accept it all. The land is in flames; blood flows on to it everywhere. Mourning and breast-beating never end. Like zombies the people wait in queues, each morning, for food. And the Earth turns and turns. Nights and days, months and years go by. Dusty winds blow through war-torn cities. The world turns and turns – impervious. Iran in its death agony. *C'est la vie!* That's life!

Jenab Vahab Soheili is headed for Washington, with £38,000 worth of travellers' cheques in his luxurious suitcase. Doctor Kiumarspur leaves the border in tears with her Microbiology PhD and her baby. In the Café de la Sanction Nader Parsi, every woman's toy, drinks double Courvoisier. Bijan Karimpur dreams of giving beauty to the concept of socialist life in Iran. Come, fill the cup to the brim ... In the Rue Saint Jacques, Mademoiselle 'Françoise Mitterand' brings life to a group of exiles come to dance and be merry. The beautiful Leila Azadeh, the genius of modern Persian literature, the jewel of every Paris party, is assaulted with a broken Johnny Walker bottle. Abbas Hekmat, in love with Immortal Iran, drunk from Amstel lager, sings a frenzied *dervish* song, from the last days of the Qajar dynasty. Ahmad Safavi, the nationalist translator, contemplates translating an American book on jogging into Persian. Dr Abdol Ali Azadeh, drunk on Irish Coffee and Château d'Yquem; Qassem Yazdani, swimming in the seas of bio-chemistry and a philosophy of world resurrection. General Doctor Qa'em Maqami Fard, ex-army veteran, and Co., chasing other men's women, with bottles of champagne in buckets of ice. Professor Ahmad Reza Kuhsar publishes his dream Manifesto 'The Free Iran, The Eternal Iran', in *LaSociété* and Nader Parsi and Abbas Hekmat fight like schoolboys over a book review, published fifteen years earlier in Tehran. Mr Biglari, ex-SAVAK, language, coding and deciphering expert, now chauffeur and errand-boy to the loaded ex-army General in Paris. And illiterate Mir Mohammadi spends New Year's Eve hunting for the Eiffel Tower ... *C'est la vie*, that's life!

In my Company house, in Abadan, the rats had swarmed through the lavatory. I closed all the doors, and poured DDT into the basin, and all over the house. The rats began to run, running, twisting, entangled, squeaking in a frenzied panic. All of them; but whichever way they scurried, the DDT was on their brains. First, most of them dashed back towards the lavatory basin, then they ran back towards the kitchen or other rooms. The nimblest leapt smack into the toilet basin, and died almost instantly. Some escaped, jumping up on to the gnawed furniture, but they, also, soon fell down, dead. Some scuttled on to the half-chewed bookshelves, tottering for a bit, then thudding down to the floor – and death.

In the Café Lafarge, in Roosevelt Avenue, Hossein Abpak, sitting behind five or six empty beer bottles, is reading an American book *A Nation of Sheep*. I sit with him for a while, asking how everything is. He tells me the book he's reading is about the people of Cambodia and Laos, victims of the imperialism and traditionalism of their own Buddhist religion. I ask after Nader Parsi. Abpak tells me Parsi has fled to London, because there's a warrant out for his arrest for evading payment of his ex-wife's alimony, and selling his Paris house illegally. Safavi too, has left, for Stuttgart; his wife's gone to Switzerland for cosmetic surgery. Abbas Hekmat has returned to London, to hospital because of hernia. Dr Kuhsar's daughter is having her first Pop Art display in *Salon les Comparaisons* at *Musée d'Art Moderne de Paris*. There is no news of Leila Azadeh.

I spend the Friday afternoon at the hospital with the Charnauts, returnng to the hotel at eight o'clock. At the reception desk, there is a note for me in Leila's writing: 'My dear Jalal, I am broken, and not well. Can you come to my rescue? I haven't the energy for anything. I die for you. Leila.'

On the downstairs phone I call her Porte d'Italie number. There is no answer. I call her sister's place. There is no answer there, either. I go upstairs, wash my face with cold water, swallow some medicines, and shave – something I have not done for two days. Then I stretch out on the bed. I don't know what to do. I decide to wait, maybe she will call. I pick up Sorraya's little book of poems, leafing through it, slowly . . . 'I build a dream-castle,/. . . And at dusk/As waves wash away my dream,/I do not cry . . . Frozen dreams,/In a shattered world,/ And we wanted no mad-house here . . .'

After an hour, I pick up the phone and give the desk Leila's number. This time, there is an answer. Oh, Leila, Leila, Leila . . . Fine and beautiful Leila. But it is her sister's voice. I tell her who I am, and that Leila's left me a note, and is apparently very upset. I ask if she knows where Leila is, and if I might speak to her. Pari Azadeh tells me she delivered that note herself because Leila is ill. At the moment, she has just taken some pills, and gone to lie down. Then I won't disturb her, I say. I only want to ask how she is. There is a silence, and I hear voices through the telphone. Then comes Leila's voice 'Salaam, Jalal . . . I called you so many times.'

'I just got your note. Is everything all right?'

'I want to see you . . .'

'Has something happened?'

'Will you come here?'

'Sure . . .'

'Please, Jalal, for God's sake, come.'

'All right, I'll be there.'

'Come here, I can't talk – not over the phone.'

'Are you all right?'

'My head, my heart, my whole soul, it's – I don't know how to describe it – everything is heavy and hardened, and smashed.'

'When did you get back from Le Havre?'

'This morning.'

'You're still all in one piece?'

She tries to laugh. 'Yes. I am still in one piece.'

'That's good.'

'Do you want me to come and pick you up?'

'Can you manage it?'

'I think so.'

'I know how to get there.'

'Dear you. You're my life-line.'

'Leila!'

'Come on, then. If you only knew how I've suffered.'

'I can guess.'

'No . . .'

'What's happened?'

'I've gone and left him, the son of a bitch. He talked so much, and nearly blabbed me to death.'

'I'll come and see you.' I say simply.

She does not even ask how Sorraya is.

'*Allo*? ... Are you still there, my darling?'

'Yes.'

'How are you, yourself?'

'Alive.'

'Look what I've done to myself ...'

'You aren't to blame ...'

'You always forgive me.'

'I always ...'

'Jalal?'

'What?'

'You said we don't have to worry about what we do – but we do.'

'Well, maybe.'

'I'm so depressed, Jalal. Do you still love me?'

'...'

'You're not thinking of going back to Iran soon, are you?'

'Yes.'

'I love you.'

'Leila ...'

'You're the best man I ...'

'All right – take it easy and have a rest now, girl.'

'Did I say the wrong thing again? ...'

'You can always come to me.' My voice shakes as I utter this idiotic sentence.

'What?'

'You can always come to me.'

'Come to Iran, in this state – me? Go to a mullah, repent of my sins?'

'I –'

'What did you say? I can't quite hear you ...'

And nothing is ever more stupid than trying to tell someone on the phone that you love her, and she replies, what did you say? I can't quite hear you ...

'Nothing. It's a bad connection.'

'Yes, it's a bad connection. Come over, I want to see you.'

'All right.'

'Are you coming at once?'

'Yes.'

I replace the receiver, and light a cigarette. Someone, wearing a black dressing gown, is sitting in front of the mirror. She is at a distance from me. Seen from behind, she looks like Leila Azadeh. She is fluffing her hair, which is cut very short, *à la garçon*, on one side of her head. She holds a brush in one hand. She turns to face me. There is lipstick fresh as blood, on her lips. There is a shining look in her eyes. She gets up and walks towards me.

Outside the window, the whore of night-time Paris is awake and rambling. Beneath my tiny balcony, the city is spread – a jungle of neon; life and art, cathedrals and museums, history, literature, poetry, tradition; reality and illusion, life and motion, light, sex, love and wine; talk, feeling and happiness, money, misery, eating and drinking... Fill the cup to the brim!... And somewhere there, Sorraya is dying. Life is simple. You are brought out from your mother's womb; shown the world's magnificence and learn to hope. Then they strike you in the teeth, snatch everything away, smash your brain into a coma; back to zilch. It's not fair. 'I want to see my child again, with my own eyes, before they wrap me in my white shroud and lay me in my grave.' Farangis, Farangis, I'm sorry ... It is not fair.

NEW FICTION FROM ZED

Ali Ghalem
A Wife for My Son
A powerful novel of conflict between the pull of Moslem tradition and the reality of modern life. The painful yet determined battle of a woman becoming conscious of her own possibilities. Ali Ghalem is an Algerian film-maker. This novel has now been translated into four languages.

Emile Habiby
The Secret Life of Saeed: the Pessoptimist
A hilarious portrayal of Saeed, a Palestinian turned Israeli informer. Combining fact, fantasy, tragedy and comedy, the luckless adventures of Saeed reveal the absurdities of the positions taken by Israelis, Palestinians and Arabs.

Enrique Medina
The Duke
Banned for seven years by the Argentinian military government, this is the shocking story of a small-time ex-prizefighter called the Duke, powerfully reflecting the brutality and excesses of his time.
Medina is the author of six other novels also once banned but now being republished in Argentina.

Nawal el Saadawi
Woman at Point Zero
Told with haunting simplicity, *Woman at Point Zero* is the story of Firdaus, an Egyptian woman condemned to death for killing a pimp. Originally published in Arabic and hailed as a major literary breakthrough.

Faarax M J Cawl
Ignorance is the Enemy of Love
An African love story. In the stormy setting of turn-of-the-century Somalia two people find love. The fortunes of Calimaax and Cawrala are followed through the war with the British, Italians and Ethiopians.
This is Faarax Cawl's first novel.

Nawal el Saadawi
God Dies by the Nile
The new novel illustrates the class dimension of the oppression of women. It can also be seen as a metaphor for the Sadat regime and landlords' oppression in general.

Gerardo di Masso
The Shadow by the Door
Introduction by Richard Jacques
An Argentinian guerrilla recalls the struggle and his dead comrades. Now in exile, he tries to keep his sanity by escaping from the unbearable present through his memories of an adolescent summer in the country and a love affair crushed beneath the weight of political events.
Winner of the Cafe Iruna Prize, Bilbao 1982.

Esmail Fassih
Sorraya in a Coma
The narrator, fresh from the chaotic experiences of the Iran/Iraq war, is plunged into the vanities and excesses of wealthy Iranian expatriates living in Paris, where his niece—Sorraya—lies in a coma following an accident.
Haunted, awake or sleeping, by nightmare memories of the war, the narrator views his self-exiled compatriots and his own predicaments with wry detachment and humour. Satire, pity and terror are skillfully interwoven in this translation of a novel by one of Iran's leading new writers.

All in Hb and Pb